The Call of Cassandra Rose

A GRIPPING PSYCHOLOGICAL THRILLER

the call of cassandra rose

Sophia Spiers

LUME BOOKS

LUME BOOKS

Published in 2022 by Lume Books

Copyright © Sophia Spiers 2022

ISBN 978-1-83901-478-9

Typeset using Atomik ePublisher from Easypress Technologies

Printed and bound by Ingram Lightning Source

www.lumebooks.co.uk

For Luciano and Arabella

This book contains images of self-harm that some readers may find upsetting.

Prologue

Eyes shut. The outside world blocked out. I was in a deep trance state, melting into myself. This was the only place where I belonged, the only place I could be me. Hypnosis had become an addiction.

'Deeper,' she said. 'Dig deep within yourself.'

I sank into her words. Her sentences were stretched, elongated. I didn't know where her voice ended and my thoughts began. We had developed a strange telepathy over the months, and I could have sworn she could read my mind. We were connected.

'It's been so long.' Did I say that out loud?

'Access your memory bank. Re-live the sensations one more time. The calm clarity it gives you.'

The knife she'd taken from the kitchen was cold in my hand. I pressed the sharp edge onto my bare leg, but not hard enough to break the skin. Tingles raced up and down my spine. Adrenaline surged through my body. I ached for the rush.

One more time wouldn't hurt.

'You're stronger now. You're in control. Prove it to me. To yourself.'

This was a test. She was testing my will. My chest tightened. Would I pass?

'Now, cut.'

Chapter One

Matt texted to say he was going to be late. Pressing shuffle on my playlist, and with Amy Winehouse belting out a song, I poured instant boiling water straight from the tap into a white china cup to make myself a tea. The sound of the water spilling into the teacup echoed around the kitchen, breaking the stillness. I leant up against the counter, crossed one foot over the other and re-read the message.

`Sorry. Late again. Don't wait up. M`

It was the third night in a row. I placed the phone back in my dressing gown pocket, discarded the freshly made tea and headed for the wine fridge instead, opting for a fancy bottle of red – Chateau something or other – and padded into the snug for the long night ahead. He liked to impress his friends and colleagues with his fine wine collection even though he hardly drank, and I'd started taking pleasure in drinking his booze when he was out.

The snug was the smallest room in the house and was just off the open-plan kitchen and living space, next to the side entrance and garage. It was the only room I actually felt comfortable in, and the only room that housed any of my pre-Matt belongings, which didn't amount to much. Fantasy and Sci Fi novels, CDs and vintage records, a second-hand sofa, travel magazines, gig tickets and a huge map of the world poster, which I'd Blu-Tacked to the wall despite Matt's protests over the years that it was a piece of junk and needed removing. He preferred to see a more 'tasteful' antique map, perhaps in a gilded frame, in keeping with the rest of the house, but I begged him to allow me to keep it. That was the one thing I wouldn't compromise on when I moved in. Everything else, Matt got his way. With the poster stuck to the wall, and my few measly belongings stuffed in the streamlined storage cupboard out of sight, the room almost reminded me of the bedsit I used to live in, although the proportions of the snug were far, far, bigger.

Kicking off my slippers, I sank into the burgundy Chesterfield, with its missing buttons, and inhaled the sofa's familiar leathery scent like I always did when I was alone, granting myself a moment to be comforted by sensations familiar from my late teens, early twenties. Joshy was sound asleep, tucked up in bed wearing his Gruffalo onesie that I'd bought him for Christmas, his bedside lantern throwing soft shapes and colours around the room. Rosita, our housekeeper, the eyes and ears of our cavernous home in one of the most sought-after postcodes in London, had only just left, after helping me put my son to bed – again.

After bath time, Joshy had been hyperactive and played up, jumping on the bed, refusing to settle. Rosita must have been upstairs, waiting in the shadows, and appeared just at the right moment, happily taking over from me. Too exhausted to argue with him, or her, I thanked her for stepping in and left them both to it. Within fifteen minutes she was back downstairs, unclipping her hair from its bun and putting on her lightweight jacket, looking content, having read Joshy two stories. I thanked her again, saying how grateful I was to have her, and she nodded her acknowledgement and walked out. When I checked in on Joshy, he was sound asleep and snoring away, clutching his teddy, the duvet tangled around his body.

Knowing that nothing would cause Joshy to stir, I turned up the music's volume a fraction and began texting a reply to Matt.

`When will you be home?`

Delete

`I'll wait up for you`

Delete

`I'm waiting for you in bed with no clothes on, hurry`

Delete

`Sometimes, I hate your guts`

Delete

`Are you screwing someone else?`

Delete

`Have you stopped loving me?`

Delete

`Come home, I miss you. I miss us.`

Delete

`See you soon. Love A xxx`

Send.

I placed my iPhone by my side, switched on the TV, pressed mute on the remote control and sipped my wine, watching the flickering images while listening to the mellow sound of Amy's voice playing in my ears.

My music abruptly stopped as a ringtone blasted through. That was unlike him, to call so soon after I'd texted. It was unlike him to call at all. I looked at my phone.

It wasn't him.

My stomach plummeted.

Sitting up to attention, I stared at the name flashing on the screen – unable to bring myself to touch my phone, as though it was contaminated or on fire.

4

No. It couldn't be. It *couldn't* be.

I blinked, clearing my vision, hoping the name would disappear and that somehow, I was mistaken, but the name remained. Like a flick of a switch, everything changed. No longer did I feel comforted and secure in my little snug, in the life I had built, in the world around me.

Someone from my past, someone I believed was dead to me, was contacting me for the very first time in years.

Someone who had the power to tear my life apart.

My shaky hand reluctantly reached for the phone. My pulse raced like crazy.

She hung up before I had the chance to drop the call. I breathed, retracting my hand, taking my glass instead. I gulped down the wine and poured myself another, filling my glass to the rim.

What did she want from me, after all these years?

I turned the music up as loud as it could go, to stop the chaos from erupting inside my head, hiding inside the noise. The call was a reminder to me that she still existed, that she was out there, that she held all the power and was able to turn my small world on its axis.

The caller knew me well enough to understand that just one phone call was all it would take to rattle me and keep me on my toes.

I'd have to start watching my back.

Somehow, I must have dozed off, because I woke to the roar of Matt's Mercedes G-Wagon jeep as it pulled up onto the driveway. The jeep vibrated and purred as it came to a halt. My playlist had ended and there was an empty bottle of wine discarded on the floor. The TV was playing an old episode of *Have I Got News For You*, and I was a little drunk. I wiped my mouth, brushed my hair down and checked my phone. There'd been no other calls or messages.

Shaking off the unease, I glanced at the time. It was past eleven. Matt's footsteps crunched across the gravel driveway. Where had he been all evening? Surely he couldn't have been working so late again? He came in through the side entrance, stealthily, like a cat in the night. I hid the evidence of my extra-curricular activity under the sofa and pretended to be asleep.

The door creaked open and he stepped into the room, nudging me gently. My eyes remained shut and I stayed statue-still.

'Annabelle?' He prodded me a little harder.

'Huh?' I peeled my eyes open.

'You've fallen asleep in here, again.'

'What time is it?'

'Late.'

He still looked well groomed.

'Have you eaten?' he asked.

'A small amount. Did you get everything done?'

'All done. We ordered takeaway and worked right through.' His phone flashed inside his trouser pocket. 'So, what have you been up to today?' He placed his hand in his pocket, stepping back.

'Oh, nothing much.'

'Nothing?'

'I tried a yoga class today.' That was a lie. Truth was, I'd run past the mums from the school who were clutching yoga mats and drinking super juices, avoiding any eye contact.

'That's promising.'

'They've been badgering me for ages, so I decided to give it a try.' Total lie. They didn't even speak to me.

'And?'

'And, that's it. I gave it a go.' I bit down hard on my lip.

'Great. Glad you're making an effort with them, and with

yourself. Yoga will help keep you nice and trim.' He smiled.

'I guess.'

'I'm really tired. It's been a full-on day. Do you mind if I turn in?' He leaned in and kissed my forehead. He smelt of aftershave, recently applied. 'Night, darling. I'll see you in the morning.'

I held my breath, hoping he couldn't sniff the remnants of the stale wine on my lips. He made his way towards the door.

'Matt?'

He popped his head back through the door. 'Yes?' He loosened his tie. 'Is there something you wanted to say?' He stared, waiting.

There was so much I wanted to say, but I struggled to find the right words.

'Annabelle?'

'Don't forget the awards ceremony at the school in the morning,' I said.

'Ahh, about that.'

'You *promised*.' I clenched my hands into tight fists.

'I don't see why we need to celebrate the achievement of six-year-old boys. It's ridiculous.'

'That's what we're paying for, Matt. It was your choice to send him there, remember? I was happy with the local comprehensive.'

'We are in a very privileged position, of course we'll provide the best start for our son.'

'I didn't mean it like that.'

'So, what did you mean?'

I looked away.

'Okay, look. I can still make my PT at seven. I'll move my breakfast meeting and see you at the school, okay?'

'Thank you.' I exhaled, allowing my shoulders to relax.

'You coming to bed?'

'I'm going to stay up a while longer.'

'Night then.'

Giving him time to fall asleep, I stumbled into the hallway with a fuzzy head, full of wine and paranoia – never a good combination. The framed wedding photo on the console table stared back at me. I picked it up and studied it. We looked happy. I looked radiant, glowing, six months pregnant and bursting with hopes for a new future together, a future I'd never anticipated. I was twenty-three, he was forty. It was a whirlwind romance.

Allowing the framed picture to slip from my fingers, I watched it smash to the floor. Shards of glass scattered by my feet. I picked up a piece and fingered the sharp edges, lightly scraping it along the length of my forearm. My body tingled. A satisfying faint white line appeared on my skin, as if traced by a crayon.

Climbing the stairs to bed, I left the broken glass on the floor.

I'd deal with the mess in the morning.

Chapter Two

Joshy pestered me all the way to the school about organising a play-date with his new best friend Leo, but I was only half listening. The unexpected call I'd received the night before had really shaken me. Thankfully, we were running late, so by the time we arrived the school doors were already open and parents were filing into the main hall for the end of year achievement assembly. Breathing a sigh of relief because I didn't have to speak to anyone, I took a seat two rows from the back and placed my rucksack on the seat next to me, to save it for Matt.

The hall filled up quickly and before I knew it there was only one empty seat left – Matt's.

The schoolboys sat silently in neat rows and Mr Johnson, the prestigious and celebrated headteacher, stood on the stage, puffed out and full of self-importance, boasting about how proud he was to have yet another successful year under his belt – due to his leadership, of course. Everyone clapped and laughed on cue and I checked my phone for any updates from my husband.

He promised.

Twenty-five minutes had passed, and Joshy had already collected his bronze medal for exceptional long distance running in PE, when

Matt bustled into the hall. I half-waved and he excused himself past the parents and sat down next to me.

'It was tricky to get away,' he whispered as he turned his attention immediately to his mobile, responding to some work email or other. 'What did I miss?'

'Joshy won an award for long distance running.'

'That's great.'

Matt called himself a venture capitalist, investing money and time into failing businesses, bringing them back to life ... yet couldn't find the time to invest in us.

'He takes after me,' I said, leaning into him. 'The running, I mean.'

'What?'

'I won an award for running when I was younger.'

'Great,' he mumbled, his head buried in his bloody phone.

'Everyone's been asking if the seat's free, it's been embarrassing.'

Finally, he put his mobile away and placed his hand on my knee. 'I was okay to stand at the back of the hall,' he said, looking behind him, giving my knee a little squeeze.

Spinning around, I saw Rachel, Leo's mum, leaning up against the back wall holding an iPad and taking photos, the device obscuring her face. She lowered the iPad and caught my gaze, staring vacantly at me. Her ombre-effect hair was perfectly bouncy, her yoga-honed arms perfectly toned, her face perfectly made up. It was hard to read her expression. I smiled, but she didn't reciprocate. I stiffened, turning back to Matt.

'I thought you'd want to sit next to your wife.'

He squeezed my knee tighter and laughed on cue at something the headteacher had said. At first, I thought the placing of his hand was a gesture of unity, to show a sense of togetherness, that we were a couple, a family. But it wasn't. He was silencing me.

10

'Darling. This is not the time or the place to make a scene. Just be normal,' he whispered, with a gritty tension to his voice.

He slid his hand away and turned around to look at Rachel. She raised her hand and waved her fingers at him in a flirty way.

We sat, mute, for the rest of the torturous ceremony until the charity bucket for some well-intentioned project made its way round, interrupting the stillness between us. Matt dropped a crisp £50 note into the bucket, kissed me on the forehead and said goodbye, telling me there was a chance he was going to be working late again.

I slipped out straight after, successfully avoiding any conversations with the other parents, ducking out of Rachel's way. I'd ask about the playdate another time. With the whole day to myself and nowhere specific to be, I trudged up the hill towards Hampstead Heath. My mind was full, weighted with worries about that call, but my diary was pathetically empty, and so I had nothing to distract my attention. No coffee dates, yoga, Pilates or personal trainers arranged, no friends to catch up with, no hairdressers, no Botox and fillers or nail technician appointments booked – nothing.

Sitting on my usual bench, in a secluded spot under a willow tree where nobody bothered me, I fished my iPhone out of my back pocket and changed my playlist to Lana Del Ray. My phone began to fizz in my hand.

It was *her*. Again!

My face flushed, my heart beat wildly inside my chest and I felt as though I was about to throw up. I looked around me, half-expecting to see *her* standing behind the bench, laughing at me mockingly, in the way she always did, like it was some kind of sick twisted prank. It was the sort of thing she'd do, to get a rise out of me, a reaction.

When she'd called out of the blue last night, I naively believed it was a one-off. But it was now clear that she wanted something from me.

I hit the end call button, cutting her off, taking the tally of her missed calls to fifteen that morning. I quickly headed home, looking behind me every few minutes.

Chapter Three

That evening, I gave Joshy extra time in the bath to play. Truth was, I was out of energy. Rosita had, surprisingly, left early, and we were alone in the house waiting for Matt to come home. I sat on the chair next to the oversized stone resin bath, watching Joshy dip his ships and sharks and little men in and out of the soapy water, while I zoned out.

My phone vibrated. A message. I pulled it out of my dressing gown pocket. Matt.

`Still here. Give Joshua a kiss goodnight from me.`
`Work meeting. M`

My body tensed. I bolted upright and paced the bathroom, immediately dialling his number, cross-referencing his story.

'Annabelle?' he answered. 'Is everything alright?'

'Yes. Why wouldn't it be?'

'You're calling me at work.'

'I know.'

'We said no calls unless there was an emergency, remember? Did you not receive my message?'

'Yes, but …' I mumbled, suddenly tongue-tied, unsure of myself.

'Is it important? I'm about to go into this meeting. Really exciting new venture. Lots to tell you when I get home.'

I tuned his voice out, straining to listen to any background noises for clues. A woman laughing, a hotelier handing over a key fob, the popping of champagne corks.

'Well?' he said.

'I was ringing to see …' I stopped mid-sentence. His business partner's voice bellowed through on the other side of the phone, giving me the confirmation that I needed.

'Matt! We're going in buddy,' Bill said.

'Look. I won't be too late. I promise. This is big. Huge. It's what we've been working on for a long time,' said Matt.

'Okay. Go. Go.' I ran my hands through my hair. 'I'll see you soon.'

'Let's speak later.' He quit the call abruptly.

The tight knot in my stomach released. I looked at Joshy, who was lost in his game. Reaching my hand into the bath, I tested the temperature. It was lukewarm.

'Time to get out.'

'I want to stay in longer,' Joshy said, as he splashed my leg playfully.

'Let me see your fingers.' I took his chubby hand. 'See? They're wrinkly,' I said, kissing his cute fingers one at a time.

'Just a while longer, Mummy. Please?'

It was hard to resist his wide eyes and big smile. He held my gaze and time stood still. For that brief moment, I forgot about everything.

'Okay sweetheart. Five more minutes,' I said, kissing his hands and sitting back down on the wingback. I plugged my earphones in.

As Joshy played his game, and the soft tunes played in my ears, I allowed myself to take the weight off my feet. Exhausted, I closed my eyes and transported myself back to when I was heavily pregnant with Joshy, advised by the doctor to take plenty of bed rest.

Matt would sometimes come home from work early, surprising me with lunch and flowers. He'd rush through the side entrance, fling his shoes off and send a sour-faced Rosita home. I'd lie on the sofa and lift my top up, allowing him to kiss every inch of my swollen belly.

With the baby safely nestled inside and the warmth of Matt's lips on my skin making me tingle, it had become the only nourishment I needed.

'You're exactly what I've been waiting for, little one,' he'd whisper to our son. The baby kicked every time he spoke to him. It was like they were secretly communicating.

My mobile started to ring. My eyes opened and the bathroom formed around me. Joshy was still happily playing in the bath, splashing and talking to himself. I pulled my earphones out of my ears, hoping to see Matt's name on my screen, praying it was him, telling me he was on his way home to us.

But instinctively, I knew.

It was *her*. Mary.

She'd been continuing to call. Bombarding me all day. For the umpteenth time, I dropped the call. Like a bad dream, the phone rang again. I declined, following it up with a message with my trembling hand.

    Please leave me alone.

Why was she haunting me?

'Is that Daddy?'

'What?'

'Daddy? Was that him?'

'No,' I said, looking around me, feeling like I was being watched.

'Then who is it?'

'No one.'

The phone rang again.

'Is it Daddy now?'

'Stop asking questions all the bloody time,' I snapped, putting the mobile in my dressing gown pocket, wanting to throw it into the bathwater. Drown it. *Drown her.*

'Okay,' he said, as he continued to play, as though nothing out of the ordinary was happening.

I tested the water. It had turned cold. 'Right. Let's get you out.'

'No, Mummy,' he said, splashing and giggling.

'Joshy. Stop it.'

He splashed again and laughed. Water dripped from my face. I wiped it away. It was all a game to him. Just a game. But I wasn't finding it funny. My temples started to ache. The room's temperature started to rise.

'Come on, let's get out.'

'No. I want to play more,' he said, slamming both hands into the bath water in protest. Water poured over the edge of the bathtub.

'For God's sake. Why don't you ever do as you're told?' I yelled, standing over him. I yanked him up from under his arm, hauling him upright. I could feel my heartbeat pounding inside my skull.

'Ow. Mummy. You're hurting me.'

Joshy began to cry. I caught a glimpse of myself in the mirror opposite. I didn't recognise who I was. Somehow, I looked older than my twenty-nine years.

I let go of him, suddenly aware of my own strength. His skin was marked red.

'Sorry, Mummy. I only wanted to play.' Tears streamed down his face.

The air was thinner. Tighter. It was hard to breathe. What was I doing to my son?

'It's okay. It's okay.' I took the fluffy towel and enveloped him. It was still warm from the heated rail. 'It's all going to be okay, baby bear. It's all going to be okay.'

I knew that it wasn't.

It took ages to settle Joshy into bed; he was being naughty, refusing to put his pyjamas on, refusing to do anything I asked and repeating back to me everything I said. He was pushing me to my absolute limits, but I was too scared to tell him off after what I'd done in the bathroom, so I sat on his bed and bit my tongue. Eventually, he tired himself out and settled down, asking me to read two of his favourite bedtime stories, *The Gruffalo* and *The Gruffalo's Child*. We snuggled in bed and I read out loud, changing my voice for all the characters in the book; but my mind was elsewhere – ruminating on the calls I'd received from Mary.

As I padded back down the stairs, a loud knock at the front door made me jump. I froze on the staircase. It was late. Past nine o'clock. Whoever it was, was using our letterbox and not the doorbell.

I sat on the step, not making a sound. My shaky hand retrieved my mobile from my pocket. I opened the security system app to check the camera at the front door, expecting to see *her* standing outside.

There was no one there. I exhaled.

I waited a while longer, staring at the black and white image of my front door on my phone. The silence in the house intensified. Minutes passed. When I felt it was safe to move, I crept down the stairs and saw a leaflet on the doormat. My jumpy heart settled. It was only a leaflet.

I picked it up, glancing at the single page, expecting to see

Thai or Chinese delivery, gardening services or another new gym opening up in the area.

Hypnotherapy: Change your life. Forever.
Cassandra Rose, Clinical Hypnotherapist.
Don't delay. Ring now.
You can change your life. Forever.

Change your life forever. Those four words bounced around in my head. I turned the one-page leaflet over. *Anxiety, Confidence, Self-Esteem Issues, Habit Breaking, Fears and Phobias. Regression. Let Cassandra Rose change your life, forever. Don't delay. Call now and book your appointment. Abbey Gardens, St John's Wood.* The leaflet was a calming pale blue, with ripples of water as a backdrop. The clinic was in Abbey Gardens. I knew that road well.

Was that a sign? My heart fluttered.

Swiping my momentary optimism away, I knew that I was being naive. Stupid. How could one person change my life? It's not as if the hypnotherapist could wave a magic wand and sweep all my troubles away, one by one. Besides, it would mean having to open up to her first, and there was no way I was going to do that.

There was nothing she or anyone else could do. I'd made my bed. I was trapped in a life I once thought I wanted and a life I believed I'd escaped from.

I'd fought relentlessly to build myself back up, after finding the courage to flee at seventeen. It had been hard to find my feet at first, but somehow I managed it. Leaving her gave me the space to reinvent myself, away from the pain and turbulence, away from her toxicity, and once I'd found my place in the world, I'd sworn to be nothing like *her*. Nothing was ever going to hold me back and nothing was going to bring me down, ever again. I was going to live a full life, see new things, meet new people, travel the world and never settle down.

I threw the leaflet in the waste-paper bin under the console table, noticing that our wedding photo had been reframed and put back in its place. I walked into the kitchen and stared at the wine fridge, which was filled to the brim. I pulled a fancy bottle out from the bottom rack and poured myself a large glass, hiding the rest of the bottle on a shelf at the back of the larder cupboard, behind the Coco Pops I'd bought Joshy about a year ago, knowing no one would look there. Matt forbade Joshy 'trashy' cereal. I retrieved a fresh bottle from one of the dozen cases in the garage and used it to fill the empty space in the fridge.

With my phone on silent, I tried to settle into the evening, alone in the snug with only my playlist and jitters for company. But I couldn't relax.

My mobile started to flash.

It was insufferable. She was insufferable.

The walls around me started caving in. I dropped her call and sent another text.

`Leave me the fuck alone!`

I watched the word *typing* dance up and down on the WhatsApp message on my mobile. Oh God, what was she going to say?

Swallowing down the lump in my throat, I began to read her reply. Her shrill voice echoing inside my head as though she was there in the room with me, sitting next to me on the sofa speaking.

`Anna. I need to see ya, girl.`

Chapter Four

Matt left for work super early, and by the time I'd made it down the stairs and into the kitchen, Rosita had already prepared breakfast for Joshy. I was secretly relieved when Joshy insisted Rosita take him to school instead of me; I was in no hurry to leave the house and was still in my nightgown, groggy and irritable from insomnia. I'd gone to bed stressing about whatever Matt was up to. When he finally came home at ten thirty, showered, and then settled into a deep sleep (which didn't take long), I'd spent the rest of the night stressing about the text message I'd received from Mary. Her words running around in my brain, over and over.

I need to see ya, girl.

What did she want from me?

Rosita was content with the school arrangement, and like Speedy Gonzales had Joshy fed, ready and out the front door within thirty minutes, all without the slightest hint of protest from him. They were both giggling away at some private joke as they closed the door behind them.

Lost in thought, I stood in the shower, turning up the dial until the water was piping hot, until my body prickled and stung, until my skin had turned red raw, until my thoughts blurred and smudged.

There had to be a way of stopping her before she caused real damage. Mary was like an unseen computer virus, her toxicity spreading fast. If I didn't do something about it, she'd destroy all my files (the few I had left).

I had no choice. I had to end it today. The calls. The past. Her.

With a new determination, I dried off my sensitive skin, threw on a pair of jeans and t-shirt and headed down Fitzjohn's Avenue towards town, towards Mary. Zigzagging across the intersection at Swiss Cottage, I played chicken at the junction of three oncoming roads of traffic, my music blasting in my ears, my thoughts tumbling around me. Cars honked and drivers yelled from their car windows as I sprinted across the road, almost getting myself run over. I wasn't paying the slightest bit of attention to them.

I turned onto Abbey Road and hustled my way past tourists and Beatles fans who always loitered by Abbey Road Studios and the iconic zebra crossing, passing Abbey Gardens, my favourite street in the area, along the way.

That's where that hypnotherapist was located.

I used to roller-skate around the area and down that very road when I was a child, and spent hours daydreaming about the lives of the people inside the fine Georgian stucco houses. I longed to live in a house on Abbey Gardens. I imagined having birthday parties; tons of friends would be invited and there'd be red balloons decorating the front door. At Christmas, there'd be a huge tree in the bay window for all to see, with beautifully wrapped presents underneath. We'd have an open fire. My imaginary family would be gathered round, singing carols. My imaginary mum would bring me hot chocolate, and stroke my flushed cheeks, making me feel snuggly and warm. I'd be loved. Wanted.

Of course, that was only a fantasy.

We never had a Christmas tree growing up, it was too flamboyant. Money was best spent elsewhere, on things like fags, weed and her endless parties. Sometimes, if she was in the mood and feeling particularly festive, I'd be allowed to hang a few tacky baubles she'd bought from the local market on the dying houseplant in the kitchen. I'm sure it was Pebbles' fault the plant never seemed to do so well, despite my best efforts to water it. The cat used it as a litter tray.

My stomach knotted at the sight of the tower blocks of Lisson Green council estate in the far distance. I inched towards it, turning my ring round so the diamond faced the inside of my palm and switching my music off.

I sat on a low wall opposite the estate, which had been my home for the first seventeen years of my life, and texted.

I'm here. A

The exterior of the estate didn't look so bad these days. A fancy facelift had been undertaken to please the neighbouring rich residents who were sick to death of looking at it. The buildings, six stories of brooding concrete, were an eyesore even after the makeover. Back in the day, long balconies joined all the high rise blocks together on the second and fifth floors. The local gangs used them as a rat run for petty crime, moving from one tower block to the next. Those more innocent, like me and my friends, enjoyed the endless summers roller-skating along the balconies, playing knock down ginger, using the same escape routes.

A finger tapped my shoulder. Looking up, I recognised the warm face. I pulled my earbuds out.

'Hello, gorgeous.'

'Uncle Jack. You made me jump.'

Jack was a market trader, had skin like leather and was wearing the uniform he always wore, come rain or shine: a flat cap and fingerless

22

gloves. A roll-up dangled from his mouth. He wasn't really my uncle, but *her* best friend, and much loved on the market and estate.

'Nice of you to contact me,' he said, smiling, his rollie hanging from his lips. He re-lit the cigarette and offered out his rusty tobacco tin.

I shook my head, no.

'Oh, check you. Smart as well as beautiful.'

'Stop it.' I laughed, pushing his hand away. 'I haven't smoked in years.'

'Na, good on ya. These things will kill ya.' He coughed.

'They certainly will.'

'You gonna see her, then?'

'I don't …' I jumped off the wall.

'Oh Anna, doll. How long has it been, now?'

The mere mention of her had my shoulders hunched up by my ears. 'Six years.'

'She's got cancer, love.'

Suddenly dizzy, I grabbed his forearm to steady myself. *Cancer?*

'It's in the lungs,' he continued.

Letting go of his arm, I scooped my emotions into a bundle, stiffening up. 'She hasn't contacted me in years. Years, Jack. And now …'

He looked at me and smiled, pulling at my heartstrings, messing with my head. 'Why don't you try and make amends with Mary, hey?'

'Don't do this, Jack.'

'She's your mum,' he pleaded.

I swallowed the grief I had for Mary. She'd been as good as dead to me – a ghost. I didn't need her resurrected now. 'I've moved on with my life, Jack.'

Silence settled between us.

'Where's the little nipper?' he said.

'At school.'

'How old is he now?'

'Six.'

'Got any photos? Bet he's got your stunning blue eyes.'

I fished my Mulberry purse out of my rucksack and flashed him a picture from the inside pocket, which was next to my credit cards. The photo had been taken last summer; the three of us eating ice cream, looking relaxed and holiday happy at a time when life felt less complicated.

'He looks like your mum, Anna.'

My chest tightened. I pulled my purse away. 'Jack?'

'Yes, doll.'

'I've been wondering about my childhood.'

'All the more you should go and see her.'

'Did Mary love me?'

He turned his gaze away from me and looked towards the grey estate, flicking his rollie to the floor.

'Did she even want me?'

He turned to me, staring into my eyes. 'Listen, love. You don't want to be dragging up the past. No good will come of it. Trust me. Best leave it alone. Concentrate on the here and now, on your future and the little future you have left with your old ma. She needs ya right now.'

I put my purse away, and pulled the rucksack back onto my knotted shoulders.

'Let's go see her together. For old times' sake. What harm will it do, doll?'

I couldn't allow myself to get sucked into the comfort of Jack. Each time I let my guard down, as far as Mary was concerned, bad things followed. They'd already started. I had to concentrate on the here and now, like he said, not the past. Forget about her. Concentrate on my family.

'Jack. I've got to go. Just tell her to stop calling.'

'Come on love. Don't rush off. Why don't we pop in together? Just for a cuppa. She won't bite. I'll come wiv'. Be your buffer, like.' He took hold of my arm. His grip was light and tender, making me melt.

I cleared my throat. 'I have an appointment and I don't want to be late,' I lied.

'No pressure, love. When you're ready, yeah?' He placed a delicate kiss on my cheek; his rough stubble scratched my skin. He smelt of a mixture of tobacco and coffee.

I missed him.

'I'll send her your regards,' he said.

'Sure.'

'Don't be a stranger,' he called after me.

I'd decided to take the long route home, detouring through Regent's Park, thinking about what he'd said to me, about Mary having cancer and how she needed me. But where had she been when I'd needed her the most? She'd never been there for me. Never.

I stuffed all notions of her and my murky past into a tiny compartment in the back of my mind and power walked the rest of the way home.

Chapter Five

Joshy was sitting on the sofa in the family room, dipping his carrot sticks into hummus while watching an over-enthusiastic goon on children's TV singing a repetitive, irritating song. Rosita was in her usual spot in the kitchen, clearing up, keeping a close eye. She seemed to be staying later and later every night. Sitting next to Joshy, I coiled myself around him, nuzzling in and inhaling his scent. He smelt of bubble bath and was wearing his snuggly Gruffalo onesie.

'*Señora*, I finish now.'

'Okay Rosita, thank you,' I said, pretending to be engrossed in the TV, clinging onto Joshy.

She hung her apron on the back of the larder door. 'You want me to put Joshua to bed again? I stay,' she said.

Why she'd recently appointed herself 'housekeeper-turned-nanny', I had no idea. Matt was really fond of Rosita and didn't seem to mind her self-appointed role – she could do no wrong as far as he was concerned.

Matt's mother, Celeste, had known Rosita's family in Spain all her life. She'd purchased Rosita's plane ticket over to London and she became the family's trusted live-in housekeeper. Matt was a young teenager at the time. Childless, and with no known romantic involvement, Rosita rooted herself deep within Matt's family unit, often claiming to me, in her distinctive Spanish accent, that she'd brought Matt up herself. When the family moved out of London, Rosita stayed by Matt's side and became his housekeeper, sometimes swapping over to help Celeste and staying at her mansion if called upon. Matt helped Rosita find a small place in Kentish Town (I guessed it would have cramped his style to have her living with him – he was a bachelor, after all), and so she moved into the reasonably priced rental studio flat above a grocer's shop and had been living there ever since.

'No that's fine, not necessary, Rosita. Thank you.' I couldn't meet her eyes. Secretly, she intimidated the hell out of me.

'I stay.'

'Rosita. I said no.'

She placed her arms on her wide hips.

'Thank you for offering. But I'll manage on my own tonight,' I said.

'Okay *señora*.'

I thought back to when I'd first met her. I had been in the kitchen, looking for the kettle so I could make myself a cup of tea, but there was nothing out on the worktops, no toaster, no jars of tea, coffee or sugar – no kettle. Nothing. The kitchen worktops resembled an operating theatre rather than a working kitchen. I'd never seen anything so modern in my life. Rosita stood watching me from the side-lines and seemed to be enjoying the impromptu show I was performing. Getting myself more and more flustered, I was too afraid to ask for help. She watched without offering a hand, until she decided to end the pantomime. Then she calmly walked over to the sink and turned one of the stainless steel taps on. Instantly, boiling water poured out. I mean, how the hell was I supposed to know?

'Okay *niño*, Rosita will see you tomorrow, yes?' She shook her long brown hair from the restraints of her bun and planted a kiss on Joshy's cheek.

'Bye Rosita,' I said, pulling Joshy in closer.

After she left, I helped myself to a bottle and settled in for another long night, deciding to keep Joshy up a while longer – it was Friday night, after all. I started to drift in and out of sleep, while he happily watched TV.

A dream slipped into my mind.

I was in a deserted playground, sitting on a swing, gently swaying back and forth. It was cold and dark. The sky was black. My bare legs were sprinkled with goose bumps. I was wearing a pair of blue striped shorts and a *Star Wars* t-shirt Uncle Jack had bought me from the market stall. The top had faded, and it was getting really tight around the arms. I had long white socks with holes, and pink and white roller skates on my feet. The wheels squeaked loudly as they rolled along the concrete floor. Imposing grey buildings surrounded me, casting long scary shadows on the ground. They looked like big monsters. Lisson Green Estate. Alone and afraid, I wanted to skate as fast as I could, away from the playground, away from the estate – but for some reason, I couldn't move off the swing. I was paralysed. Gripped with fear, my body started to shake, and my heart thumped hard.

'*I want my mummy,*' I whimpered. '*I want my mummy,*' I cried.

'Daddy's home.' Joshy leapt from the sofa, jerking me awake.

My eyes sprang open. My chest contracted as I gasped for air.

The remnants of my dream lingered in my mind. It was the same nightmare I used to have as a teenager, waking night after night drenched in sweat, crying. I'd no idea why I was having such dreams, or what it meant to me. Like a broken record, the scene of me as a child in the deserted playground haunted me every time I closed my eyes. When I ran away from home at seventeen, the dream started to dwindle away, eventually stopping.

But now it had returned.

Shaking the dream away, I rubbed my eyes and watched Joshy crash into Matt's open arms, nearly clotheslining him to the floor. I watched their embrace as if they were someone else's family. They had such a special bond.

What was Matt doing home so early? I glanced at my glass of wine. It was too late to hide it.

'Hey, little fella.' Matt steadied himself.

'Daddy look, I've got a party invite.' Joshy ran out of the room and reappeared with a professionally printed and laminated invitation, waving it around Matt's face. Matt smiled as he struggled to read.

'Wow, a party.'

'It's Leo's birthday, he's going to be six.'

'Leo's birthday, huh?' Matt looked over and smiled at me. 'And where's Leo having his birthday?'

'In the garden. Look.' Joshy snatched the invite back from Matt. 'A Mad Hatter's tea party,' he read out loud.

His reading was coming along, and I was bursting with pride.

'Adults invited,' Joshy continued. 'That means you can come too, Mummy and Daddy.'

'Sounds like fun to me,' Matt said as he winked at me. 'We haven't been to Rachel's in a while. It would be nice to catch up.'

Shrivelling into the sofa, I felt myself diminish. The party was three weeks away – plenty of time to work myself up into a frenzy. I hated going to any of his friends' social events or gatherings, even the kids' parties. They always made me self-conscious, as though I was on display. Usually, I'd spend the entire time mute, refraining from saying anything at all just in case I sounded dumb or said something out of place or inappropriate, constantly in fear of embarrassing Matt and exposing myself in the process. I struggled to relax and be myself at the best of times – whatever being myself meant, these days.

'Can I wear a big hat?' Joshy lifted his little arms high in the air, demonstrating how large he wanted his hat to be. 'This big, pleeeeaaase?'

'You can wear anything you want,' Matt said in his goofy voice. He stood up from the floor, took his pin striped suit jacket off and folded it neatly, shoulder to shoulder with precision, and draped it over the back of the armchair so it wouldn't crease.

'Can Mummy have a Mad Hatter's tea party too, for her birthday?'

'I have other plans for your mother's birthday, don't you worry. Big plans. Huge.'

'Please don't go to any trouble,' I said, forcing a smile onto my face. 'You know I'd be happy with a meal at home. Just the three of us.'

'Only the best for Mummy. Isn't that right, Joshua?'

Joshy wrapped his arms around Matt, satisfied.

'I tell you what Joshua, why don't you run upstairs and brush your teeth? Daddy will be up in a minute to tuck you in,' said Matt. 'And if you're quick, I'll read you a bedtime story.'

'Two stories?' Joshy beamed a toothless grin.

'Whatever you want.'

Matt took his shoes off and placed them by the side entrance in an orderly fashion as Joshy ran out of the room quick as a flash. His footsteps could be heard above us as he engaged in the task of brushing his teeth while jumping up and down. I loved the fact that he couldn't stand still for a second. So much energy bursting out of his tiny body.

The chandelier lights flickered every so often as he bopped around above our heads. Matt spotted the bottle of wine as he loosened his tie and unbuttoned the top button of his crisp white shirt. 'It's fine, Annabelle. Enjoy it.'

'I needed to unwind.'

He topped me up. 'You look beautiful tonight.'

My finger traced my lips. I'd forgotten that I'd applied lipstick.

'It suits you,' he said.

'Thank you.' My cheeks flushed. It had been ages since he'd paid me a compliment.

'You should wear make-up more often, like you used to.'

We locked eyes.

His phone pinged a text. He prised it out of his trouser pocket and read the message. I studied his features closely for clues, but his expressionless face gave nothing away. He focused on texting whoever was on the other end of the phone.

I wanted to know what was taking his attention away from me, what was so important. What was always so bloody important.

'Rosita's prepared us dinner. It's one of her Spanish specialties,' I said, desperate to break his concentration. Craving his focus.

His eyes lit up with pleasure. The last time I cooked dinner, I burnt the oven chips, overcooked the sirloin steaks and served up soggy tomatoes. Matt said it was endearing and called Rosita to come over to rustle something else up for us. That was five years ago.

He sat down next to me and placed his mobile phone face down on the coffee table. I placed my feet up on the same table, obscuring the phone. Matt rested his hand on my thigh, and I bit my lip, resisting the temptation to pull my dress down to cover my pimply flesh.

'Joshy will be waiting for you,' I reminded him. 'Why don't you put him to bed? I'll set the table and dish up the food.'

'Sure, I'm on it.'

'And then hurry back to me.'

'Hold that thought.'

'Daddy, I'm ready,' Joshy shouted from upstairs. The lights flickered above our heads as he jumped.

'Coming,' Matt shouted back.

Distracted, he left – without his precious phone. It had worked! He'd be down any minute. I didn't have long.

A part of me wanted to leave his phone alone, to trust him, to be the good dutiful wife. Play my role and make him happy. But another part of me, the weaker and insecure part, wanted to know exactly who he'd been texting.

I stared at the iPhone in my hand.

No. It had to be done. There was just enough time.

He had a new fancy phone with face recognition, but you could still punch in the code to open it. He'd been trying to persuade me to get the same phone, but I thought it unnecessary. My phone worked perfectly well and had done for years. With clammy hands and my heart beating wildly, I swiped up. A wide-eyed Joshy grinned back at me from the screensaver, making me feel bad for what I was about to do. I had to be quick.

Face ID or Enter Password

My fingers fired out 151515.

The phone shook. The image of Joshy disappeared and was replaced by a black screen.

Face ID or Enter Password

Had my finger slipped? I tried again, 151515.

The screen shook again. We had agreed to have the same passcodes for everything. That was the deal. No secrets, that's what he'd said to me when we'd first got together. *No secrets.*

The chandelier stopped flickering. The footsteps from above became distant, the voices further away. They'd moved into Joshy's bedroom. Would the mobile lock me out if I tried once more? The risk was far too great.

Placing the phone down exactly as I'd found it, I gulped wine, paced the room and put music on to settle my nerves. I laid the table, placing the large red Le Creuset dish with Rosita's chorizo, bean and potato concoction on the table. Fifteen minutes later, Matt reappeared, our son was tucked up in bed asleep. Easy listening music pumped through our Bose speakers. My stomach twisted into a thousand knots.

'Dinner smells great,' Matt said.

I dished up the food onto the stupid black slate plates which looked like roof tiles, hoping he wouldn't notice my trembling hands.

'Leave it. What's the rush? Come sit with me.' He patted the sofa. 'You look sexy tonight. You haven't worn that dress in a long time.'

I stopped what I was doing and padded over to him, sitting down. 'It was in Sardinia.'

'What was?'

'The last time I wore the dress. It was in Sardinia.'

'Wow, that long ago. That was a great holiday. Amazing to think Joshua was with us all along, growing in your tummy. Our little miracle.' He stroked my midriff, leaving his hand to linger. 'Maybe we could recreate that holiday,' he said, leaning into me.

It had been our first holiday together and I hadn't known I was pregnant. He'd whisked me away as a surprise, his way of wooing me. We'd only just started dating and were getting to know one another. We'd spent two weeks entwined. Life was put on hold while we fell madly in love. When we returned, someone had pressed the fast forward button, and everything spun out of control. Before I knew it, I was pregnant, married and moved in – with a huge ring on my finger and a brand-new life that Matt had sculpted for me.

'Annabelle. Relax,' he said, inching closer, cupping my face in his hands.

My face felt fragile in his grip.

His grey eyes looked deep into mine. 'What's the matter, darling?'

'Nothing's the matter.' His phone was in my peripheral vision.

'Mmmm, you smell so great.' He closed his eyes, trying to kiss me.

Pursing my lips, I moved back a little. 'Can we have dinner, and then maybe after?'

'It's been so long, Annabelle.'

It was hard not to allow my imagination to spiral, not to picture him with someone else. Desiring another woman, touching another woman, whispering into another woman's ear, having sex with another woman. If he was having an affair, would I be to blame? Was I pushing him into someone else's arms?

I wanted his love, his attention. I did, more than anything in the world, but sometimes I questioned whether I deserved any of it. I couldn't live up to the person he expected me to be. I was a fraud, constantly pretending to be someone else in order to please him. To cover up who I really was.

'What's wrong?' he asked.

'It's nothing, I mean it's something. Look, can we just chat?'

'You've got me all worked up.' He kissed my tight lips. 'You're so beautiful.' He kissed harder, lost in the moment.

Parting my lips, I allowed his tongue to slip into my mouth.

I felt acid churn in my stomach. I couldn't relax. I couldn't. Again, I pulled away.

'Why are you brushing me off?'

'I'm not trying …'

'Why are you teasing me in this way?'

His lips were back on mine. His eyes shut. His hands all over me, travelling underneath my dress and up my thigh. The more I tried to relax, the more rigid I became.

Mary played on my mind. Her cancer. Had it changed her? Mellowed her out?

Was it even the truth?

My mind moved onto the dream I'd just had, desperately trying to capture the finer details, willing it to come back to me clearly so I could make sense of it all. Why was I alone in the playground at night feeling afraid? And where the fuck was Mary?

'You're so tense, darling.' His hands travelled further up my thigh.

'Matt, stop ...' I forced the words out of my dry mouth.

He threaded his fingers inside my knickers, attempting to pull them off.

'I can't breathe. Matt. I can't ... Please Matt. Stop!' I pushed him off me and hugged myself.

'What the hell is *wrong* with you? I thought this is what you wanted!' Matt said, standing up and rearranging himself. He picked up his phone. 'It's as though I repulse you.' He started for the side entrance, putting his shoes back on. 'You know, you've been impossible to live with recently. I don't know what's going on inside your head half the time. And quite frankly, my patience is wearing thin.'

'Matt, please! Let me at least explain.'

I was met with silence.

'I need to tell you something.'

Silence.

'We never talk about anything. Please? Matt?'

Silence. Silence. Silence.

'Where are you going?'

'Out!' he said, slamming the door behind him.

I pressed my head into the cushion and screamed, 'I'm sorry.'

His car's engine fired up. The house rattled. He was gone.

Chapter Six

I sliced the loaf of bread on the thick wooden chopping board my mother-in-law had bought for my birthday last year. It was a rough, ragged cut: thick on one end, super thin on the other. It didn't bother me that the bread wasn't sliced evenly and that I wasn't even using the correct knife, despite having been told off a million times by Matt. The way I saw it, it was going straight into Joshy's mouth anyway.

Joshy had woken up moody and I wanted to cheer him up with one of my special childhood sandwiches – the sort I used to make myself when I was his age – for his Saturday treat. Using the same sharp blade, I smeared lashings of butter and strawberry jam all over the bread, making a sloppy jam sandwich – just how I liked it.

'Morning darling,' Matt said.

He came up behind me and kissed the nape of my neck, making me jump and accidently nick myself with the knife. 'Shit!' The knife clattered as it made contact with the granite worktop.

'Language, darling,' he said, acting as though nothing had occurred between us the night before.

Where did he go, after he stormed off last night?

'Daddy!' Joshy bounced up and down on the breakfast stool at the kitchen island, super excited to see his dad.

Matt placed a kiss on Joshy's forehead.

Blood dripped from my finger onto the sandwich, ruining it. I stared at it, transfixed for a while, my thoughts elsewhere.

'Darling. You're bleeding,' Matt said, turning his attention back to me. 'Quick, run your finger under the tap.'

I rushed over to the sink, leaving the bloodied sandwich behind, and ran the cold water over my wounded finger. I watched the blood and water mix into a muted pink colour.

'You okay?' he asked.

'It's only a small cut.'

'Darling, you've made a mess of the loaf,' Matt said. 'It's because you're using the wrong knife. How many times do I have to explain?'

Only when I turned around to face him did I realise that he was sporting his Ralph Lauren navy polo shirt, khaki trousers, white soft shoes and a navy cap. Another Saturday of golfing. My heart sank.

'Annabelle. Please pay attention. Firstly, you need to turn the loaf on its side and then you take the serrated knife to slice, using a sawing motion. Then you should use the butter knife to spread.'

'Okay,' I said, turning away from him. 'I'll try and remember.'

'And this is a butcher's knife ...'

I clutched the marble sink, my knuckles turning white. 'I get it,' I snapped.

Silence followed.

'I'm sorry. You know I've never owned a fancy set of knives before. And I get confused with which one to use. They all look the same to me,' I said, fetching a Gruffalo plaster from the medicine cupboard and wrapping it around my index finger.

'Right, well,' he said, looking hurt.

'Matt.'

'It's fine. All fine.' He plastered a smile back on his face. 'I must head out. Meeting Bill and the others for a round of golf at The Grove hotel.'

I bit down on my lip to stop myself from blurting out what I was really thinking: that he was always playing golf, or at work, or at some swanky dinner schmoozing his clients, or … I tailed off to stop myself spiralling.

'See you all later.' He blew us kisses and disappeared through the side entrance of the house. Rosita appeared from the utility room. They were like a tag team. One in, one out. The roar of Matt's Mercedes G-Wagon fired up, vibrating through the house as he pulled off the driveway.

'Fancy going to the playground?' I asked Joshy, trying to keep my voice steady.

'I take, *señora*,' Rosita said, filling the space in front of me.

'That's okay. I can manage.' I squeezed past her wide frame, avoiding her gaze. 'Thank you for offering. Come on, Joshy.'

'But Mummy, I haven't eaten breakfast.'

'I make,' Rosita said, as she started to heat up oats on the hob, making porridge within moments, sprinkling a handful of mixed berries on top.

'Yay, porridge,' Joshy bounced up and down.

I sat on the stool beside Joshy and picked at my nail varnish, waiting.

I'd decided to take Joshy to the less popular playground, hidden in the middle of Hampstead Heath amongst acres of meadows and trees. It was a fair walk, but that was okay, I needed to clear my head and I loved the smell of the trees in the summer. It soothed me. We strolled hand in hand with the warm sun heating our faces. Joshy, for once, didn't ask me a million questions about this and that, and was content to chat to himself, playing a make-believe game about the Gruffalo living on the heath.

As Joshy continued to chatter, I started to wonder about my own childhood. I had no recollection of going on long walks with Mary, of being taken anywhere special, or going on any day trips or camping holidays. There were no fond memories of spending any extended period of time together whatsoever. On a Saturday morning, I usually played maid, fetching her a cup of tea and some digestive biscuits while she stayed in bed, having a long lie-in. I'd wash the dishes, fold the clothes and clean the toilet with bleach, then I'd head out to meet my friends on Church Street market with my roller skates glued to my feet.

Joshy made a beeline for the empty swing in the playground. I sat on a bench opposite and plugged my earphones in, pressing play on my playlist. I watched him as he swung up and down, swinging higher and higher. Higher and higher. Higher and ...

My eyes shot open.

My skin sprinkled with goose bumps from the sudden cold snap. The sun had been replaced by heavy rain clouds and it was getting dark. I pulled my earphones out of my ears. The air was thick and unclean. Grey high-rises surrounded me. The soft wood chip beneath my trainers was now replaced by concrete.

My body stiffened. My toes curled.

The playground ahead of me was barren, void of children. The terror of my nightmare was back.

A scream caught in my throat.

I swallowed down the panic and blinked hard to clear my vision. My surroundings came back into focus. The trees, the meadows, the sunshine and the playground. Children played, parents chatted on their mobiles and to each other and the birds continued to chirp in the trees. What the hell just happened? Did I fall asleep and slip into a dream? I stared ahead at the playground.

The swing, the one Joshy was playing on, was empty.

Joshy had gone.

I stood up from the bench and scanned the playground: slide, climbing frame and seesaw. He was nowhere. I spun on my heel. My mouth dried out. 'Josh …'

I caught a glimpse of his red t-shirt on the other side of the fence, standing next to another boy and a woman. *Oh, thank God.* I scrambled out of the gate, racing over to him, grabbing him by the shoulders. 'Don't you ever do that to me again. You hear?'

'Are you okay?' said a familiar voice.

I looked up. Shit! Rachel. 'I'm alright, I thought for a second. I …'

'You lost your son?' She flicked her ombre-effect hair with her hand and then crossed her yoga-toned arms, staring down at me. She was sporting Sweaty Betty gym gear with the perfect thigh gap.

I straightened up and smiled. 'Hi, Rachel.'

She nodded.

'I closed my eyes for one second and then when I opened them, he was gone.'

'Hardly gone. He spotted Leo and came running over. No harm done.'

'Yeah, lucky you ain't a child abductor,' I said with a weak smile, attempting to break the ice.

'You are not,' she said.

I cocked my head to the side.

'Lucky you *are not* a child abductor,' she said, correcting my grammar.

'Oh, of course,' I said. My face flushed.

'Mummy. Leo says I can go to his house and play. Can I go now?' Joshy asked, tugging at my arm. 'Pleeeaasse?'

'I, err. Well, we …'

'I'm afraid Leo has a private tuition shortly. Another time, maybe?' Rachel said, stooping down to Joshy's level and ruffling his hair.

I fiddled with my phone, wrapping the wires from the earphones around it. A ringtone interrupted the silence.

'Well?' Rachel said, 'Aren't you going to answer?'

I smiled at Rachel, fighting the nausea down.

'Your phone?' Rachel said, taking Leo's hand and guiding him away.

'Oh. It's not important. It's nothing,' I said, dropping the call. 'It's no one.'

I didn't need to look. I knew who it was.

'Right, well. We'd best be off,' she said, walking off, not even saying goodbye.

'See you at school,' I mumbled.

Chapter Seven

'Mummy, it's raining,' Joshy said, as we entered the school playground.

It was Monday morning and we'd rushed out the door, forgetting his reading bag.

'It's only a sprinkle.' I fumbled with his school blazer, like that would help somehow.

Instantly, the playground became a sea of brightly coloured umbrellas. How the hell were they all so prepared for rain? My weather app had said bloody sunshine. Staring at the large wooden arched doors, the main entrance to the school, I willed them to open. The teachers surely wouldn't leave us hanging around in the drizzle for too long.

As I drew Joshy in closer, he started to squirm his way out of my grip. He ran off, heading straight to his friend, Leo. I took in some deep breaths and, mentally preparing myself, walked towards Rachel and the other mums. Rachel saw me approaching and rolled her eyes at the others.

An awkward silence followed. Hovering next to them, I fixed a smile on my face.

With a practised hand, Rachel tilted her umbrella, blocking me, and continued with her conversation. 'As I was saying, Leo breezed through the homework, but of course he's super smart, and naturally gifted.'

She'd known Matt for years and was a recent divorcee. Her divorce, as far as I knew, was lengthy and costly – for her ex. She'd caught him red handed with his pants wrapped around his ankles, while their young cleaner performed a sex act on him. After that, she went on the rampage and keyed his beloved Aston Martin, threw him out of the family mansion, and if the rumours were true, had subsequently slept with half the male population of Hampstead.

'It wasn't challenging enough for Alexander,' said Saskia, her face expressionless due to all the Botox.

'Leo is so enthusiastic; he achieves far more in an hour with the private tutor than in a week at school. I'm confident he'll surpass his own tutor soon,' said Rachel, shaking her umbrella my way.

They continued to fire statements at one another, ignoring me. The message was loud and clear, I didn't fit into their clique. I stood on the periphery of the group, waiting to miraculously find the courage to say something, smiling like an idiot, by which point Leo had managed to get Joshy in a headlock, looking very pleased with himself. Joshy didn't mind, but from where I was standing, it looked like he was being strangled.

'Joshy, it's time to go in,' I said.

The boys laughed. Leo shoved him towards Alexander. The game had turned into a tennis match, with Joshy used as the ball. I reached out, hoping Joshy would take my arm. 'Come to me, honey.'

The boys got rowdier.

'Mummy?' Joshy's eyes welled up.

Alexander pushed him back to Leo, harder this time.

I crouched down to Joshy's level. The mums towered over me, staring as the rain started to come down heavy.

'Mummy?' Joshy whined.

'Why don't we stop playing this game now?' I meekly said.

Leo bulldozed him into Alexander, their little bodies crushing him.

'The school is opening,' I said a little louder.

'Mummy, they're squashing me.'

'Please leave him be. Leave him be!' I snapped, pulling them apart and landing on my bum on the wet ground.

At last, the school bell rang and the doors opened. Leo ran towards Rachel, tugging at her hand. She leant over me, the rain dripping from her umbrella hitting my head. 'You should try yoga. It may help "zen" you out. Come, Leo. Let's go, baby.'

The mums, like a pack of wolves, turned in unison to gather their young. In pairs, they disappeared into the school. Joshy reached his hand out to me, helping me up. We walked into the school in silence, his chubby little hand protectively clutching mine.

As I arrived home, I could hear the sound of Rosita's competence as she vacuumed upstairs. I walked straight into the kitchen, leaving wet dirty shoe prints on the newly washed floor. With a trembling hand I opened the kitchen drawer and stared at the stupid Japanese chef knives. I squeezed my eyes tightly shut as a flurry of thoughts rushed my brain.

The growing distance between me and Matt. My desperate attempts at motherhood. Rachel. News about Mary's cancer and her sudden bombardment of phone calls after years of silence. The playground. *The playground.*

Call it gut instinct or a sixth sense or intuition, I knew my brain was desperately trying to communicate something to me about when I was younger, and it was something bad. Real bad.

My mind clung onto the oversized map of the world I'd stuck on the wall in the snug. When I was living in my bedsit, I'd pinned all the countries I'd been planning to visit. Brazil, South Africa, Canada, Thailand, Japan. Sydney, Australia was going to be the first stop. I wanted to start my travels as far away from *her* as possible.

'You won't be needing this anymore,' Matt had said, the day he moved me into his house, ripping the pins off the countries, peeling the poster off the wall.

'Please Matt, please let me keep it!' I'd begged, tears filling my eyes, as the gravity of my impending situation hit me square in the face.

'*Señora?*'

I opened my eyes.

Rosita's horrified face stared back at me. Blood dripped down my arm and two splotches fell onto the floor. I looked at my forearm. Fuck. I'd cut my skin with the small vegetable knife I was holding. I wasn't even aware I'd taken the blade from the drawer.

Rosita gawked with one hand clasped to her chest.

Frozen to the spot, I was unable to meet her eyes. Ashamed. Confused. 'It was an accident,' I eventually said, covering up the blood on the floor with my wet trainer, smearing it around and making it look far worse. 'I'm sorry I made a mess.'

'*O Dios mio.*' She handed me the tea towel she was holding.

'Thank you.' I pressed it hard against my arm. It stung, sobering up my thoughts.

She moved her big capable hands onto her hips and looked at the floor in dismay.

'It was only an accident,' I repeated tearily, as if my words would make it better, make everything vanish. 'Rosita. Matt doesn't need to know about this. It was a mistake. An accident, you understand. He has enough to worry about without having to worry about me as well. Okay?'

'*Si.* Okay. I no tell *Señor* Clarke.'

45

'Thank you,' I breathed.

'*De nada*,' she said.

Was she warming towards me?

'Rosita. Can you pick up Joshy from school later? It's been hard recently and, well …'

Her eyes had hardened. I stopped myself from saying more and pressed the towel onto my cut.

'What I mean to say is, he loves it when you collect him from school.'

'*Si. Señora.* I do,' she said, waving her arms in the air and looking towards the messy floor again.

'Thank you.'

With one speedy movement of her hands, she tied her hair up in a bun and stomped heavily into the utility room, reappearing with a mop and bucket.

'Oh, please. Let me help you clean the floor,' I said.

'No. *Señora.* No. I do.'

As my playlist and bottle of wine came to an end, the quiet house was awakened by a roaring engine. Matt was home. He flung open the door to the snug.

'Everything okay?' he asked, breathless.

'What do you mean?' I said, trying to steady my voice, hoping he hadn't clocked the empty under the sofa.

'Rosita called me, concerned. She said she'd witnessed something… alarming.'

She'd betrayed me. I slouched.

'Well?'

'It was nothing, she's being silly. Only an accident. That's all she saw. I don't know why she even bothered telling you.'

'An accident?'

'That's right. Clumsy me. Nothing to worry about.'

'Are you sure?'

'Of course I'm sure.' I sat upright.

'Perhaps we should get Rosita to help out more? Lessen the burden for you. Would that help?'

'Why? No. I'm fine.' My mouth had gone dry.

'Annabelle, you must understand that I have to put the needs of our son first.' He took in a long deep breath and ran his hand through his hair. 'I worry that things are getting tough for you … like the last time …' He trailed off.

'What "last time"?'

He paused, searching for something in my eyes.

'Matt?'

'Look. I'm going to take a shower and head to bed. I have another early start tomorrow. Are you coming up?'

'No, I think I'll stay up a while longer, watch some TV,' I said, staring at the mute TV.

He left the room, closing the door quietly behind him, leaving his fresh aftershave to linger. Then something caught the corner of my eye. A blue leaflet, on top of the TV unit. I stood up.

The blood drained from my head. How could it be?

My phone started ringing, vibrating violently inside my pocket. It was *her*.

Inching across the room, ignoring the call, I picked up the leaflet, feeling stunned. Confused.

Had I fished it out of the trash? I'd no recollection of doing so, but that didn't mean it hadn't happened. Things had become blurry for me lately. My brain was a muddle, the pressure building, and it was having an effect on me. My nightmares were seeping into my waking life and now I was cutting myself, unaware.

47

The phone finally stopped ringing in my pocket.

Suddenly I could breathe.

I stared at the blue calming hypnotherapy leaflet in my hand.

Change your life. Forever. Call Cassandra Rose, now.

It had to end. Tonight.

Pulling my phone out of my pocket, I dialled.

Chapter Eight

Looking down the steep staircase towards the basement clinic on Abbey Gardens, a wave of nerves came over me. Gripping the railing to steady myself, I inched down the steps towards the front door, wondering if I'd made the right decision by booking the appointment.

Last night, she had answered the phone straight away and I immediately hit the end call button. It took four attempts before I plucked up the courage to even say hello. When we finally spoke, her voice was soothing and reassuring. She was patient with me, listened to me mumble on incoherently and wasn't in the slightest bit irritated by all the missed calls she'd received. She didn't ask any awkward intruding questions, instead saying, *let's see if you like it. No pressure, okay?*

Change your life forever, the leaflet had promised. Well, let's see.

With sweat trickling down my back, I stared at the front door to the clinic. Below the brass plaque, engraved with her name, was the intercom. I pressed it before I could change my mind. The buzzer made a noise and the door automatically opened. I wiped my clammy brow and entered. There was no turning back.

The front door didn't lead to a reception area. Instead, I walked straight into a large open-plan room, which was both cool and airy, a welcome relief from the oppressive heat outside. There was no therapy couch in sight, not what I'd been expecting at all. A white egg chair was positioned to my right by the window and next to it, a stylish gold-trimmed side-table. Beyond that was a two-seater cream sofa and coffee table. On the crisp white wall, above the sofa, a large exotic moth was framed in a black box. It reminded me of the framed moth Matt had on his desk in his study. The opposite wall was bare, apart from a single certificate in a gilded frame, *Diploma in Hypnotherapy*.

The hypnotherapist, or someone I assumed to be the hypnotherapist, sat – with an air of glamour and sophistication – behind a large glass desk positioned in the middle of the room. She had dark eyes and black hair in a razor-sharp bob with a middle parting.

'Welcome. I'm Cassandra Rose, the hypnotherapist,' she said, standing up and brushing down her pencil skirt. Her calves were lifted by 4-inch black stiletto heels, which clicked as she walked across the room to shake my sweaty hand. She asked me to take a seat, gesturing to the fancy egg chair, and offered me a drink. On the side-table sat a jug of water, with slices of lemon and lime, a single glass and a box of tissues.

I said no, even though I was gasping. Sitting on the edge of the chair, I watched her open a leather notepad and take her seat elegantly. A strange ornamental blue and white glass eye chime was hanging from a hook on the ceiling behind her, next to the French doors that led to the garden.

'Have you visited a hypnotherapist before?' The tone of her voice was rich, like velvet.

'No, I haven't. I've seen stuff on TV but ...' I cleared my throat. God, I sounded weird. Alien-like.

'Well, forget everything you think you know about hypnotherapy.

It's all staged for entertainment. My sessions are nothing like that. My goal is to work with my clients, giving them gentle yet powerful suggestions, to change unwanted habits and install healthier ones. It's like re-wiring a brain.'

'Oh.'

'Hypnosis is an extreme state of physical relaxation, with heightened mental awareness. From this deep state of calm, the subconscious is willing to accept ideas and suggestions that the conscious mind might normally block out.' She spoke methodically, as though each word had been carefully selected before escaping her plump lips.

'Right.' My jeans made an embarrassing noise on the chair as I shifted position.

'As I explained over the phone, my clients must have faith in the process and trust that the work undertaken will benefit their lives.'

'Okay,' I said, nodding, not quite understanding what she was saying, nor why I'd put myself in such a stupid situation. What was I thinking?

'You seem nervous. Are you okay?'

'Well. It's just … I've never done anything like this before.'

'I understand. This is a new experience for you, and it should be a positive one. I'm here to help in any way I can. It's my job,' she said, smiling. 'I can help you achieve the life you want, the life you desire, but in order to do so, you must be a willing participant. Does that make sense?'

The hypnotherapist crossed her hands and waited. Her nails were painted crimson. I nodded, even though I was unsure.

An uncomfortable silence followed. My mouth had completely dried out and I desperately needed water but was too scared to help myself. God, I was pathetic. The hypnotherapist stood up, picked up her notebook and wheeled her office chair along the squeaky-clean floor, positioning it opposite me. Then she poured water from the jug, offering me the glass.

'Thank you.' I gulped it down.

Cassandra sat down, placed her notebook on her lap and linked her right ankle over her left. I noticed the red soles of her stilettos – Louboutin.

'Annabelle. The short conversation we had on the phone suggests you may be suffering from a little anxiety. More water?'

'No, thank you.'

'Perhaps you're also suffering from mild depression?'

I looked away, staring at the jug of water.

'Take all the time you need.'

'I'm not sure. Maybe. Yeah, maybe.' How could she deduce so much from one tongue-tied phone call?

'Do you have any children?'

'I have a son.'

'How old is he?'

'Six.'

'What a lovely age.' She leaned further in. 'Are you married?'

'Yes.'

'Does your husband offer you support?'

'What do you mean?'

'Do you get the support you need at home?'

'Of course, he supports me.' I tugged at my clammy t-shirt, hot again despite the cool clinic. 'I'm very lucky, really. I have a lovely home, a lovely family. Everything I could wish for …' I paused, looking away.

Silence crept into the room and lingered thick, like a poisonous gas, filling up the crevices and gaps in the cool clinic space, filling up inside my lungs. I tugged at the neck of my t-shirt. The appointment was a mistake. A terrible mistake.

'Annabelle. I'd like you to view this space as your safe place. I want you to feel as though it's a place where you can let go and be yourself. Say what's on your mind. I want you to have the freedom to be open about your feelings.'

I sat on my hands and made tight fists.

'You can gain control of your life,' she said. 'It's not that hard to achieve.'

Tears started to tumble from my eyes, rolling down onto my cheeks. 'Sorry, I don't know why I'm crying,' I said. 'I haven't cried in years.'

'No need to apologise. Feel free to express yourself in any way you desire.'

'Thank you.' I unclenched my fists and wiped my eyes with my arm roughly.

'Why don't we begin with something fun? A manifestation exercise. You can practise this on your own, whenever you feel like it.'

'Okay.'

'This will help you relax. Are you ready?'

'I'm not sure. I think so.' I'd no idea what she meant by manifestation, no idea what was coming next.

'Humans have the power to manifest anything they want in their lives. If we believe in it strongly enough, it'll happen,' she said, smiling, as though she was letting me in on a secret. 'Okay. Let's start. Don't be nervous. It'll be fun. Just listen to my instructions. That's all I ask of you.'

I nodded.

'I'd like you to take in a long, slow, deep breath and close your eyes. Visualise something that comforts you, and hold that image in your mind. Make it strong. Vivid. As though it were real.'

'Now?'

'Yes please.'

I sat back in the chair.

'You can shut your eyes, Annabelle.'

'Oh. Okay.' Cassandra disappeared from my vision as I closed my eyes.

'Think of the first thing that pops into your head, something that is reassuring. Picture something that makes you feel safe and secure. Comforted. Something you want, or have wanted in the past. It doesn't even have to be real. Hold the image in your mind's eye,' she said. 'Do you have an image?'

I decided to give it a try. What did I have to lose? It's not as if I'd ever see her again. I'd already made up my mind that I wasn't coming back.

'Nod, if you have something locked in your mind.'

I nodded.

For some reason, the first thing that sprang to mind was my imaginary family, inside my imaginary house on the very same road I was currently sitting in. It was Christmas, and we were sitting around the open fire, singing carols. The fireplace glowed with warmth, and our cheeks were pink from the heat. The brightly decorated tree stood proudly in the bay window. Presents, wrapped with large pretty bows, sat under the tree, waiting to be opened. My imaginary mother handed me a hot chocolate. My chest swelled. 'Thank you, Mummy,' I said to her.

Time passed.

Relaxing further into the chair, I lost myself in the perfect scene I'd conjured up in my mind's eye. I was locked inside a snow globe with my imaginary family.

'Annabelle, how do you feel now?'

I peeled my eyes open. 'Warm and fuzzy.'

'Fantastic,' she said, purring like a cat.

Cassandra and everything else in the room came back into focus. 'That was so nice,' I said, smiling back at her. 'So, so, nice.'

'You see? Nothing to worry about,' she said, grinning from cheek to cheek. 'Shall we proceed with some light hypnosis and see how we go from there?'

'Yes. Okay. I'll give it a try. Why not?'

'Brilliant, Annabelle. You won't regret your decision,' she smiled. 'I promise.'

She adjusted herself in her seat. Cleared her throat.

'Now,' she said in an even deeper, richer tone, 'take in some more long, slow, deep breaths for me ... long, slow, deep breaths, in and out ...I want you to concentrate on your breathing ... nothing more, nothing less. Focus on my voice.'

Here I was, about to put my trust in a complete stranger.

She slowed her own breathing down, and before I knew it, we were both breathing in perfect synchronicity. With each breath I watched her take in, I sank further into the chair, watching her chest rise and fall as she breathed in time with me. In and out.

I waited for more instructions, but no instructions came. My eyes began to feel heavy ... they wanted to close ... I couldn't fight it, even if I tried ... I allowed my eyes to ... close.

'That's right. Let it all go. Keep your eyes closed.' She sounded out every syllable.

My eyelids were heavy, like lead. The pressure inside my brain released, like air escaping. I was melting into the chair, as the outside world shut down around me.

Her words floated in and out of my brain. It was narcotic.

'Relax ... there's no agenda here ... all you need to do is let go ... let my voice travel with you ... breathe in and out ... letting go ... heavier and heavier. Reee-laaaaax ...' she said, stretching out the words like an elastic band.

Believe, trust and let go. Those were the words that settled inside my head. I couldn't tell when one sentence ended and another began, it all merged together. Breathe in and out. Believe, trust and let go.

Strange sensations washed over me. One minute, a wave of sleep carried me into my imagination and the next, I became acutely hyper-sensitive to my surroundings, as though I'd be able to hear a pin drop in the street outside. I wanted to vanish inside her words.

I wanted to vanish.

'That's it, breathe … in and out … breathe in time with me, Annabelle … focus on my breath … let it become your breath … drifting away … I'll take you to a happier place … deeper and deeper. And sleep …'

Her voice entered my mind, and my thoughts became her voice.

'I'd like you to imagine a time and place in your life, where you were at your happiest. Picture a time and place where you were independent. A time before you met your husband, before you had your son. Carefree and happy. I want you to search your mind for a specific time and place. Do it now. Picture it in your mind. Relive that wonderful special moment. Where are you? What are you doing? How do you feel? What colours do you see? What sounds do you hear? Is there a particular smell? Feel secure in this environment – alone, by yourself. You are a strong independent woman, Annabelle.'

The tiny hairs on my arms stood on end.

I drifted back in time, to the summer I worked in the Greek islands, when I was nineteen. It was the first time I'd ever been abroad. I was in Crete and I'd discovered a secluded, enclosed, beach. It was my secret. The sea was a beautiful turquoise and I'd never seen colours like that before. The waves lapped gently against the shore and I could smell the pine trees in the hills above. The strong midday sun recharged the cells of my body, I was alive and at peace with my surroundings. The soles of my feet were burnt by the hot sand as I walked towards the sea, then dipped my toes into the warm foamy waves. The cheap toe ring I'd bought in the market reflected back at me. The water was inviting. I took off my sarong and dived in. I began to swim out, deeper and deeper. Far from the shore. I lay on my back and floated out towards the anchored yachts. I drifted off.

Drifting, drifting, drifting out to sea.

'Counting back up from one to ten. Coming back to reality. One, feel yourself becoming more alert. Two, climbing up the stairs of your conscious mind. Three, becoming aware of the room.'

No. No. No. My brain scrambled. *I don't want to leave.*

'Four, waking up. Five, you're now more alert. Six, moving your fingers, your toes. The sensations are coming back. Seven.'

I'm not ready.

'Eight. You're almost back in the room with me.'

I want to go back to the beach.

'Nine. Prepare to open your eyes.' Her voice was crystal clear. Sharp. The image of the beach disappeared.

'Ten. Wake up. Eyes wide open. Welcome back to the room.'

We stared at one another.

No words were exchanged, no words were needed.

Exhilaration stirred inside me. It felt as though I was high. Awakened. Seeing clearly for the very first time. My mind had opened.

She gave me homework to do. I was to say positive affirmations to myself as often as possible until the next time I saw her. She explained that the positive suggestions would take time to become fully effective, but they would eventually stick because something called synapses in the brain would have been created, forming new thoughts and habits.

I'd no idea what she was on about, or how it all worked, but I trusted that she knew what she was doing. From the moment she had pulled me out of hypnosis, and I'd opened my eyes, I knew I wanted more. I was hooked.

She'd done the impossible: she'd helped me to escape.

Chapter Nine

I woke to the sound of Joshy chirping downstairs about having outdoor PE, Matt talking loudly on the phone about another new investment he was interested in, and Rosita clinking and clanking, loading the dishwasher while singing some Spanish folk song to herself.

I looked at my alarm clock. It was 7.45am. Damn it. I kicked my legs out of bed, forcing myself up and out.

It had been a few days since my hypnotherapy session with Cassandra, and the high I'd initially felt had diminished. I'd slipped back into my funk. My nightmares had continued, night after night, and Mary had continued to call, day after day. Her constant barrage was making it impossible to think, to breathe, to live. It was suffocating.

When I finally plucked up the courage to answer her call, I experienced a physical reaction and couldn't go through with it. My hands shook violently, my body tensed, and a sense of doom gripped my throat so tightly it constricted my breathing. It was a full-blown panic attack.

Then there was Matt. Staying later and later at the office. In the evenings, I'd work myself into a frenzy, convincing myself he was having an affair, but come the morning, after having hardly any sleep, I'd dismiss my paranoia, making up excuses for him. I'd no solid proof. Rosita didn't help matters either of course, compounding my inner feelings of hopelessness, and I was beginning to wonder whether Joshy preferred her over me.

Matt knew nothing about my hypnotherapy appointment. Cassandra suggested I wait a while before telling him. It would help empower me, help me to take back control of my life, she'd said. To be honest, if Matt had known, he would not have reacted well. He hated all the 'mumbo jumbo' stuff that had been passed down by my sorry excuse for a mother. He didn't believe in crystals, chakras, tarot readings or any form of alternative healing. If it wasn't on Harley Street, then it wasn't legit.

By the time I'd braved it down the stairs, Rosita had Joshy dressed, teeth and hair brushed, and was making him a healthy breakfast of porridge and berries. His reading bag and PE kit were waiting by the front door.

Her competency highlighted my failings.

'Thought I'd let you lie in,' Matt said, sipping his super green energy juice. He was suited and booted, ready for work.

'Thank you,' I said, sitting next to Joshy by the kitchen island.

'Is everything okay? You were tossing and turning all night long.'

'Yes, fine.'

Joshy tucked into his healthy breakfast, kicking his legs against the bar stool as he ate. I placed my hand on his leg to stop his fidgeting.

'You still look tired. Why don't you allow Rosita to do the school drop off and pick up?' Matt said to me.

Rosita nodded in agreement as she walked into the utility room, holding the wash basket. Joshy started kicking his feet again, catching me in the leg. I turned my body slightly to avoid any more boots and looked at the wall clock. 8.10. I had just enough time to throw on some jeans and get him to school for 8.30.

'I can take him,' I said, glancing at Rosita in the utility room, who was already undoing her hair from the restraints of its bun. I stood up.

'*Hermoso niño*. Come on Joshua,' she said, instantly appearing in the kitchen. 'Let's go school.'

Joshy squealed with delight and jumped off the stool, running to get his shoes. I sat back down.

'Annabelle. Take the day off for yourself,' Matt said.

I pulled the belt to my dressing gown tightly around my waist.

'Maybe it's time for you to take up a hobby?'

'I guess,' I said, fiddling with my fingers. 'You know, there's something I've wanted to do for a long time. Something that is long overdue. Since I'm turning thirty, an' all, I thought maybe I could start driving lessons. What do you think?' I sat upright, hopeful.

Matt noisily slurped his green super juice, draining the glass and turning away, placing the empty in the sink. 'Right then. I'm off to work,' he said.

He walked over to Joshy, who was sitting on the floor putting his Velcro-fastened school shoes on, and leant in, kissing his forehead. 'I may be home late tonight, darling,' he said, like a broken record, looking at his Rolex. 'Make sure you eat dinner with Joshua.' He then padded over to me and kissed me on the forehead, as though I was his other child, not his wife.

His skin was soft; he'd shaved, and his aftershave lingered on my cheek. 'Okay,' I said, through gritted teeth.

Within fifteen minutes, Joshy and Rosita were on their way to school, and Matt's jeep rattled the house as he drove off to work. They were gone.

Everything fell eerily silent.

I Bluetoothed music through the speakers, hoping to break the stillness and fill the void. With everyone gone, the expansive space which I called home became a universe, with me a grain of sand. Even after seven years my house didn't feel like a home to me. I didn't fit comfortably inside. It was like wearing oversized baggy clothes and clown shoes. I felt more like a house guest than a permanent resident.

I knew I was lucky. Never in my wildest dreams had I expected to live such a privileged lifestyle. The house. The car. The clothes. The diamond ring. The housekeeper turned nanny. The whole thing was nuts to me, and I still had to pinch myself on a daily basis. I didn't want for anything. Matt made sure of it.

Loading the washing machine with clothes, I was determined to do something useful, throwing items from the basket inside, mixing the colours and whites together. I'd managed okay on my own before I met Matt, before my life had been micromanaged, and I could certainly manage now. I'd do the laundry, get myself showered and changed, and perhaps search online for a driving instructor. I didn't need Matt's permission. Maybe after that, I could go shopping, buy something new to wear, something more sophisticated and glamorous.

Matt's Armani jeans were at the bottom of the pile. I checked the pockets out of habit and retrieved a receipt, eyeballing it. It was dated a few nights back, when he was supposedly working late.

The receipt was for dinner at an intimate restaurant. He has taken me there once for a romantic meal, when we'd just started dating. The only problem was, the restaurant was located on the other side of town in Chelsea – nowhere near his offices on Baker Street.

I collapsed onto the hard tiles, staring at the receipt in my hand.

My mind began to spit out excuses for him.

There had to be a logical explanation. The receipt didn't prove anything. It was dinner with Bill, his business partner, or maybe it was with a new associate he was schmoozing. It was Celeste, his mother. He'd forgotten to tell me she was in town. But no, she would have wanted to see Joshy.

I analysed the contents for clues, but it only made my suspicions worse. The meal had been for two people. Prawns and scallops, followed by two plates of sea bass and samphire, washed down with a bottle of white Burgundy. The wine, predictably, cost a fortune.

The walls to the utility room started to close in, as my paranoia began to swell. Larger and larger my suspicions grew, squeezing out the oxygen from my lungs. I threw his trousers into the machine and put the wash on an extra-long cycle, tearing the receipt up into tiny pieces.

Stumbling out of the utility room, I gasped for breath.

Memories rushed my brain as I mourned my old self, the person I used to be before I met Matt, and after I had fled Mary and the estate. The in-between. That short moment in my life where I actually thought, truly believed, that everything would turn out okay. I'd had big dreams. I was saving money so I could meet my girlfriends in Oz. It was going to be amazing – the beaches, the parties, the boys. The freedom. All I had to do was save enough cash to tide me over once I got there … but then I met Matt, and everything changed.

My best friend Kat never understood why I cried down the phone to her the day I found out I was pregnant, and Matt had proposed. She said I was lucky to have bagged a millionaire. Wasn't that every girl's dream?

Kat was always the scared one, not me.

'You can do it, Kat! You can do anything,' I'd said to her.

'I can't go to Oz alone. We're a team.'

'You're not alone. The others are already out there. Why wait? Just think, I'll be there a few months after you.'

'You promise?'

'Promise. I'm going to be drinking beer and enjoying barbecues on the beach with you all soon. I just need to save a little more money first.'

'Okay. Okay. I'm going to do it. I can't believe it. I'm gonna book a one-way ticket to Sydney,' she asserted. 'Thank you, Annabelle. You're such an amazing friend.' She hugged me tight and called the girls in Australia.

She wouldn't recognise me now.

Opening the kitchen drawer, I stared at the stupid chef knives lined up in a neat row from largest to smallest. The longer I stared, the more unbearable the urges became, overriding the little logic and dignity left inside me.

It could ease the pain, I told myself.

It *would* ease the pain. Fix things. The only way I knew how.

My hand inched closer to the blade. My finger ran along the cold sharp edge. Ice ran down my spine. I shut my eyes. Cassandra came to mind.

My eyes sprang open and I scrambled for my phone.

```
Hi Cassandra. Sorry to bother you. I know my
appointment is not for a couple of days, but I was
wondering if you have any space today. It's an emer-
gency. I'm super low and I'm having bad thoughts. I'm
worried I'm going to do something stupid. Annabelle
```

Three dots danced on my iPhone. She was replying.

```
Why are you so down? What's prompted these nega-
tive feelings?
```

The dots appeared on my screen once more.

```
What are you worried you'll do exactly? Cassandra
```

My heart raced as my fingers fired across a quick response, grateful she was on the other end of the phone. Grateful to have someone.

```
Something I'll regret.
```

Fumbling with my phone, I located my music app so that I could switch the music off. The quiet returned, and this time it was a welcome break. Sitting on the heated kitchen floor, I drew my knees into my chest, waiting for her response.

What's happened to make you feel this way? You were very positive when you left the clinic the other day. Why the sudden U-turn?

Things aren't so great at home I texted.

She was taking her time to respond.

I re-read the message I'd sent and imagined her eye-rolling, thinking I was another bored desperate housewife, dissatisfied with my privileged life. Boohoo me. What did I have to complain about? On paper, my life was perfect. A dream come true. But it didn't feel like a fairy-tale. It felt like a trap. My fingers found my voice and typed out another text.

Sometimes, I get urges. Bad urges. And they're getting harder to resist.

Holding my breath, I stared at the phone, waiting. I typed another message.

I don't know if I can wait until my next appt. Please. If you have any space for me today.

My eyes welled up.

Annabelle. This is very concerning. Firstly, you must promise to keep yourself safe from any harm until we meet. Secondly, I will re-jig my day. Come to the clinic at midday. Don't be late.

Yes. Yes.

Thank you so much. A

I held my phone close. She'd no idea what a lifeline she was.

It's nothing. I am your therapist after all, and I must ensure that you are safe at all times.

She was a guardian angel. Thank you I typed.

Until midday. Cassandra R.

Chapter Ten

Cassandra sat behind her glass desk, serene and sophisticated, not a damn hair out of place. She was together in every way I wasn't. She welcomed me with a warm smile and the tension in my body started to lift. I wanted to thank her for offering me the emergency appointment and being there for me when I needed it, but I didn't know how to do that without drawing attention to the bad stuff I'd texted her about.

I was an idiot for sharing so much.

Taking my seat, I started twiddling my long hair. Fresh white lilies on the side table had opened and their scent tickled my nose. Next to them, a box of tissues, a replenished jug of water with slices of lemon and lime, and a single glass.

'I'm so thankful you could see me at such short notice,' I said.

'I have a duty of care to all my clients. My clients can call on me at any time. I'll always try my best to make space.'

'That's really kind of you and reassuring to know.'

'Not at all.' She folded her hands on the table and breathed in, looking serious. 'May we discuss your messages?'

I nodded and stared down at my white mottled legs which never seemed to tan. It was a stupid idea to wear jean shorts for the appointment.

'You mentioned you were concerned about doing something bad?'

'I'm sorry if I worried you. It wasn't my intention.'

'Is there something you'd like to share with me?'

My face flushed.

'Do you sometimes hurt yourself,' she said, 'on purpose?'

Feeling like a little girl, I shrank into the seat.

'It's okay to talk about it. You're safe here with me,' she said, the softness in her voice choking me up.

'It's nothing,' I finally said, dismissively.

'You don't self-harm?'

My hands trembled as I reached for the water, taking a swig. The silence started to build in the room, like an intense pressure. I sat still, convinced that any micro movement I made would give my state of mind away.

'I need to understand your behavioural patterns in order to help you.' She sat back, examining me.

'I don't know how to explain it.'

'Try me,' she said.

'I …'

'Consider me your friend, Annabelle. A friend who offers you help and guidance. If you view me as a friend, as opposed to your therapist, it'll help you to lose your inhibitions.'

The tone of her voice was syrupy and warm, comforting, making me want to open up to her. I wanted to let go and give myself away. It was so hard holding onto the baggage all the time. It was eating me up inside.

Could I let my guard down? Could I trust her?

'I do hurt myself,' I eventually said, clenching my hands. 'Sometimes.'

She opened her leather notebook and picked up her pen. 'Do you know why?'

'It stops me from feeling other bad stuff.'

She scribbled something in her notebook.

The room fell quiet. I drank water. 'It's only happened a couple of times. It's something I should never have started up again,' I said.

She looked up. 'Started up again?'

The blood swished around inside my head. 'I did it as a teenager. It was a silly phase.'

'I see.' Her features were soft, her face filled with empathy. Her back remained poised and upright, like a ballerina. Her nails were painted bright red, matching the colour of her lips. The large emerald ring on her middle finger glistened from the lights above. She had a delicate gold chain on her slender wrist. There was no wedding band.

'Really, it's nothing. I've stopped before, and I can stop again.'

'Why do you dismiss it as nothing?' She twirled her pen around in her fingers.

'I'm not suicidal, if that's what you're writing in your book.' I pointed.

She put her pen inside her pad and closed the book, placing it aside. She looked into my eyes. 'I believe you're a highly sensitive human being with complex needs. Needs that haven't been met yet,' she said. 'We'll work together to meet your needs. Here, in this clinic.'

I could feel my face turning pink. No one had been that nice to me before. I pulled a few tissues from the box and blew my nose.

'Was there something that happened to you when you were younger, perhaps? Something that compelled you to hurt yourself?'

I shook my head.

'Okay,' she said, keeping her facial expression neutral. 'Okay.'

I let out a deep sigh, I hadn't realised that I'd been holding my breath.

'Let's explore another avenue. Feel free to stop me at any point.'
I nodded.

'Are you concerned the bad urges you have may extend to others, such as your son, for example?'

'Sorry. I don't understand what you're saying.'

'Do you believe that you're capable of hurting your son?'

'What? No!' My stomach knotted tightly. 'I would *never* harm my son. *Never*. I'd die for him. *Never*,' I repeated.

'You understand, that as your therapist, I need to ask these awkward questions. It's important to get a rounded picture of what is happening.' She re-crossed her legs.

'Of course. I'd never harm him. He's my life.'

'I understand.'

'It's just that sometimes ...' I paused.

'Sometimes?'

'Sometimes I feel a little distant from my son. Detached.'

'I see.'

'God. That sounds so bad, doesn't it? I didn't mean it in a bad way. I don't know why I said that,' I mumbled.

'It's okay Annabelle. This is your safe space, now. You can unload any way you wish, even if you don't quite understand what you're saying,' she said, softly. 'May I ask, how is your relationship with your husband?'

'Well, he supports me.'

'What about love?'

'He says he loves me. He says it all the time.'

'Go on.'

'I don't know, maybe it's me, maybe I'm misinterpreting everything. Maybe I'm going mad?' My mind rested on the receipt. There had to be a logical explanation for it.

'In what sense?' she said in a soothing tone.

'I'm finding *everything* hard at the moment.'

'I can see that. Perhaps if you can elaborate a little more, we can get to the bottom of …'

'Intimacy,' I whispered, looking down. 'The thought of being intimate with my husband at the moment sends my head into a spin. I freeze. Clam up,' I said. 'There's all sorts of stuff cropping up from my past and it seems to be getting in the way of me living my everyday life. Things that I don't want to deal with now. Can't deal with. Things I can't explain to you.'

'I understand, and I won't probe if it makes you uncomfortable,' she said, thoughtfully. 'How about you tell me *when* these negative feelings started to occur? Can you do that for me?'

'Everything was fine until she started to …' I tailed off, focusing my gaze on the hypnotherapy certificate on the wall.

'Annabelle?'

'Look, everything is getting to me because I'm not sleeping very well. I've been having nightmares lately.'

'Nightmares?'

'They're nothing. Just stupid childish dreams. Nonsense.'

She shifted in her seat and cleared her throat. I could sense her frustration. I wasn't giving her anything to work with. I wasn't quite ready. All I wanted was to fall into the trance state and float away to Greece, escaping from my problems.

'We can move on from the dreams, for now,' she said.

'Thank you,' I said. 'I'm sorry I'm so hopeless today.'

'Annabelle. Do you have any friends you can turn to? Anyone else you can speak to?'

'No. Not really. It's tragic I know.'

'Not at all. These things happen. People drift. Circumstances change.' She smiled broadly, making me feel more at ease. 'Let's explore your relationship with your husband a little more. Is that okay?'

'Well, we don't spend much time together. Not like we used to.' I took in a deep breath. 'We seem to be growing apart.'

'I see,' she said, with a heavy nod.

'He works so hard and he does try his best. For instance, he's finding the time to organise my thirtieth birthday celebrations. That's something, right?'

'That's very thoughtful of him.'

'I'm sure whatever it is he's planning, it will be big, flashy. Expensive.'

'You're very lucky.' She smiled.

'Sometimes, I feel like he doesn't know me at all.'

She stood up, picked up her notebook and pen, wheeled her office chair across the room until she sat opposite me and crossed her legs.

'Don't get me wrong, I'm grateful for all the amazing things we have. I don't come from much. In fact, I come from nothing at all. It's such a privilege to give Joshy everything he needs and more. Give him the things I only dreamt of as a child. An amazing home, a good education, a family that wants him. But that doesn't mean I'm comfortable with it all. Do you know what I mean?'

She nodded and started scribbling in her notepad. I picked at my nail varnish, hoping she wouldn't probe into my background. I'd slipped up again.

She stopped writing and looked straight at me. 'Tell me, what would you like for your birthday?' she asked, warmly.

I relaxed my shoulders and cleared my throat. 'What I'd like more than anything is for him to come home early and to tell me he loves me. That would be enough.'

A beat of silence followed.

'That doesn't sound too unreasonable,' she finally said. 'What else would you like him to do for your birthday?'

'Maybe a dinner at home, no fuss. Just the three of us. I'd rather that, than go out to some fancy restaurant where I don't know which fork or spoon to use. I'd be happy with a small gift, like a necklace, something understated, something that doesn't scream money.' I paused. 'My husband screams money all the bloody time and I'm struggling with it. It's the only way he knows how to communicate. Believe it or not, I feel we may have been happier without it.'

I looked at the clock above the door. The session was up, and I'd been talking for ages and ages. We hadn't even done the hypnosis. 'You know, I'm known as Annabelle, wife of a successful businessman. I have no identity of my own. I used to be somebody. I used to matter. Now, I'm only a wife and a mother – and I'm pretty crappy at both.' The words spilled out of me before I could swallow them up.

'Maybe you could speak to …' she paused. 'You haven't mentioned your husband's name.'

'I'd prefer not to say. Just in case. You know what the Hampstead community is like. You might even know him,' I laughed nervously.

'Yes of course, you're quite right. It's best to keep things separate,' she said. 'The space we've created here, inside these four walls, is for you and you alone. It's designed to make you feel secure, with no outside influences.'

We sat facing one another in silence. I looked at the wall clock.

'Don't worry about the time, Annabelle. I can offer you an extra session, free of charge.'

'Oh, thank you so much. That's so generous.'

'Not at all,' she smiled. 'In a moment, we'll begin the hypnosis which will help get you back to a positive frame of mind.'

I breathed into my belly and rested my hands on my lap, waiting

72

for her to begin. An excitement started to build inside of me. I wanted to escape back to Greece, back to the place where no one could find me. Disappear inside myself.

'Are you ready to begin?' she asked, softening the tone of her voice. I nodded.

'Close your eyes and let go.'

I closed my eyes and began to drift. I did not quite understand the mechanics of hypnosis, all I knew was that it was something I was good at, and it felt magical to get away and escape from all of my mounting problems.

Chapter Eleven

CLINICAL NOTES
Mrs Annabelle (surname not disclosed)
D.O.B: 28.07.89
ADDRESS: Marsefield Crescent, Hampstead, NW3
Session date: 04.07.19
Session time: 12:00
Sessions: Session 2.

Client reports experiencing 'bad urges' – self-harming.
Client claimed urges have 'started up again'. These habits started when she was younger. Why? How?
Self-punishment flared up recently. Evident there's a trigger – query recent triggers.
Client reports harming stops her 'feeling bad stuff' – what is she blocking?
Self-harm used as coping mechanism.
Note – pattern of self-harm associated with guilt / shame.

Annabelle reports problems with love and intimacy. Husband – not close.

Guarded about family life. (Question, could her son be in danger?)
No friends or allies. Clearly lonely. Needs a friend. Confidante.

Bouts of depression. Suffering insomnia and nightmares. Consumed by a constant stream of negative thoughts. This all results in low self-esteem.

Today's hypnosis: *Calming down of nervous system. Breathing techniques. Deeper hypnosis work for self-esteem and self- image, using strong visualisations.*

Trouble sleeping – a continuation of relaxation techniques during hypnosis, helping to reduce anxiety and promote better sleep, possibly eliminating nightmares.

Follow-up session/s:

Challenge self-perception and offer alternative possibilities.
Boost confidence.
Build more trust in therapeutic relationship.
What happened when she was younger? Find the trigger/s.
Are the nightmares significant?
Break unwanted destructive habits.

Homework given:

Continue with positive affirmations for empowerment,
'She is strong, she is independent, she can make her own positive decisions, she can take back control over her life.'

Note to self. Annabelle's birthday – necklace.

Chapter Twelve

I'd showered, dressed, applied some make-up and was downstairs making breakfast for Joshy before Rosita had a chance to tie her hair up in a bun and put on her apron. Joshy's reading bag was waiting by the front door. Rosita had sensed my shift in mood and seemed to busy herself with household chores around me, hovering close by on standby, like an annoying fly. Determined to stay on top of things, I wanted to prove to Rosita, to Matt and to myself that I *could* cope. And I did cope – I didn't screw up once. With a new spring in my step, I walked him to school without any protests from him demanding Rosita take him instead. He bounced all the way to the school gates, his little hand nestled in mine.

Was the hypnotherapy working? My tummy fluttered at the prospect.

Rachel, Saskia and the others, all sporting gym gear, were in the playground in a wolfpack huddle. My stomach churned at the sight of them, but I managed to stay focused on the job at hand. I couldn't avoid Rachel and the others forever. Plucking up the courage, I followed Joshy through the playground, with my head held high, fixed on showing them I was as normal as they were.

Rachel smiled, 'Hello.'

'Hi.'

'So?' she said, glaring at me and then looking around her, waiting for me to make the first move and speak.

My mind had gone blank within seconds of approaching. I smiled, cursing myself under my breath. Rachel made a face at the others and they began to giggle awkwardly. Within moments, my emotions started to betray me, stupid tears formed in my eyes. I couldn't quite believe what was happening. I was a grown woman, for Christ's sake. All I wanted to do was say hello, RSVP to her kid's birthday party and ask for a frigging playdate for Joshy. How hard could it be? A simple task was escalating into a nightmare.

'Are you okay?' Rachel asked.

'I was …'

All eyes were on me.

'I'm RSVP-ing for Leo's birthday party. We'd love to come.' I breathed a sigh of relief. There, I did it.

'Your gorgeous husband has already replied. He texted me the other night,' she snapped back in a self-assured way.

'Oh, okay. Great. That's great.' I stumbled back, feeling disorientated, knocking into Joshy who was standing behind me.

WHEN did he text her and *WHY* was he texting her? What else did they text about late at night?

The school playground spun around me.

'Finally, the school's opened. They think we don't notice, but we do. We notice EVERYTHING,' said Rachel, taking Leo's hand and brushing past me. 'Come, baby.'

The rest of the school run turned into a panicky blur. Did I hook his reading bag onto the right peg, or had it slipped from my fingers in the busy corridor? Did his teacher ask to speak to me after school, and had I agreed? Did I even kiss Joshy goodbye?

All I could think about was Matt and Rachel. Rachel and Matt. Matt and Rachel.

I scrambled out of the school gates as quickly as possible, catching my breath outside. There was no way I was going back to the house and Rosita, the super woman, I'd only spiral further. Thank God I had an appointment with Cassandra at noon, but what was I supposed to do in the meantime while my mind raced uncontrollably?

Blood pumped around my body as I paced up the hill towards the high street, hoping the exercise would snap me out of my rapidly descending mood. I stopped at the cash machine, clammy and out of breath, standing in the long queue of people suited and booted, about to get on the tube to go to work. While I waited in line, I typed *Cassandra Rose hypnotherapist* into the search engine on my phone and waited a few seconds for the page to upload.

There were no page results apart from a link to her website with the caption, *Website Under Construction.* I then opened WhatsApp, found Cassandra's name and zoomed in on her profile picture. It was a professional black and white head shot, like you'd find on an acting CV. She was looking sideways over her shoulder towards the camera, her hair was black, shoulder-length, longer than it was now, glossed to a shine, and she was sporting a short fringe. She had a hint of a smile on her face and a sparkle in her eyes.

Embarrassed by my own picture, I scanned my photo album and replaced the awful selfie I'd taken a few months back in the park with Joshy, to a shot of me sitting solo on a beach in a sarong and vest top. Matt had taken the photo when we were on holiday, making me pose like a model. Even though I felt stupid at the time and was as white as snow, despite having been in the sun for nearly a week, at least I looked relaxed and happy.

It was my turn at the cash machine, so I placed my phone in the back pocket of my jeans and rifled through my rucksack, trying to locate my purse. I pulled my credit card out of the slip of the purse and noticed that the family portrait of us on holiday that I usually kept there was missing. Had I dropped it someplace?

After withdrawing cash, I walked along the high street aimlessly waiting for the shops to open. I passed an artisan baker, ice cream parlour, independent bookstore and a charity shop filled with second hand top designer goods, all the while focusing on anything other than my husband and his female bestie texting sweet nothings to each other late at night. I stopped outside a hairdresser's a few doors down from the tube station. It was still early and there were no customers inside, but the sign on the door said *open*.

Taking in a deep breath, I stepped inside.

A little bell rang as I entered. The walls were bare brick, the mirrors were silver gilt and the waiting area seats were French Louis XV in style, with grey fabric upholstery. Breakfast radio played loudly in the shop. One stylist was coiling a hairdryer wire near the slinky curved reception desk and another was sweeping the floor at the back of the shop, where three sinks were located.

'Yes, my darling,' the woman with the hairdryer said, chewing gum. 'How can I help you?' She looked to be around my age, had a platinum blonde pixie cut, lots of piercings in her ears and was wearing high waisted baggy jeans and white trainers.

'I don't have an appointment, but I was hoping you could fit me in?'

'Why don't you take a seat? Tell me what you want,' she said, placing the dryer on the reception desk and walking over to the black hydraulic chair by the first workstation near the window. She pumped up the chair.

'I was wondering if you could trim my hair. Cut it shorter,' I said, taking my rucksack off my shoulders, feeling a little more confident about my sudden spontaneity.

'Not a problem, my darling. You sure you don't want to try something more adventurous?' She gestured to the seat.

'What if you cut it just above the shoulder? Maybe give me a fringe?' I sat down on the chair and stared at my reflection.

She scrunched her nose and cocked her head to the side, analysing my 'dreary look' through the mirror. 'Okay. That could work. That could work. What about some blonde and auburn highlights, to create depth to the mousy colour, lightening it up for the summer?'

'Actually, I was wondering if you could dye my hair darker. Much darker.'

As the stylist cut my hair, I began to feel a little less burdened, as though I was shedding a layer of skin. Screw Matt and screw Rachel!

The clinic was exactly as I'd left it. Lilies in a vase, box of tissues, jug of water with slices of lemon and lime bopping inside, a single glass. Sat behind the glass desk was Cassandra, smiling warmly at me. 'Wow. You look great, Annabelle,' she said, as I took my seat.

My face flushed. I'd decided to go for a warmer hair colour, called cocoa, a shoulder-length choppy bob and no fringe.

'How are you?'

'This morning started off well. I forced myself out of bed, walked Joshy to school and as you can see, had a haircut,' I smiled. 'But then ...'

I thought about Matt texting Rachel. Did it actually mean anything, or were they just friends? After all, friends often texted one another late at night.

'I had an embarrassing moment with the mums at the school gates. I seem to lose my confidence when I'm around them,' I said. 'I'm sorry if it all sounds trivial.'

'Ahh, the infamous school playground. It's like being back at school, is it not?'

'Exactly,' I said, wondering if she had any children of her own. 'They huddle together in a close group, like wolves, and it's hard to get on the inside of their pack and gain their acceptance.'

'Do you believe you're not good enough for them, perhaps?' she said, opening her pad, jotting something down.

'I don't know. Maybe?'

'The irony is, Annabelle, you *are* good enough to be in their company. You *are* good enough to be in anyone's company. In fact, they'd be lucky to have you as a friend. From the little I know of you, you seem kind and considerate, sensitive towards others' wants and needs. Selfless. These are amazing traits to have. You're perfect friend material.'

My face flushed bright pink.

She stood up, wheeled her chair across the room and sat opposite me. She crossed one leg over the other, swinging her foot up and down. I had begun with a misconception that all therapists were stuffy looking and old, but she was the polar opposite. Confident, sophisticated and glamorous.

'Why don't I give you some hypnotic suggestions to help manifest more positivity into your life? Let's just focus on you for today. Only you.'

I eased further into the chair, preparing myself. 'Shall I close my eyes now?'

My eagerness made her giggle. Her husky laugh echoed around the room. It was infectious, and I began to giggle too. It had been a while since I'd heard my own laughter. I'd no idea what we were both giggling about, but it felt great to let off some steam and to be myself, without any snobby judgement from others.

It felt as though we were old friends and had known one another our whole lives.

'Okay, okay.' She calmed her giggles down, wiping under her eyes to make sure no mascara had run. Her mascara was fine. She was fine. Her eyes fixed on mine. 'Let's try something different today, make it a little fun. Hold out your hand.'

'Both hands?'

'Just the one. I'm going to shake your hand, like a greeting. This is called a rapid induction technique. Just go along with it. Okay?'

She took my hand and stared deep into my eyes. Electricity crackled through my body as she started to shake my hand gently. Convinced she had the power to read my thoughts, I tried to empty my mind of clutter. Slowly, slowly, I began to lose myself in her black crow-like eyes.

She yanked at my hand unexpectedly, slapping it down onto my lap. 'Now sleep,' she commanded.

It was a complete shock and I was startled. But my eyes immediately closed.

'You'll now be in a deep trance state. Transported to the depths of your subconscious mind within minutes. Seconds. I'm going to begin counting down from ten, nine. Rapid trance, deeper and deeper you go ...' Her voice faded into the background and everything slowed down, stretching out in front of me, until it felt as though time stood still.

My body swayed to the tempo of her voice as her words and sentences and their hidden subtexts filtered into my brain.

'You will grow in confidence, with my guidance.'

'You will begin to concentrate on what is right and let go of what is wrong.'

'Flush out the negativity that surrounds your life. Flush it out.'

As my confidence grew, Greece appeared to me once more. The lapping of the waves, the anchored yachts, the smell of the surrounding pine trees. I breathed in deep and slow, filling up the cells in my body with her words of confidence. All my worries about Matt's supposed affair with Rachel had disappeared. All my stresses about my childhood and Mary had trickled away. All my urges to hurt myself had vanished. I was restored once more.

'I will steer you to a better life. A happier life. An independent life. I'll be there for you, if you need me. Always.'

Chapter Thirteen

'What's taking so long? Hurry up, for crying out loud,' Matt shouted from downstairs.

I'd locked myself in the en suite bathroom and was psyching myself up to leave the house, repeating the positive affirmations Cassandra had given me over and over again. It was the day of Leo's birthday party – the social gathering from hell – and we were running late.

As I climbed into the front seat of the jeep, I was feeling a little more hopeful. They were just normal people. It was only a kids' party. I had nothing to worry about. It was one afternoon. If I could get through this, I could get through anything. I could do this! I really could. I turned to Matt and smiled, placing my hand on his lap. The muscle in his leg twitched beneath my hand and he kept his gaze straight ahead, his jaw tight. He fired up the engine and pulled off the driveway. He hated being late for anything.

By the time we drove onto the private road in Frognal, towards Rachel's house, my confidence had dwindled. Beads of sweat appeared on Matt's brow as he struggled to park the G-Wagon in between a Range Rover and a Bentley, swearing under his breath, which was something he'd never normally do. He was flustered, too.

We walked through the iron gates and along the gravelled driveway, past the newly wrapped Aston Martin and towards Rachel's magnificent arts-and-crafts-era house, in complete silence. Joshy was sandwiched between us. My anxiety mounting with every step, I wanted to be anywhere but there.

A hired butler greeted us at the arched front door with stained glass. He took the birthday present and ushered us into the house. We walked through the expansive hallway, with its Versace wallpaper, white marbled floor and a showy chandelier centrepiece, and out to the garden where all the guests were. Rachel's home dwarfed ours in size, it was on the next level. Her entrance hall alone was bigger than Mary's entire flat.

Matt encouraged me never to say anything about my social background. '*It's best they don't know,*' he'd said, '*I'm doing this for you of course, considering your feelings. I wouldn't want them to think any less of you.*' But even though I'd never disclosed anything personal about myself to his circle of friends, my differences were obvious, no matter how much we both tried to mask them.

The park-like garden was ablaze with balloons, bunting and fairy lights. An extended table with a lace tablecloth was laid out, displaying endless cakes and desserts. Brownies, fudge and fairy cakes, mini kid-size Battenbergs, Swiss rolls and Bakewell tarts, with a choice of organic, gluten and sugar-free. Scones with jam and clotted cream on top, dainty cucumber and smoked salmon finger sandwiches with the crusts cut off.

She'd gone all out, and it looked like half of Hampstead had been invited.

Everywhere I glanced there was something going on; jugglers, clowns, a man in striped trousers on stilts, a lady making balloon swords and flowers. A live jazz band played at the back of the garden on a makeshift stage, and waiters in black uniforms walked around with silver trays offering champagne and sushi. She'd hired an army. Kids screamed and howled as they threw themselves against the padded walls of the bouncy castle, as if they were high on crack.

Kids' parties should be about pass the parcel, jelly and ice cream. But this wasn't just a children's party. It was a coming together of Hampstead high society, the elite. Matt always told me that, in the background at such events, deals were made, favours were offered and returned, backs were scratched.

Joshy spotted the birthday boy. He let go of my tight grip in favour of joining his friend and the other kids in the long queue for the balloon lady. My security blanket, gone. His black top-hat bobbed up and down as he ran. Matt scanned the garden, stopping at Rachel. He straightened up, cleared his throat, his eyes fixed on her. She wore a figure-hugging red backless dress.

He never looked at me in that way anymore.

My black skinny jeans, long sleeved white top and flip-flops did little for my confidence and I wished I'd plucked up the courage to wear the pretty dress Matt had laid out for me. The problem was, the dress exposed a small scar on my arm, and I didn't want to draw attention to myself. I'd marked my flesh like a tattoo out of protest four nights back when Matt called to say he'd been invited out for dinner by some work colleague or other. That night, in a moment of complete desperation, I allowed my feelings to run away from me and I self-harmed. Ashamed of my actions, my mind turned to Cassandra. I knew she'd be disappointed, so I kept it from her. I wanted her to be proud of my progress.

Matt took my hand and steadily guided me through the guests, towards the host standing in the gazebo. My heart pounded as we waited our turn to say hello. A waiter offered us a drink. In the time it took Matt to decline the offer of champagne, I'd placed my empty glass back on the tray and accepted a second. It was the nerves. I wanted to click my heels like Dorothy and be transported back home.

'So lovely of you to come.' Rachel air-kissed Matt on both cheeks and turned to me. She looked me up and down. 'Love the hair. Who cut it?' she said, in a snappy sort of way.

'A hairdresser?' I said, not quite understanding how she expected me to respond.

Matt had been a little freaked out when he first saw my new cut and had said that he preferred it much longer. I wondered how long. As long as Rachel's?

Rachel screwed her face up as if there was a bad smell hovering beneath her nose. 'Are you feeling better?'

'Better?'

'Yes,' she said, the sides of her lips curling. 'We haven't seen you at school for a few days. We've been worried about you,' she said.

'I'm fine,' I said, through tight lips.

She spun on her gold canvas Gucci wedges and turned her attention back to my husband. 'So, anyway,' she said, as she threaded her arm through his in a single effortless glide.

He didn't seem fazed by the close physical contact. In fact, he looked more than comfortable.

'Where's your Joshua?' she asked Matt.

'He's over there, wearing that ridiculous top hat. Look at him. It's so big, it's covering his eyes.' He beamed back at her.

Was he flirting? My blood was on the boil. I looked around for a refill.

'He looks so funny,' said Rachel. 'Adorable. He reminds me of that guitarist from that hideous rock group, what were they called?' Her ombre-effect long hair swished as she threw her head back.

'Guns N' Roses,' I said.

'Noise, that's all they were,' Matt said, directly to Rachel, ignoring me.

My temples throbbed from the pressure of heat pushing down on my head. I opened and closed my mouth a few times, attempting to release my locked jaw, but it didn't help.

'Joshy looks like you,' she said to Matt. 'Handsome.'

Joshy was hitting Leo over the head with a balloon sword. I smiled to myself. At least Joshy wasn't a pushover like me. One of the hired servers appeared and I helped myself to another glass.

'We must have him round one afternoon,' Rachel said, spinning back to face me with her arm still glued to my husband.

Now was my chance to ask her about the playdate. Instead, I excused myself and headed to the loo, downing another glass of champagne along the way. The downstairs toilet was occupied. The house was empty inside, even the butler had disappeared, so I made my way up the grand circular staircase in search of another toilet. I needed some head space away from everyone.

There were many doors leading off the first-floor landing. All of them closed. Not knowing which door led to a bathroom, I opened the first one in front of me. It was the master bedroom. Rachel's private space. My head ordered me to go back downstairs to Matt and the others and to stop being a snoop. But there was a small part of me that was curious. What was it like being her?

My heartbeat quickened as I closed the door behind me and crept inside.

It was a boudoir in every sense of the word, the essence of feminine glamour. A blend of pinks, silvers, glitters and feathers. I walked over to her dresser and picked up a perfume which had been decanted into a crystal bottle. I twisted the lid and smelt the fragrance. The scent was floral and citrusy, a combination of femininity and sass, like Rachel. The super king four-poster took centre stage and was adorned with dozens of plumped up sequined cushions. I traced my fingers along the satin sheets and sat down on the edge of the bed. The mattress was soft and bouncy. The bedsheets luxurious.

The sounds of the children playing outside trickled through the window. A light breeze danced on my cheeks. I had the urge to lie down and close my eyes.

Quickly, I leapt up from the bed. What was I even doing in her bedroom? I'd had way too much champagne and was behaving recklessly. As I started straightening the bedding, I heard voices fast approaching. Too late to exit her bedroom, I rushed into the en suite bathroom, closing the door behind me.

'I wanted to check everything was okay,' Rachel said. 'You don't seem yourself.'

Silence followed. I knew she wasn't on the phone because I'd heard more than one set of footsteps.

'Come on, darling. You can't lie to me. I know when there's something playing on your mind,' she said.

'I don't know what to do anymore,' the man said. 'Everything's a little …' he paused. 'Strained.' I recognised the man's voice.

Matt.

'She's not herself,' he said.

My stomach clenched tightly. He was talking to her about me.

'Trouble in paradise?' she asked.

'It hasn't been paradise for a while, and you know it,' said Matt.

The large bathroom became devoid of oxygen.

'That's what you get when you net yourself a pretty young bride. I did warn you.'

'You're the devil in disguise, Rachel Montgomery-Jones.'

'Drop the Jones part, please. It's just Montgomery from now on,' she said. 'Good riddance to bad rubbish, I say.'

'He didn't deserve you.'

'And who does?' she said, softly.

'Rachel. Let's get you downstairs before you cause trouble and people start to talk.'

They giggled like a pair of fucking hyenas, leaving the bedroom, and me, behind.

Fighting back angry tears and totally desperate for the toilet because of the copious amount of fizz I'd just downed, I had no choice but to pull my knickers down and squat over the toilet seat to do a pee. I noticed a speck of blood on my knickers. My period had come. God damn it, could I not catch a break? It was hard to keep track, my cycle had been so irregular lately. With my knickers wrapped around my ankles, I waddled over to the extended wall cabinet with the Hollywood style lights in search of a tampon.

The cabinet was filled with luxurious items, expensive face and body creams, and oily hair treatments. All items lined up in neat rows. The packet was right at the back. I dipped my finger inside, fishing out a tampon. The tampons and other items cascaded to the floor and a pill bottle tumbled out, hitting me over the head.

I wanted to scream, shout, hurl everything from her cabinet across the bathroom and smash the place up. Destroy it all. How could Matt say those things to her about me?

I picked up the bottle. Prozac, prescribed to Mrs Rachel M-Jones.

My ribcage squeezed inside my chest.

I stared at the pill bottle until the word Prozac blurred and my eyes stung. How long would it take for someone to notice me gone? Would anyone even care? He'd have been much happier married to someone like Rachel. I started to imagine them on Rachel's bed together, naked and entwined, making love. I couldn't compete with the likes of her. Never.

Trouble in paradise? It hasn't been paradise for a while, and you know it.

My jaw tightened. I opened the bottle, dropping a bundle of pills into the palm of my hand. It would be so easy to swallow one pill after the other after the other, ending the pain and turmoil.

Joshy, being the air that I breathed, pushed his way to the forefront of my mind.

He was something to live for.

Clawing onto his image inside my mind, desperate not to let him go, I came to my senses and poured the pills back into the bottle, making sure not to spill any. Jostling on my hands and knees, I picked up all the spilt contents from the floor and placed everything back how I'd found it. I inserted a tampon and got the hell out of there.

Downstairs, I brushed my hair down with my trembling hands and took a glass of champagne from the kitchen island to calm my nerves. I ambled towards the bi-fold doors which overlooked the garden. Matt was surrounded by all the mums, and in his element. He looked as though he was recounting some funny story. Everyone was relaxed and laughing. Rachel, still by his side, giggled the hardest, flinging her head back and swooshing her long wavy hair about, her face erupting in contortions of delight.

Joshy tugged at Matt's trousers, competing for his dad's attention. Matt was too engrossed to notice, more interested in his attentive audience. Standing solo in the kitchen, I watched the display, while their intimate conversation in the bedroom became the soundtrack in my ears.

You're the devil in disguise, Rachel Montgomery-Jones.

'Daddy?' Joshy continued to tug at Matt.

My poor, poor baby. I was about to rescue Joshy when I suddenly stopped in my tracks, not quite believing what I was witnessing.

Matt's hand glided down Rachel's exposed back, resting inches above her bum. The waiter walked past and offered me a fresh flute. I took the glass and stood on the spot, downing the drink to stop myself from screaming.

His hand was frigging all over her! It made my skin crawl and my stomach turn.

Something about what he was doing reminded me of the very first time we'd met. I was smoking a cigarette outside the kitchen of the hotel I was working at. It was late at night and the evening was coming to an end. I needed a break. My feet were killing me because of my heels, and I was shattered from working seven days on the trot. Kat had only just left for Australia and I'd taken over her shifts as well.

This man appeared out of nowhere and stood beside me. I was leaning against the wall and couldn't see him properly and I'd assumed he was one of the managers of the hotel. I'd no idea he was a guest at the black-tie charity function which was taking place inside. He'd taken his bow tie off.

'I've been watching you,' he said.

'Oh really?' I replied, raising my eyebrows. 'And? Do you like what you see?' I turned my head to face my companion.

'A rare beauty like yourself, I'd say, very much so,' he said.

His dark hair was luscious and thick, his jaw strong, his grey eyes intense and serious. They pierced right through me. I couldn't look away. He had this air about him, a self-confidence I hadn't experienced in a man before. Commanding and forceful and really, really sexy.

'Oh please! Spare me the cheese.' I flicked my cigarette across the floor.

'It's true.'

'Thank you for the compliment,' I said, peeling myself off the wall and taking a bow, making him laugh. He had one cute dimple in his cheek. 'Well it was lovely chatting to you, but I have work to do, so I'm going to take my beautiful arse back inside.'

'You know, I usually get what I want,' he said, as he held onto my arm, stopping me from moving.

'And what is it you want?'

He had a glint in his eyes. 'You!' he replied.

'I wouldn't be so sure of your ...'

Before I could finish my sentence, he pulled me in closer and glided his other hand delicately down my back, making me tingle. My breath caught in my throat. When his fingers trickled down my spine, my whole body came alive and my world tipped upside down.

'Daddy? I need the toilet. Daddy?' Joshy cried, breaking my thoughts.

The blood drained from my head. Matt's hand remained. Everyone continued to chatter and laugh. Rachel was shrieking with laughter, her head flinging back, her long hair swishing around, clearly enjoying my husband's attention.

'I need the toilet – Daddy?' Joshy held onto his shorts and started crying.

I squatted down, breathless, placing the empty glass on the floor beside me.

I knew it. I fucking *knew* it. How much more proof did I need? The receipt, late night texts, openly flirting with one another, private little chats.

They were screwing each other and parading their affair in front of everyone. In front of me. In front of Joshy!

When I glanced back up, Matt and Joshy were fast approaching, coming straight for me.

'Right. Birthday cake!' Rachel snapped, in the garden.

'Annabelle,' Matt said, as he neared.

'Mummy. I need the toilet.'

'Quick. In here.' Matt pointed to the loo next to the utility room. He watched Joshy close the door behind him. The guests in the garden had started to sing happy birthday.

'You okay?' Matt crouched down to my level and touched my forehead. 'You're pale.'

'I'm fine.'

He shot me a look. 'Are you drunk?'

'I'm fine. I …' I stumbled. 'I'm fine. Give me a moment,' I said, pushing his hand away from my face.

'Annabelle. Have you had too much to drink?' he barked.

'What do you care, anyway?'

'It's a children's party for heaven's sake.'

'What else was I supposed to do? Stand around on my own, while you … while you … openly flirt with her.' The champagne had given me a false sense of confidence.

He stared, wide-eyed. 'What in God's name are you talking about?'

'I've been watching the pair of you,' I said, pointing towards the garden.

'Are you out of your mind?' He stood up and scanned the empty kitchen.

'Oh, here we go, again. I'm the crazy one. It's always me.'

Everyone cheered the birthday boy outside. I attempted to stand, but my legs gave way. The room moved around me. I held onto the wall for support as I crouched.

'You're a mess,' he spat.

'I've worked it out. I've worked it all out. I saw the receipt. I saw you two together. I heard. I *know*.'

'Who are you talking about?'

'Rachel!' I spat.

'She's a good friend.' His face turned crimson. 'You're clearly drunk and don't know what you're saying.'

'I know, Matt. I know you're hiding something.'

'Annabelle. Stop this at once. This is unacceptable behaviour.' He grabbed me under the arm and attempted to haul me upright. 'Go outside and wait for me there. We're leaving.' His face was beetroot. 'Now!'

I shook my head, no. I may not have been the brightest spark, but I wasn't bloody born yesterday.

'Go. Outside.' He pulled me up. 'You need some fresh air to sober up. Go! Pull yourself together before the others see you. Now!'

I stood up, planting my feet on the ground, hoping to steady myself.

'I'm going to check on Joshua. Our son. And then, we're leaving.' He smoothed his hair with his hand. 'Wait for me outside.' He stormed off towards the toilet.

The guests from the garden had started to disperse and were heading towards the house. He was right, I had to get out. *Run. Run. Run.*

The last thing I remembered was tripping over my flip flops along Finchley Road and falling into a heap on the pavement. Hands were on me. A passer-by tried to offer help. I yelled, convinced I was being mugged. A small crowd gathered. People stared. Someone laughed. I cried.

After that, everything was blank. Nothing.

The next thing, I found myself sitting on a swing in the playground on the council estate where I grew up, staring at the grey tower block ahead of me and towards Mary's flat on the fifth floor. It was dusk, the last remnants of a pink hazy sunset had almost disappeared behind the buildings, and the night sky was engulfing the city. London felt sinister and dangerous. The estate menacing.

Alone and afraid, sitting on the swing, my mind struggled to join the dots from the past two missing hours of my life. My memory was firing blanks. I'd never felt so out of control. Why had I ended up in the place of my nightmares? To where she lived. And what happened in those two missing hours? I checked my phone for clues. I'd called Cassandra, but judging by the call duration, we hadn't talked. The only other activity was from Matt, who'd clogged up my phone with messages.

I'm looking for you, where are you?

I'm furious you left without us. Come home immediately.

Where are you? I'm in the car driving around aimlessly.

This is unacceptable. Come home.

I'm concerned. CALL ME.

Call me. I'm back home. Joshua is asking questions.

I've called Rosita, she will put Joshy to bed. I'm coming to look for you again.

Annabelle, it's been two hours. Where are you? Call me.

I'm back. If you don't come home soon, I'll have no choice but to call the police. Ring me.

My phone vibrated. Matt was calling. 'Hi,' I said.

'Are you okay?' His voice was steady.

I checked myself over, looking for any cuts or bruising. My feet were dirty and scuffed, but that was about it. My diamond ring was still on my wedding finger. 'Yes,' I said, twisting the ring round and looking behind me.

'Don't ever do that to me again.'

'Okay,' I said, feeling disorientated.

'I'm coming to get you. Tell me where you are.'

'No. No, don't. I'm okay to walk. I'm coming home now.' I quit the call.

Despite my best efforts to push my past to the very far corner of my mind, something bad was resurfacing from when I was younger, and it wasn't going away. There was a reason I'd ended up in the playground.

Taking my phone, I scrolled through my contacts, stopping at Mary, but I couldn't bring myself to call her.

I sucked in the stagnant dry air and dialled the only person I could count on. My anchor. It went straight to voicemail, so I left a message.

'Cassandra. Hi, it's me. Annabelle. Sorry to bother you on the weekend.'

I paused to compose myself. It was now or never.

'You were right. Some of my current problems stem from when I was younger.' I glanced up toward the imposing tower block ahead of me, towards Mary's flat. Her light was on. She was home. I swallowed the nausea down and continued. 'I think something bad happened to me when I was a child and I think it has something to do with my mum. We've been estranged for a while, haven't spoken in years, and she got in touch recently out of the blue. She started calling, but I've been too scared to speak to her, so I've blanked all of her calls. It's a complicated relationship. Really damaged. Anyway, ever since the calls, I've been experiencing a recurrent nightmare. It has something to do with the playground from my childhood – on the estate I grew up in. I believe the nightmares could be a memory. A memory … a memory that has been forgotten,' I stammered. 'Can you please call me when you get this? No. Actually, don't call. Please message me instead. I'll be at home with my husband.' I shuddered. 'I think you may be able to help me uncover what happened to me when I was younger. I know you can help me find the truth. I know you can.'

Saying those words out loud, even in a voicemail, reaffirmed what

I'd been thinking for a while. It was time I sorted out my problems. Some of my problems, anyway. I silenced my phone and started power walking home, getting the hell away from the estate and my past, walking back home to Matt – my other problem.

Judging by the tone of his voice on the phone, this wasn't going to be pretty.

Chapter Fourteen

Matt paced the kitchen, holding a glass of whiskey in his hand, and I sat on the breakfast stool, in silence, picking at my chipped nail varnish.

'Why didn't you wait for me outside?'

'I don't know.'

'Where did you go?'

I scraped the last bit of red varnish off my fingernail.

'Annabelle, why did you get drunk?'

'I don't know.'

'What about the things you said?' He gulped down his drink, tipping his head back, draining the dregs from the glass. He poured another generous measure from the crystal decanter he'd taken from the drawing room. 'Your paranoia is getting out of hand,' he spat, his glass of whiskey securely in his grip. 'You're not in the right state of mind.'

I sat very still, too afraid to move.

'Does Joshua ever cross your mind when you're having these ridiculous outbursts?'

There was more than just a look of deep disappointment in Matt's eyes, there was judgement. Disgust. Fury.

'What do you think it's like for him, having a mother like you?'

Similar words had come out of my mouth once, '*do you know what it's like having a mother like you?*' I'd cried to Mary.

I swallowed down the huge lump in my throat. 'Matt, what are you trying to say?'

'You know exactly what I'm saying, Annabelle.' He swished the whiskey around in his glass and then poured the neat alcohol down his throat.

He hadn't drunk that much in years.

Joshy was tucked up in bed so thankfully couldn't hear Matt's rant, and Rosita had been smart enough to make herself invisible, although it wouldn't have surprised me if she'd been earwigging outside the door.

His eyes fixed on me. 'Tell me, where did you go after the party?'

I chewed on my lip.

'You don't believe your behaviour warrants an explanation?' he asked. 'You can't behave as though you're from a council estate. Not anymore. You've changed. Your circumstances have changed.'

Each word he spat was a sucker punch to the gut.

Even if I attempted to explain the stuff with Mary to him, my past, my dreams, and the paranoia I'd been experiencing, he wouldn't want to understand. He wanted a trophy wife who remained quiet, looked pretty and behaved in a socially acceptable way. Not a spouse who was unravelling before his eyes, swamped with suspicion and emotionally scarred from childhood issues. He should have married someone like Rachel.

'Where did you go?'

'I don't know.'

'What do you mean, you don't know?' he said. 'WHERE WERE YOU?' He stood over me. His hand gripped the glass, as though a simple squeeze would shatter it to pieces. He placed it down on the breakfast table beside me.

The room spun around me, echoing the disorientation inside my head. Their private little chat. His hand trickling down her back. Two hours missing from my life. The playground on the estate. Mary.

He placed both his hands on the island, next to me, and leant forwards so our noses almost touched. 'You're becoming a liability to yourself. To me. To Joshy.' He peeled himself away. I could smell the alcohol on his breath.

'I'd never harm Joshy. Never,' I said, tearfully.

'You need professional help. Let's see if that makes a difference.' He walked over to the sink and started to wash his hands. 'You've got to get a grip. You need to get help, otherwise ...' He stopped himself from saying more.

Matt scrubbed his hands thoroughly like a surgeon about to perform an operation. It was an annoying habit he had when there was something on his mind or he felt under pressure.

'I saw my mum,' I said under my breath, with no idea why that lie escaped my mouth.

He froze, leaving the tap to run.

Although I'd never opened up about my upbringing (he never asked), he was no fool. He'd worked things out for himself. It wasn't hard. The first time they met, she embarrassed herself in true Mary fashion. She'd been invited to the house for dinner. At first, she happily showed off her very best self. She used a voice I'd never heard before, paying close attention to her pronunciation, minding her Ps and Qs, but as the evening progressed and she started to get hideously drunk on Matt's fine wine, she slipped. She became rowdy and super flirty with him, dancing around the dining room table like she was on some podium in a sleazy nightclub, and even managed to spill red wine on Matt's precious sheepskin rug. At the end of the night, she disappeared into the toilet. The smell of weed drifted through the gap beneath the bathroom door and permeated the rest of the house. I was mortified. She left with one of Matt's expensive African figurines, which she'd stolen from the drawing room. I could see it poking out of the fake Louis Vuitton handbag she'd bought from Church Street market. Needless to say, she was never invited back.

The tension intensified when Joshy was born. Matt pretty much put an end to the microscopic traces of relationship we had left. There was no doubt in his mind; Mary spelt trouble and he didn't want me or Joshy anywhere near her, or the council estate. Of course, I tried my best to keep the peace for as long as I could, tried my best to hold on, but it was no use. When Joshy was a baby, she completely disappeared from our lives and I eventually let go.

As much as he had tried to erase her from our lives, he couldn't control the fact that she was still Joshy's grandmother. Flesh and blood. They shared genes. He couldn't wash that away, could he? Whether he liked it or not.

He turned the tap off and dried his hands. His body became stiff as he approached.

'She has cancer, Matt.' My voice trembled as I spoke.

He poured himself another measure, loosened his tie and tipped the neat whiskey down his throat, slamming the glass on the island, empty. The crystal met the marbled top with a slam, and I jumped. The noise echoed around the room.

'Why have you defied me?' He inched closer.

'I didn't stay long. I was in and out within minutes.'

'So, if you were there a matter of minutes, what happened to the rest of the time?'

I remained quiet.

'Are you antagonising me?'

'No. I promise. I'm not.'

'You know that woman will get inside your head and fill it with trash. Is that what you want? To get worse?' He began to pace. 'I can't trust you anymore. I can't trust you with anything. I'm going to need to keep a closer eye on you.'

'I'm trying. I am.'

'Really, Annabelle.'

'Yes. I promise.'

His words to Rachel bounced around my head; *it hasn't been paradise for a while*. Maybe I was the problem, not him. Maybe I was seeing things that weren't even there, making up his supposed affair and using it as an excuse to derail further.

'So, let me get this straight. We go to a children's party, you get drunk – bearing in mind it's the afternoon. You make a complete embarrassment out of yourself. You accuse me of having an affair with one of my oldest and dearest friends. Then you go missing in action. And here's the best part, you go and visit your crazy pot-smoking, self-obsessed, foul-mouthed sorry-excuse for a mother. Great work, Annabelle. That really is trying. Well done. Bravo.' He clapped.

'I'm sorry.' I looked away. He was right. He was right.

'I don't want you near her or that damn council estate. You stay away. That's over with now. Your life is with me, with us. This is your family. Here.' He paused. Breathed in. 'You leave me no choice, Annabelle. I'm going to contact Dr Jacobs. He's helped once before and will help again. He'll know what to do.' He took his phone from his pocket. 'He'll prescribe something to calm your mania down,' he muttered to himself, scrolling through his phone.

Breathing in deep and slow, I tried to calm the panic from erupting, just as Cassandra had taught me. I drew my breath into the pit of my stomach and held it for five counts. I released the air through my mouth and imagined my anxiety escaping.

'Matt. Listen to me, please. I beg you. I agree with you. I do need someone to talk to. But it has to be someone I trust. Someone I'm comfortable with. Someone who will take the time to listen to how I'm feeling. There's a reason why I've been overwhelmed lately.'

He wasn't paying the slightest bit of attention to what I was saying. Striking while the iron was hot, he was probably texting the doctor.

'I swear, I'm going to change. But I have to do it my way.'

He continued to ignore me as his fingers fired out a message on his phone.

'Don't shut me out. Don't do this to me. I need time to sort this out, by myself.'

Paranoia crept in. What if he was texting Rachel? Even if he wasn't sleeping with her, one thing was certain, he confided in her and not me.

I swiped my paranoia away. 'I'm going to get the help I need. I promise,' I said.

He remained quiet. The silence was punishing.

'I've found someone. She's good. An alternative therapist. She's going to help me,' I blurted.

'What did you say?'

'It's nothing. No one. Promise me you'll give me time to sort this mess out my way.'

'What alternative therapist?'

'Does it matter? Just as long as I get the help I need. Look, I want to take the initiative and do something about my problems. That's what you want, isn't it?'

My phone buzzed on my lap. I looked down.

Hello Annabelle. I've noticed your missed calls and picked up your voicemail. I'm concerned. Please contact me to let me know you're okay. That you're safe. Cassandra.

'You'll stop all this nonsense at once. You will see Dr Jacobs and get the proper help you need. I will make sure of it. If that doesn't work, then, and *only* then, we may consider other options.'

I started blind texting a response from beneath the breakfast bar.

I'm v shaken. Need to see u. Are u free tomorrow?

'I'm sorry Annabelle, am I boring you?'

'What? No. No. I'm listening.'

Matt stood over me, looking dumbstruck.

Ready to confront past. Need to get to truth. Running out of time. Pls help me.

'What the hell do you think you're doing?' he spat.

Staring at my phone, I waited for her to respond, my leg jigging up and down.

'Annabelle?' he asked again.

At last.

Okay. We have much work to do. Come on Monday at 12pm. I will see you then. C

'Annabelle? You will see Dr Jacobs and that will be the end of it,' he said.

THANK YOU. You've saved my life. A x

I glanced up. The room was empty. Matt had left.

Chapter Fifteen

Sunday dragged on forever. Every minute was painful and drawn out. Matt continued to ignore me, using his silence to punish me, knowing it would eventually get to me. As the day progressed, I became more and more teary, more and more paranoid about my own behaviour – disregarding his – and by the late afternoon, had fallen into a depressive black hole, battling strong urges to self-harm.

The problem was, there was nothing I could say or do to make things better between us. There were no grey areas when it came to his thinking, only black and white, and as far as he was concerned, any discussion about the day before was now closed and off limits.

He'd spent most of the day conveniently locked away in his study, pretending to work, appearing for lunch without muttering a single word to me, only speaking to Joshy in his goofy voice. He hated anyone going inside his office and disturbing him, so I just gave up and let him be, pretending to Joshy that everything was fine, that Matt had work on his mind.

Joshy, on the other hand, didn't stop talking, jumping around, crying, singing, screaming, repeating the same words over and over again, refusing to eat his cucumbers at lunch time, throwing them on the floor in protest, and for some unknown reason thought it would be fun to see how much toilet roll it would take to clog up the downstairs toilet, explaining it was a very important experiment. To top it all off, Rosita had been given the day off by Matt.

Exhausted and at my wits' end, I was counting down the seconds for the weekend to be over with so I could see Cassandra and get some guidance as to what to do about my situation with Matt.

'I'm off out.' Matt appeared in the open-plan family room.

I was startled. 'What? Now?'

'I have to iron out details with Bill for a meeting we have first thing tomorrow.' He'd changed out of his casual lounge wear and was now sporting a smart pair of trousers and a crisp white shirt. The room stank of aftershave.

'But it's five o'clock on a Sunday.'

'Are you going to start with the paranoia again?' he asked. 'I have to work. Simple as that.' He picked up his keys from the coffee table in the TV area.

That was the first thing he'd said to me all day. At least he was communicating.

Joshy and I were at the kitchen table attempting his 'save the planet' art project. The table was covered with my old travel magazines, glue, scissors and colouring pens and pencils. We were cutting pictures out of the magazines and sticking them onto cardboard. Images of mountains and forests, beaches and clear turquoise seas, dolphins and turtles.

'Matt. I'm sorry about what happened yesterday. I was out of order. It was the alcohol. It made me loopy. I know Rachel's just a friend. Please stay home so we can talk things through.'

'I'll see you later,' he said, stopping at the side entrance door.

'Bye, Daddy.'

'See you later, Joshua,' he said warmly. 'Annabelle. I won't be late.'

With the second comment his voice returned to ice and his features once again seemed brittle. He walked out. The jeep fired up and he was gone.

Was he lying about seeing Bill, or was I going completely crazy? I picked up my phone from the table and opened WhatsApp, to check when Matt was last online. Five minutes before he had appeared in the family room. I checked Rachel's status. She looked picture perfect in a pink Chanel suit, kitten heels, her ombre hair in a sixties updo, holding a glass of champagne in her hand. Her plumped up lips were a soft pink and her face flawless, devoid of wrinkles. She was currently online.

Joshy started laughing.

'What's up?' I said, turning to him, placing my phone back on the table.

'Look, Mummy. I pulled it off.'

With a wide toothless grin on his face, his blue eyes sparkling, he held up a clipping, which I'd stuck down onto the cardboard moments earlier, in his chubby hands.

'Why did you do that?'

'It's not glued properly. Look,' he said, pulling another image off.

'Joshy!'

'They're coming off in my hands.' He pulled another image off. 'I can do it better.'

'You're doing it on purpose. Stop it.'

'It's funny,' he giggled. He peeled off a picture of a beautiful, deserted beach.

'Joshy. Stop. We've worked really hard, now you're ruining it.'

'Sorry. I will glue.' He picked up the Pritt stick and started smearing the backs of the images, as well as the glass table.

'Not like that. You're making a mess. Look what you've done.

There's glue all over the table, now.' I could feel the pressure building inside my head.

'Sorry, Mummy,' he said, chuckling to himself.

'It's really not funny, Joshy.' I pulled at my neckline, suddenly hot.

'It is, Mummy. It's funny. It's funny.'

I pushed the chair back, away from me, and stared at my phone.

Joshy pulled another image off, giggling away to himself. There were no images left on the cardboard. 'Why have you ruined the project we made together?'

'It's okay. We can ask Rosita to do it tomorrow.'

'What do you mean, ask Rosita? Why should we ask her when you have me doing it right now? Why do you always rely on her instead of me?' I said, raising my voice and planting my feet firmly onto the ground.

'I'm sorry,' he said, shrinking into his seat.

Without thinking, I picked up the piece of cardboard in one hand and the scissors in the other and tore into the project, cutting it up. 'Well, let her bloody do it then!'

Joshy's eyes grew wide as he stared at me in disbelief. For a split second, everything went quiet. A beat passed. I was punishing Joshy because of Rosita. I was punishing Joshy for my troubles with Matt. With Mary.

'Oh Joshy,' I said. 'I'm so ….'

He howled – an ear-splitting scream, like he was in pain – and ran out of the room, bursting into tears. 'I want Rosita. I want Rosita. I want Rosita.'

As Joshy wailed upstairs, I took the scissors to my upper arm, scraped it across the skin, over and over until I drew blood, until all the anger and hurt that was tightly bundled up in a knot subsided and everything had turned quiet inside my head.

An overwhelming sense of guilt followed. The scissors slipped from my fingers. Blood dripped onto the table.

What the fuck was I doing? Joshy needed me!

I pressed a tissue onto my arm and bounded up the stairs, two at a time, to his bedroom with a bar of Toblerone in my hand as a peace offering. He didn't deserve a shitty mum like me. He deserved better. He hugged me and told me he was sorry for ruining the project.

Once he was asleep, I opened a bottle of wine and attempted to remake the art project, sticking pictures of freedom and escape onto a new piece of cardboard, but I couldn't concentrate. I knew in my gut Matt was lying.

I was tempted to text Bill's wife to catch him out, or maybe 'accidently' dial Rachel, but as soon as the idea entered my head, I squashed it. What use was it if I had my suspicions confirmed? I clearly wasn't strong enough to take care of my son, not on my own. I had to get stronger.

That night, Matt came home smelling different from how he had smelled when he left. No longer smelling of his aftershave, but of something else I didn't recognise.

I woke to find Matt already gone and Rosita in the family room, sticking new images onto a fresh bit of cardboard, finishing the art project to Joshy's delight. My travel magazines in tatters. How the hell did she know what to do for the project? I thanked her for her trouble, and she quickly dismissed it as nothing, telling me that Matt had instructed her to do the school run, showing me his text as proof.

When the house fell silent, I went upstairs to get ready for my appointment, running over what I wanted to say to Cassandra in my head. Did I really want to dredge up my past, bad memories and recurring nightmares? Did I really want to dredge up Mary? And should I even mention Matt?

I applied make-up, masking the bags under my eyes, styled my hair, and with no idea why, stepped out of my comfort zone, choosing to wear a black and white geometric A-line skirt I'd never worn before, matching it with a white t-shirt and black cardigan (to cover up my new cut) and brand-new wedges on my feet.

Chapter Sixteen

'Okay. Now that you're calmer, let's start from the beginning. So, you believe your husband is having an affair with this …?' Cassandra sat opposite me, back upright, one leg crossed over the other, swinging her foot up and down.

'Rachel.' I wiped my swollen eyes. They stung from crying. The tissue was streaked black from my mascara which had run down my face, ruining my carefully applied make-up. It was embarrassing.

'He's seeing Rachel behind your back?'

'Yes.'

'And you believe this, because …?'

'I have no proof. None. Apart from some flirtation between them and a stupid receipt I found in his pocket for some swanky dinner for two.'

Her eyes narrowed and two faint lines appeared on her forehead. Her face turned serious. Was she doubting me, too?

'That doesn't prove anything, does it? A receipt and some minor flirting. Big bloody deal. God, what if I'm making this all up in my head? What if I'm tormenting myself over nothing? What if I'm going nuts?'

'I don't think you're crazy, Annabelle.' Her features softened as she fixed a warm smile on her face.

She did believe me.

'On the contrary. I think you're quite extraordinary.'

My face flushed. No one had ever called me extraordinary before.

She stood up, brushed her skirt down and walked over to the glass desk, retrieving her leather notepad and pen, her glamorous high heels clicking on the floor, the sound echoing around the room. The strange ornamental eye chime – which was hanging from the ceiling next to the French doors leading to the courtyard – spun around. She returned, sat back down gracefully, poised, and opened the pad on her lap, jotting down notes. Her hand glided gracefully up and down, like a calligrapher's.

I'd arrived at the clinic half an hour early and paced the pavement, waiting. She'd spotted me outside and took pity on me, calling me in. As soon as I walked down the steep steps towards the clinic, clinging onto the banister for support because of the stupid shoes I'd decided to wear, and saw the concerned look on her face, I burst into floods of tears. So much for composing myself.

'It's going to be okay,' she'd said, as she opened her arms, allowing me to fall into her embrace. Once I'd eventually stopped crying, I took my seat and was completely mortified about my arrival. To mask my embarrassment, I started blabbering on and on and on, spilling the beans about Leo's birthday party, my suspicions about the affair, and the awful weekend I'd had with Matt.

'I'm curious to know what it would mean to you if he were having an affair – and I'm not suggesting for one moment that he is,' she said, not looking up, continuing to write notes.

'I guess I'd be betrayed.'

'Let's unscramble your thoughts further. Anything else?'

'Well, I'd probably want to harm myself,' I sniffed, pulling at my cardigan sleeve. The cut on my arm, beneath my cardigan, throbbed.

'The idea of him being with someone else makes me want to reach for the knife and do some damage. I'd blame myself, because deep down, I'd know it was me who pushed him away. Pushing him into someone else's arms.'

She stopped writing and placed her pen inside her notepad. 'It's interesting you would choose to harm, rather than stand up for yourself.' She placed the notebook on the floor.

I scraped the heels of my hands down the fronts of my legs. She leant in, took both my clammy hands in hers and stared into my eyes. She wore thick black liquid eyeliner which accentuated the shape of her oval dark eyes. I was suddenly conscious that I looked a mess.

'Why do you not love yourself?' she whispered. 'You're a beautiful woman, inside and out. You should love yourself.'

I looked away.

'What prompted you to feel this way?'

I shook my head. 'I don't …' I held my breath.

'Annabelle, I'd like you to repeat after me: I am safe in this room,' she said, squeezing my hands.

'I'm safe in this room.'

She let go and I sank back into the egg chair, breathing evenly.

The room fell silent.

'Annabelle. We must talk about the voicemail you left me. It's important we don't avoid the underlying issues any longer.'

'I'm feeling much better about everything now we've spoken and …'

'I can give you empowering suggestions and induce hypnosis which offers light relief,' she said, cutting me off. 'However, you must understand that it's only a temporary fix for you. There's something dark lurking beneath the surface and we must uncover what it is. Otherwise you'll be forever chained to your past. Chained to your destructive habits, unable to move forwards.'

I gulped down water, draining the glass, thinking about when I took the scissors to my upper arm. She was right. I couldn't avoid it any longer. God, why did it have to be so complicated?

'The question you need to ask yourself is whether you want to make a permanent change to your life.'

'I do. I really do.'

'Then with your permission, I'd like to explore your childhood and uncover the reasons why you feel the need to harm yourself. I believe it's something we can no longer ignore. You confided in me for a reason.'

She stood up, leant across me, and poured water from the jug into the glass. I could smell her exotic perfume. The lemons and limes bobbed up and down in the jug as she poured. 'It'll help us have an understanding as to why you allow others to hurt you, and it could stop the destructive cycle. There is no other way,' she said, handing me the glass and sitting back down. 'Do you consent?'

I nodded, taking a sip.

'In your own time. You mentioned in your voicemail, something bad happened when you were younger. Is this correct?'

'Yes,' I whispered.

'And it has something to do with your parents?'

'I never knew my dad.'

'I'm sorry to hear this. Would you like to talk about your father?'

'There's nothing to talk about. Don't even know who he is. He left shortly after I was born. He could be dead, for all I know.' I pulled another tissue from the box and blew my nose.

'I see. That must be very painful for you.' She uncrossed and re-crossed her legs. The slit of her black pencil skirt revealed a small star tattoo on her thigh. 'Can we talk about your mother, then?'

115

'Let's just say, me and my mum have some deep-rooted issues,' I said, stiffening up.

'Can I ask, do you fear that you will repeat the same mistakes with your son that your mother made with you?'

'I … well …' I said, tongue-tied. 'Sometimes. Yes.'

'Annabelle, we need to explore your relationship with your mother, as well as what happened to you in the past. The two are connected somehow.'

'Look. Can we do this another time?'

The wheels of her chair squeaked as she pulled in even closer, giving me hardly any space. 'We have to confront our past in order to move towards the future in a positive way. You hinted so yourself.'

It was as though annoying flies were buzzing around inside my head, meddling with my thoughts. I needed time to think without interference.

'You can't bottle it all up, Annabelle. It's not healthy,' she said.

'I know,' I said, inhaling deeply. I looked up to the ceiling and then back at her. 'Something terrible happened to me when I was younger. I know it did. The problem is, I can't remember the details,' I said, fidgeting with the scrunched-up tissue in my hand. 'I think I've blanked the memory out.'

'So, what *do* you remember?' she whispered softly.

'I was in the playground on the council estate where I grew up and it was cold and dark. I was alone and afraid, crying out for Mary. I had to be about ten years old, or thereabouts, because I was wearing roller skates at the time, which Mary had bought me for my tenth birthday.'

'Mary?'

'My mother. She insists I call her by her name. Says the word "mum" makes her feel old.'

'Any other details about this "lost" memory?' She bunny-eared the word lost.

'No. I don't think so,' I said, trying to pull fragments from my mind.

'I see,' she said.

'This whole thing is affecting my moods, how I parent, even affecting my marriage. Matt's noticed that something's not quite right with me, and he's naturally worried about Joshy.'

'Matt. Is that your husband's name?'

'Yes.'

'Have you spoken to him about any of this?'

'You're the first person I've spoken to about any of my problems.'

'I'm honoured you're putting your faith in me,' she nodded. 'I want you to know that we all have demons from our pasts we can't escape from. What's important is dealing with our past effectively so it doesn't affect our present day or our future.'

'I don't know how to fix things.'

'That's why you have me. We can work the pieces of the puzzle out, as a team,' she said, reassuringly. 'I believe that the stars aligned, bringing us both together for a reason.'

My heart skipped a beat. Mary had always talked about the alignment of stars and destiny.

'Are you familiar with the hypnotherapy practice of regression?'

'No.'

'It's a technique that hypnotherapists use to help clients travel back to a particular past event.'

'I'm not so sure about this. What will happen to me?'

'Nothing will happen. I'm in total control at all times, and I can bring you back into the room at any point,' she said, picking up her notebook. 'Why don't I show you? Close your eyes, relax and allow me to do the rest,' she said in a soothing tone. 'Trust me. I'll keep you safe.'

Chapter Seventeen

Shutting my eyes, I focused on Cassandra's soft lullaby voice as she induced me into the trance. The hypnosis state had become easier to achieve. When the tone of her voice changed, nothing else mattered and I knew it would only be a matter of minutes before I was transported someplace else. However, this time, I wasn't escaping, I was going back to my childhood, back to my nightmares.

'Allow my voice to travel back through time with you. I want you to regress back to the images which have been haunting you in your sleep. Back to when you were a child. Go back as an adult and see if you can uncover what happened to you. Why you were in the playground on your own. Hidden memories that you've buried deep inside of you will unfold and appear to you, visually, like a dream. Let your brain explore and search, allowing my voice to be your guide.'

I squeezed my eyes tightly. Was I ready?

'Annabelle, I have a technique if you're frightened. Visualise me in your mind standing next to you. Visualise the two of us holding hands, together. It'll offer you support and safety. You can take me back in time with you. Take me back to your past.'

My brain floated in and out of consciousness.

'Understand this one truth, nothing will come between us, not now, not ever. Nothing will break the special bond we have. Together, we are united, and we are stronger. You will feed off my strength, and it will transfer over to you, as if it were your own. Are you ready?'

'Yes.'

She lifted my hand off my lap and enveloped hers around, offering me encouragement and support. 'Ready now. Deeper and deeper. Take us back to the place that holds significance for you. Do it now.'

The descent into my subconscious was quicker than I'd expected and the images in my mind came to me, like a lucid dream. In the depths of my imagination, Cassandra and I were standing side by side, holding hands. Her grip was strong. Tight. I felt protected.

'What do you see?' Her voice penetrated, slipping inside my mind as though it were my own thoughts.

'It's dark. I don't know where I am,' I heard myself say.

'Am I with you?'

'Yes.' I wanted to tell her how beautiful she looked in my imagination. How graceful she was. Radiant, like a pinprick of light, hope. 'You're wearing a white summer dress. It's so bright, it's offering us light. Shining like a beacon.'

'Good work. Strong visualisation is a powerful tool. Keep me close to you. Keep me near.'

I waited for more instruction.

'Explore your surroundings. What's ahead? Is there anything of significance?'

As we walked, hand in hand, prisms of light bounced off her dress, shining a spotlight. In my imagination, a clearing appeared ahead of us as though a dense fog was lifting. I paused, but the tight squeeze of her hand reassured me, reminding me that I was safe. We continued on, inching forward, together.

We were outside. Not on a beach or in a pretty meadow but surrounded by a concrete landscape. Imposing high-rise blocks appeared, their grey, ugly form growing from the ground up, leaving a metallic taste in my mouth. The dense London smog in the air around us. Lisson Green council estate. My heartbeat accelerated.

Cassandra's gaze fixed on something ahead.

The playground. My chest tightened.

Glass crunched beneath our feet as we approached the rusty gate to the playground. It squeaked open on its own. Inside stood a solitary swing. It was windy, making it swing solo, the chains creaking as it moved up and down. The climbing frame, roundabout and slide had vanished. Empty beer cans littered the floor and an abandoned car tyre leant against the fence.

'We're in the playground where I used to play. There's a swing up ahead.'

'Is there anyone on it?'

'It's hard to see, it's hazy.'

We drew closer.

'Wait. There's someone there.' The fog unveiled and everything became clearer. 'It's a woman. She has her back turned.'

Taking in short shallow breaths, I began gasping for air. 'Cassandra, I'm finding it hard … Shit … It's getting hard to breathe.'

The squeeze of her hand made me feel safe, again. 'Stay calm Ann-a-belle, stay focused. Remember I'm here for you,' she said. 'You're doing great. I'm standing with you on the inside and I'm sitting opposite you on the outside. I'll be with you every step of the way both consciously and subconsciously. There's nothing to fear.'

My breathing evened out, back to a steady rhythm.

'Try and identify the woman.'

The sun dipped out of sight and was replaced by thick clouds. The temperature turned cold. Suddenly I was afraid again.

It was all in the past. It couldn't harm me. It was all in the past, I reminded myself.

My legs trembled. 'I'm sorry. I can't do this,' I said, my voice breaking. 'Please take me out of the trance state.'

'Who is she?'

'I don't know. I don't know … She has her back to us.'

'Ask her to turn around.'

'Can we leave now?' I tried to move, but my feet were cemented to the ground. I looked down. The concrete was covered by thick squelchy mud. It was rising all around us. The woman contorted her body like a corkscrew. She continued to twist round, but it was impossible to make a face. Her features were blurred out, like someone had smudged them and she was crying black charcoal tears. Hollows for eyes.

She reached a wrinkly arm out towards me, excess skin dangled from under her arm. 'Help me, Anna,' she cried. 'Help.'

I froze. 'I can't do this,' I cried. 'I can't do this. I can't.'

'Okay. Stay calm and focus on my voice. Let's take you back to a happier time in your life. Go further back to when you were really young. Is there such a time where you felt happier, more secure, as a child?' Cassandra said.

'Yes.' A new image appeared in my mind, and suddenly I was safe from harm.

'Great. Picture such a time and place in your mind now. Transport yourself there. Go back and allow that child to speak to me. Can I speak to you as a child?'

I nodded my head.

'Good. Tell me, where are you now?'

'I'm in the kitchen in Mum's flat.' I looked around, Cassandra wasn't there, but that was okay because I had to go to school anyway, and she couldn't come with me. 'I have my uniform on.'

'How old are you?'

'Six,' I said in my six-year-old voice. It soothed me, being six. It was the same age as Joshy.

'And what are you doing?'

'Making a sloppy jammy sandwich. Just how I like it. It's called a sloppy jammy because the jam always slops out.'

'Is your mother there with you?'

'She's in bed. She's tired. Always tired. Oh no. I slopped my sloppy all over my school shirt.'

'Is that a problem?'

'No problem. It's okay, there's slops from yesterday too. Here she is. Mummy!' I cried, as Mary entered the crammed kitchen, clad in her dressing gown. Her hair matted; her mascara smudged. She was still wearing yesterday's lipstick.

She yawned a big yawn and put the kettle on, fiddling with the radio antenna to find her favourite station. 'Mr Boombastic' started to play. That song made me laugh. Bombastic Fantastic. I giggled.

'Sit down, Anna. Let me brush your hair,' Mummy said.

She took the hairbrush and I sat down by the round table, waiting. I loved the way she brushed and brushed my hair, making me all sleepy, like I was ready for bed instead of school. School – yuk.

She stroked my hair with the hairbrush, getting the knots and tangles out from the bottom. She was very good at it, the brushing. It was such long hair, nearly Rapunzel long. Mummy wanted to cut it, but I said, no, not on my life, not ever. I wanted it to grow and grow and grow until it reached the floor. If it grew long enough, it could hang over the balcony and all the way to the playground.

'There you go. All done.'

'Mummy, look at my sloppy jammy.' I held the half-eaten sandwich up.

'Good work, Anna. It looks delicious.'

'Are you taking me to school today?'

'Not today. You're going with Helen.'

'When, Mummy? When can you take me?'

'Anna. I said you're going with Aunt Helen. Now, eat up.' There was a rap at the door.

'Only me, Mary. Are you ready, Anna darling?' Helen said, walking straight into our kitchen. The door was always open for all of Mummy's friends. It was okay, because nothing bad ever happened and I liked her friends. Some of them, anyway.

Helen was our next-door neighbour, with the biggest and bestest hugs on the whole estate. She opened her arms to me. I quickly stuffed the jammy into my mouth, pushed the chair back and bolted straight into her big arms for a squidgy cuddle.

Mummy and Helen talked for a moment and I bounced down the stairs, in our crazy upside down flat, to get my school bag and shoes from my little bedroom. I squeezed my feet into my shoes with holes in the soles and raced back up the stairs as quick as I could, counting in my head. One. Two. Three. Today was the fastest time ever. I was getting good at running.

'See you later, Mummy.'

'Later, gator,' Mum said.

Pools of tears formed in my eyes.

'Bringing you back into the room. On the count of five, coming back to the present day. Four. Three, almost awake. Two, get ready.

Move your fingers and toes. One. Open your eyes. Take a good stretch. Welcome back to the room, Annabelle.'

My face was soaked with tears.

'How are you feeling?'

'I'm okay.' I looked away and took another tissue, dabbing my sore eyes.

'That was great work today, Annabelle. You should feel proud of yourself.'

'Thank you.' I looked at the wall clock.

'Stay longer if you wish. We can talk through what we've uncovered.'

'You know, I'd best be heading back. It's getting late and I promised Joshy I'd pick him up from school,' I said, trying to stop my lips from quivering.

A heaviness I'd never felt before weighed down on me as I carried myself back up the hill, towards the school to collect Joshy. I had to make a choice: either ignore my suppressed memory, hoping it would go away in time, or delve further in and sort my messy life out.

Nearing the school, I checked my phone and noticed three missed calls from Uncle Jack. I pressed call back. 'Uncle Jack, it's me.'

'Hello love. Glad you got in touch,' he said. I could hear him drag on his roll-up. 'Your mum needs to see ya, love. She isn't in a good way. You have to come.'

I leant up against the wrought iron gates to a mansion block besides the school.

'Anna. Did you hear what I said, doll?'

'Tell Mary, I'm coming to see her.' I took in a deep breath. 'Tomorrow.'

It was time.

Chapter Eighteen

CLINICAL NOTES
Mrs Annabelle Clarke (Note – she finally disclosed family & husband's name)
Sessions: Session 5.

Client contacted me over the weekend, distressed. She reports experiencing a traumatic event when she was a child. Suppressed memory stored in subconscious, blocked from conscious recall. Annabelle asked for my help to recover memory.
There's a link between her mother, Mary, recurring dreams and the suppressed memory.

Client was agitated and upset upon arrival. Bad weekend – family time problematic.
Client reports husband doesn't believe she's a good mum and fears husband is having affair. No proof. Fabrication or truth? Who is Rachel?

Client says she's comfortable in clinic space. This is superficial. She is not fully relaxed, nor fully trusting. Not yet – must work on this.

Annabelle needs more coaxing to open up in order to unlock past.
Need to build on trust and security. Must compound, safe space = clinic.

Reluctant to speak about her mother. Nervous upon questioning.
Mother has cancer – could cause Annabelle tremendous guilt. Is her mother an aggressor?

Today's hypnosis: *Client verbally consented to regression.*
Annabelle was anxious during regression work, so I requested her to visualise me standing next to her while regressing back to childhood to offer emotional support. Experimental technique, never been used before. It worked – well done me.
Visited childhood as an adult. She grew up on a council estate. The playground is the setting.
Woman on a swing. Is she a friend or foe?
Breathing became rapid as she approached woman. Hyperventilating during session. Could not continue and run the risk of actual physical harm.
Client experienced an overwhelming sense of fear, so I requested she regress to a 'happier' time.
Six-year-old Annabelle is making her own breakfast, her mother is in bed – childhood neglect.

Note - Annabelle is confusing abuse with false sense of love.
Annabelle's weaknesses – her mother / trauma suffered as a child.

Follow up session/s:
Regress back, find out who the woman is on the swing?
Build on trust. Compound safe space in clinic – Annabelle's sense of security.

Agreed to see client more often upon request and increased weekly sessions.

Homework given: *Continue with self-care and affirmations. Note – Changed appearance. Mimicking?*

Note to self – Next time, must strongly advise Annabelle against any contact with her mother for the time being. Explain that she runs risk of jeopardising treatment plan and spiralling into a fixed state of mania if contact is negative and / or aggressive.

Chapter Nineteen

I was standing outside Chetwode House tower block in the Lisson Green estate, waiting for the external lift to reach ground level, hopping from one foot to another. Every fibre in my body was agitated, on edge. It had started raining and I could feel the playground's dark presence behind me. Three hoodies on push bikes began to slow ride around me, circling like vultures. They were trying to suss me out. Keeping my head down, I waited for the lift. The smell of weed clung to the air, thick and fragrant, overpowering the smell of urine coming from the lift shaft.

'You slipped?' One of them swooped his bike to a sharp stop, to my right. He reached over to touch my hair, making me flinch. Grime music pumped from his mobile.

'Sweet,' another one said as he scooped to a tight halt, to my left. 'The gal is boujee, fam.'

Both bikes crisscrossed me, trapping me.

'What's happening?' The third called out in a heavy eastern European accent, as he continued his circuit, making a figure of eight behind me.

The only escape route was the lift. It seemed stuck on the fourth floor. The lifts were notorious on the estate for breaking down. Come on! Come on! I'd left all my jewellery at home, dressed down in a pair of jeans, a tatty jean jacket and Converse trainers, but it didn't seem to matter; they'd immediately sniffed the strong scent of money and it had led them straight to me. My hair was glossy, my skin clear and my perfume expensive. Real, not like the cheap watered-down rip offs from the market, which lasted an hour if you were lucky.

Taking a gamble, I looked over to the hoodie to my right, holding his gaze. 'I'm going to see my mum,' I said, hoping he didn't detect any weakness in my voice. 'Mary,' I confirmed, straightening up. 'She's my mum.'

It was a bold move. Hopefully one that would pay off. I had to prove to them I wasn't scared and that I belonged on the poxy estate, somehow. I was just like one of them. An insider, not an intruder. My legs trembled, about to give way and I was shaking. The lift shaft juddered, making its noisy descent.

'Alright,' he drawled, tipping back his hood to reveal his face.

I knew him. Oh, thank God, I knew him. His name was Tommy and he lived in Dinton House, two blocks away. I knew him from when he was a baby in nappies, being pushed around in a buggy by his teenage mum, Isla. We went to the same school and she was two years above me. Her parents, being strict Catholics, made her keep the baby. Tommy never knew how close Isla was to having him aborted.

'She's safe,' Tommy signalled to others after studying me long and hard.

I let out an exhalation.

'Mary's some crazy bitch, fam,' the hoodie to my left snorted. He spat on the floor, missing my trainer by an inch. 'Some crazy bitch.'

The doors to the lift opened and the smell of ammonia hit the back of my throat, making me gag. I stepped inside, pounding the button to the fifth floor hard. Their laughter drowned out by the closing doors.

Stepping out of the lift, I looked over the balcony towards the London skyline. It always took my breath away; one of the bonuses of being an inner-city girl. I reached my hand out to trace the buildings and the sky beyond. As a kid, I used to believe that if I reached out far enough, I'd be able to touch the BT Tower.

Below, on the ground floor and into the distance was the playground. I could still hear Mum's shrill voice inside my head as she yelled out from the window on the fifth floor, 'Anna! Get your backside upstairs, your dinner's ready, girl'.

Stiffly, I walked along the balcony, forcing one foot in front of the other, towards number thirty-three, Mary's flat, feeling less brave than I had done moments earlier. Drum and bass music played from one of the neighbouring flats. Helen appeared like a ray of sunshine from number thirty-one.

'Anna. It's been so long.' She embraced me tightly. She'd gained a few pounds, so her hug was more comforting than ever.

Even though Helen had four kids of her own and lived in a small three-bedroomed flat, she always had space for me. I'd often have sleepovers, maybe once or twice a week, and at night we'd all squeeze tightly together on the red leather sofa covered in plastic, eating dinner from trays on our laps watching 'The Fresh Prince of Bel-Air' and 'Buffy the Vampire Slayer'. She'd cook us the most amazing Cypriot dishes, recipes passed down by her mother, such as stuffed vine leaves and pastries filled with spinach and cheese. Sometimes the smell of her exotic food would waft along the balcony, making my stomach growl angrily at me.

Growing up, I loved spending time at hers. It always felt homely, with her plumped up cushions, colourful beaded room dividers and constant cooking smells, not forgetting her securely locked front door. Not like my home, which was like Piccadilly Circus on most days, with the comings and goings of everyone on the estate, because of Mary's ridiculous open-door policy. Our flat always reeked of fags and weed, the fridge was mostly bare, and the cupboards full of tins of unbranded spaghetti hoops and baked beans, which were my staples.

'Let me take a good look at you.' Helen peeled herself away and held me out at arm's length to inspect me, looking me up and down and twirling me around, with only the purest affection pouring from her big brown eyes. Her love was always non-discriminatory, she had enough for everyone.

'You're as beautiful as ever. A face that lights up this whole damn estate.'

I blushed.

'How are you?'

'I'm okay,' I lied. Standing two doors away from Mary's flat, I could sense a dark and sinister aura like thick gas, circulating. 'How's she been?' I asked, pleading with my eyes, hoping she'd read my signal and say something that would discourage me from going inside Mary's flat.

Sadness cast a shadow on her face. 'My darling, she's been really bad.'

Swallowing down the huge lump in the back of my throat, I straightened myself up, pulling myself together. I would NOT allow myself to get sucked in. Not anymore.

Helen patted me on the back. 'Don't be a stranger, now,' she said, as she retreated back into her flat, closing the door quietly behind her.

As I stood outside Mary's front door, psyching myself up, Pudding – mum's smelly stray cat and replacement for my childhood cat Pebbles – approached from behind, weaving in between my legs, brushing her bushy tail against me. She scratched at Mary's front door, wanting in. The door was, predictably, on the latch. *My place is your place* had always been her mantra.

Saying a secret prayer, I pushed the door open, allowing Pudding to enter first. My legs turned to jelly as I followed the cat inside.

I had no master plan.

Pudding stopped by my feet and sprawled across the threadbare carpet in the compact landing. Her belly sloshed over to one side as she rolled onto her back, inviting strokes.

'Is she looking after you okay?' I whispered, tickling her tummy.

Pudding purred but quickly lost interest, swiping at my hand with her front paw. She arched her back and waddled off into the kitchen next door, in search of food.

Familiar voices boomed from next door. Mum's was naturally the loudest. Her deep throaty voice vibrated through the paper-thin wall, straight into me, making me shudder. I could picture them all in the kitchen, sitting around the small round table, talking rubbish and drinking gallons of tea or rum, or both. They'd be Uncle Jack, Lloyd and his wife Sonya. Mary would be reading a palm or telling a fortune from the tea leaves. She'd be wearing her favourite gypsy skirt, the one with bells on which jangled every time she walked – the noise always irritated the hell out of me – and she'd be smoking her 'wacky-backy', as she liked to call it, claiming it was for medicinal purposes. Her stash was kept in a pretty jewellery box I'd made in primary school for Mother's Day. I'd decorated it with glitter and star stickers.

Jack had told me that the cancer had aged her. Apparently, she was looking gaunt and frail. It was hard to imagine her that way, she'd always been so robust and unbreakable. Nothing could knock her down. I was sure that the cancer wasn't real. It couldn't be.

The hideous patterned wallpaper in the landing had almost been stripped off. Each time I walked past when I was younger, I'd rip a piece off. She'd caught me once and walloped my hand so hard, it stayed numb for an hour. That didn't stop me from wanting to do it more. Tiny victories helped.

I pressed my ear against the cold damp wall. Someone cracked a joke, maybe it was Uncle Jack, and an eruption of laughter followed. She was naturally laughing the hardest, the loudest, and judging by the sounds of her rowdy cackles, she sounded exactly the bloody same. The cancer hadn't changed her at all. Not one fucking bit.

Her laughter reverberated through the thin wall that separated us, leaving a nasty taste of bile in the back of my throat. The image of a sick old lady shattered in my mind, like shards of broken glass.

A fire ignited inside my belly. I was suddenly furious with her.

How did she manage to get on with life, finding the time to have fun, despite the fact that she was dying? Despite the fact she had no relationship with her daughter and didn't even know her own grandson? How could she act as if everything was normal? Did I not matter to her? Did Joshy not matter?

After I ran away from home, we didn't communicate for years. She wasn't even that bothered. However, it bothered me. Eventually, I plucked up the courage to visit her and worked really hard to make amends and build a bridge – rickety as that bridge was, at least it was something. I naively believed that we'd get on better as adults, as friends, as opposed to mother and child. Her friends always meant so much to her. It wasn't much of a relationship and not much of a friendship either, but it was all I had.

What a fool I was.

She was nowhere to be seen when I was struggling to find my place as a new mum. I needed my mother by my side more than ever. It wasn't only Matt who'd kept her away, she'd kept herself away. *She'd kept herself away!*

She could have fought for me, fought for Joshy, for her family. She could have made the effort to change, to prove to Matt and to me that she cared, that she was capable of putting someone else's needs in front of her own. Instead, she'd chosen not to. Instead, she'd chosen to give up on us, without a fight.

The more she chortled in the kitchen with her pals, the more I thought about her neglectful behaviour and the more my bitterness soared out of control.

Underneath the thick layer of pain was a deep layer of contempt.

Every cell in my body came to the boil. I punched the wall as hard as I could. The pain, instant and gratifying, made me yelp out loud. I doubled over, clutching my hand. The laughter coming from the other side of the wall stopped.

'Who's there?' Mary called.

My knuckles bled. My heart pumped. My vision blurred.

'What happened to me when I was younger?' I cried.

'Anna? Is that you, girl?'

'I can't do this,' I said, stumbling back outside, breathing in the smoggy London air. 'I can't do this.'

With my adrenaline jacked and my muscles tight, I took flight and ran as fast as I could. I got the hell out of the estate and sprinted towards the clinic.

I had to see Cassandra.

Chapter Twenty

'Dear God, what's happened?' asked a panicked-looking Cassandra.

I was sitting on the bottom step outside the clinic, waiting for her to answer the door. By the time she'd appeared, I was shaking, and my teeth were chattering, my hair was soaked and my knuckles were a mess from punching Mary's wall.

'I went to see my mum. I thought she could help.' The rain dripped from my forehead into my eyes. I blinked away the raindrops and tears. 'I didn't know where else to go or who to turn to. I'm sorry I've turned up on your doorstep unannounced.' The rain had penetrated my jean jacket and t-shirt. 'I'm sorry,' I said, holding my head in my hands.

'It's okay,' she said, kneeling down beside me, peeling my hands away and exposing my face. Exposing me.

She was barefoot. Her toenails painted black. Her feet long, slim and tanned. Her skin, velveteen.

'Let's get you inside so you can dry off. You can tell me all about it.' She hoisted me up, like I was a ragdoll, keeping watch for any signs of the neighbours. She was really strong for her lean, slender frame.

Unsteady on my feet, I leant on Cassandra for support as we walked inside. The clinic was cold, and it was dark. The lights flickered as she turned the switch on, a soft ambience returned to the room, bringing some artificial warmth. She helped me with my wet jacket, taking it off and hanging it on the back of the door.

'You've hurt yourself. Let me take a look.' She stared at my smashed knuckles.

'It's nothing,' I said, pulling my hand away.

'It's not nothing, you're bleeding,' she said, taking my hand back. This time, I didn't stop her.

'And you're shivering.' She guided me to the two-seater sofa against the wall.

I'd never sat there before and slumped down clumsily, feeling it sink beneath my weight. It was much lower than I'd anticipated, and it made me feel like a child.

'I'll fetch you a blanket and a warm drink from my home upstairs.' She crossed the room with natural grace and elegance. Unlocking the internal door to the right of the sofa, she turned to me and said, 'Are you okay if I leave you alone? I won't be too long.'

'Yes, of course. Thank you for taking care of me.'

'Sit tight, I'll be right back,' she said in a satisfactory sort of way. 'I'll take care of everything.' She beamed a huge smile.

It was only then I noticed her hair was tied away from her face with a colourful headscarf, making her cheek bones prominent, and she was wearing an electric blue kaftan adorned with pretty beads running down the sides. She looked exotic. Avant-garde. Nothing like the therapist I'd gotten to know, with her sharp crisp suits, glossed hair and professional mask.

I realised then that I knew so little about her.

She disappeared through the internal door, not quite closing it behind her. An unusual herby scent lingered in the room long after she'd gone. Her footsteps lightly ascended the stairs to her home. Another door closed. A lock turned.

Determined not to think about Mary for fear of spiralling, I scanned the clinic to ground myself. Everything was in its place: flowers, tissues, a glass and jug of water with slices of lemon and lime. I breathed. I was safe, that's all that mattered. Cassandra would know how to fix things. She always did.

I sat waiting for her to return, drumming my fingers on my lap. She was taking her time.

Getting slightly impatient, I walked over to the door she'd disappeared through and peeped up the narrow winding staircase. There wasn't much to see, just another closed door at the top of the stairs. Who did she live with, I wondered. She didn't wear a wedding band, but that didn't mean there wasn't someone special in her life.

Behind the glass desk, French patio doors overlooked a small outside space. I pressed my face against the door and fogged it with my breath. The garden was small and unkept, an overgrown mass of weeds and grass. A storm had developed and the wind pelted the rain sideways against the panes, making the flimsy glass rattle. So much for summer.

A draught from the French doors made the mysterious blue-and-white-eye chime, which hung from the ceiling, twirl around. Whichever way you looked at it, the eye followed. It must have been some kind of hypnotherapy reference, but I found it creepy.

On her desk, there was an appointment book, a leather-bound notebook which she'd often write in, and a diamond-encrusted Montblanc pen. All three items perfectly aligned in order of size. Running my finger along the desk, I picked up a thin layer of dust. I opened the A4 appointment book and tilted my head, peeking at the random page I'd selected. There were no names, no appointments, no entries written inside. I flipped through and settled on another page. It was empty. I continued to scan the pages, one at a time. Each time I turned there was nothing. The pages were blank.

Closing the diary, I stared at her leather notebook and traced my finger around the design, feeling the grooves of the intricate swirly pattern. When I picked up the book, it seemed to pulse in my hands. There was a connection. A bond. Inside were the clinic notes she'd written up about me. Her analysis and thoughts.

Cassandra's book of secrets.

I shouldn't have been snooping, but I couldn't help myself. I was drawn to find out more about her, compelled to find out what she really thought about me. The book was pulling me like a strong magnet. I had to know.

But before I had a chance to steal a look inside her notepad, the loud clicking of heels started down the staircase towards the basement clinic. Placing the notepad down where I'd found it, I raced back to the sofa, trying to settle my rapid breathing, hoping that I'd put everything back exactly how I'd found it.

I gasped, noticing wet shoe prints on the floor. A visible trail of betrayal. Idiot.

Cassandra entered the clinic and had changed into her usual attire; black pencil skirt, white blouse and patent black heels, her hair was brushed to a shine, sporting a centre parting, and she'd applied red lipstick. She was starched, yet glamorous. In one hand, she was holding a first aid box and in the other, a mug of something. Draped over her arm was a woven blanket and hand towel. An earthy smell wafted from the steaming drink as she placed it down on the coffee table in front of me. I didn't have the guts to tell her I hated fancy teas.

She was taking care of me and there I was snooping! Guilt gnawed.

Cassandra wrapped the musky blanket around my shoulders and handed me the small towel to dry my hair. Allowing her to play mum, she applied an alcohol-based ointment from the first aid kit to some cotton wool and dabbed my smashed knuckles lightly.

It stung like hell, making me flinch. She raised an eyebrow and smiled, playfully.

'What?' I grinned back. 'It hurts.' The irony was not lost on me.

Cassandra finished up with my hand and placed the bloodied cotton wool onto the coffee table. 'If the swelling doesn't go down by tomorrow, you'll need an X-ray. We wouldn't want anything broken, now would we? Drink your Chinese herbal tea, it'll help warm you up.'

'Thank you.' Not wanting to disappoint her, I picked up the mug and blew on the hot drink to cool it down, sipping a small amount at a time. It tasted bitter, like mud. I placed it back down on the coffee table.

'How did you hurt yourself?'

'I'm too embarrassed to say.'

'Don't be afraid to open up, Annabelle. You can tell me anything.'

'I punched a wall in my mum's flat,' I said, lowering my head. 'As soon as I heard *her* laughter coming from the kitchen, on the other side of the wall, I lost it. It was like a switch. I couldn't control myself. Suddenly, I was angry. Hurt. I didn't even get to see her. I punched the wall and ran away like a coward.' I smiled, hoping she wouldn't judge me and would understand why I acted so recklessly.

'You can control and channel your hurt and anger in more positive ways,' she said as she turned her body to face me.

Our knees brushed slightly. She picked up new cotton wool, took my hand and dabbed the wound, not noticing the brief contact we'd made, tending to my sore knuckles, swabbing the grazed area.

Mum had never tended to my smashed knees from the countless roller-skating accidents I'd had growing up, or offered me plasters, or even made me hot milk or chocolate to help soothe me when I was in any pain or feeling low.

'I'm feeling really angry towards her,' I spat. 'Despite the fact

I should be more empathetic because of her situation. You know, what with the cancer an' all.'

'Why do you have bitterness, Annabelle? Tell me.'

'I don't have many fond memories of growing up,' I said. 'A lot of my memories consist of her trying to push me onto other people, getting me out of her hair so she could entertain her friends. As a teenager, I'd be out all day and night. Gone for hours. She never once asked where I'd been or who I'd been with. She didn't even know if I attended school or not. Just as long as she had a little peace and quiet, that's all she cared about. She never took an interest in me or my life. One day, I left home without even telling her. According to Uncle Jack, it took her a couple of days to realise that her small stash of money she kept in a jar for weed had been raided and that my clothes had been emptied from the wardrobe. I was seventeen. I never went back.'

'This is very sad to hear,' she said.

Silence settled in the room.

Cassandra walked over to the desk to retrieve her leather notebook. I held my breath. She had a steady focus about her and didn't seem to notice the wet footprints on the floor. She returned and sat down next to me, placing her notebook on the coffee table beside my tea. I stared at the book, transfixed for a while.

'I thought that by seeing Mary, it would be a fast track to some answers.'

I waited for Cassandra to respond, but she remained quiet, clasping her hands.

'The last session threw up a lot of questions for me and I know she's hiding something. I sense it in my gut. She knows the truth. She knows what happened to me. What do you think?'

'You can't go looking for answers on your own. You're too vulnerable.'

She was right, as always. I'd made a mistake the moment I'd stepped foot inside Mary's flat and I knew it. There was too much baggage for me to deal with all at once.

'You and I have made a pact.'

'We have?'

'I'm bound to you, as you are to me. It's a contract.' Her tone changed, becoming more business-like.

There was a flash in her eyes. No smile. Something in her manner made me sit up to attention.

'There has to be a level of trust,' she said, as her eyes darted across the floor, settling on the wet footprints near her desk.

I lowered my head. 'I know.'

'Good. I'm glad to hear this,' she said, her voice light and steady again.

I took another sip of the disgusting bitter tea to mask the shame I felt.

'We've embarked on this journey of new discovery and healing. I am invested in your truth, and in you. And with me by your side, you'll be able to recover your memories. But it's important you heal emotionally before you confront your mother. If you have any questions, you must come to me first.' She patted my knee, reassuringly.

'Okay. I promise.'

She was so wise. Worldly. Always knew what to say to make me feel better. I'd never met anyone quite like her before. She fascinated me.

'Now drink your tea.'

I sipped some more, pulling bark-like sticks out of my mouth.

'Forgive me if you think I'm speaking out of turn here, but I must say what's on my mind.' She crossed her hands.

I placed the cup down on the table.

'I don't believe your mother is capable of loving you, not like a real mother should.' Her face was soft while she delivered her sting.

I looked away and stared at the framed hypnotherapy certificate on the wall opposite.

'I don't believe this woman has ever loved you. Her love is disingenuous.'

'But she must love me in her own way, surely? I'm her daughter. Her flesh and blood.'

A quietness spilled over us. Did Mary not love me?

'You deserve to be loved properly, Annabelle,' said Cassandra.

Her unexpected words crashed into my thoughts, making my cheeks burn.

'Is that new?' She pointed to the cut on my upper arm where I'd taken the scissors to my skin.

I looked at her wide-eyed, placing my hand over it, to cover it up. 'It was an accident.'

'Don't be ashamed of who you are, Annabelle. You must learn to embrace every aspect of your personality.'

She leant in and pulled my hand away from my arm, exposing the lumpy scar.

'There's something beautiful about scars,' she said.

'Beautiful?' I laughed nervously, not knowing where to look.

'There's beauty in everything if you look hard enough,' she said, locking eyes with me. 'A scar is a manifestation of past pain. Past hurts. It's part of who we are. In time, some scars heal, and some don't. Each scar tells a story.'

Placing my hand over the scar again, I rubbed the rough damaged skin beneath my fingers. My scars had always been a stark reminder of my failures, how I'd lost control, my hopelessness, a reminder of her, Mary, forever letting me down, a symbol of my marriage breaking down, failing Joshy, my world falling apart. How could it be a beautiful thing?

Where others saw a freak show, Cassandra strangely didn't. She saw beauty. She thought I was beautiful, but not in a sexual or artificial way, she saw beauty hidden underneath damaged layers of hurt and pain and anger, she saw beauty beyond the scars, beauty I was unaware of. Beauty I could never see, no matter how much she tried to dress it up.

'May I ask about the sensations you experience when you cut?'

My shoulders tightened. I sat upright.

'It could reveal some answers as to why you're compelled to do so.'

Her openness about the subject gave me some confidence to explore depths of myself that I'd always shied away from. Cassandra was giving me permission to be me, without judgement.

'At first, there's a build-up of pressure which you can't ignore. It's like you're about to pop. It's hard to think of anything else. It becomes an obsession. Your mind goes into overdrive.'

'So, the only way to release the pressure is to give in to your urges?' she asked.

'Exactly.'

Her eyes fixed on mine. 'Please continue.'

'When I was younger, Mary filled our tiny living room with balloons for one of her parties. She told me not to touch any. Imagine telling that to a child!' I laughed. 'She left me alone in that room and it was torture. Hell. It was like she'd done it on purpose and was testing me. The urge to play with the balloons, to pop them, became overwhelming. If I didn't pop at least one, I was sure to faint.'

'And did you?'

'Of course. I couldn't help myself,' I laughed, giddy and lightheaded. 'In the end, I popped each and every one of them.'

The clinic filled with laughter, as she giggled alongside me. It was strange and comforting. I realised that I couldn't remember the last time I'd laughed out loud with Matt. Had I ever with Mary?

'Did you get into trouble?'

'Yep. She gave me a good hiding and said I always ruined everything for her.'

'That's a terrible thing to say.'

'Yeah, well. That's Mary for you.'

'Talk to me more about the urges, so I understand.'

'Okay, so you know you have to cut yourself, or you'll explode. There's no other way out. It's done, you've decided,' I said, bolder, growing in confidence, swelling.

I'd never described how I felt about harming before. It had always been hidden – my dirty little secret.

'The next thing you do is find an implement, a penknife, kitchen knife or even scissors. Nothing too blunt, it has to be sharp. You break the skin. You slice. You cut. A nick satisfies, but sometimes you need to cut deeper. It depends on how low you're feeling.' My heart raced as I relived the sensations like it was happening in real time.

'And then?'

'Obviously, you feel the acute pain, but that gets dulled out because it's the rush that really gets to you. For that split second, you're on top of the world. You're winning. You feel a release. After the pain and the rush, a weird sense of calm follows and you're at peace. You know what I mean?'

She nodded. 'What happens after that?'

'Well, that's the shitty part. The come down. The same old feelings return, the same old crap. Self-loathing follows you around, no matter what. It doesn't solve a thing, and I guess that's why the cycle continues.' I was suddenly spaced out. Wired, yet sleepy.

'Thank you for sharing.' She picked up her notebook and jotted down notes.

I glimpsed at the clock. I'd been there for almost two hours. 'Can I stay a while longer?'

'Yes. Stay as long as you need. I have nowhere specific to be.'

'That's so kind. Thank you for looking after me today.'

'Not a problem. It's what I'm here for.'

My mind percolated what had been discussed in session while we sat in comfortable silence. Cassandra was right about Mary. She never cared for me, not really. Not like a real mum should have. My thoughts turned to Joshy. My chest felt heavy. Tight. Would he grow up with feelings of bitterness and anger towards me?

'You look tired. Why don't you close your eyes? Drift off, Annabelle.'

She was right. I was exhausted. My mind quietened down and I closed my eyes.

'Sleep,' she said soothingly.

Chapter Twenty-One

I was slouched on Cassandra's sofa with my eyes shut, not yet asleep, nor fully awake. In that tranquil in-between stage where your mind roams and wanders freely, not fixating on any specifics or worries, stresses or anxieties, nor in the deep slumber of sleep where you find yourself floating in a dream, or worse, disappearing into the depths of a nightmare.

'We should explore.' Cassandra's velvet voice pulled me back into the room.

'Huh?' The lids to my eyes were too heavy to lift open.

'Explore your childhood once more. Let's see whether we can work out what is troubling you.'

'But I'm so tired,' I said, melting like butter.

'Yes, I know. But you're susceptible to suggestions right now. Your mind is open. We should use this golden opportunity to explore new avenues. Talk it through while you're comfortable and deeply relaxed.'

The notes of her voice went up and down, making me sink further into myself.

'Annabelle, can you recall the first time you harmed yourself?' she asked.

Cassandra's words echoed in my mind: *don't be ashamed of who you are.*

'Tell me how it all started. How old were you when it first happened?'

'I was fourteen when I first cut myself. The harming didn't last that long, and I stopped shortly after I left home at seventeen. My urges evaporated when I wasn't around Mary.'

'Annabelle. Take me back to when you were fourteen. When it first began.'

'She was supposed to be there with me.'

'Who?'

'Mary,' I said, swallowing down the sharp pain. 'She promised me. It was sports day at school, and I was the house captain. She was the only parent not there.'

'And how did that make you feel?'

'Angry. Really angry.'

'I see.'

'It happened after art class, during lunch break.'

'What did?'

'The first time I cut myself on purpose. It was stupid, really. More of a dare. I was showing off to my friends.'

I'd stolen the scalpel from the art room. Me and the others, Siobhan, Betsie-Jane and Shadi, all huddled in the art supply cupboard after the lesson, during our lunch break. We were supposed to be on prefect duty. Shadi, the most handsome guy I'd ever seen in my life, had his big size ten feet up against the door, holding it shut so no one could barge in on us.

It was a hot afternoon, stuffy, and someone's BO wafted under my nose. I think it was Siobhan, because I'd spotted sweat patches under her arms during art. She caught me glancing at her and two minutes later she'd put her school blazer back on.

'Go on, then,' Betsie-Jane whispered. 'It's your turn now.'

'I don't know if I can,' I said.

'Chicken,' snapped Siobhan, forever the mouthy one of our group.

'*Sssh*. Someone's coming,' Shadi said, his hazel eyes sparkling in the dark.

We all froze, remaining silent. We could hear footsteps outside. I'd already got done by Sir the week before, for bunking double science.

'That was Miss McDonnell. I think she's gone,' said Betsie. 'Phew. That was close.'

I'd held up the scalpel in my hand, secretly praying that somehow the others would bottle it, opting for lunch instead. I didn't want to go through with the ridiculous dare anymore. It was so stupid. Why had I opened my big gob? Always wanting to act the big shot. The big shitter, more like.

We'd agreed to play dares to spice things up during class. We were bored. Siobhan's idea! Her dare was to hum each time the classroom went quiet, Shadi had to put his hand up and speak to Miss in an American accent, asking whether he could skip class, and Betsie-Jane had to laugh loudly each time Miss said something. Like an idiot, I'd decided to take it to the next level. I picked up the scalpel from the stationery tray, vowing to cut myself deeply enough that I'd be sent to the hospital, missing the rest of school.

'Miss might come back,' I said.

'Nah,' said Siobhan. 'She probably forgot her fags or something. She loves to smoke in the staff room.'

It was getting hot and sticky, and I could feel a wet patch spreading on my back. Maybe it was *my* BO?

'It's all clear,' Betsie whispered.

They all stared at me, waiting. My heart leaped.

'Do it. Do it. Do it,' said Siobhan, egging the others on.

They all joined in, in unison. Shadi hiked my skirt up, to reveal my skin. My body tingled like crazy. 'Here. Do it on your leg. Right here,' he said, as he dragged my hand onto my upper thigh showing me where to cut, making the briefest of contact.

'She's too chicken,' said Siobhan, 'wasting all our time. Come on. It's now or never, Anna. We ain't got all day.'

'I mean, I don't see the point to be honest with you,' Betsie said, the voice of reason. 'The dares are over with, now.'

'Not hers. She said it. She's got to do it,' said Siobhan, having none of it.

At the time, there was a point to my dare. A huge point. I was pissed off with Mary. Fed up. Raging with hurt. She'd let me down, again. It's not like I was doing well in other areas of school, so sport was my thing. I was good at running. Really good. I wanted her support. I wanted her to be proud of me. She never seemed to be there at the crucial moments in my life. A theme I was forced to get used to.

'Now, cut,' said Siobhan.

Everyone gawked at me. The art cupboard began to close in.

You'll be sorry Mary. You'll all be sorry.

Squeezing my eyes tightly shut, I sliced right through the skin on my upper thigh. Nothing happened for a second. Everyone in the art supply cupboard remained still. The quiet thrummed in my ears. Everything slowed down as everyone waited silently. When I opened my eyes, everything sped up, as if on fast forward. A rush like a wave rippled through my entire body, goosebumps appeared on my skin and for a brief moment, all eyes were on me, and it felt good. So good. The pain, which swiftly followed, was sharp and zingy, like lemon being squeezed on a paper cut.

'Oh *shit*,' said Siobhan.

Blood dripped from the scalpel onto my white sock, down on my shoe and onto the floor. Blood gushed from the open wound. The cut was unintentionally deep. I slid down the wall onto the floor.

'Anna? Are you okay?' Betsie said, panicked.

'Say something. *Fuck*!' exclaimed Shadi.

'Is she gonna die on us?' asked Siobhan. 'Quick. Let's get out of here.'

'We can't leave her,' said Betsie. 'Anna? Are you okay? I think you've hurt yourself. Anna?'

'I'm going to get Miss,' Shadi said.

He opened the door, letting the light flood into the cupboard. I squinted as tears misted my eyes. My white sock had turned red. The scalpel dropped to the floor. My leg hurt like crazy and I was shaking uncontrollably.

'Annabelle. Annabelle. Can you hear me?'

Whose voice was that?

'Annabelle. Stay calm. Stay focused. Remember to take in some slow and deep intentional breaths. In and out. Nice and slow, calming your system down. I'm going to take you back to your happy place. Annabelle. Nod if you can hear me?'

It was Cassandra. My pinprick of light. I was safe. Secure. In the clinic.

'Annabelle, find your happy place. Go to your happy place. Go now.'

Like a break of sunlight filtering through rain clouds, her voice calmed me down and my breathing regulated. My nightmare evaporated and my happy place returned. I was back in Greece.

The hot sand prickled my feet, my toe ring glistened in the sunshine and the turquoise sea sparkled. The midday sun sizzled on my skin, warming me up. I took off my sarong and entered the warm calm water, swimming out toward the anchored boats.

'Counting backwards from ten. Nine. Eight, coming back. Seven, bringing you back. Six. Five ...'

A little while longer.

'Four. Three. I'm bringing you back to the room.'

Not yet. I'm not ready.

'Almost back, listening to my voice. Two …'

No. No. No.

'One. Open your eyes and take a good stretch. Welcome back, Annabelle.'

The lace veil lifted.

Everything came back into a soft focus. I checked to make sure everything was in its place, for reassurance. The jug, the glass, the box of tissues was on the side table next to the egg chair. Cassandra sat next to me on the sofa, jotting down notes in her pad.

'How are you feeling?' She closed her booklet, placing it on the table.

'I'm okay. I think.' I stared at the notebook. 'I've never told anyone what happened to me when I was fourteen before. Even when Matt asked about my permanent scar, I said it was a stupid accident in art class.'

Cassandra placed her hand on my knee. 'Take all the time you need to adjust back to your surroundings.' She pulled her hand away and walked over to the side table and poured water from the jug into a glass, the lemon and lime slices bobbed up and down. Her heels clicked as she came back.

My leg zinged long after her hand left it. I sipped water and placed the glass back down on the coffee table next to the half-finished mug of herbal tea and glanced at the wall clock, feeling spaced. Fuzzy.

It had to be a mistake. It had to be.

'Is that the right time?' I asked, the fog in my brain still heavy.

'Yes of course, why?'

'Oh my God, no!'

151

'What's the matter?'

As I stood up, the room spun around me. I hurtled myself towards the front door, almost tripping over my feet, grabbing my jacket from the hook. 'It's Joshy,' I wailed.

'Slow down. Slow down! What's wrong with Joshy?'

'His school ended forty-five minutes ago. I've forgotten to collect him. This is the excuse Matt's been waiting for. He's going to send me to see that doctor for sure.' I opened the front door. The rain had stopped, and a gush of humid air greeted me. It was suffocating.

'Annabelle. Please stop. You're in no fit state to walk. Let me get you a taxi. Perhaps you should call your husband and let him know. It'll be okay. The school will protect him.'

'I'll call Rosita,' I said, not quite believing what was happening to me.

Matt was going to kill me.

Chapter Twenty-Two

The traffic was really heavy and the taxi I was in crawled all the way to the school. A two-mile journey took twenty-five bloody minutes. It would have been quicker to run. My poor baby. He deserved better than this. It was the excuse Matt was looking for to send me to that doctor. I'd just proven him right. I was a bad mum. Joshy was going to grow up hating me.

A few yards from the school, the cab came to an abrupt halt as it waited for a woman to cross at the zebra crossing. Every second that passed became unbearable. It didn't help that the woman walked at a snail's pace across the road. Sitting in the back seat of the cab, my legs jigged up and down and I chewed on my fingernails. Come on, come on!

She stopped midway and turned to face the taxi, staring straight at me, making eye contact. The blood drained from my head. I put my hand over my mouth to stop myself from belting out a scream. There was no mistaking. It was her. The woman on the swing with the matted hair and blacked-out eyes.

The driver looked ahead, not fazed by the horror that was before us. I shook my head from side to side. No. It couldn't be. It couldn't be. The hybrid car started up and continued on its way. I stared out of the side window, the woman had already crossed and was walking up the hill at a speedy pace.

She was a young girl in jeans and sneakers.

I was losing my mind.

We pulled up outside the school gates. An Aston Martin with its front wheel touching the yellow zigzags was being ticketed by a traffic warden. Rachel. Quickly darting past the warden, I accidently knocked him into the car, setting off Rachel's car alarm. It shrieked loudly. 'Hey lady,' the warden shouted at me.

'I'm so sorry. My son. I'm sorry,' I said, as I ran through the front playground, the car alarm shrilling in my ears.

Rosita emerged out of the building with a teary Joshy in tow. His eyes were swollen and red, his nose snotty from excessive crying. Rushing over, I cradled him in my arms. He burrowed into my chest as Rosita took a step back, crossing her arms.

'I'm sorry, baby bear. I'm so sorry. I didn't realise the time.' I'd never been late for Joshy before. Even when I couldn't manage the school run, and things were bad, I always made sure he was collected by Rosita. 'Are you okay?'

'I played football with Leo in sports club,' he stammered.

'You're such a big boy.' I kissed his forehead, his cheeks, his chubby hands. 'Does Matt know?' I said, turning to Rosita. Afraid of the answer.

'*Señora*, the school call Mr Clarke. *El esta en casa*. Home. He already home.'

'Thank you for getting Joshy,' I said, my voice breaking. I was in deep shit.

'*Señora*?'

'Yes?'

'You no good. You need doctor? You sick. You sick.'

I stood up and brushed myself down. 'I don't know what you're trying to say to me, Rosita, but I'm fine. I forgot the time. Okay.' I took hold of Joshy's hand.

Rachel came bounding out of the school in a sprightly way, full of energy. She was in her gym gear, hair bouncing with every step, holding a mobile in one hand and car keys in the other, Leo following closely at her heels. My grip tightened around Joshy's hand as I rushed him out of the gates, passing the bleeping Aston Martin and down the hill towards home, leaving Rosita a few paces behind, struggling to keep up.

'Come on, Joshy,' I said, hurrying him up. 'We've got to get home.'

'But Mummy? Rosita. She's behind us. Let's wait.' Joshy reached his hand out for Rosita, wanting to make a chain. I kept on power walking, ignoring him.

'It's fine. Come on. We've got to get home.'

'But…'

'JOSHY! Enough.' I gripped his wrist and started to lightly jog.

Matt held the front door open as he eyeballed me long and hard. I sheepishly entered the house, avoiding his glare. His face was pinched. His jaw locked. His hands were tight fists, by his sides. I'd messed up, big time. I knew it, he knew it, Rosita knew it, God, even Joshy knew it. Wiping my brow, I lowered my head and followed him into the kitchen, keeping mute. Rosita, all sweaty and flustered from her brisk walk, entered a few minutes after me. She was thanked for her duties and sent home with an envelope of cash.

I'd rummaged through my brain, trying to come up with a suitable excuse for why I'd forgotten Joshy at school, just in case Matt wanted to talk it through, just in case he asked how it happened, just in case he dared to speak to me, look at me, acknowledge my bloody exist-ence. Just in case he wanted to know why the hell I was derailing in front of his very eyes, why I was falling apart, why I couldn't sleep at night and couldn't function during the day, and why Joshy was now suffering because of it. Why I was secretly worried that I was turning into my mother, convinced Joshy would grow up despising me.

But he didn't ask anything.

With my head still fuzzy, stuffed with cotton wool from the deep hypnosis session, I tried to push the incident to the back of my mind, for Joshy's sake. I wanted to prove to Matt that I was capable of looking after Joshy without any more mishaps. After clearing away dinner, I bathed Joshy, tucked him in and read his two favourite bedtime stories, all the while fighting the urge to scream, cry and run away for good. Fighting the urge to harm, hurt myself so badly, do some real damage. Resisting the temptation to call Cassandra, my light, to help guide me out of the dark.

The tension in the house was oppressive. The silent treatment from Matt, torturous.

Time ticked on slowly. I ran a hot bath and lay in the tub for some time, feeling the prickly heat envelop my body, listening to my pulse thump inside my temples, too afraid to go downstairs and face Matt without having Joshy as a buffer. I ducked my head under the bubbles, willing myself to be still, willing my thoughts to stop for just one damn second – but the session I'd had with Cassandra pushed its way to the forefront of my mind. Her words swam around my head. *Don't be ashamed of who you are.*

I *was* ashamed. Deeply ashamed. Deep down, I knew that I was a terrible mother to Joshy, just like Mary was to me.

I was startled as I came up for air. 'Matt? I didn't know you were standing there.' The bubbles had disappeared. The water was luke-warm. I covered my breasts with my hands.

Matt was standing over the bath, with a thunderous face. 'Enjoying your soak?'

'I thought maybe ...'

'I'm taking you to see Dr Jacobs tomorrow,' he said, icily. 'Your appointment is at 9.00 am.'

'Matt. About today. It was a genuine mistake...'

'Save it. We'll talk tomorrow with the doctor. See if he can make sense of it all, because I'll be damned if I can.'

I sat up. Water spilled over the edge of the tub. 'Matt, I can explain.'

It was too late. He'd already walked out of the bathroom, leaving the door wide open.

'Why don't you ever want to talk things through?' I yelled.

A cold draught swept through the room, making me shiver.

Dr Peter Jacobs was scruffy and unshaven, wearing corduroy trousers and an off-white creased shirt. He wore two sets of glasses, neither pair on his eyes. One pair was propped on his head and the other dangled around his neck on a stupid gold chain. He had a long pointy nose and the worst comb-over I'd ever seen in my life. He smelt of strong mints, and I wondered whether it was to mask his bad breath because there was a faint smell of halitosis in the air. The clinic was on Harley Street, boasting a grand reception area, a central staircase and two receptionists with headsets, which led to all the treatment rooms upstairs.

His office was in complete disarray, with stacks of paperwork and reference books piled everywhere. The desk behind him was cluttered and next to it two grey filing cabinets stacked on top of one another looked like they were about to topple over. Bookcases lined one side of the room, filled with psychology books, and on the opposite wall, tasteless paintings of horses – a show of masculinity? – shared the space with dozens of framed certificates for qualifications in medicine.

He was a bloody shrink!

Swallowing the nausea down, I stiffly took my seat next to Matt, opposite the doctor, and stared at my feet.

'How's your mother, Celeste?' The doctor asked Matt.

'Very well, thank you, Doctor Jacobs,' Matt replied.

'Do send her my regards, and please call me Peter. We've known each other a very long time. Annabelle?' He extended his hand to me.

Matt nudged me.

'Hello,' I said.

'Charming, charming.' The doctor's beady eyes fixed on me. 'So, Annabelle.' He smiled, revealing coffee-stained teeth. 'Matt tells me you're having some difficulty.'

'Doctor Jacobs, we've come for your help.' Matt jumped in before I could even answer, taking my hand to show solidarity. 'Annabelle's not been herself lately, and, well, I'm a little concerned for her well-being. I was wondering if you could help, perhaps even prescribe her something to help her manage on a day-to-day basis.'

I wondered whether the man who called himself my husband knew me at all. He hadn't the foggiest idea what I was really going through and he wasn't in the least bit interested in finding out, either. All he wanted was to bully me into an appointment that I didn't want, and bully the doctor into plying me with drugs that I didn't need, in order to silence me so he could get on with his life – and his damn affair – without any interruptions. I was well aware that he wasn't doing this for me. He was doing this for him.

'Well,' the doctor said, thoughtfully. 'I'll need to learn a little bit more about Annabelle and the situation.' He smiled. 'I need to make an assessment, gather some information.' He cleared his phlegmy throat and stared at me.

'Of course. Of course,' Matt said, sheepishly.

Even though our chairs were adjacent, the distance between us was an ocean, and it was growing. I slipped my uninjured hand away from his, leaving his to dangle over the side of the chair, solo. The doctor clocked the awkward exchange and cleared his throat.

'Tell me, Annabelle. How are you feeling?' He squinted, looking my way, assessing me.

My stomach clenched. I turned my attention to one of the ugly pictures on the wall. One particular horse looked double-jointed, its head twisted round a full 180 degrees.

'Why do you believe you are here?' His eyes narrowed further.

Matt sat, rigid. 'Annabelle?'

My body stiffened.

'It's okay. Speak, dear,' the doctor urged.

I turned back to face the doctor. He put on a pair of glasses, making his tiny eyes almost disappear. He leaned forward. I inched back. My hands gripped the arms of the chair.

'Well ... I think I'm fine.' I gave a half smile. 'There's nothing wrong with me,' I said, straightening up and looking the doctor square in the eyes, trying to keep my facial expression neutral. 'Matt's exaggerating.'

'Doctor Jacobs,' Matt interjected. 'I am NOT exaggerating. I promise you. There's been a huge change in her. An alarming change.'

'Tell me, Matthew. What concerns do you have, exactly?'

I could feel Matt's glare on my face.

'She's behaving erratically and sometimes, well, sometimes she's ...' Matt put his hand to his mouth and coughed. 'She's neglectful of our son.'

The doctor pulled a face that I couldn't quite read and sat back, crossing one leg over the other. I kept my gaze straight ahead.

'Annabelle. Would you care to elaborate?' asked Jacobs.

My cheeks flushed. 'I don't know why I'm here, to be quite honest with you. It's a waste of everyone's time.'

'Why do you think your husband thinks differently?'

'Honestly. I couldn't tell you,' I said through gritted teeth.

'Annabelle. Please tell the truth,' Matt said, his voice clipped. His face screwed tight with tension. 'Explain to the doctor what's really been going on.'

'Would it be easier if we arranged another appointment for you … to come alone?' The doctor asked, ignoring Matt.

'I don't think so. I'm not quite sure why I needed an appointment in the first place. I'm fine. Everything's fine. It's all fine.'

'Annabelle. Please tell the truth,' Matt said softly.

I turned to look at Matt, remaining mute, my blood beginning to boil.

He shifted in his seat and brushed his hair with his hands. 'Please open up to the doctor and tell him what's been happening to you, so we can get you the help you need.'

I turned away and stared at my feet, shrugging my shoulders. 'Why don't *you* tell him, Matt. Go on, go ahead.'

'Doctor?' Matt said. 'May I?'

How could he tell the doctor anything when he didn't know himself, when he never bothered to ask? He didn't have a clue.

The doctor nodded his approval to Matt.

Matt adjusted his tie and cleared his throat. 'In the last week alone, she has got drunk at a children's party and started accusing me of ridiculous things in front of our friends. It was totally out of character. She was behaving in a wild, crazy way, shouting loudly and slurring her words. There was no consoling her. Not to mention, this erratic behaviour was in front of our son Joshua, in front of other young children. I asked her to wait for me outside so she could calm down and get some fresh air, sober up a little, but instead, she disappeared and went missing for hours. We didn't know where she was or what

160

she was doing. Joshy was naturally upset seeing his mother in such a state. She didn't answer any of my calls. After I had settled Joshua at home with the nanny, I had to drive around the area looking for her. I was worried that something terrible had happened,' he said, as his voice broke.

He was playing the poor worried husband card, and the shrink was falling for it.

'Annabelle eventually came home, very late, looking a complete wreck, and wouldn't offer an explanation. She didn't even ask if Joshua was okay. She brushed the whole thing off as if nothing out of the ordinary had occurred.' He paused. 'Yesterday, she forgot to collect our son from school. He was abandoned at school, crying and afraid. The school tried to contact Annabelle, but her phone was switched off. They called me instead. Imagine how frantically worried I was. Again, I believed something terrible had happened to her. She turned up outside the school gates over an hour late with no explanation. Her hand was bleeding, as though she'd been in a fight of some kind,' he said, fiddling with his tie again. 'Annabelle. Show the doctor your hand, so he knows I'm telling the truth.' He turned and pointed towards my hand.

I covered my hand with my sleeve, keeping my gaze at the floor while both the doctor and Matt waited for me to speak.

'Doctor, please. As you can see, we clearly need your help. Your guidance. Before things worsen. I don't want the situation to escalate like … like … *the last time*,' Matt whispered.

What the hell was he talking about? What last time? Why was he lying like that?

'I understand, Matthew,' the doctor said, nodding his head sympathetically, as if he could relate to Matt's misery, knew what Matt was talking about – like they were in on something together. The doctor stretched out his legs in front of him and then retracted them. 'Annabelle, would you care to respond?'

Breathing deep into my tummy, I closed my eyes for a second to steady myself. When I opened them, I stared the doctor straight in the eyes, without blinking. 'I don't know what he's talking about.'

In my peripheral vision I saw that Matt cradled his head in his hands.

'Yes, I got drunk at a kids' party. That was a mistake, I admit. The booze went straight to my head. I hadn't eaten breakfast you see, and, anyway, it was only a couple of glasses of champagne.'

'Oh, it was far more than that,' Matt interjected.

'How would you know? You spent most of the day ogling Rachel.' I stared at Jacobs, too afraid to look at Matt. 'You forgot to mention your own behaviour at the party, didn't you?'

'Annabelle!' Matt exclaimed.

'He was being super flirty with the host and I got upset about it, so decided to leave the party. *That's* why I left. I didn't go missing, I went for a long walk and popped in on my mother. She's dying of cancer.'

I could feel Matt's face turning beetroot red.

'Yes. I did forget Joshy at school,' I said, looking down at my lap. 'This is true. And you can't make me feel any worse than I already do, but it was a genuine mistake. I thought yesterday was Wednesday, and Joshy has music club on Wednesday. As soon as I realised, I called Rosita and rushed over to the school. I honestly thought it was Wednesday, Matt,' I said, turning to my husband, teary eyed, playing my part to perfection.

He stared straight ahead, clenching his jaw. He was furious.

'And as for my hand, I clumsily tripped over because I was in a rush to get to Joshy.'

The room fell completely silent.

Dr Jacobs, pink-faced and lost for words, crossed his legs and then his arms. It was clear to the doctor that we needed marriage counselling, not a shrink.

'I'd like to go home now, please,' I said, standing up, unable to look at either of them.

Matt stood up, stiffly. Fury oozed from his pores. 'Doctor Jacobs, I'm sorry for wasting your time,' he mumbled.

I'd dodged a bullet.

Matt clutched the steering wheel of the jeep, his knuckles white. 'Why are you backing me into a corner like this?'

'I'm sorry,' I said, absently looking out of the window, numbed from the whole experience. 'I don't think he can help me.'

'So, who can help you? Hmm? Tell me,' he said. The traffic lights turned green and he honked his horn at the car in front of us. 'You don't even know, do you Annabelle?' He beeped his car, again. 'You don't even know,' he said, as he sped off.

'What would you know?' I said, under my breath.

Chapter Twenty-Three

'Annabelle? Annabelle?'

My eyes pinged open. 'Annabelle?' Shit. Matt was calling.

I turned on my side, glancing at the alarm clock on the bedside. 9.35 am. Shit. Shit. Shit. Joshy's giggles boomed from downstairs. It was Saturday, and all I wanted to do was curl up in a tight ball, pull the covers over my head and go back to sleep.

'Annabelle, I'm making pancakes.' His voice sang from downstairs.

I didn't think he knew how to make pancakes. I clambered out of bed and took a quick shower.

It had been three days since the awful appointment with Dr Jacobs. Matt had me under virtual house arrest and had asked Rosita to move in. I'd convinced myself she'd become his surveillance camera, reporting back to him when he wasn't around. I made sure I was on my very best behaviour at all times, using Rosita as my weapon, subtly feeding her information about my positive state of mind. 'I feel great,' I'd say out loud, pretending to be on the phone to an imaginary friend. 'Today is a good day, isn't that right Joshy? Rosita, can I help you with anything?' I went through the motions of my confined life pretending to have my shit together, waiting for the day I could leave the house and have an appointment with

Cassandra to sort out the bloody mess I was in. She was the only person who could help.

There was a WhatsApp message waiting for me when I got out of the shower.

`Good morning. How are you today? Cassandra`

She'd been checking up on me every day and her messages were keeping me sane.

`Better than yesterday. Thank you for asking. Feeling more optimistic today.`

I deleted the correspondence and placed my phone on the dresser. I dropped the towel that I had wrapped around me and stared at my porcelain flesh in the full-length mirror, tracing my finger over the familiar route of my c-section scar. I recalled the day Joshy was born, when he was ripped from my body, taken away from me. The obstetrician and midwives attempted to resuscitate his lifeless blue body, while I lay in bed screaming, yearning to hold him in my arms, believing somehow it was all my fault that he wasn't breathing.

My eyes skimmed past the other permanent scar on my upper thigh – my first cut. I didn't need to look at that one. I'd learnt every groove, every mark, every inch of it off by heart. It was embedded in my mind. The other self-inflicted cuts on my body had started to heal and were barely visible on my skin, now. The culmination of all my past hurts and pain carved into my flesh, like some kind of horror story. A destructive cycle, finally breaking. I hadn't cut myself for a while. Each time the urge gripped me, I thought of Cassandra. Thinking of her gave me courage to stop harming, it offered me a glimpse of hope.

She'd said that scars were beautiful, but what did she mean, exactly? I turned away from my reflection and threw on some clothes.

'Annabelle? Are you coming down?' Matt chirped from downstairs, breaking into my thoughts.

'Just a moment,' I chirped back.

My phone flashed a message. Cassandra.

How does Matt seem today? she texted.

Happy. I haven't seen him yet, but he's whistling to himself and making pancakes. He's in a relaxed mood ☺

Her reply came instantly.

Do you think his change of mood is suspicious?

I tried to read between the lines, deciphering what she meant by the message.

I thought it was my good behaviour paying off. Is this not the case? Should I be worried?

She didn't respond. I brushed my teeth, creamed my face and pulled a brush through my hair, checking my phone for updates every few minutes. Finally, a response came through.

Ignore my last comment. I don't want to imprint false impressions onto you. Matt's change of mood is a good thing. It's progress. He's letting go of his control over you. Stay positive. Stay strong. Have a nice day. Cassandra

I texted. Thank you so much for your support. I don't know what I would have done without you. Hoping to get an appointment with you soon. A

I deleted all the messages and went downstairs.

Matt was hovering over Rosita as she beat the batter for the pancakes. Joshy was seated by the island, scraping his knife and fork along the empty plate. He was chatting to Matt about football summer camp. Matt took the frying pan from the hob and flipped a pancake into the air. He caught it in the pan, stealing the glory from Rosita. Both boys let out a heroic cheer.

'Morning, baby bear.' I kissed Joshy, breathing him in.

Matt turned to me, 'Annabelle, you look great. You have some colour back in your face.' He sounded surprised.

I blushed, taking a seat next to Joshy. Matt's Burberry overnight bag and golf clubs were by the side door. His good mood was suspicious.

'Pancake?'

'No, thanks. You off somewhere?'

'I'm meeting Bill and the others at The Grove for some golf. It's a team building thing. Did I not mention it?'

There was a sour taste in the back of my throat. I shook my head no, fiddling with my phone under the breakfast table.

'It's been arranged for a while now. I'm sorry if you weren't made aware.'

'Mummy, when do I start camp?' Joshy cut in, bouncing up and down on the stool and waving his cutlery in the air.

I turned to Joshy, placed my phone on the table and retrieved the knife from him. I didn't want any accidents, now that Matt was leaving us. 'Well, you have almost three weeks left until you break up for the summer, so that means you start camp the week after that.'

'Mummy, will Leo be at football camp?'

'I'm not sure.'

'Mummy, where are my studs?'

'Your football boots don't fit you anymore. You need new ones.'

'Leo has orange ones. I want orange ones, too.'

Matt flipped the pancake into the air, making Joshy squeal and jump with excitement.

'Are you staying overnight?' I asked Matt, cutting through Joshy's noise.

'Two nights, actually. Would you rather I stayed home?'

'Mummy, can I buy some new ones?'

'You don't usually stay overnight for golf,' I said to Matt.

'Annabelle. Do you want me to cancel?' he asked, with a hint of irritation in his voice. 'Should I rearrange my plans?'

With him gone, it meant freedom for me.

'Annabelle?'

'Huh? No. Please, go. Go. Have a good time. I'll be fine. Besides, Rosita is here to keep me company,' I said, forcing a smile onto my face.

'Mummy, what about my boots?'

'We'll buy new ones. Maybe Rosita can take you today, baby bear?' I said.

Joshy's little face lit up.

'I tell you what, why don't you all go shopping together and make a day of it. You need to get out, Annabelle. You've been stuck at home for days.'

Matt walked towards us with the frying pan in his hand and flopped a pancake onto Joshy's plate. Joshy jumped up and down, almost toppling over. I steadied him back onto the stool. Rosita, always on standby, appeared from behind Matt and took the pan from him, washing it up straight away. I opened the jar of Nutella, his Saturday treat, and spooned it out, spreading it onto the pancake with the knife.

It was as though nothing had happened over the past week. Life was back to normal. For Matt, anyway.

'Here. Take my credit card. We can cash in on the airmiles.' He handed me his American Express gold card. 'Get something nice to wear for your birthday. We have big plans for Mummy's birthday, don't we, Joshua?' Matt put his finger to his lips. 'Ssshhhh. Remember what we spoke about. Don't tell Mummy anything, okay?'

'Daddy is doing secret things,' Joshy said, turning to me, bouncing.

'I don't want a fuss made of me,' I said to Matt.

Joshy seemed disappointed. I put my arm around his waist and gave him a little squeeze.

'Nonsense, Annabelle. It's your thirtieth and we're going to celebrate in style.' Matt walked over to the sink and started to wash his hands. 'So, you'll be okay if I go to The Grove?' he asked, with his back to me.

'Yes. Of course. Don't worry. Go. We will be fine.'

'I'll stay if you need me to. If you're not up for it.'

I stared at the back of his head. 'But won't Bill be disappointed?'

He stopped scrubbing his fingers. His shoulders rose an inch. Something was on his mind.

'Matt. Go. Have a good time. I'm feeling more myself again. You have nothing to worry about. I promise.'

'That's great.' He wiped his hands with a tea towel and walked over, placing a kiss on Joshy's forehead. 'Take care of Mummy for me.' He turned to me, taking my chin in his hand. 'I'm glad to see things are getting better for you.' He kissed me on the cheek. His face was smooth. He'd shaved and smelt of strong aftershave.

He walked over to his bag, waving one last time before leaving through the side entrance. I waited until I heard the roar of his engine and messaged Cassandra.

`I'm free. May I come for an appointment today? A`
Rosita reappeared in the kitchen, holding a wash basket.

'Rosita, I need your help.'

She sighed as she put the basket down and unclipped her hair, releasing it from the restraints of the bun.

Chapter Twenty-Four

I asked Rosita to take Joshy shopping to buy football boots, telling her I was meeting a pal for lunch. Rosita was more than pleased with the arrangement. It meant she could adopt the role of Joshy's mother without any interruptions from me. She agreed to take Joshy to Brent Cross shopping centre, promising him Lola's cupcakes if he behaved.

I was free, but my window of opportunity was small.

Cassandra had read my last message but hadn't responded. She would have said no if there was an issue with me turning up, surely. I took her silence as a green light and decided to head down to the clinic. She'd been encouraging me to become more assertive, so here I was, doing just that.

I'm coming to the clinic. I need a walk to clear my head after being cooped up in the house for days on end. Let me know if it's not a good time. I'm on my way now. Annabelle

My heart sank as I realised that she wasn't at work. I pressed the buzzer again, hoping that she was taking her time because she was upstairs in her home, but still – nothing. I dialled the clinic number and could hear the office phone ringing. Peeping through the window,

I saw that the lilies on the side table had wilted and the jug was empty of water. Very much empty.

I'm outside the clinic. Is it not a good time?

No blue ticks appeared. I was beginning to feel really foolish.

Next, I tried her mobile. It went straight to voicemail. Damn it. I paced up and down the pavement, chewing on my fingernails, plucking up the courage to knock on her front door. With my heart in my mouth, I climbed the white steps to her three-storey Georgian home. I really needed to see her. The closer I got to the front door to her house, the more uncertain I became. I knew what I was doing was wrong; I was crossing the line and overstepping my boundaries, but I'd come so far, I couldn't back down now. Besides, I was checking to see if she was okay, being a good friend.

The red paint was peeling off the front door and there was no bell or door knocker. I peeped through the letterbox, but it was too dark to see inside. All internal lights were off and the doors leading off the corridor were shut.

'Cassandra, are you home?' There was no answer or movement inside. 'Cassandra?' I let the letterbox slam shut.

'What are you doing?'

I turned around to see where the voice was coming from. An elderly neighbour, hunched and frail, was staring over at me. He was standing in his doorway and using a Zimmer frame for balance.

'Hi, there,' I swallowed. 'I'm looking for my friend.'

'You want to stay away from that place. Nothing good happens inside those four walls. Mark my words. Nothing good,' he said in an accent I couldn't quite place. Perhaps Norfolk?

'Excuse me?'

'Nothing good happens inside.'

I peered through the letterbox, again. 'Cassandra. It's me. Is everything okay?' I said, projecting my voice into her hallway. I could sense the neighbour glaring over. I cocked my head round to look at him.

'Nothing good,' he repeated, waving his forefinger in the air. He turned and shuffled his way into his house, slamming the door behind him. I could hear the locks turn, as he secured himself inside.

Freaked out, I bolted down the steps and started down the road. My phone buzzed violently in the back pocket of my jeans. My excitement faded as soon as I saw the name flash up. I gripped my phone, tightly. Mary's persistence was insufferable.

There was so much I wanted to say to her, so many questions I wanted to ask, so many things I wanted to hear Mary say to me, but I knew I shouldn't have any contact. Not yet. Cassandra had advised against it. Dropping Mary's call, I stared at my phone, willing Cassandra to get in touch. Everything made sense when she was around. She filled my lungs with oxygen, making it easier to breathe.

Taking long determined strides, I headed towards the market to speak to Uncle Jack. Maybe he could get through to Mary for me, tell her to stop calling, to give me the head space I needed.

I turned onto Church Street market; I'd forgotten how busy it was on Saturdays. The crowds, the noise, the smells from the food stalls. It was heaving. A melting pot of nationalities, all bagging a bargain. You could get anything you wanted, from fruit and veg to electronics and fake gold jewellery. Stalls were lined up in rows, selling cheap clothes, unbranded toiletries and tacky mobile phone accessories. Familiarity tugged at my heartstrings.

Every Saturday, I'd be down the market, without fail, weaving in and out of the stalls on my roller skates, hanging out with my pals by the music stall, sometimes even helping out Uncle Jack for pocket money. He'd often give me some change so I could get myself salt and vinegar crisps, a Lion bar and a can of pop as a treat. If he was selling really well, I'd get ten whole pounds and some flowers to take home to Mary.

The antique shops behind the stalls told a different story. Those shops were reserved for the snotty-nosed super-rich, who were sold over-priced gems, not the average bric-a-brac you'd find along the stalls or pound shops. You needed an appointment to get through those doors. My mother-in-law often frequented the antique shops, 'bagging' herself a priceless gem to help fill her Hertfordshire estate.

Jack was wrapping a bouquet of flowers, a roll-up dangling from his mouth. I walked towards his stall with a sense of nostalgia. It was sandwiched between the record stall pumping out '90s house music and a burger van pumping out the smell of fried onions. It comforted me, watching him work his corner. He'd had his stall for as long as I could remember.

'Hello, Uncle Jack.'

'Is that my gorgeous girl?' he smiled, his yellowed uneven teeth clenching his brown rollie.

My heart swelled.

'Let's get a coffee,' he said, flicking his cigarette onto the pavement. He gave his money pouch to his neighbour who ran the record stall.

We crossed the road and I followed him into the café. It was a regular workman's café, what you'd call a greasy spoon, a million miles away from the yummy mummy places of Hampstead that served falafel, couscous and Ottolenghi-style salads. At this place they had full English breakfasts, builder's tea and instant coffee on the menu, with no avocados in sight. I used to buy my chips from the café at lunchtimes when I was at secondary school. I'd use a fake pass for home dinners to lie my way out of the school gates, and meet the hot boys from the local Catholic school who congregated outside.

I buried my memories as soon as we took our seats by the window, which was dripping with condensation. Now wasn't the time for reminiscing. A waitress with pineapple hair and hooped earrings trudged towards us, dragging her squeaky trainers across the sticky floor. She slumped our piss poor coffee onto the table, spilling some of it as she went. She didn't seem to care. I pulled my elbows away.

'A bacon sarnie, doll,' Jack said.

She shrugged and walked off, unimpressed.

'Listen Jack. I'm just going to come out and say it. You've got to tell Mary to stop calling me,' I said. 'It's borderline harassment.'

Jack's eyes were still on the waitress.

'It's the cancer, love,' he said, turning to me.

'What?'

'The cancer has got her good an' proper.'

'Don't do this to me, please Jack. Not now. I can't deal with the guilt as well as everything else. I can't. I'm overloaded as it is.'

'The chemo isn't working.'

My mouth dried out.

'She's not got long to go.'

'Has she lost her hair?' I said, fighting back tears.

'Wears a headscarf.'

'Bet she loves all the attention that brings her.'

He smiled, knowingly. 'Don't be so hard on her, hey.'

I shrugged my shoulders, unable to look him in the eye.

'What is it, love?' He searched my eyes. 'Yeah, so, she wasn't the best of mums. But she tried. In her own way, she did try. Being a single mum an' all, ain't easy.'

There was ringing in my ears. He was getting inside my head. Confusing me into thinking that she cared. That she loved me. I checked my phone to see if Cassandra had read my messages.

'Why are you running away from the truth?'

'Jack, you have no idea,' I said, my voice trembling.

'She feels like she doesn't know you anymore. None of us do. She misses ya, misses the kid. Ever since you fucked off with old money-bags, you ain't been around much. What's happened? You get this fancy life and all of a sudden, we ain't good enough for ya, is that it?'

He was only half joking, and I bolted out of my seat.

'Look, I didn't mean to have a go. Sit. Come on, sit with your old uncle. That's a good girl.' He held onto my arm, pulling me down.

The waitress reappeared with a doorstop sandwich. I sat back down and rubbed my temples.

'That's my girl,' Jack said.

He squirted ketchup onto one side of the bread, brown sauce on the other, squishing the sandwich together, offering me a bite. I shook my head. He took a huge chunk out of it, munching nosily. He reached over to the adjoining table, grabbed a napkin and wiped the cracks of his mouth. I checked my phone again – nothing.

'Tell your uncle what's going on.'

'Honestly Jack, I'm fine,' I said, bursting into tears.

He grabbed another tissue, passing it over. I dabbed my eyes. The texture against my skin was hard and scratchy.

'Why are you crying doll? Is it your little man? Has something happened?'

'No, no, it's nothing like that.'

'Is it to do with your ma?'

'Yeah. But it's not what you think, Jack. It goes much deeper than that. Much deeper.'

'What do you mean?'

'It's like I'm in a black hole and I'm worried I can't get out,' I sniffed, cupping my hands over my eyes.

'What's scaring you, Anna?' he asked, peeling my hands away.

I stared at his familiar leathery face. 'What should I do? Tell me what to do. Everything's such a mess,' I said.

'With what, doll? Talk to me. You're not making any sense, love.'

'Matt.'

'Why, what's he gone and done?' He stiffened, visibly.

'He's having an affair. I know he is.'

'That fucking prick! How dare he treat you like that. You deserve more than that.'

'Do I?'

'Where's the feisty girl I used to know, roller-skating around the estate and turning everyone's heads? She wouldn't take shit from anyone.'

A sense of sorrow for the girl he thought I was started to overwhelm me. That feisty girl was lost to me. Lost.

He extracted a flask from inside his body warmer, slipped whiskey into his coffee, then poured some into mine. 'That prick has sucked the life out of you,' he muttered.

I took a sip. It burnt on the way down, warming me up. 'It's not all his fault. Maybe it's me. I haven't exactly been easy to live with.'

'That's an excuse, Anna, and you know it.'

'I wonder what he saw in me in the first place. Some ex-council flat girl with a foul mouth and no table manners.'

'Don't put yourself down. You're as good as he is. Better. You hear?' Jack said, sharply. He poured another drop of whiskey into my mug. 'You should get the fuck out of that place, and fast. You'll have no peace living with him.'

'But it's my home.'

'Home?'

I couldn't look at him.

'That ain't no home for you, Anna. No matter how lah-di-dah and fancy it is.'

'I've got nowhere else to go.'

'You'll figure something out.'

My phone flashed on the table. Cassandra had messaged. It couldn't have come at a better time. Blinking away the tears, I swiped my phone open.

'Everything okay?' Jack asked.

```
Annabelle. I won't be able to meet today. It's
the weekend. I have plans. Please arrange to see me
during clinic hours. Cassandra
```

The mobile slipped from my fingers and dropped onto the table. What did I expect her to say? *I'll drop everything to accommodate you, come now?*

'I'm fine,' I said to Jack, focusing my attention on the droplets of water falling onto the window ledge from the condensation. 'Honestly, I'm fine.'

Beads of sweat formed on my brow. Everything started closing in. The noise in the café, the smell of bacon, Jack. It was hard to breathe. I stood up, placing my hands on the table for support.

Breathe in, breathe out, breathe in, breathe out.

'You alright, love? You don't seem fine to me. Drink some water … take a sip of this … is there someone I should call?'

His voice sounded as though it was under water. The noises from the café were muffled. He picked my phone up off the table.

'No!' I snatched it back. 'I have to go.'

I darted out of the café, pushing past some bloke in a Puffa jacket and baseball cap. I turned the corner and stopped in the alleyway, breathless and sweaty. Leaning both hands on the wall out in front of me, I dropped my head in between to catch my breath. After a few moments, I pulled myself up straight and sent her a response.

Okay. I'll call on Monday morning. I really need a friend right now. Annabelle

Chapter Twenty-Five

Like an addict, I tried to fight off the urge to harm, but every passing second that became more unbearable, and the pressure built until I couldn't take it anymore and I snapped. Rosita was downstairs with Joshy baking a cake, getting mucky with the flour and the eggs. I'd locked myself in the en suite, and with Matt's razor blade in my hand and tears clogging up my sight, I sliced into my forearm. A bitter-sweet release followed. Matt called while the blood, still fresh, dripped from my forearm onto the heated tiles. He said that he missed and loved me, and in return, I told him that I missed and loved him.

Cleaning myself up, I watched the blood and tears drain down the plughole.

Matt came home unexpectedly on Sunday with flowers, having cut short his golfing trip. Was he guilty, or was I being paranoid over nothing? That night, for the first time in a month, we made love.

Sex with him was always safe, conservative. He practised the same sterile moves again and again. But this time there was a shift in him, he acted forcefully, with urgency. When he looked at me there was a hunger burning in his eyes. He wanted me. Desired me. He pinned me down with the weight of his body and gripped my neck lightly, thrusting himself inside of me, pushing himself as far into me as he could. I lay on my back and put my hands over his, making him squeeze tighter and tighter until I felt a whooshing flow of blood rush my brain, swishing around inside my temples.

'Did I hurt you?' he whispered, rolling off me.

'I'm okay,' I said, staring up at the ceiling.

'Things will get better, won't they? Between us, I mean,' he said. We lay side by side. 'Of course.'

'You're so beautiful, Annabelle,' he said, turning his head to face me. His eyes soft. He reached his hand over to my face and stroked my cheek.

Numbed, I gazed back up to the ceiling.

'I'm going to put things right,' he whispered as he turned over.

How was he going to put any of it right?

The night clogged up with paranoia and nightmares, and somehow it rolled into morning. The weekend was, thankfully, over. As soon as I was alone, I dialled Cassandra. The tone of her voice was soft and mellow, and instantly I felt soothed. She offered me an appointment straight away. Breathing a sigh of relief, I sent Rosita on a huge food shop and got myself ready. I rushed over to the clinic, feeling a fraction lighter.

'Matt went away for the weekend. Golfing,' I said, looking around the clinic to re-familiarise myself. Fresh flowers. Tissues. A jug of water with the lemon and lime slices. God, it was good to be back.

'You don't believe him?'

'How can I trust anything that comes out of his mouth? He's so secretive all the time.'

'And you think he lied and was with his mystery lady instead. Rachel, perhaps?'

'I can't tell for sure. He came home early, cutting his trip short.'
'I see.'

'He said he missed and loved me. Maybe he was telling the truth about golfing, or maybe he was feeling guilty about cheating and came home early to fix things? I don't know what to think. It's driving me mad.'

'Or perhaps he had a disagreement with his mistress?'
'What?'

'There could be a number of reasons why he came home early, Annabelle. The point is, you don't trust him, do you?'

'True,' I said. 'He's moved Rosita into the house, did I mention this to you? Matt's using her to keep tabs on me, yet I still don't have the foggiest what he's up to, who he's seeing, or what he's thinking, for that matter.' I continued: 'Rosita's in her element, taking over my role. She's really getting on my fucking nerves. I'm sorry, I know I swear a lot.' I drew in a deep breath.

'No judgement. Remember?' she smiled.

'Thank you.' My shoulders relaxed.

'As you were saying …'

'I saw Uncle Jack on Saturday and he told me Mary hasn't got long to live, and I'm starting to feel guilty about it all.'

Cassandra forced a smile onto her face, but I could tell by her eyes she wasn't happy.

'I'm sorry. I know it's not a good idea to see her, I totally get that, and I won't contact her, I promise. Jack just makes me feel bad about it.'

'That doesn't sound like an ideal weekend,' she said.

'There's something else.'

'There's more?' She crossed one leg over the other, shaking her foot up and down.

'I cut myself.' I hung my head.

181

Her foot stopped moving.

'I wasn't in a good head space, and everything came crashing down.' I looked away, ashamed.

'I'm not surprised that you self-harmed this weekend. Everyone has a breaking point. The people surrounding you are unreliable and make you feel bad about yourself.'

My hand reached to my throat. I rubbed it gently, thinking back to the intimate yet distant moment I'd shared with Matt. It had left a bitter-sweet taste in my mouth.

She uncrossed her legs, leant in and peeled my hand away from my neck, placing it down onto my lap. 'What is it? Is there more on your mind?' Cassandra asked softly.

'We slept together.'

'Oh.' She leant back and folded her hands on her lap neatly, re-crossing her legs.

'He was different somehow.'

'In what way?'

'Well … he was … kind of forceful,' I said as my cheeks burnt.

'Please don't feel embarrassed to speak.'

'It's hard to explain,' I said, looking away. 'It felt as though he wanted to consume me. Like he actually wanted me.'

A beat of silence followed. Her features remained neutral. 'Annabelle. Is there a chance you're associating the act of being forceful with a false sense of love?'

'I don't know. Maybe. Maybe I am. I'm so confused right now.'

'Perhaps being forceful signifies his ownership of you.'

She stood up, brushed herself down. My eyes followed Cassandra as she walked gracefully around the room, lost in thought. The only sound came from her Louboutin heels clicking on the wooden floor.

She sat back down. Her back remained upright. 'I'll help you get to a positive head space,' she said, her voice now light, her features soft, her eyes filled with empathy.

'I'm so grateful for everything you're doing for me,' I said, breathing a little easier.

'It's my duty to care for you,' she said, looking deep into my eyes.

I felt safe around her, like I was home. I could tell her anything, anything at all. I trusted her. 'I'm still having nightmares, Cassandra.'

'Annabelle. Please listen to what I'm about to tell you. The nightmares won't stop.'

I swallowed hard, fighting back the tears.

'Neither will the harming. None of it will stop, unless …' she took a breath, 'unless you confront your past and unlock your suppressed memory. *That's your trigger*,' she whispered.

'I'm scared to face the past alone.'

'You're not alone, Annabelle. You have me.'

'What will I find?'

'Only you hold the answer.'

'If it's been buried for years, it's going to be bad, like, really bad.'

'You can't live in chains. You must push past your fear.'

She folded her hands neatly on her lap and stared intensely at me with her black eyes, making me feel as though I was melting, already in the trance state.

'Okay, so let's begin.' The tone of her voice changed now, as it always did when she was about to induce me.

Her chest rose and fell as she slowed her breathing down, lulling me into deep hypnosis. I breathed in time with her. A nervous energy raced through my body. I was ready to go under. Ready to let go. Ready to confront my demons.

'Now, close your eyes and take me back to your past, back to your nightmares. Visualise me standing next to you for support.'

I slipped easily into the hypnotic state and drifted back through time.

In my mind's eye, Cassandra stood by my side. We walked together, towards the playground, hand in hand. It was empty apart from the woman on the swing. Her eyes, as before, were blacked out, and she was crying charcoal tears. Glass crunched under our feet as we walked. We stopped at the gate of the playground. I looked over to Cassandra.

'You'll need this.' She held out a stainless steel knife.

'I don't understand,' I said. My hand trembled as I took the knife from her. It was cold and heavy in my hand. The metal blade reflective.

'Added protection,' she said. 'It'll keep you safe.'

My heart beat faster.

'Go and see what she wants,' she said, urging me to continue solo.

Ice trickled down my spine as I inched through the gate into the playground. A tidal wave of mud crashed in from behind, covering the ground at rapid speed. It worked its way up. The taste of mud hit the back of my throat. The woman started swinging, her feet brushed the mud each time she swung low.

Her skirt had bells on and jingled when she moved. My stomach convulsed as I joined the dots.

It was *her!*

The mud continued to rise, and debris floated to the top. Beer cans, syringes, a doll I used to play with. Her name was Melissa and I'd given her a bad spiky haircut. I'd cried for weeks and weeks afterwards, regretting what I'd done. Mum refused to buy me a new doll, to teach me a lesson. I pushed Melissa's head back under and worked my way across the playground, in the thick sludge.

The woman stopped swinging, parted her lips and screamed, making every fibre in my body tense up. Dozens of moths flew out of her gaping mouth. She began choking on them. The swarm surrounded me and started to attack, blinding me, preventing me from moving further forwards. I batted them away with the knife. Chaos unfolded all around me and in my panicked confusion, I let go of the blade. I scrambled to retrieve it, but it disappeared into the mud. No more protection.

'Help me ... help me,' the woman cried.

'She needs my help,' I shouted above the noise.

'Who does?' Cassandra asked. 'Annabelle? Can you hear me? Who needs your help?'

'Anna, help ...' the woman said, gagging on her own words.

The sea of sludge continued to rise and rise.

'Who is she, Annabelle?'

The moths. They were everywhere. I couldn't see. But I knew. I knew who she was.

'It's ... it's ...' I stammered. 'Mary.'

'Annabelle. Calm down,' Cassandra commanded. 'Caaaaaaalm,' she said, stretching the word out.

In my mind, Cassandra stood by the gate, serene and unaffected.

Cassandra – my future. The woman on the swing – my past.

'Go to your happy place. To that beautiful beach in Greece. Only this time, make sure I'm standing with you. I want to be there with you, by your side, protecting you. I want to experience the sea lapping on my feet, feel the sun on my skin, smell the pine trees. Take me with you,' she said.

Letting go of my murky past, I escaped to Greece with Cassandra. She watched me as I peeled my sarong off and dived into the turquoise water. I lay on my back and floated out while I listened to the sound of her voice, drip feeding me positive affirmations.

Layer by layer, she pieced me back together.

Chapter Twenty-Six

CLINICAL NOTES
Annabelle Clarke (Note – mother calls her Anna).

Annabelle contacted me over weekend, asking for another emergency appointment.
An invitation to cross professional boundaries. I declined. Annabelle displaying strong signs of dependency. Lack of mother figure means Anna needs to obtain nurturance elsewhere. Anna actively solicits approval from care givers.
Dependent personalities prone to be in abusive relationships.

Bad weekend. Husband is having an affair. Anna convinced.
How long will she allow him to use her? Intimate with him – low self-worth.
Mother's chemo not working – Anna is guilt ridden.
Housekeeper taking over mothering role.
Unreliable people surrounding her. Habits resurfaced. Pressure built.
Inevitable – cut herself.

Anna opening up fully in session. She is now comfortable in clinic space, enough to speak candidly. Trust. Bond has been built between client and therapist.

Today's hypnosis: *Regression.*
Revisited childhood trauma.
Asked to imagine holding a knife, for extra protection – unsuccessful.
Woman figure from childhood is her mother.

Follow up session/s:
Encourage Anna to stand up for herself more with husband.
Self-harming cycle – must be broken. Need the trigger. Why does her mother ask for help?

Homework given: *Become active in daily life.*
Make decisions for herself. Get involved.
Make new friends and an effort with the mums at school. (Rachel – keep friends close and enemies closer.)

Note to self, re: regression. Some of Anna's imagery taken from things she has seen in everyday life, i.e. moths (taken from my picture in clinic?).

Anna is now fully susceptive – golden opportunity for suggestions to stick.

Chapter Twenty-Seven

Over the weeks, Cassandra and I worked closely on boosting my confidence, and for the very first time since therapy had started, life – on a superficial level – was ticking along nicely. Matt seemed less controlling of me, too preoccupied with work or whoever was his fancy bit on the side; Rosita had moved back into her own flat and I was really trying to make an effort to bond with Joshy. I also hadn't cut myself, which was a huge triumph. Having Cassandra by my side, cheerleading me on, really helped to silence the urges.

But still, no matter how much therapy I undertook, my underlying issues remained; Mary and what happened when I was a child—the *trigger*, and the big question mark over Matt's 'infidelity'.

Cassandra had encouraged me to make an effort with Rachel and the other mums at the school. She said that befriending Rachel would help settle my suspicions and put my mind at rest. So, with my newly acquired electric pink mat and Sweaty Betty gym gear, I decided to try out the yoga class the mums always talked about. It was an opportunity to get to know them a bit better, and to arrange that long-overdue playdate I'd promised Joshy that I would organise before the school year ended.

The first thing that hit me as I walked into the room was the heat. The temperature felt as though it had been jacked up to 1000 degrees Fahrenheit. God, they didn't mention it was that *hot* bloody yoga! The room was humid, stuffy and smelt of sweaty bodies, and we hadn't even begun.

Rachel and the rest of the mums were lined up at the front. I hurried past them, head bowed, avoiding eye contact, wondering what I'd got myself into, and positioned myself at the end of the row next to Saskia.

'I didn't realise this was your thing,' Saskia smiled.

'I'm not sure it is,' I said, relaxing a little. The baby hairs on my forehead were clinging to my skin.

'Fair enough.' She stretched forward, folding the top half of her body onto her legs. She had the agility of a cat.

Rachel sat, cross-legged, 'quietly' chatting to the others. She was speaking just loudly enough for the rest of the room to hear.

'It was a total surprise, him whisking me away like that. We had the best weekend. The best.'

'Congratulations,' the woman to Rachel's right said.

'Thank you,' she gushed, as if she was being congratulated on winning an Oscar, as opposed to a sleazy weekend.

'You're falling for this mystery man. I can tell,' Saskia said as she uncurled herself and sat upright.

My ears pricked and my eyes burnt from the heat and my mounting paranoia.

'I wouldn't go that far.'

'Rachel Louise Montgomery-Jones, are you in love?' Saskia said.

'Stop it,' Rachel said. 'It's nice to be treated with respect.'

'You deserve happiness.' Saskia repositioned herself. 'Are you excited about your party?' She lifted her head and stared straight at me.

I turned behind me to look at who she was speaking to, my mind still fixed on Rachel and her mystery man. Saskia was looking at me.

'Oh, bless her. She doesn't even know,' Rachel said, stretching behind Saskia to catch my eye. 'Your adorable husband is planning a birthday party for you.'

'He is?'

'Don't look so shocked,' she laughed. 'Really! You guys should learn to communicate better.'

Blood swished around inside my head.

Saskia caught my eye and smiled. 'Why don't you join us next Thursday for a drink, to celebrate the end of the school year? It's a tradition for the mums to meet,' she said, compensating for Rachel's bitchiness. 'It would be nice if you could come, even for one. We've reserved a table at The Ivy in St John's Wood, 8.00 pm.'

Rachel's eyes grew wide as she glared at Saskia. She was pissed off.

'Thank you. Yeah, maybe I will join you,' I replied, grateful for Saskia's kindness. The drink-up was the perfect opportunity for further fishing. Rachel couldn't keep her mystery man a secret forever.

The tall, long-limbed instructor waltzed in, wearing a headset and sporting bright orange hair. She had orange lycra leggings and a matching sports bra and consequently resembled a giraffe. She looked super-humanly strong, with muscular arms. Everyone hushed as the instructor stood on a box, taking centre stage. She put her hands on her hips and spread her legs apart, assessing the class.

'Okay, people. Who left the window open?' She jumped off the box and took three long-limbed strides toward the far end of the room, securing shut the top window which had been left open by a crack. Whispers of disapproval from the yogis echoed around the room. I began to perspire from every pore in my body.

'Who would be mad enough to open the window in a Bikram session? Kind of defeats the purpose,' Rachel snapped. 'If you can't handle the heat, get out of the kitchen,' she said, leaning back and staring at me.

Was she digging me out?

'Okay. Okay people. Let's settle down. First time?' The instructor looked at me.

I sat up to attention and nodded, as sweat poured out of every orifice of my body.

'Any injuries I should know about?' she asked, as she extended one of her long legs out in front of her. 'Well?'

I cleared my throat 'No.'

'Great. Welcome to the class …'

Why was she still staring?

'Your name?'

'Oh. Annabelle. It's Annabelle.'

Somehow, I wasn't in the mood for yoga anymore. My mind was on other things. Rachel and Matt. Matt and Rachel. Together. At The Grove.

'Welcome to Bikram, Annabelle. You've come to the right place, it's a fantastic way to detoxify and heal your body. It helps us relieve all the stresses that come with day-to-day life, am I right people?'

The room responded with yesses. It was a cult.

'It builds strength, tones your muscles and makes you stronger. Trust me, this will become your new addiction. One last thing, Annabelle. Don't breathe through your mouth, you could hyperventilate. *Capice?*'

I nodded.

'Great. Okay. Let's begin.'

Fifteen minutes into the class, sweat poured and I started to pant wildly, breathing through my mouth, hyperventilating. It was an inferno.

I had to get the hell out of there! My feet squelched on the wet mats as I stepped around the sea of sweaty bodies and I exited as quickly as I possibly could, swearing never to return, even more convinced that Matt was seeing bloody Rachel behind my back.

Chapter Twenty-Eight

I was on my favourite swing, swinging up and down, my legs weighted down by my roller skates. The wheels squeaked as the skates rolled along the concrete floor. My knees were scuffed from falling over earlier in the day when I was bombing it around the estate balconies like a lunatic, playing knock down ginger with my friends. But now, the playground was deserted, everyone had gone, and it was getting dark. I was glad the playground was empty, because I hated the older kids who came later, smoking drugs, drinking cans and making out. They always teased me about Mum and liked to call her stuff, like 'slag' and 'skank'.

The tower block ahead of me was blocking the pink sunset. I looked up towards my mum's bedroom window. The light was on. She'd be calling me up for dinner soon. I was getting cold and was only wearing shorts and a *Star Wars* t-shirt. My tummy rumbled when I remembered it was fish finger Friday.

'Is she there?' Cassandra asked the child in me.

'She's at home, getting food ready. It's fish finger Friday. My favourite.'

There was movement at the window. Someone was silhouetted behind the thin net curtain. I stopped swinging and stared, waiting for her to yell my name out. Any minute now. The curtain twitched and pulled aside to reveal a face. The hairs lifted on the back of my neck. The woman in the window had blacked-out eyes and was crying black charcoal tears.

'No!'

'What's happening?' asked Cassandra.

'It's her,' I said. 'The woman. She's in the window.' Panic stuck in my throat.

My legs were sprinkled with pimples from the sudden cold snap in the air. The creepy woman opened the window and peered out, opening her mouth to speak. Dozens of moths flew out. Flying down the building and swarming around me, obscuring my vision. I gripped the chains of the swing more tightly. Crying, I let go of the swing, trying to bat the moths away from my face. The back wheels of my skates skidded, making me lose my balance.

'Anna!' Mary shouted. 'Help me.'

'Get me out of the trance. Get me out. Get me out,' I yelled, pulling myself back up onto the seat of the swing, not sure whether I was screaming out loud, or inside my head.

'Help me.' Mary's voice bounced off the buildings, echoing around the estate.

'Annabelle. Stay calm, remember everything I've taught you. Breathing in and out, nice and steady. Deeper and deeper you drift …'

Breathe in, breathe out, breathe in, breathe out.

'What are you so afraid of?' Cassandra asked.

'There's something inside the flat. It's evil. It's evil. It's evil.'

Breathe in, breathe out, breathe in, breathe out.

'Okay. That's enough for today. Bringing you back into the room with me, where you are safe and secure. Counting up from five. Four. Three. Climbing the stairs to your conscious mind. Two and one. Open your eyes and welcome back to the room. Take a good stretch.'

My eyes pinged open and everything slowly formed around me.

My hands ached as I uncurled the tight fists I'd made. Cassandra was only inches away from me, sitting on her office chair, our knees almost touching. Her perfume smelt exotic and tickled my nose, making me want to sneeze.

'I'm sorry. I'm such a failure.' I looked down towards my feet and my new open-toed kitten heels.

'Annabelle, you're not a failure,' she said. 'Look at me.'

We locked eyes.

'I think you're very brave to embark on this journey.' She patted my knee, leaving her hand to linger. Her fingernails were perfectly manicured and filed to sharp points, like triangles. The emerald ring on her index finger sparkled. 'Many of us have painful pasts. It's important not to run away from them. Be brave. Be strong.'

I folded my fingers to hide my own bitten down fingernails and looked up at her. 'I'm worried I'm wasting your time.'

'Nonsense. Something will present itself,' said Cassandra, gliding her hand away and crossing one leg over the other. 'Something always does.'

Glancing at the clock, I noticed that I'd been there for hours. 'Is it okay if I stay a while longer? I'm worn out and I don't want to go home. Not just yet.'

'Stay as long as you need. I have no one after you,' she smiled. 'This is your special place. For you, alone.'

'I never see any of your other clients.'

She sat up to attention. 'I space everyone apart so there's no cross-over.'

'Do you see many people in a day?' I glanced over at the appointment book on the desk.

'Why all these sudden questions?'

'I'm curious, that's all.'

'You know what curiosity did to the cat?' She fixed a smile on her face, but somehow it didn't reach her eyes.

A beat of silence followed.

My heart started pounding.

'Oh Annabelle, relax,' she laughed, breaking the quiet. 'I'm messing with you.'

'Oh!' I faked laughter.

'You must understand, I cannot possibly disclose any information about my clients.' Her features softened again.

'I'm sorry. You're right. I shouldn't have asked.'

She wiped down her skirt with her hands. 'So, tell me. How do you feel the therapy is going?'

I eased back into the chair, allowing my body to relax. 'It's weird, when I regress, I'm scared – helpless, almost. The danger is real. Whatever is lurking inside that flat frightens the hell out of me, but as soon as I hear your voice, I know I'm safe.'

'I'm glad to hear this.'

We sat quietly for a while.

'Does that mean my past can't actually harm me?' I asked.

'The past will only harm you if you allow it to. You're a strong woman, stronger than you give yourself credit for. I believe that once we uncover your memory, the trigger, you will be at peace and everything will slot into place.'

We lapsed into another silence.

It was a comfortable stillness between us and liberating to sit quietly in calm and tranquillity without feeling the need to talk, fill the space with niceties, or feeling awkward and anxious.

'May I share something with you?' asked Cassandra. 'It has something to do with my own past.'

I looked at her, stared in anticipation, wondering if I'd heard correctly.

'We have something in common.'

'We do?'

'Our mothers,' she said, uncrossing and re-crossing her legs the other way.

I was taken aback. I knew nothing about her. Nothing.

'The parallels are quite astonishing. My mother has died, but when she was alive, she behaved in a similar way to yours.' Her eyes teared up.

Her professional mask had slipped, exposing a vulnerability I'd never seen before. Were her barriers finally coming down, revealing her true self?

'I can't help but draw on the similarities to my own personal experiences.'

'Are you okay?'

'Thank you for asking. Yes, I'm quite alright,' she said, laughing it off, but I could see a deep sadness reflecting in her eyes. 'I'm sorry. This is highly unprofessional of me,' she said, turning away from me and picking up her notebook from the floor, placing it on her lap.

'Oh God. Cassandra. I don't mind. It doesn't always have to be about me. In fact, I'm sick to death of all of my problems.'

'Another time.' Her eyes had already hardened.

The mask was back on.

'No, please, I'd like to hear. Maybe it'll help me in some ways? The comparison I mean,' I said, not sure what I was saying.

I wanted to be there for Cassandra like she was for me. I wanted her to be comfortable around me so she could open up. I wanted her to trust me, like I trusted her.

'My mother wasn't like all the other mums I knew. She was different. She stood out from the rest.'

'Like Mary, you mean?'

'Yes,' she said, pausing, lost in a memory of her own. 'People say that a bond between a mother and a child is unbreakable. An umbilical cord, linking both together. The attachment is forever there. But as I matured, I realised that the bond I shared with my mother wasn't one of love, it was one of control. She controlled every aspect of me. How I felt, behaved, and how I thought. All I ever wanted to do was appease her. Her needs took priority over my own.' She straightened herself up.

I stayed statue-still, hardly taking a breath, completely captivated by her story.

'My mother was an amazing artist. She'd often make me stand for hours as a child, so that she could paint me. I wasn't allowed to move, not even to go to the toilet. For a long time, I looked back on those memories with fondness, and as a child I'd often look forward to those sessions. It meant quality time, just the two of us. Our special bubble. It was the closest thing I ever got to her love. Do you see?'

'I think so. I think I can relate,' I said, piecing her story together, attempting to weave it into my own experience. 'No. No, I don't. I'm sorry.'

'Here's the point I'm making,' she said, as she crossed her hands, business-like.

I sat attentively.

'Do you remember when I regressed you back to a happy memory from your childhood?'

My brain scrambled to the earlier days in session. 'To when I was six years old, you mean?'

'Yes. You were sitting at the table before school, waiting for your mother to brush your hair. An intimacy shared between the pair of you which you fondly recalled.'

Suddenly, I could feel Mary's tender brush stroke on my hair, as though she was there in the room with us.

'It's exactly like me standing in front of my mother, while she painted me.'

197

I stared at her, confused.

'This so-called happy memory you have, is a false sense of your mother's love. This is not real love.' She paused, waiting for me to digest her words. 'Let's look at the evidence. You're alone in the kitchen making your own breakfast at the age of six. Your mother brushes your hair, but is not dressed to take you to school. Your neighbour takes you to school, instead. Do you see now? This is not a nurturing mother. You have somehow associated this memory as an act of her love. It was not an act of love.'

My body collapsed into the egg chair.

'Do you see now?'

I wanted to probe further but was too afraid to ask. Too afraid of the answers. Why hadn't I seen this before? Why? She'd never loved me. Not even when I was a child. I swallowed down a lump in my throat.

Cassandra was writing something down in her book. Her hand glided up and down the page, like an artist's hand, and I wondered if she painted like her mum. When she finished jotting down notes, she placed her leather pad on the floor and looked up at me, folding her hands neatly on her lap. 'How are things at home?'

I cleared my throat. 'You mean with Matt?'

'Yes.'

'Okay, I guess,' I said. 'We're co-existing. Living together but not together, if that makes any sense. Just as long as I don't complain and carry on pretending everything is fine, that I am fine, he's happy. It means he can get on with whatever it is he is doing without any interference. He'll never change. Never.'

'Does that upset you?'

I thought hard about her question for a while. 'Sometimes yes, of course it does. But sometimes, no it doesn't. I'm starting to detach.'

'Detach?'

'From him. From my old self.'

'That's interesting.'

'I've come to the realisation that it's me who needs to make the changes, not him.'

'That's positive to hear.'

'I guess it is,' I smiled, thinking about the shift happening inside me. Excitement zinged around my body, replacing the despair from moments earlier.

She smiled broadly, holding my gaze. As we stared at one another in silence, time stood still. Her eyes were like black marbles, drawing me in. Sucking me into her vortex, and for that brief moment in time, it felt as though we were the only two people on the planet.

I peeled my eyes away and took in a deep breath, running my hands down my legs.

'So, tell me,' she said, after a while. 'What makes Annabelle Clarke happy?'

'Joshy. He always makes me happy.' I smiled, thinking about his big blue eyes and chubby hands.

'Hmm,' she said, almost dissatisfied with my boring, predictable answer. 'What about the new Annabelle? What makes the new Annabelle happy?'

My hand went to my mouth, but it was too late, the words were spilling out of me. 'Being here with you makes me happy. Really happy,' I said. 'I feel good when I'm around you. Safe. You know? You're the only person I can rely on. The only person I can trust. I could never speak to anyone the way I speak with you, and it's not because you're my therapist. It's more than that.'

'Having you here with me makes me happy too,' she said, beaming. 'Very happy.'

This was true contentment, I thought.

Chapter Twenty-Nine

Multicoloured football cones marked the different activities for the children's end-of-term sports day. Whistles blew and kids in team shirts yelled for their team-mates, waving flags adorned with the school logo in the air. Oak benches ran along the sides of the playing field for the injured and parents. But not one parent was seated. We all stood, shoulder to shoulder, filming and cheering our offspring.

The morning started off civilised, but it didn't take long to descend into a highly competitive arena. Some over-enthusiastic dad ran onto the field, shouting 'cheats' during the wheelbarrow race – pointing to a pair of twin brothers who had bright red hair and bright red cheeks, as everyone stared, horrified. The twins were the darlings of the school! Once he'd realised that he was acting like a buffoon, he tried to pass it off as a joke, but we all knew he was serious.

Of course, Matt wasn't there. He let me down at the very last minute – via text. I stood solo, adjacent to the other parents, for two hours watching Joshy under the scorching sun with a fixed smile on my face, very much a single parent.

Mr Johnson, still in his headmaster's gown despite the stifling heat, was in his element. 'And now, onto the penultimate race of this morning. The big one. It's ... drum roll please ... the relay. Boys! Take a moment to quench your thirst and take your marks,' he bellowed, projecting his deep voice through the speaker.

Joshy was competing in the last race. He'd not done very well so far and was upset about his performance. His hand waved up and down as he screamed to his team-mate and waited for the passing of the baton, 'Come on Alex. Come on. Hurry.' He was in the final quarter of the race and the responsibility was all on him to take his team over the finish line and to a possible victory. I wasn't hopeful.

The boys made contact. Alex passed the baton over, and Joshy, all fingers and thumbs, fumbled with it, almost dropping it. I held my breath and watched as though it were in slow motion. They eventually made solid contact and Joshy gripped the baton, making a run for it. But it was too late. The other three boys had already sprinted off. All four boys stampeded towards the finish line, Joshy being the last. His poor face was pink from frustration.

Then the boy in front of Joshy toppled over his feet, grazing his knees. He threw the baton in the air, letting out a cry of pain. His elimination took Joshy to third place; I couldn't believe his luck. Leo snatched the victory and Rachel, clad in her gym gear, rushed over to her son to congratulate him and share the limelight. I gave Joshy a thumbs up from the side-lines, mouthing, 'so proud.'

'What's the time?' I asked Saskia, who was standing next to me.

She looked at her dainty Cartier watch. 'It's almost 11.30.'

'Thank you,' I said, as I started towards Joshy.

'Hey. You're not going already?' She placed her hand on my shoulder. 'Come on. Stay. We're going for a coffee afterwards. Why don't you join us?'

'I have an appointment.' It wasn't exactly a lie, I did have Cassandra that day, but not until the afternoon. The plan was to attend the sports day, get my nails done on the high street, rush home, change, and get a taxi to Cassandra's. Rosita had agreed to collect Joshy from school, so I had the whole afternoon free.

'It's the moment we've all been waiting for. The most exciting race of the day. Children. Take your seats. It's the mothers' race,' Mr Johnson's voice vibrated through the speakers once more.

The kids cheered.

'See? You can't leave now,' Saskia smiled.

'But ... I'm in my jeans,' I said, as I looked at Saskia, who was wearing the tiniest of shorts, which resembled a pair of hot pants I used to wear in my clubbing days with my friend Kat.

'It's only a bit of fun. Come on!'

Rachel bustled over to us. 'Ready, ladies?' she said, as she cracked her knuckles and clenched her toned thighs.

'Ready,' Saskia nodded. 'Come on, Annabelle. You can't be the only mum not racing.'

As I followed the small cluster of women towards the starting line, I wondered why I'd always found it hard to say no.

The mood shifted, suddenly everyone was serious. I pulled my t-shirt down over the waist of my jeans and wiped my brow. I breathed into my tummy to steady my nerves and focused my gaze on the finish line, blocking out the noise from the frenzied kids and parents. It'd been years since I'd raced. Only 20 seconds of my life and then it would be over with.

'On your Marks. Get Set. Go!'

My trainers pounded solidly against the grass and my arms pumped hard as my stride increased. Adrenaline rushing to every single cell inside my body. A strange hyper focus, which I hadn't had since my school days, took over and everything around me was blocked out. I became calm. At one. Nothing else mattered apart from that finish line. Before I knew it, my foot had crossed over. I doubled over with a stitch, catching my breath. Shouts and cheers rang all around me. I turned and saw the others crossing over the line behind me.

I'd won! I'd won the race outright! They didn't even come close.

Joshy sprinted over and we hugged. 'You won. You won!' he said, grinning from cheek to cheek. 'Super, Mummy. You won.'

I was exhilarated, on a natural high. I'd done something that my son was proud of. I couldn't quite believe it.

'Good going,' Saskia said, patting me on the back.

'She has youth on her side,' Rachel sneered. 'Are we going for a coffee?' she said, turning her back to me, masking the fact she was breathless.

My skin prickled from irritation.

'Annabelle?' Saskia peered behind Rachel. 'Are you joining us?'

'Maybe. Yes, why not? Yes, I'll come.' I wasn't going to let Rachel win. I could do my nails another time! I fished my phone from my back pocket to check the time.

Four missed calls. Cassandra.

'I have to go. Sorry.'

'Suit yourself,' Rachel sniggered.

I gave Joshy a kiss goodbye and dialled Cassandra as soon as I got away from the crowd.

'Annabelle. We need to pause,' said Cassandra. Her voice clipped.

'Sorry? What?'

The noise coming from the playing field was so loud, I couldn't hear properly.

'Hang on. One sec,' I said, jogging through the school and out the other side, through the main door, into the front playground and stopping outside the gates near the zebra crossing. 'Sorry. I couldn't hear. You were saying, we have to pause?'

'Correct. Our sessions. We can't continue,' she said in a staccato.

I swallowed her words, one by one. 'What do you mean, can't continue? I have a session with you today.'

'I've been doing a lot of thinking. I fear that you're developing a dependency, and it's not, how can I put it? Healthy. It's not healthy for your recovery,' she said, bluntly.

'I don't understand.'

I thought our friendship was growing. She'd said she liked being around me. I believed we were connected.

The line went quiet.

'You're my therapist. I rely on you. I need you. You know I need you.'

'Exactly, I'm your therapist,' she said, 'and I'm doing this for your benefit.'

'What do you mean, my benefit? How is it benefiting me when you're stopping the sessions? I need my sessions,' I snapped. 'Surely we should continue?'

'Annabelle. Take a breather and listen to what I'm about to say. I'm not stopping the sessions, per se. The sessions are being put on hold. Paused. Until I work out a better way to treat you. That's my final decision.'

'It doesn't make sense. I'm getting better. I'm feeling better. This morning, I said hello to Rachel and the others at the sports day event, and I stood next to them without getting flustered. And guess what? I competed in the mums' race and I won, Cassandra. Can you believe it? I won the race. Rachel came second. And Joshy was so proud of me. That's what I was going to tell you today. Can you imagine me doing that a month ago? I'm even going for a drink with everyone next Thursday. You encouraged me to make friends with her and the others, and I'm doing it. That's progress, isn't it? Please don't stop my sessions. What's going to happen to me if we stop?' I pleaded, holding back the tears. 'I don't want to go back to the way I was before I met you.'

'You have to trust me.'

'I do trust you.'

'We're not making the progress we need.'

'So then, why drop me like this? Why not increase the sessions instead?'

'I have to work out a more constructive way to treat you.'

'What do you mean?'

'Like I said, you're not making progress.'

'I don't understand.'

'Annabelle, you will. Don't come to the clinic. Don't contact me. I'll be in touch and let you know what I've decided the best course of action will be.'

I stayed silent.

'Bye for now.'

And just like that, she hung up the phone and dumped me.

Every day she didn't make contact sent me deeper into a paranoid hole. I couldn't eat, I couldn't sleep, I couldn't think straight. It was clear I couldn't function without her.

Four agonising days later, a message came through:

Please come to the clinic this Thursday at 8pm. There is something I'd like to discuss. I have a solution. Cassandra

It was vague and formal, and offered no explanation at all.

Can we meet sooner? Thursday is tricky. I'm supposed to be meeting the mums for a drink after school. It's also my birthday eve. A x

She never replied.

Chapter Thirty

It was Thursday, the annual end-of-year drink-up with the mums, my perfect excuse to leave the house and meet Cassandra without Matt quizzing me. In fact, when I told him I was off out, he seemed somewhat relieved that I finally had something resembling a social life. I guessed he wanted me out of the way so he could prepare for my secret birthday party. The one I was dreading.

The night was muggy. The air was dense with humidity. I took a cab to the clinic and waited outside until 8.00 pm on the dot, reapplying my lip gloss about a million times. By the time she greeted me at the front door with that perfect smile of hers, kissing me delicately on both cheeks, I was a clammy mess. She looked crisp and fresh, dressed in a navy trouser suit, and wasn't fazed by the stifling heat whatsoever.

'Let's sit here,' she said in a friendly but formal manner, pointing to the two-seater cream sofa.

A beautiful scent from the fresh flowers filled the room, and an array of travel magazines had been arranged like a fan on the coffee table, alongside them a box of tissues, the usual jug of water and two glasses. My eyes darted across the table to a small jewellery box with a red bow, placed to the left of the magazines. I slumped on the sofa and she elegantly took her seat beside me. Placing my phone on the table next to the pretty box, I desperately tried not to fidget with my hands.

'So good of you to come this evening. How are you?'

Something felt off. I couldn't quite put my finger on it. She was behaving differently towards me, a little distant, cold. It was as though we were strangers and had only just met. It made me self-conscious.

'I'm good, thank you for asking,' I said, cringing at my response.

'You're looking chic,' she said, pouring water into two glasses, avoiding my eyes.

My hand reached to my new hair. I'd had it cut even shorter the day before, into a tight bob, giving it a blunt, razor-sharp effect like Cassandra's.

'Thank you,' I said, half smiling, feeling totally sick.

'Your husband must like it.'

'He was a little taken aback when he saw me,' I said, 'but I didn't do it to please him.'

'I see.' Her voice was steady.

I started fidgeting with my hands.

'Do tell me. How are you *really* feeling?'

'It's been hard since our sessions suddenly came to an end,' I admitted. 'I get myself worked up, in a muddle and I panic. I don't cope so well. I haven't harmed, so that's a positive, right? I mean, it's been hard, but somehow I've managed to resist the temptation.'

'That's good to hear, Annabelle.'

It was a catch-22. If I could manage on my own, she'd stop the treatments, and if I seemed to be getting worse there was a good chance that she'd refer me on.

'Do you have any idea why I asked to see you this evening?' Her eyes rested on the little box on the table.

I shook my head.

She cleared her throat, took a deep breath in, steepled her hands. 'I've given your situation a lot of thought and I'm concerned that we're not getting the results we need quickly enough. The main objective has always been to help you regain a healthier state of mind, so you can become an effective mother to your son and reclaim full independence from your controlling husband, as well as to resolve the underlying issues from your childhood and mother, Mary.'

'Yes. Yes, I know …'

'I have many concerns,' she said, cutting me off, 'some of which extend beyond yourself. Do you understand what I'm saying?'

I nodded, but didn't understand what she was getting at. Not one bit.

'It's my duty of care to inform social services if I ever suspect that a child's safety is at risk. It's my job. Of course, this is not applicable to you, right now. I don't believe that your son is in any immediate grave danger. However, if we are unable to get to the root cause of why you harm, we run the risk of you slipping into your destructive habits again and things may worsen. You run the risk of adopting the role of your mother, the learnt behaviour from your own childhood, and you may become neglectful towards your son. Worse than that, your destructive habits may possibly extend to those who are vulnerable in your life.'

My hand went to my chest.

'As you know, I believe you have the potential to be a good mother to your son. A great mother.' She sipped water and paused. 'Your phone flashed a message,' she said.

'Huh?'

'Your phone.' Her little finger brushed past the jewellery box as she picked up my phone, handing it over.

My mind chewed the words, social services. I was suddenly nauseous and dizzy. In a fluster. What was she trying to say to me? That I had the potential to harm Joshy? That I was morphing into Mary? Was it inevitable? My destiny?

I looked at my phone. A message from Matt.

Any idea what time you'll be home? Don't drink too much. I don't want you hungover for your birthday. M

'Important?'

'It's nothing. The hubby's checking on me.' I placed the mobile back down on the table.

'Is he missing you?'

'I doubt it. What were …'

'Strange to be texting when you've only been out for a short while.'

'I guess. But what were you saying?'

'The more you take charge of your own life, the more he'll begin to take an interest in what you're doing. Trust me. Men are simple creatures.'

'Sorry. What were you saying about social services?'

My thoughts were jumping all over place, rewinding back to when Joshy was born, when I was struggling as a new mother, fast forwarding to the present day and how I still struggled with motherhood, now. Had I been neglectful towards Joshy when he was a baby? Was I ever a threat to him? Could I be a threat now? Maybe in the future? Thinking back to my own childhood, I wondered – if social services had been called on Mary, would they have taken me away?

'Okay. Here's the point I'm trying to make. We've worked hard over the sessions to build your confidence. We've worked hard on your anxieties and your social phobias and issues. We've even managed to contain the negative habits such as the self-harming, to a certain degree. But I fear this is not a permanent state for you.'

I was convinced she was going to dump me, refer me on, tell me there was no hope for someone like me, tell me I was a bad mum, like Mary. Call social services.

'The bottom line, Annabelle, is that we need to put an end to your self-destructive behaviour once and for all.'

Silent tears spilled out of my eyes as I tried to digest what was happening.

'You have a trigger. Until we work out what the root cause is, you will continue to slip into your destructive ways. It may not be tomorrow or next week, but at some point, you will slip. Mark my words. It will happen. It's self-sabotage,' said Cassandra. 'Perhaps one day you'll slip too far, and the damage will be irreversible.'

'Are you about to tell me something awful?'

'It depends on your perception.'

'Please get it over with,' I said, wanting to belt out a scream.

'I wanted to discuss a treatment plan that will see a permanent change in you. I'm talking about real progress, here. Quick progress.'

'I am making progress!'

'The hypnosis is not having the desired effect it once had. The regression work is slow. We need to take more drastic measures.'

'I'll try harder. I promise.'

'Wouldn't you like to see a real difference?'

'Of course, but like you said to me once, these things take time.'

It was fine. I was fine. Everything was fine.

'I know another way.'

I swallowed hard. Took a moment. 'What other way?'

It was coming. The end to our sessions.

'It's an effective solution, and something I wanted to run past you.'

'Please. Just tell me.'

'It's radical.'

'I don't understand.'

She folded her hands on her lap. 'A while back, I designed an intense hypnotherapy programme for a client of mine and saw great results very quickly. It was very powerful. Very effective. I believe you could benefit from it, too.'

'Right,' I said, not sure what she was selling me.

'This particular client was in a similar situation to you. When she first visited me, she was in a bad way, desperately low. Our twice-weekly sessions were not helping quickly enough and her recovery was slow.' Her black eyes glazed over. 'I devised a treatment plan specifically tailored to her needs.'

'Okay,' I said, still none the wiser.

'We embarked on an intensive course of hypnotherapy and within a week, we saw positive results. It was remarkable to watch her transform into the healthy person she is today.'

Had I got it wrong? Was she offering me more therapy?

'It's a residential programme, you understand?'

'Yes,' I said. 'Yes. Wait. No. I mean no. What do you mean?'

'You will have to come and live with me during the programme.'

'Oh.' My body fizzed as I swallowed down the words – *live with me*.

'My client's treatment plan consisted of three sessions of intense hypnotherapy a day, and the rest of the time was spent doing mindful activities such as deep meditation, self-affirmations and lots of sleeping in order to heal. By the end of the week, she was unrecognisable. A new person. She's now living a happier, more fulfilled life and is a highly successful lawyer. We still stay in touch to this day and have become close friends.' She looked at me and smiled. 'However, your current circumstances differ. She didn't have any children or a partner. She was alone.'

'Oh, I see,' I said. 'But it could work for me?'

'It would be a life-changing experience for you.'

'How long will I need?'

'At least two weeks. It's a huge commitment. You'd have to leave your family and move in with me.'

'But it's not as if I'm leaving them forever.'

'Exactly.'

'So, I have nothing to lose.'

'With my expert guidance and intense hypnotherapy plan, we will get you on the right track. For good,' she said, in a satisfied way.

'I think I want to do this,' I said. 'I think I could do this.'

'Annabelle, this will not be a walk in the park. It's a very intense programme. I will need your full cooperation. The first week is going to be very tough. Very tough indeed. There's a lot of issues we need to work through. The second week, things will start to ease and slot into place.'

'Okay.'

'There are strict rules to abide by. You mustn't question my methods, but trust in the process.' She locked eyes with me. 'Perhaps you'd like to take some time to think about it?'

'It seems I don't have much choice. I want to get better, more than anything.'

'Can you tear yourself away from your family for two weeks? Would you be able to cope without any contact from the outside world? We cannot have any distractions during the therapy.'

'Yes.'

'You're certain?'

'I am. Yes,' I said.

'There'll be no turning back.'

'The way I see it, it's no different from going away on a retreat or going into rehab, right?'

'The break alone would be beneficial.'

'I could lie, tell Matt I was staying in a spa hotel or visiting an old friend. To be honest, he wouldn't even notice my absence. It would do him some good to miss me. And as for Joshy, he has football camp for two weeks, so that will keep him occupied. I could get Rosita to help. She could move back in. By the time he starts to miss me, I'd be returning home, good as new,' I said. 'Once I return home, I'll get rid of Rosita and finally deal with my cheating husband. I'll sort things out with Mary, once and for all.' My mind was a flurry of activity, plotting and planning.

My phone flashed on the table. Another message from Matt.

`Annabelle? Everything okay?`

I switched off my mobile. 'Okay. Let me get this straight. I'll be participating in a two-week hypnosis programme and staying with you, at your house, in your home, with you?'

'Correct.'

'Would I be imposing? I mean, what about the other people you live with? How would it all work out?' I asked, drumming my fingers on my lap.

'Annabelle, I live alone. There will be no distractions. It will be only you and me.'

'What about your clinic work? Will I be getting in the way of that?'

'So many questions,' she giggled.

'I think I want to do it.'

'Congratulations,' she smiled, patting my knee. 'You won't regret this.'

She picked up the pretty box on the coffee table and handed it to me. 'Many happy returns for tomorrow, dearest Annabelle.'

My eyes widened and my cheeks flushed. 'Oh my God, I don't know what to say.'

'It's only a gesture.'

I pulled at the pretty red bow and opened the box. It was a dainty gold necklace with an eye pendant. The eye was encrusted with small diamonds circling it, the iris a brilliant emerald green. It was the most unusual and beautiful piece of jewellery I'd ever seen. The stones dazzled me under the glare of the lights. A note inside the box explained the significance of the eye as an ancient symbol of protection.

Protection.

She stood up, walked around the table and came to me from the other side, fastening the necklace around my neck. All the tiny hairs on the back of my neck stood on end. I pressed the pendant close to my chest, with conflicting feelings about the gift. It was the most thoughtful present anyone had ever gifted me, it was perfect, and beautiful, and dazzling and understated and truly personal, and I was touched by her generosity and kindness, but somewhere deep in the back of my mind, a little nugget of doubt niggled away.

Should I be receiving such a gift from my therapist?

'It's beautiful on you.' She sat on the edge of the coffee table in front of me and held my hands.

I blushed, swiping away my doubt.

'Do you want to change your life forever?'

'I think so.'

'You will not regret your decision.'

I smiled at her.

'We will begin the programme this coming Saturday. Make the arrangements you need to.'

Everything was moving at super speed. This Saturday?

She stood up, smoothed down her trousers with her hands and walked over to her desk, picking up a paper-bound document and Montblanc pen. 'This is the contract,' she said, walking back, perching on the table. 'It's pretty boring stuff. The formalities. Terms and conditions. A liability waiver. The contract lists in detail the treatment plan, but of course it's subject to change, according to how well you respond. It's all stated inside. Read it if you must.' She flipped through the paperwork. 'When you're ready I'll need your signature at the bottom, here.' She pointed at the dotted line on the final page, with her black nails filed to a point. 'Payment can be arranged after the programme is complete and you're satisfied with the results.' She handed me the pen and glanced at the clock on the wall, drumming her fingers on her lap.

As she sat there quietly, continuing to drum her fingers, I leafed through the paperwork quickly, my mind too busy to absorb any words on the page, my heart fluttering like crazy. I settled on the last page with the pen in my hand.

What could go wrong?

I scribbled my name down on the dotted line. It was a done deal.

'I'll see you on Saturday at 10.00 am.' She stood up, looking content. 'Don't be late.'

Saturday was only two days away. Tomorrow was my birthday. All I had to do was find a way to tell Matt that I was leaving him and Joshy for two weeks.

Chapter Thirty-One

The bright sun glimmered through the curtains, waking me up. It was the morning of my thirtieth birthday. With my eyes remaining shut, I patted Matt's side of the bed. It was empty. I'd had a fitful night's sleep, worrying about how I was going to tell him about the programme. I'd turned every imagined conversation between us over in my head, none of them panning out well.

Chaotic sounds boomed from downstairs. I placed the pillow over my head, dampening the noise. Matt was barking orders to what sounded like an army of people in the house. My secret birthday party. I sighed and retreated to the loo, checking my phone. There was one birthday message.

```
I need to see ya. I know I haven't been the best
of mums, and I'm sorry girl. I need ya to forgive
me. I want to put things right before I cark it. I
don't have much time left. Come on girl, it's your
ma. Happy birthday. Mary x
```

My hands shook as I resisted the temptation to respond. I deleted the message, blocking her number altogether. She'd have to wait two weeks, until I was better.

Downstairs, strangers were crawling all over my home. Furniture had been moved to make space for the makeshift dance floor and a bar had been erected. Helium balloons were tied up around the house, numerous mini disco balls hung from the ceiling, flowers were arranged everywhere, and large super-sized lanterns had been strategically placed in the garden.

I should have been grateful and honoured that my husband had gone to so much trouble for me. I'd never ever had a fuss made of me before – ever. I was more used to being one of the staff members at such events, as opposed to being centre stage. But the truth was, the whole thing made me angsty. I didn't want to be the centre of attention. I didn't want his flashy displays of affection. The whole thing felt fake, lacking in sincerity. What I really wanted, more than anything, was a husband who didn't cheat, a husband who listened, a husband who loved me for who I was and a husband who didn't try to control my every move.

Matt was in the garden, holding a clipboard and having a go at some helper. 'I specifically ordered crystal champagne glasses, these are not crystal,' he bellowed at the poor woman, who seemed to be shrinking in size with every word he spewed.

Another helper, struggling with a stack of chairs, walked past me.

'Can I help you?' I asked.

'No thank you madam, I've got this,' the pretty girl confidently said. She placed the stacked chairs against the wall and walked out of the room to get more.

There was something about the girl that made me recognise something of my early self in her. Was it the glint in her eye, or her fresh face filled with hope and aspirations for her future, or was it the way she strutted across the room, so self-assured and confident despite the fact that she could hardly see over the stacked chairs, and was struggling with the weight?

A grinning Joshy hurtled towards me, carrying a super-sized

envelope. I gave him a tight squeeze, nestling into his smell. The hug felt good, and a wave of guilt swept through me. He showed me the inside of the card, *I love you, mummy bear. Hope you have a good birthday today.* The message was bunched up on the right-hand corner of the card. His handwriting was miniscule. It was the sweetest card I'd ever received and was exactly what I needed.

I buried my head into his chest.

'Why are you crying, Mummy?' he asked, pulling himself away from my tight embrace.

'Tears of happiness, baby bear.' I wiped my eyes and straightened up. It was only two weeks, for Christ's sake.

'Look!' He pointed to the big balloons that said *30*.

'Wow!'

I wasn't abandoning him. I was going away to get better. To be a better mum.

'It's the birthday girl!' Matt stiffly crossed the room, pushing past the pretty helper struggling with a new stack of chairs. 'Surprise! I wanted to celebrate your thirtieth in style.' He kissed my forehead. 'I've organised a small gathering.'

'That's so kind of you Matt. You shouldn't have,' I said.

'Rosita's prepared your favourite breakfast. Here, come sit down.' He gestured to the stool and placed the clipboard with the excel spreadsheet on the counter. He padded over to the sink and started to wash his hands. After scrubbing his hands, he poured coffee from the De'Longhi machine into the *best mum* mug Joshy had bought me the previous year, and unfolded a napkin onto my lap. 'Breakfast is served,' he said.

I looked down at the plate of avocados and scrambled eggs. My stomach turned.

'So? How was your night?' Matt asked.

I froze.

'Your drinks with the mums?'

'Oh, yeah. It was good, thanks.'

'So happy you're all getting along. Rachel and the others might pop by tonight.'

My heart squeezed inside my chest.

'You two are getting along now, yes?'

I nodded, clenching my teeth. Was he playing games with me? Testing me?

'Good. Good. I'm glad you stopped all that paranoid nonsense.'

Rachel. The other woman. The woman with all the power. She had the potential to ruin everything for me tonight by exposing my lie to Matt. The thought of seeing her at my party made me want to throw up.

Joshy fastened and unfastened his Velcro trainers. The noise grated. He ran outside to play on the trampoline. Rosita appeared from the utility room, putting her apron away.

'*Feliz cumpleaños.*'

'Thank you, Rosita.'

'*Hermoso niño. Ten cuidado*, be careful outside, Joshua,' she shouted to Joshy, who was attempting somersaults. She waved her arms in protest.

'What would we do without her, hey?' Matt looked over at Rosita and then back at me, smiling.

'She is good,' I agreed, pushing the eggs around my plate. She was the glue that would hold the operation of mine together.

'What's that?' He pointed to my neck.

Damn. The necklace. 'Oh. Nothing. I found it the other day, it's old.' My hand twiddled with it. 'Why are you looking at me like that?'

'Hmmm. Never seen it before, that's all,' he said, his gaze fixed on my neck. 'Any thoughts on your actual present? You said I should ask before buying you something.'

'I thought, maybe. Well …' Now was my opportunity to tell him about my two-week holiday. 'Driving lessons,' I said, with no idea why I was chickening out.

His expression was blank.

'I could take one of those intensive courses. Pass my test in six weeks. It'll give me a focus. Independence, too. It'll be good for me. What do you think?'

'Annabelle, darling. You don't need to waste your time on that. I told you we were getting a driver. It's something we can afford now. Wouldn't it be nice to be driven around in luxury? Surely there's something else you want?'

'But it's something I'd like to do,' I said, 'for myself.'

'Let's not talk about this now. I don't believe now is a good time to overload your head with other nonsense. You seem too fragile,' Matt said steadily.

'What do you mean *overload my head*?' I stood up from the stool. My temples throbbed. Any smidgen of doubt about leaving was squashed there and then.

'Why don't I organise something indulgent for you? Nothing too taxing. A break of some kind?'

We stared at one another in a stand-off. My blood was boiling.

'Annabelle, drop it.'

My heart pounded inside my chest.

'A break sounds nice,' I said, looking away and sitting back down. 'Maybe that's exactly what I need.'

'Is that the time?' He glanced at his £150k diamond-encrusted Patek Philippe watch, which only came out on very special occasions. God, that meant the party was going to be bigger than I'd expected. 'I'd better get on, plenty more organising to be done. I can't leave it to these idiots. Say, why don't you have a soak in the bath and relax. I've arranged a beauty team to help you get ready. Rachel gave me their number.'

Rachel this. Rachel that. Rachel. Rachel. Fucking Rachel!

'They're very good, apparently, and will do hair, make-up and nails. You need to be ready by 4.00 pm sharp.'

I gave a half smile.

'It's going to be a real pamper day for you. I've picked out an outfit. Did you see it?'

I shook my head.

'It's in the dressing room. I want you to look your very best. Happy birthday my darling wife. Am I, or am I not, a fantastic husband?' He turned away, returned to the garden and started yelling at the staff.

'The best,' I said to myself.

Three women, armed with beautifying products, stared at me. 'Is there something specific you had in mind?'

'No.'

I sat on the chair like a dumb mannequin while the hairdresser pulled and tugged at my hair and burnt my scalp with the dryer. The make-up artist stabbed at my eye with a black kohl liner, making my eyes water, and plucked my eyebrows only to draw them back on again. The nail technician clipped my chipped nails and glued long fake nails on. I squeezed my feet into a pair of silver Jimmy Choo 6-inch stilettos and one of the girls helped me squeeze into the silver sequined dress that Matt had chosen for me.

I realised then that I'd always been one of Matt's many acquisitions, just like one of the failing businesses he revamped and resurrected.

Chapter Thirty-Two

The house was packed. Gifts were stacked up high on the table despite the invite saying no presents. Everyone was being kind and polite, wishing me well and paying me compliments. I stood by the Veuve Clicquot bar most of the night, nursing my drink from an inadequate champagne glass and smiling inanely at the guests, trying to relax. I knew they were all there because of their loyalty to Matt.

Matt slipped his arm around my waist and kissed me on the cheek, whispering into my ear, 'You look beautiful tonight.' He was happy and, on the outside, we appeared to be like any other normal loving couple.

Rachel said hello, air kissing both Matt and I on the cheeks and then took herself to the opposite side of the room. Every so often, I'd catch her slyly glancing our way. Was it because my husband was glued by my side for once? Did that surprise her? I guessed she'd decided not to stir up trouble for me, and was keeping quiet about me missing their drink-up the night before, but I was suspicious about her motives, and I couldn't quite work out why she wasn't taking the opportunity to openly flirt with Matt and rub my nose in it. Whatever the reasons, her sheer presence made me feel like a jumpy cat.

There was the usual commotion as Celeste made her entrance.

Late as always, she paraded into the house like Hampstead royalty, wearing a full-length fur coat, despite the heat. She wasn't your typical seventy-five-year-old grandma. She'd had every single plastic surgery procedure on offer: face-lift, eye bag removal, tummy tuck, nose job, boob lift. Even her hair was fake: long, full-bodied auburn hair extensions which accentuated her skeletal frame. Everyone fussed around her, but to me, she was just my snotty-nosed mother-in-law. I knew she believed that I was inadequate for her son, just like the glass I was sipping my champagne from.

'Darling child.' She double kissed me, making the briefest of contact.

'Hello Celeste, thank you for coming.'

'Oh, I wouldn't miss this for the world. Are you enjoying your party?'

'Yes, thank you.'

'He is a good boy. My Matthew is very kind. Some might say *too* kind.'

Sipping my drink, I smiled, mentally preparing myself for the onslaught. There was always something well-rehearsed she had to get off her chest.

'When he was a boy,' she began, 'he brought home this little stray dog. Endearing little thing it was, but nevertheless, a stray. He begged and begged for us to take him in, he explained that all the dog needed was a loving home and to be looked after.' She paused, making sure she had my full attention.

'Did you keep it?'

'No, my darling child. We couldn't possibly take in all the strays. Where would we be if we did?'

'What happened to it?'

'I had the dog taken away the moment Matthew was at school.

Goodness knows what diseases were lurking on that creature. I told Matthew that he'd run away. Do you know what happened next?'

'No. What?'

'The very next day, Matt completely forgot about it.'

'I see,' I said, fighting back the urge to scream in her face. It was yet another one of her warnings.

'Yes, I'm sure you do, my darling. Matthew is very kind,' she said. 'If you'll excuse me.' She waltzed off.

I'd been swimming against a strong current ever since I'd met Matt. I'd never *ever* belonged, and Celeste was always the first to remind me. I touched the necklace Cassandra had given me and secretly prayed for the strength I needed to get me through the rest of the night.

One of Matt's awful song choices, which belonged in an American diner or a shopping centre and not at a thirtieth birthday bash at all, was playing. I looked around the party. Everyone looked stuffy and serious, speaking in hushed tones. It felt more like a funeral wake than a party. It was doing my head in. Matt was so buttoned-up he wouldn't know fun if it punched him in the face.

I remembered our first holiday together in Sardinia. It was late at night and we were going for a stroll after dinner. I tried to tempt him into making love to me on the deserted beach, but he refused point blank, walking us back to the safety of our hotel room. With locked doors, the lights off and his clothes neatly folded over the chair, we made love.

Pulling up my playlist on my phone, I Bluetoothed it through the Bose speakers, overriding his song choice. Amy Winehouse's 'Valerie' belted out. The song, being upbeat, had an immediate effect on the party. Suddenly guests were less sombre and more animated. Feet tapped, voices raised, and laughter bounced around the room.

The music took a hold of me, lifting my spirits. I started to sway my hips against the rhythm. I shut my eyes and a weightlessness, which I'd only experienced a few times in the trance state, took over, as though a balloon was lifting me up, higher and higher. My feet no longer hurting from the high heels. The ground beneath me disappeared and I was free.

A hand pressed heavily down on my shoulder, bringing me back down to reality. I opened my eyes. 'Annabelle?' Matt glared. 'What *are* you doing?'

'I'm dancing.'

'You're embarrassing yourself. Come with me. How much have you had to drink?' He whispered into my ear.

'I'm not drunk!' I protested.

'You need some fresh air. Let's go into the garden.' He gripped my arm.

'Quit telling me what to do,' I whispered, yanking my arm back. I could sense Rachel glaring at us from the bar area.

'Annabelle, stop.'

'I want to go out the front of the house for a cigarette.' I'd stolen a Marlboro out of Bill's packet earlier and slipped it into my shoulder bag. I hadn't smoked in years, but I knew I'd need a cigarette after telling Matt I was leaving him for two weeks. I opened the magnetic fastener to my sequined handbag and placed my hand inside, fidgeting with the lighter.

'You're smoking?' His mouth gaped open like a fish.

'It's a new hobby,' I spat, walking away from him, seeing a glimpse of my old self.

He remained rooted to the spot. All heads turned my way. He didn't have the balls to follow. He was too gutless. Terrified of making a scene in front of his high society pals, in front of *Rachel*.

I walked into the hallway and leant my head against the wall, taking a breather. Rachel appeared, cornering me.

'You're a sly fox,' she slurred.

I looked around. We were alone.

'So? Why are you lying to your darling unsuspecting husband? And where *were* you last night?' she snapped.

'I don't know what you're talking about,' I said.

She'd obviously spoken to Matt about the drink-up and found out I'd lied. Why was she covering for me?

'You're a naughty girl.' She moved in closer, placing her hands against the wall, on either side of me. I could smell the alcohol on her breath.

'It's not what you think.'

'I'm intrigued.' She inched her head closer.

'It's nothing.' I ducked under her arm. She stepped back.

'Doesn't seem like nothing to me,' she sneered. 'So? Who is he? We're all dying to know.' She linked into my arm, like we were suddenly the best of friends. 'You can tell me.'

'There's nothing to tell.'

'I always knew there was something strange about you. Is this it? Your dirty little secret? You know, I'm very good at keeping secrets.'

'I don't know what you *think* you know, but you've got it all wrong. Okay?' I pulled my arm away and started for the front door. She grabbed it back and squeezed her manicured nails into my skin. 'I wonder what Matt would think, if he knew you were lying to him.'

I turned to face her head on. 'What have I ever done to you?'

'Well, it's only fair that one should know when one's partner is playing around.'

'It's not what you think,' I said, through gritted teeth.

'Looks like you're the perfect home-wrecker to me.'

Before I could rein it in, I bit back. 'You'd know all about that wouldn't you!'

'Excuse me?'

'Nothing. Forget I said anything. I'm drunk. Being stupid.'

'No. No. Come on, do tell. I want to hear it. I want to hear what *you* have to say to *me*.'

'You've slept with half the men in that room, even the married ones. You're probably sleeping with my husband, right now,' I said, shaking.

'How dare you accuse me of such vulgarities,' she said, her lips curling to a smile.

She was actually loving this!

Standing my ground and trembling from the core, I held her gaze. She broke first, diverting her eyes as she slowly inched back, one foot at a time.

'You're a waste of space.' She turned away, moving with prissy speed back to the party where the music had been changed back to Matt's diner style.

Bitch!

Chapter Thirty-Three

Stumbling out of the front door, I gulped in the crisp air. The temperature had dropped, and the fresh summer night felt cooling on my face. I sat on my doorstep and fished the cigarette out of my bag, sparking it up. My hand was shaking. Inhaling the smoke deep into my lungs, I hoped I hadn't fucked things up by opening my big mouth to Rachel. I could just picture her inside the house, blabbing to Matt about me being a liar.

Was I mistaken about their affair? I didn't know what to think anymore.

One thing was for certain, I'd had enough. Enough of my stagnant life, surrounded by stagnant people. The liars and the cheats and the fakes.

The smoke entered my bloodstream and a rush flooded my brain, making me lightheaded. I looked up to the yellowy moon and stars littering the sky. Tomorrow would mark a positive change in my life. Changes had already begun.

Back inside, Matt was hitting the top shelf and had become engrossed in some kind of row with Bill. Rachel had – suspiciously – left early, claiming a headache, and Celeste stayed as far away from me as possible, avoiding me like the plague she thought I was. I spent time chatting to Saskia, who turned out to be surprisingly nice. She was easy-going, not how I'd imagined at all, and she didn't once ask about me missing the drink-up at The Ivy, nor did she refer to my alleged infidelity that Rachel had 'covered for'.

The evening came to an abrupt end. Bill shouted at Matt, claiming that he'd been impossible to work with the last few weeks and that he'd changed recently. In return, Matt told Bill he had no idea how to run a business and then did something inexcusable; he marched Bill out of the house and told everyone to go home.

While Matt made a complete arse of himself, I somehow managed to stay stone cold sober. I was mortified. Guests felt awkward, saying goodbye to me, avoiding Matt. After they left, I helped Matt up the stairs and into our en suite. I sat on the heated tiles and watched him retch into the toilet bowl, planning my next move. He wouldn't just allow me to leave.

The noose around my neck tightened.

When he'd finished vomiting, he brushed his teeth and wobbled back to the bedroom. He stripped off all his clothes, still managing to fold them neatly on the chair, and threw himself on top of the bed, leaving his phone behind on the vanity unit. 'Come to bed,' he slurred.

His phone lit up. A message flashed onto his locked screen. No name attached to the message, just a number I didn't recognise:

Do you think she knows?

I stared at the phone, reading the message over and over again.

Do you think she knows?

Placing the phone face down on the unit, I walked into the bedroom.

I finally had proof. I wasn't going mad.

He was sprawled on the bed, butt naked in a star shape. 'Take your dress off,' he mumbled.

Staying rooted to the spot, I watched him as he lay on the bed, a total mess, pathetically fighting off sleep.

I knew there and then that I'd never let him hurt me again.

The following morning, while Matt nursed a hangover in bed and my house filled up with professional cleaners, I crammed as much as I could into a weekend bag and crept out of the house by the side entrance, undetected, bypassing all of my unopened presents as I headed to Cassandra's. I left a note on the kitchen island for Matt to read. I was riddled with guilt for not saying goodbye to Joshy, my heart broken for abandoning him in such a way, but I couldn't face it. He was too young to understand. Besides, I couldn't run the risk of Rosita raising the alarm.

I'd be back soon. I'd come back and be the mother that Joshy deserved, and the strong independent wife Matt had not expected.

Matt,

    Things have been unbearable lately, so I've decided to take the initiative and sort my head out. I need some time to work out what I want.

    I'm embarking on a self-help therapy programme. It lasts two weeks. I'll text you in a few days to let you know how I'm getting on. Please do not try and find me, or bully me into letting you know where I am. Please don't persuade me to come home. I'll come home when I'm ready and when I'm feeling better.

    I know you'll be angry at me for upping and leaving you without even discussing it, but this is something I need to do for myself. I can't live my life pleasing you. I suggest you take this opportunity, this break, to think about our marriage and our family, and what it really means to you. Do you really want to make things work between us? Are you willing to change and make sacrifices yourself?

Please make sure Rosita looks after Joshy and takes him to football camp. Maybe she can move in again?

A break would do me some good, you said so yourself. Goodbye, your wife, Annabelle.

Chapter Thirty-Four

I expected Cassandra to be waiting for me at the clinic, but instead, she was sitting on the front doorstep of her house, looking glamorous in dark shades and red lipstick, like she belonged in a Hollywood movie. My tummy somersaulted as I began to climb up the concrete steps towards her. I thought back to when I was a kid, wanting to get away from the estate, desperately wanting to live in one of the fine Georgian houses on Abbey Gardens.

It was like I'd come full circle.

Be careful what you wish for, girl. Mary's shrill voice echoed in my head, warning me. *Be careful what you wish for.*

Dragging my wheelie behind me, I reached Cassandra, silencing Mary's voice.

Cassandra remained poker-faced. She took my case without saying a word and led the way into her home. She locked the door behind us, taking the key out of the keyhole, placing it inside a key box in the dark hallway.

Her home smelt of damp and cigarettes, in need of airing. It was a complete contrast to the bright and airy clinic space in the basement. The walls of the narrow hallway were painted navy, and large moody oil paintings of barren dusty landscapes and blood orange skies hung from the picture rail. A long red Persian runner covered the black and white decorative tiles, and two pendant lanterns dropped from the ceiling, casting prisms of colourful light on the walls, although offering little illumination. All the doors leading off the hallway were closed. It was cocoon-like, and reminded me of the lower deck of a ship. My luggage was left at the bottom of the stairs. I followed her towards the back of the house, into the kitchen, in silence.

The bohemian-style kitchen also took me by surprise. It was tired. Old wooden cabinets, doors coming off their hinges, stained work-tops, and an old-fashioned freestanding upright cooker with a grill on top, which looked grimy from years of use. A cactus plant in a bright green pot next to a jar of wooden spoons had completely dried out. I thought it was impossible to kill cactuses.

She gestured for me to take a seat at the small pine table next to a floor-to-ceiling window, which overlooked the courtyard garden below. The window's paint was flaking off and another ornamental eye chime hung from a hook attached to its handle.

It should have been a relief to be in a home that wasn't immaculate and filled with ostentatious crap, but something felt off, and I was far from feeling relaxed. My hand went to the pendant around my neck that she'd gifted me, twiddling it with my fingers.

She leant up against her kitchen counter, took her sunglasses off and sparked up a brown cigarette, while she held my gaze. There was so much I didn't know about her. She inhaled slowly and seductively. Sucking in the smoke as it wafted across the room, the earthy sweet scent hit the back of my throat, making me cough. It was some kind of exotic cigarette, not your usual kind, and it gave me an overpowering sense of *déjà vu*, like I'd smoked one of those when I was younger or smelt it someplace before.

Cassandra ignited the hob with a clicker and placed a brass kettle on top, which whistled once the water boiled. I continued to fidget with my necklace while she made tea. I had the urge to fill the silence with small talk, but nothing came to mind. The only sound in the room came from the boiler, rattling away as it struggled to work. She placed a steaming cup on the table, which was stained with cup rings. It was that weird herbal drink. I looked around for a coaster but couldn't see any. Every inhalation of smoke Cassandra took was deep and slow, methodical, like she was sucking it down to the pit of her belly.

'Thank you for my tea.'

She smiled, but the smile didn't reach her eyes.

'What type of tea is it?'

'You're drinking Chinese herbs. This particular batch is designed to take the heat out of your body and cleanse your liver. It's detoxing and may cause you to feel drowsy.'

'Oh.' I burnt the tip of my tongue as I took a large gulp. The tea tasted as horrible as it did the first time.

'I love my necklace,' I said.

'I'm glad.'

'I had a good birthday party in the end.'

'That's nice.' Her expression was pinched.

Continuing to play with my necklace, I battled away tears as the doubt in my mind mounted. It was a blip, I reassured myself, only a blip. My emotions were heightened, and I was reading the situation wrong.

'I like the paintings in your hallway.'

'They were painted by my mother.'

'Wow.'

She glared.

'They're amazing. Do you draw?'

234

'Annabelle, I haven't brought you here so we can talk about me or the damn paintings.'

'I'm sorry,' I quivered.

'You need to take the programme seriously.'

'I do. I'm so grateful to be doing this.'

She rolled her eyes.

'Cassandra, have I offended you in some way?'

'You were late,' she clipped. 'I expected you at 10.00 am sharp. One thing I will not tolerate is tardiness. The hypnotherapy programme needs to be taken seriously. Do you understand?'

I nodded.

'You must stick to the rules and do as I say no matter how things may appear.'

I stole a quick glance at the dirty wall clock next to the boiler, it was only 10.26 am. I decided not to press further. She took the programme very seriously, which meant I had to. It wasn't a jolly, after all.

'I believed you weren't going to show,' she said, her features softening, her hard expression relaxing.

My heartstrings pulled. 'Oh my God, I'm sorry if I worried you. It was tricky to get away, that's all. I'm here now, and I promise to take it deadly seriously.'

'This is good to hear,' she said, stubbing her cigarette out in the overflowing ashtray on the table. 'Now, why don't you drink up and tell me all about your birthday? I want to hear every single detail,' she said, pulling up a seat next to me and sitting down. Her back remained upright and poised.

'Lots of people came. Matt, being Matt, made a huge deal about the party and invited the whole of Hampstead, including his pretentious mother.' I laughed. 'And then there was Rachel, of course. But thankfully she didn't stay too long and didn't cause too much grief.'

Her face twitched.

'To be fair, it was a really nice party and I had a better time than I expected. Everyone was generous and kind and seemed to be having a good time. But come the end of the night, it all went pear-shaped. Matt got hideously drunk, which was not like him at all, and started to have a pop at his business partner,' I said. 'It pretty much ended the party.'

'That does not sound like the controlled person you've described,' she said, leaning in.

'He was anything but controlled. He was acting like a complete prick.'

'Oh dear.' She laughed, and I laughed, and suddenly we were two best friends gossiping over a cup of tea.

'So, tell me. What did he buy you for your birthday?'

I put my hand to my necklace. 'He hasn't given me my present yet.'

'That's a shame – he doesn't appreciate you as much as you deserve,' she said.

My stomach fluttered.

'So? Shall we make a start?'

I cocked my head to the side, confused.

'With therapy. We can have your first hypnotherapy session right here, right now.'

'In the kitchen?'

'Is there a problem?' She took my empty mug and walked over to the sink.

'No, not at all. I just imagined settling in first and assumed the sessions would continue downstairs in the clinic.'

She turned to face me, leant against the counter and crossed one foot over the other. 'In order for this to work, you need to take instructions without questioning. Can you do that for me?'

I nodded.

'Hypnosis can be done anytime, anywhere, and when I decide you need it. Don't resist me, because if you do, the programme will fail.'

I nodded, again, and a rush of nerves flooded my system.

'Good. I'm glad we've cleared that up,' she said, in business-like tones. 'Now, I'd like you to close your eyes, and relax ...' Her tone changed and her words stretched out.

My eyelids were heavy, and I was suddenly exhausted.

I closed my eyes and started to drift off there and then, sitting on the hard pine chair, listening to the rattling boiler and inhaling the dense exotic cigarette smoke.

Chapter Thirty-Five

I startled awake from a coma-like sleep. It was pitch black. The bedsheets were tucked tightly around me. I was groggy, my mind cloudy, as though I'd been drinking heavily. I pulled myself upright, releasing myself from the restraints of the sheets. My head pounded with the slightest of movement. I leant up against the soft headboard for support. That wasn't my headboard. That wasn't my bed. I wasn't at home.

Memories resurfaced as I mentally worked backwards, retracing my steps. I'd left Matt and was at Cassandra's on the therapy programme. The kitchen was the last thing I remembered. I didn't even recall the session that followed. When had I fallen asleep and how had I ended up in bed? I swiped at my face as though bugs were buzzing around and kicked the sheets off, freeing my legs. Fumbling in the dark, I reached over to the bedside table, knocking something heavy over. The loud thud made me jump. It was probably the table lamp. Patting the table blindly, I searched for my mobile so I could use the flashlight. I don't know why I expected it to be there, maybe because it was always on the bedside at home, but it wasn't there now.

As I stumbled out of bed, I stubbed my toe on the corner of the bedside table. 'Shit,' I said out loud. The sound of my own voice broke the eerie stillness in the room. My toe hurt like hell as I blindly hopped across the bedroom. When I reached the far end, I padded my hands along the textured wall until I located the light switch. A stained-glass lantern lit the room, offering barely any light, bouncing pretty colours around. I opened the shutters to the small window. Sunlight flooded in, making me squint and my eyes water as I tried to adjust to the brightness.

The sun was still high in the sky. The window overlooked the terraced gardens below. It seemed that I was at the top of the house. I peered out into Cassandra's unkept garden and spotted the neighbour next door tending his vegetable patch. His garden was immaculate. I inched away from the window, but it was too late, he'd spotted me. He froze, his eyes grew wide. I smiled and waved, but he didn't respond. Instead, he stood staring for a while, then shuffled back inside his house, leaving the basket full of runner beans behind.

The room was old fashioned and sparsely furnished, with only a double bed, one bedside table and a mahogany wardrobe. The wallpaper was hectic, maroon patterned swirls, making the room feel busier than it should have been. I placed the bedside lamp, with its frilly fringe, back on the side table and scanned the room for my mobile, but I couldn't locate it anywhere. My suitcase had been opened and all its contents emptied. I checked inside the armoire and found my clothes hanging alongside an array of glitzy ballroom gowns. My clothes were drab in comparison. My underwear was neatly folded at the bottom of the wardrobe, next to lots of glamorous high heeled shoes. Fingering the sequinned garments, I wondered whose room I was in and who owned the pretty dresses.

My toiletries had been unpacked in the cramped en suite bathroom, which led off from the bedroom under the eaves. My toothbrush and toothpaste were placed in a water-stained frosted glass on a dusty shelf above the sink. Alongside it were my face cream, make-up bag and hairbrush. A rim of dirt circled the inside of the porcelain sink. My shower gel and sponge were in a small tray attached to the shower pole in the tiny shower cubicle.

I stared at my reflection in the round mirror above the sink and noticed I was wearing white collars. My breath caught. *What the hell?* My eyes travelled down my body. I'd changed into silk white pyjamas which didn't belong to me. I'd no recollection of changing.

I ran a cold shower to stir myself awake, in hope of sparking my memory. I stood under the icy cold water, which virtually dripped from poor water pressure, until I couldn't take it anymore and my skin stung like I had bad sunburn. The holes in my memory remained. Brushing my wet hair away from my face, I changed back into the clothes I'd been wearing when I arrived.

The smell of coffee hit my nose as I started down the creaky stairs. Cassandra was in the kitchen. She'd changed, and was now wearing a bright green kaftan, humming to a jazz radio station. She broke three eggs into a bowl and started beating, oblivious to me as I stood in the doorway. A newspaper was open on the kitchen counter and there was a cafetière on the hob. I coughed to make my presence known.

'Goodness. You gave me a fright. Come in, come in.'

'I didn't mean to scare you.'

'Sleep okay?'

'I think so,' I said, unsure.

'Fabulous.'

'Hope you don't mind. I decided to take a shower. I was feeling a little spaced out after the hypnosis session.'

'Not at all. My home is your home. Come. Sit down. I'm making breakfast, although it's a little late for breakfast now.'

'Breakfast?' I'd had breakfast at home, a slice of toast with marmite.

240

'Well, let's call it brunch,' she said, as she poured the eggs into a pan and swirled them around with a wooden spoon to make them scramble.

I glanced at the clock. It was 10.50 am. 'Brunch? How … how long was I napping for?' I stuttered.

'Napping?'

I scratched my head.

She took the pan off the hob and placed it on the counter, lit up a cigarette, and turned to face me. 'My dear. It's Sunday today.'

'What the …?'

'Sunday,' she repeated.

'But it can't be,' I said. 'How can I lose a day like that?'

'You were exhausted,' she cut in, blowing smoke from her cigarette my way. 'I helped you up the stairs and put you to bed myself. It was quite easy really. You were still under hypnosis and highly suggestible at the time. I hope you don't mind,' she smiled. 'Remember, mental exhaustion can play havoc with your mind. You obviously needed the sleep and I'm sure you feel better for it. You *look* better for it. Fresh as a daisy. I do hope you were comfortable in that room.'

I slumped down onto the pine chair. She had a point; living with Matt over the years had taken its toll. Maybe I was more wiped out than I'd imagined?

'The room was comfortable,' I said. 'In fact, it's the best night's sleep I've had in ages. I didn't even dream.' The tension began to ease from my shoulders.

'I'm so pleased. The room you slept in belonged to my late mother. She adored that bedroom.'

'Oh God. I'm sorry, I shouldn't have slept in there. To be fair, I don't really remember much.' It was wrong and felt icky. 'I can sleep someplace else, the sofa maybe, I don't mind, whatever you prefer.'

'Nonsense. A bedroom is a bedroom,' she continued. 'Besides, she didn't die in there, so it's perfectly fine.'

I blinked, processing the information. She may not have died in there, but judging from what Cassandra had said, she must have died somewhere else in the house. 'Can I help you with anything?' I asked, shaking the mental image of her dead mum sprawled across the kitchen floor from my mind.

'You'll do nothing of the sort. You're my house guest and you'll allow me the privilege of spoiling you rotten.'

My heart leaped with joy. After years of being under Matt's thumb, under the watchful eye of Rosita, and experiencing years of neglect from Mary, I'd finally found myself a true companion.

'I hope you don't mind me unpacking your belongings. You didn't bring a lot with you. You can borrow whatever you need from me.'

'Thank you.'

'In fact, tonight, you'll need to wear something lavish. We will have a celebratory meal to welcome you into my home to mark the official start of the programme, and our journey of discovery together.'

'That's amazing. Thank you.'

'I've made scrambled eggs and sliced-up avocado. Your favourite, I believe.'

'How did you know?' I cocked my head to the side.

'You told me.'

'Huh! Strange. I don't remember saying,' I said, grappling with my unreliable memory.

She placed the avocado and eggs, a fork and a cup of coffee on the table in front of me. My tummy rumbled. I waited for her to take her seat.

'Please start. I never eat breakfast. Straight coffee for me in the mornings.'

'Oh. Okay. Thank you. Do you have a knife?'

'It's best we keep you away from any sharp objects. For the time being at least. I'm sure you understand.'

'Oh. Okay.'

I tucked into the food, using my fork and finger to scoop, shovelling the egg into my mouth. It was bland and under-seasoned, but I didn't want to ask for salt and pepper. Matt had once said, when we were dining at a two Michelin starred restaurant, that it was rude to ask for salt and pepper. It was an insult to the chef.

'Have you seen my phone?' I asked.

'It's here with me. You left it in my care yesterday. You asked me to take it from you.' She picked up the phone from the counter, making no attempt to pass it. 'No one called,' she said.

'Oh.'

'You seem disappointed.'

'No. No, I'm not,' I said, avoiding her eyes and stuffing more egg into my mouth. Was it too much to ask of Matt to check up on me?

'I suggest you embark on a digital detox while you're here. It'll help to focus your mind solely on the programme. We don't want any external influences interfering with the therapy.'

Even though every cell in my body wanted to please her, I wasn't quite ready to give up my phone. Not yet. I wanted to hear from Matt, see what he had to say for himself and besides, my phone was the only link I had to Joshy. All my pictures of him were on there. And then there was all my music, which kept me sane on many dark days.

'Can I have a couple of days to settle in first, and then maybe I could give it to you?'

'I'll leave you to make the right decision. I can only offer you advice.' She flicked her cigarette stub into the sink, ran a tap over it and walked towards me, handing me the phone. She patted my

243

shoulder and walked towards the door. 'I need to get ready. I have a few errands to run. When I get back, we can have the first session of the day, Anna.'

My body stiffened like a corpse.

She'd just called me Anna.

'Okay,' I said.

Maybe she didn't realise what she'd said?

Chapter Thirty-Six

Drinking my coffee alone in the kitchen, I listened to the faint sound of the children playing in the small playground next to Cassandra's house. It made me pine for Joshy, and I began to wonder what he'd eaten for breakfast and what he was doing. It was a beautiful sunny day and he'd enjoy having a run around on the heath. Would Rosita take him out and would she remember to take a snack? Leaving Joshy was not a permanent thing, I reassured myself. I'd be back taking care of him myself, very soon.

How had I got it so wrong with Matt? He'd shown me glimpses of tenderness in the past, but was that even real? I checked my mobile, again. Cassandra was right, there were no messages from him. Had I given him the green flag to play away from home? He clearly didn't give a shit about my well-being. If he did, he would have messaged me to see if I was okay. All that talk about wanting to fix things and make things right between us was utter bullshit. I should have known better.

Do you think she knows?

I looked out of the window and down below into Cassandra's garden, fantasising about the new and improved Annabelle, the one that was going to take control of the situation with Mary, take charge of Rosita and kick Matt's cheating butt into shape.

I had to make the two-week programme work.

Stupidly, I hadn't brought anything to fill my time between sessions, and with time to kill I was at a loss. I washed the dirty dishes with an old sponge that needed throwing away, cleaned the sink, watered the cactus, emptied the stinking ashtrays and wiped down the worktops. I thought about going for a walk but dismissed the idea. Cassandra hadn't given me a house key, and I didn't know what time therapy would start. She had a stack of magazines in the clinic, so I guessed there'd be some lying around the house somewhere. Cassandra hadn't set any house rules, which rooms I could or couldn't enter, so I assumed it would be okay to search.

As I stood in the hallway, everything was still, silent. Assuming that she'd left the house, I padded along the corridor and opened the creaky door to the front room. The room was a mismatch of furniture and styles from different eras. An oval mahogany table in the middle of the room was set for a dinner party. Silverware, off-white stiff linen napkins, a candelabra and plates with decorative gold rims all laid out. Dust had settled inside the wine glasses. A brass chandelier with lights that looked like candles hung from the ceiling, and more oversized moody oil paintings filled the wall spaces.

Books and ornaments cluttered the bookshelves. An eye sculpture was on the mantelpiece above the decorative fireplace, and on the vintage G-plan sideboard was a record player, alongside tons of LPs. Making a beeline for the records, I fingered through the titles. Disappointingly, there was nothing modern, it was all either '70s disco music, the likes of Hot Chocolate, Abba and Gloria Gaynor, or stuffy classical symphonies and concertos.

I was in a time warp.

Everything was preserved, distilled, like life had been put on pause. But as I continued to circle the room, I noticed a pair of red sparkly high heels discarded in the corner and a hypnotherapy reference book called *My Voice Will Go With You*, turned over on a green velvet wing-back chair by the window where a large spider was busy weaving its web. I traced my finger along a dusty sideboard cluttered with booze and hordes of framed family portraits. The images had faded from the light and looked an age away. An exotic dark-haired lady, with olive skin and black eyes, featured in all of them. She was smiling in every snap. Cassandra's mum – I could see the resemblance. The images captured seemed to dance as though alive, her mother was fluid, like she'd been pictured in motion with every shot.

In a couple of photos, that woman held hands with a young girl with dark eyes and long black hair. The girl looked sad, solemn and seemed to disappear into the background, overshadowed by the glamorous woman standing next to her. Blink and you'd miss her. Cassandra as a child. My heart ached for that little girl as I recalled her melancholy story about her mother making her stand still while she painted her for hours on end.

At the back of the cluster was one picture of a much older man, looking stern, stiff and serious, sitting behind a glass desk in a white room with his hands clasped together and a frown upon his face. Standing behind him was Cassandra's mum, her hand resting on the man's shoulder, flinging her head back in the shot, caught in mid laugh. I recognised the room they were in. The basement clinic. That must have been her father.

Closing the door behind me, not wanting to intrude longer than necessary, I padded towards the room adjacent to the kitchen. The door was locked. Peeping through the keyhole, it was too dark to see inside. As I straightened up and turned around, I bumped straight into Cassandra. She was standing directly behind me.

'Hello, Anna.'

'Gosh, you shocked me,' I said, taking a step back, placing my hand on my chest. 'Sorry. I didn't mean to pry. I was looking for something to read.'

'That's okay. I understand you're curious. We all are, it's human nature.' She was dressed in a crisp suit, ready for work.

'Why is this room …'

'Locked?'

'Yes.'

'It was my mother's studio.'

'I'm so sorry.' I fiddled with my necklace, cringing at how many times I'd used the word sorry since arriving.

'Don't be. It's locked for a reason. It's filled to the brim with all her things. Paintings, sketch books, her ridiculous outdated self-help books. I've yet to find the time to clear it away. One day, I will,' she smiled. 'Mother was flamboyant, fiery. Father said the reason she was such a hot head was because she was Persian. Fire ran through her veins. In her blood. However, we soon realised she had serious mental health issues. The weird mood swings, the erratic behaviour, the deep lows and the euphoric highs. Once, we caught her walking along the road completely naked in the middle of the night. Can you imagine what the neighbours thought of us?' She laughed, but there was a strain to her voice. 'Father was a psychiatrist. He started treating her, but it was no use. She was lost to us.' She smiled. 'You see? We both have mummy issues.'

'How did she …'

'Die?' She inched back and leant against a painting on the wall. It slanted sideways, but she didn't seem to notice. 'She took her own life. Slit her delicate wrists. In that very room.' She gestured towards the locked room.

'I'm sorry.'

'Don't be. In a way, it set her free from her sickness. She's at peace now.'

'I guess you're right.'

'Don't look so glum, Anna,' she laughed. 'It was a very long time ago.'

A beat passed.

'Can I ask you something?' I said.

'Yes. Of course.' She folded her arms.

'Why are you calling me Anna all of a sudden?'

She smiled. 'Does it bother you?'

I cleared my throat. 'No. No … well … it's just that …' I couldn't form the words and articulate why it was unnerving me so much. Why it creeped me the hell out. Why it felt wrong. Strange.

It was as though my past and future lives were crossing over somehow.

She cocked her head to the side, waiting for an answer.

I shook my head, dismissing my jitters. 'It's nothing. It's fine. Not a problem. Not a problem at all.' I smiled. 'You can call me Anna if you wish.'

'Great. Shall we get started then, Anna?' She retrieved the large set of keys from the key box. I stepped aside as she unlocked the door to her mother's studio, then opened it. 'Let's have the next session in here. We can make use out of this redundant room. Take a seat over there.' She pointed to a red velvet chaise.

Chapter Thirty-Seven

My nose wrinkled at the musty smell as I followed her into the art studio. It was stale inside, stagnant. She folded back the original shutters, letting light from the outside in. Dust particles hit the back of my throat, making me cough. I sat down on the threadbare chaise and a plume of dust escaped from the material, evaporating into the thick air. Wiggling myself back into the seat, the springs beneath me poked hard into my bum.

I had the urge to scratch my skin, itch my scalp and wipe my face clean.

Dozens of large paintings leant up against odd bits of furniture. There were two sideboards, a large antique desk in the middle of the room and a coffee table to my left, next to the chaise, that was cluttered with knick-knacks, framed pictures, ashtrays and books. An easel stood near the desk by the floor-to-ceiling window, its painting covered by a dust sheet; next to that, an artist's stool with an adjustable seat. Paint brushes in glass jars littered the floor along with dirty rags, cardboard boxes, and empty mugs. Every inch of wall space was covered up, either by shelving units, paintings or exotic tapestries. The ceiling wasn't spared either, with more ornamental eyes hanging down from the ceiling like icicles. Dozens of them, everywhere.

Instead of feeling protected, I felt as though I was being monitored from every possible angle.

A faint noise, like electricity humming, buzzed around the room and I could feel a slight pressure building inside my head as I sensed the weird interference. There was an odd energy surrounding us, like a force-field. I'd never believed in ghosts before, but Cassandra's mother's studio had a weird vibe to it.

'Are you comfortable?' she asked.

'Yes.' I tapped my fingers on my lap.

'Why don't you put your feet up? Lie down.'

My head eased onto the green scatter cushion beneath me.

'Relax and let go. Deeper and deeper, you will travel into your subconscious.'

As her voice changed, I was comforted once more. Enveloped in the soft blanket of familiarity – the warm tone of her voice and the hypnosis state that would soon follow. I turned my head to face her. She picked up her leather-bound notepad from the desk and dragged the office chair along the multi-layered Persian rugs on the floor, manoeuvring it around the clutter. She positioned the chair opposite, like she did in clinic, and took her seat, brushing her skirt down.

'Deeper, you will sink into the trance state. Quicker. Faster and more immediate. Now, sleep.'

I closed my eyes, blocking the world out. My mind started to drift.

'Anna, I'm going to begin by asking you a series of questions. Is that okay?'

'Yes.'

'It'll be done in quick succession, and you must answer without conscious thought, saying the first thing that comes to mind. Do you understand?'

'Yes.'

251

'Empty your mind of thoughts. And try to answer my questions as honestly as you can.'

'Okay,' I said, drifting further.

'Are you happy that you are on the programme?'

'Yes.'

'Are you optimistic about making progress?'

'Yes.'

'Are you ready to change?'

'Yes.' My tummy somersaulted with butterflies.

'Do you believe I have the power to help you?'

'Yes.'

'And do you trust me?'

'Yes.'

'Good. Good. Now, do you have an understanding as to why you've been self-harming?'

'It helps silence the chaos inside my head.'

'Excellent analysis, Anna, excellent.'

My shoulders relaxed further into the chaise.

'Now, tell me this, when was the last time you harmed yourself?'

'When Matt went away to The Grove hotel on his dirty weekend.'

'Why did you stop harming?'

'Because …' I couldn't get the words out. 'Because …'

'Anna. Why did you stop?'

'Because the urges go away when I'm with you,' I blurted out, 'because when I'm with you there's no chaos, only calm.'

'This is positive news. However, you believe this a permanent state?'

'I'm not sure. You said it wasn't. That's why I'm here. But … I don't know. I believe I can stop.'

'How?'

'Just as long as you're there to help guide me. Then, I know I can.'

'And if I'm not around? What happens then?'

'I don't know if I'm strong enough to resist without you.'

'So, you're saying you need me to help you?'

'Yes.'

'And you'll follow my lead and my direction?'

'Yes.'

'Anna. What would happen if I asked you to do something that you didn't agree with, would you do it then?'

'Yes.'

'Why?'

'Because I trust you and you know what you're doing.'

A quiet wrapped itself around the room.

'What are you thinking, Anna?'

'I'm thinking that I want to make you proud of me,' I said.

'I am proud of you. Very proud.'

Her soft words burrowed inside my brain, making a home.

She woke me after what felt like an eternity. My neck was sore. I pulled myself up to sitting and rolled my shoulders out, waiting for my blurry vision to come back into focus.

'How are you feeling?'

'A little spaced out, but good. I feel calm. At peace.'

'Excellent.'

'Thank you for offering me a safe place to stay while I sort my life out.'

'Not a problem at all, Anna. Now, would it be okay if I put you under again?'

'Yes,' I said, lying back down and shutting my eyes.

Chapter Thirty-Eight

'You're going to regress, back to your childhood, to unravel more truths. Are you ready, Anna?'

'Yes.'

'Take me back to the council estate, when you were younger, to that eventful day.'

I listened to her voice and melted back into the chaise.

The years peeled away as I sank into a deep layer of my past.

'Where are you?' she said.

'I'm inside someplace. It's dark. Smells bad. It's making me feel sick and I can't breathe. If I breathe in, I'll vomit. I need, I need …' The doors opened and light flooded in. I was in the lift. I stumbled outside into the fresh air. 'I'm on the fifth floor of the tower block.'

'Excellent.'

'There's a girl on roller skates. She's darted right past me.'

'Is that girl important?'

'Yes.'

'Follow her.'

'She's too quick. She's skated round the bend, towards Mary's flat.' I had to catch up with her. 'Anna! Anna!' I called after her, but it was too late.

I ran along the balcony towards Mary's flat. The front door was on the latch. I pushed it open and hesitantly inched inside. The girl had discarded her skates at the top of the stairs and there were muddy skate tracks on the carpet in the compact landing. Mary was going to be so mad about that. I poked my head through into the kitchen to see if the girl was there. The sink was filled with dirty dishes and music played on the radio: Prince, '1999'. The Armageddon countdown. The girl was nowhere in sight.

Bad noises started echoing around the flat. Crying. Yelling. It was coming from downstairs. Bad, bad, noises.

The girl. I had to save her.

My pulse raced as I tried to move, but my feet were cemented to the cheap lino floor. I looked down; thick gloopy mud surrounded me. No. NO. NO. There was mud on the kitchen floor, as well. She was going to be mad. So mad. An earthy taste hit the back of my throat.

'Where's the girl?' Cassandra asked.

'Downstairs. I can't reach her. I can't move. Help. I can't move. Help.'

'Take one step at a time.'

'I can't move …' My chest tightened. My breathing became rapid.

Down the stairs to Mum's flat, where the horror that had been gathering dust for twenty or so years, awaited me. But I wasn't ready to face it. I wasn't ready. I wasn't ready.

I wasn't ready.

Chapter Thirty-Nine

CLINICAL NOTES
Anna admitted to not wanting to self-harm while under my care. Sense of wanting to please me.
Self-harming – attention seeking behaviour?
Q: If the focus is redirected from her, will she harm again?

Anna seeks a primary caregiver for comfort, affection and nurturing. Not independent.
I have filled the role of her mother.
It's exhausting and testing for me as her practitioner, yet I will push on, regardless.
In her mind, my house has become the childhood home she has always craved. Offers security and safety.
But why does she continue to block childhood trauma? Self-sabotage?

Today's hypnosis:
Fire round questions – effective. True insight into how she's thinking. Will use again.
New set of affirmations given while under a much deeper level of hypnosis.
Displayed somnambulistic hypnosis – rolling of the eyes – not witnessed

before. (Well done to me for achieving this profound state of mind.)
Suggestions are now bypassing conscious thought and going straight into
the subconscious.

Note to self – she seems unsteady and forgetful of things.
Grasp of reality could be slipping, like years back when she suffered PND
and manic episodes.

Save the girl – Save Anna!

Chapter Forty

'Open your eyes. Welcome back to the room, Anna. Take a good stretch.'

My feet were elevated on two yellow scatter cushions with bright orange buttons. My neck had stiffened, my legs were numbed with pins and needles and I'd been crying. Tears had escaped my eyes and had run down my face, wetting my neck. I peeled myself off the chaise. My vision was like a sepia Instagram filter. It felt as though days had passed. I was disorientated and had lost count how many times she'd put me under in that one session.

Cassandra sat opposite, her legs crossed, looking serene yet business-like. She closed her notebook, placing it on her lap. 'Are you okay?'

'I think so.' I stared at the pad and wondered what she'd been writing.

'That was ground-breaking work. A step closer to uncovering the truth. You should feel a tremendous sense of achievement.'

I smiled, feeling happy that I'd made her happy, but deep down, I didn't want to admit my frustration. What did it all mean? The noises, the crying, the sense of doom when I entered Mary's flat. What was lurking down the stairs?

'I've made you tea,' she said.

'Thank you,' I said, wondering when she'd made the drink.

The herbal tea was on the cluttered coffee table, next to a lit cigarette resting in the marble ashtray. I scanned the retro self-help books piled on the table, feeling a little dazed. *The Power of Positive Thinking*, *The Power of Now*, *The Celestine Prophecy*.

'Why don't you take the tea upstairs? You must be exhausted. You'll need time to process the session. Let it settle.'

'Okay.' I stood, wobbly on my feet.

'Remember, we're celebrating the start of the programme tonight. I expect you to be downstairs in the dining room, 8.00 pm. Sharp. You can choose one of my mother's outfits. I want to welcome you into my home in style. Tonight is about fun,' she said, smiling broadly. 'Therapy will resume tomorrow.'

My tummy fluttered, warming the chill left in my bones.

Sitting on my bed, I set an alarm on my phone for 7.30 pm. I didn't want to be late. Not again. Choosing an acoustic guitar playlist on my phone for a mellow vibe, I began to scroll through my photos while I sipped my tea. Seeing pictures of Joshy made me teary, I didn't expect to miss him as much as I did, and so soon after leaving.

Matt was a different story. He still hadn't messaged. No guesses as to how he felt about me being away from home.

A recent family photo of us sitting in Celeste's Hertfordshire garden, having afternoon tea, caught my eye. In the snap, I was sandwiched between Joshy and Matt, Celeste sat at the head of the garden table. I zoomed in on Matt's face. He was looking in my direction with an angry expression on his face. The photo was taken only moments after he'd complained to me about being too soft on Joshy, saying I'd allowed him to eat too many of Celeste's sickly sweet cakes, even though she'd been encouraging Joshy to try a little of everything, and

I was only following on from that, thinking it would please her. His dad, Ralph, a rotund man with pink cheeks and a full head of silver hair, took my phone and snapped away, capturing Joshy having a tantrum, Celeste, upright and regal, grinning like a Cheshire cat and me fighting back the tears, while Matt looked as though he wanted to kill me.

At least Joshy had one set of grandparents who were in his life. My dad had been absent all my life and Joshy didn't know Mary, having only met her a handful of times when he was born, which didn't really count. There were no photos of her with Joshy in my phone. In fact, there were no photos of her at all. There should have been a ton of happy family snaps of us together, pictures of the picnics we'd had in Regent's Park and the birthday parties she'd attended and the unexpected visits, turning up on our doorstep with a carrier bag full of chocolates for Joshy.

She'd been gone for six years and had kept herself away, like a dirty secret.

But secrets had a habit of exposing themselves.

The fast track to my buried secret would be to ring Mary and have it out with her. The whole repressed memory was still coated in thick fog. I could demand she spill the beans and tell me everything that went on when I was younger. I hovered my finger over her blocked number, knowing that one phone call was all it would take for the nightmare to be over.

Placing my phone face down on the side table, I knew that any contact with Mary was, for the moment, forbidden. I'd have to get the answers Cassandra's way. She knew best.

The alarm sounded, waking me up. I must have dozed off. I hadn't even managed half the tea, it was stone cold, sitting on the side table next to my phone. Classical music played from downstairs. I scrambled out of bed and quickly showered to wash away the brain haze and ogled the lavish gowns in the wardrobe, bewildered.

What the hell was I doing dressing up in a ball gown?

Not wanting to disappoint Cassandra, I settled on the most conservative dress in the wardrobe, a black full-length figure-hugging dress with silver sequins on the shoulders. It was far too long and too loose for my frame. The high heels in the wardrobe were far too big for my feet and I hadn't brought any extra shoes with me, because I didn't think I needed anything glamorous, so I decided to stay barefoot. There was no way I was going to pair the dress with my trainers.

I scooped the bottom of the dress up so I wouldn't trip over it on the steps and walked down the creaky stairs in my bare feet, completely weirded out, like her dead mother's spirit was somehow draped over me, her ghostly energy seeping into me.

Chapter Forty-One

The music was coming from the dining room. Inside, Cassandra was twirling around like a ballerina, flinging her arms in the air in a theatrical way, lost in the music. She was also barefoot and wore a red strapless mini dress, exposing her long, lean, tanned legs. The sequined motif of a rose on the front of her gown sparkled from the candlelight. Thick black cat-like eyeliner accentuated the blackness of her eyes. Her irises matched her pupils. She moved with a sense of freedom that strangely reminded me of a child in dress up, despite her height.

She noticed me standing in the doorway and smiled broadly, showing off her white pearly teeth. She wasn't in the least bit embarrassed by her flamboyant display but revelled in the spotlight, putting on a show as she pirouetted towards me, giggling like a schoolgirl. I humoured her with a clap, she bowed, and then burst out laughing. I mimicked her laughter and was convinced she could tell I was faking.

'Isn't this fun?' she shouted over the hectic music. 'We can do whatever we want. Be whoever we want to be. Live however we choose to live.' She threw her arms up in the air. 'No rules apply tonight. Isn't it liberating?'

She danced and spun and twirled around, and I was giddy watching her. Drunk on her spirit.

'Enjoy yourself, Anna. Be free.' She spun on her toes, around and around she went, flinging herself onto me, almost knocking me backwards. I caught her in my arms.

'I feel dizzy,' she said. Her black vortex-like eyes smiled back at me. Cassandra peeled herself off me and straightened her wild hair with her hands. It had gone frizzy. 'Ahhh, the Givenchy dress. You have great taste.'

'I wasn't sure what I should wear, there were so many choices.' I blushed.

'You carry my mother's essence well.'

'Thank you,' I said, shuddering inside.

'It suits you,' she said, turning on her toes and swaying towards the record player. She turned the volume down. 'Let me pour you a drink.'

On the dining table was an opened bottle of wine. She filled two glasses. We sat down at the table and clinked our glasses together. 'To us,' she said.

'To us.' I took a big gulp to settle my nerves.

'I have a confession to make,' she said, suddenly serious. 'I haven't made us any supper. I'm hopeless at cooking. I hate it. I can just about make eggs.' She flung her head back, laughing like it was the funniest thing ever. She looked like her mum in the photos.

'Don't despair, we have wine!' She held the bottle up. It was almost empty. 'Let's drink and be merry.'

She shook out a Gauloise cigarette from its packet and lit it from the candle flame, offering it to me. Without thinking, I took the cigarette and inhaled the smoke deep into the pit of my stomach. It was acrid with a strong herbal flavour and was unlike any cigarette I'd had before. I didn't care whether it tasted foul. I wanted to experience what she was experiencing. See the world through her eyes, even if it was for a fleeting moment. Her energy was infectious.

'Can I ask you something?' I asked after a few puffs.

'Of course,' she said, turning to face me, her elbows resting on the table as the cigarette dangled from her hand.

'Am I making progress in therapy? Like real progress?'

'Why do you ask?'

'I want to make sure I have a real chance at getting better and I'm not making any mistakes.'

'This will not do!' she snapped.

'Sorry?'

'I forbid you to talk shop. Not tonight. Tonight is about letting go,' she said. A smile crept across her face. She placed the cigarette to her red lips and blew a singular smoke ring into the air in a playful, flirtatious sort of way.

I drank to mask my bumbling nerves, and soon found myself easing into the night and losing my inhibitions, forgetting the fact that I was at my therapist's home on a self-help programme, getting plastered and wearing her dead mother's ballgown. It'd been so long since I'd let my hair down. I missed being free. Reckless.

'Anna. I want us to get to know one another and the best way to do that is to have a little game of Q and A. What do you say?'

'Yes, okay.'

She topped me up, finishing the bottle, and strolled over to the dusty cabinet, fetching another one. 'It's important we have playtime, don't you agree?'

'Yes. I do,' I smiled to myself, not quite believing how the evening was panning out.

'So much depression. On and on and on it continues. Further and further, we descend into the darkness. Sometimes, we need to come up for air, sometimes we need lighter moments.' She uncorked the bottle and poured us both two generous glasses.

If Matt could see me now, dressed in a fancy frock and having the time of my life, feeling very much like a decadent princess. I smiled to myself as I butted the cigarette out.

'Ask me any question you like, and I'll answer as honestly as I can. Go,' she said.

'Okay.' I drank quickly. The wine tasted luxuriously rich. 'What's your favourite colour?'

'Boring. Next question.' Cassandra's smile crinkled her black eyes.

My face flushed. I took another sip. 'How old are you?'

'Boring. Next.' She drank.

'Is there someone special in your life?' I asked, instantly regretting my forward question. I picked up my glass and realised it was empty.

'Now, that's better.' She topped me up. 'There was someone. Someone very special.'

'Was? Is it over?'

She began to play chicken with the candle flame, dipping her hand in and out of the fire. 'Would you like to know something interesting?'

'Yes.'

'He was cheating on me.'

'Wow.' I sat back into the wingback chair. 'Were you heartbroken?'

'I was. For a long while.' She lowered her head and looked up at me. Shadows from the candlelight danced on her face. She looked beautiful, serene, almost vulnerable, suddenly shrouded in a heavy melancholy.

'What an arsehole,' I said.

'Indeed, he was.' She tilted her head up, sat herself upright and within an instant, she looked different. Strong and confident, unaffected by her story of heartache. 'Now, I believe it's my turn to ask the questions. Drink more wine first.'

She offered me another cigarette, but I declined. The wine had quickly gone to my head and I knew that smoking would make matters worse. The last thing I wanted to do was embarrass myself by throwing up in her toilet or passing out in front of her.

'Has your husband contacted you at all?'

'No. He hasn't messaged me.'

'Not once?'

'No.' I hung my head.

'Oh dear.'

Sensing her judgement, I was too afraid to meet her eyes.

'I believe now is the time to stand up for yourself, to tell him it's over. Take that positive step today.'

'I … well …'

'Anna?'

'But that's so final.'

'Haven't you considered leaving him?'

I stared at her face. She looked serious, like she did in session, the childlike woman had evaporated and was replaced by my therapist. I was in session.

'Well … Truth is, I haven't really thought that far ahead,' I mumbled. 'There's been so much going on with other stuff. You know, like my mum and the past and how I'm parenting Joshy. The harming which has flared up again. It's been full on and really hard to focus on what I should *actually* do about Matt.'

'Come on, Anna. Where's my strong independent woman gone?'

'Well …' I was starting to sweat.

'It's a simple formula. You must decide on a course of action in order for things to change.'

'I know.'

'It's lucky you have me to guide you.'

'Thank you. I really appreciate all that you're doing for me.'

'Well, let's do something about your problem, right now.'

'What do you mean?'

'We can make a positive decision today, can't we?'

'We can?' I shuffled in my seat.

'Certainly. Give me your phone.'

I handed it over to her.

'What's the code to your phone?'

'Why?'

'I need to unlock it, silly.'

'Oh. Of course. 151515.'

She tapped the code in, gaining access. 'Let's see.' She started to scroll. 'Anna. Do you trust me?' She looked up, holding my gaze tightly.

'Yes.'

'Great.' She turned her attention to the mobile and fired a message, her nails clicking on the screen as she typed. She handed the phone back to me.

I looked down, staring at the message she'd written, but hadn't sent.

It's over.

'It's as easy as pressing send,' she said, referring to the two words she'd typed.

I swallowed away the sudden sick feeling I had. How would I cope with Joshy on my own?

I needed to trust Cassandra. Had to trust her.

'Anna. It's easy.'

Before I could change my mind, I pressed send.

'Are you okay?'

'I ... I think so,' I said, as tears spilled out of my eyes.

'Don't cry over him. Please don't cry. It's for the best,' She cupped

267

my face in her hands. 'Anna. My darling. This is a good thing. This is a positive step forward.' She wiped my tears.

'I don't know why I'm so weak. I should be happy. He's done nothing but cause me pain.'

'Exactly. Stick with those strong feelings. You knew this was a long time coming but were too afraid to face the music. Now you're on the programme and here with me, you can start to make the right decisions for yourself.'

I looked up.

'You know, I'm so very happy you've come to stay with me,' she said. 'It's wonderful to finally have some company again. It's been so long.'

'I like being here with you.'

'Whoops, looks like we've managed to finish another bottle. Naughty us,' she giggled. She stood up and glided towards the drinks cabinet to retrieve another bottle.

Chapter Forty-Two

My head was throbbing from all the booze we'd sunk, spinning from what went down the night before. On the bedside table was a cup of Chinese herbal tea and a note in spidery handwriting saying, *Drink up. I'm running errands, see you shortly for the first hypnotherapy session of the day. Cassandra.*

Pulling the covers up to my chin, I winced at the thought of how last night had, unexpectedly, panned out. We drank, we laughed, we talked, and we danced around like a couple of schoolgirls. It had been one of the strangest evenings I'd ever had. Ever. I'd been so tightly wound recently, I'd forgotten what it was like to let my hair down – and I worried that maybe I'd let my hair down too much. Had I overstepped the mark?

She was my hypnotherapist after all.

But what of *her* behaviour? She didn't behave like my therapist and was unlike anyone I'd ever encountered before. Last night, she'd become infectious, and I was totally intoxicated by her. Had we both crossed over into the friendship zone? And wasn't that what I wanted? To have a true friend, a confidante.

My mind darted to the text message I'd sent Matt. At some point, I knew I'd have to deal with the aftermath. I pulled myself up to sitting and took a sip of tea to ease the knot in my stomach. It tasted like dishwater and I instantly wanted to spit it back out. Maybe it was the hangover making it taste foul? No matter, I knew I'd only throw up if I drank any more, so I poured it down the sink, cleaning around the bowl afterwards, and took a long shower to clear my head.

I was ravenous and in desperate need of coffee. I changed, then walked down the stairs, the floorboards creaking with every step, towards the kitchen. The house was quiet and the fridge almost empty, with only two eggs, a small carton of semi-skimmed milk and two lonely carrots in the bottom tray. The bread in the breadbin was mouldy.

I wanted to make myself useful, so I cleared up the mess we'd made in the dining room, clearing the ashtrays and throwing away four empty bottles of wine into the recycle bin. I took the front door key from the key box in the hallway and stepped outside into the bright sunny day, stopping by the gates to the basement clinic, looking down the steep steps. I'd never seen any of her other clients before and wondered what type of issues they had.

Did Cassandra form a close bond with all of her clients? Would she be offering the residential programme to anyone else? Would I be replaced in two weeks? My hand gripped the railing, as I stood there for a beat. I swallowed down my flash of jealousy and headed towards the yummy mummy café at the end of the road.

As I stepped off the pavement to cross over, Cassandra's neighbour came steaming round the bend in his vintage Jaguar. He mounted the kerb as he attempted to park his vehicle outside his house, almost running over my toes. He manoeuvred the car backwards and forwards, oblivious to the near miss. Once parked, he flung the door open and gripped the edges of the car, hauling himself out. He waddled up his external concrete steps towards his front door, carrying a Waitrose shopping bag. I watched half in shock, half in amusement.

'Hello, sir,' I said, loudly.

'You be careful with that one,' he said without turning to face me. He fumbled with a set of keys which were attached on a long chain to his high waisted brown trousers. 'You be careful.' He opened his door and shuffled inside.

I could hear the locks of his front door, turning, one by one.

'Okay. Have a nice day,' I said, shaking my head and walking off in disbelief.

Fuelled with take-away coffee and a salmon and cream cheese bagel, I decided to stop in the park next to the house. It was the perfect summer day, warm and breezy. I found an empty bench in the shade under a tree and watched the cute toddlers and their nannies in the playground. I missed Joshy.

My mind moved onto Matt and the text. I couldn't delay the inevitable any longer. It was time to check whether he'd replied. I took my mobile from my back pocket and switched it on. The apple icon burst into life. I tapped in the code. The phone shook as the six-digit code was rejected. Access denied. Incorrect code. I tried again, but the same thing happened. I couldn't understand it.

It had got messy towards the end of the night, maybe I'd changed the code and couldn't remember? I'd have to ask Cassandra, see if she knew. I walked back to the house, puzzled.

Cassandra was standing on her doorstep with her hands on her hips. As I walked up the steps towards her, she turned on her heels, leaving the front door ajar. She was rigid. Cold. Nothing like how she was the night before. There was immediate tension in the air. I followed her through the house and into the kitchen, in silence. What had changed?

She sparked up a cigarette, leant up on the counter and closed her eyes, inhaling slowly and deeply. 'Where were you?'

'I assumed you were working, and I was hungry, so I decided to go to the café. I didn't think it would be a problem. Did … did you want a sandwich too?' I said, standing at the foot of the kitchen door. 'I can go back and grab you something if you're hungry. It's not a problem.'

She stared wide-eyed, unblinking, her black eyes penetrating right through me, making me shiver.

'Cassandra. Is everything okay?'

'No. Not exactly.' She blew smoke my way.

The smoke filtered into my lungs and I started coughing.

'Can I have my keys back?' She held out her hand.

Stepping into the kitchen, I handed over the set with my suddenly shaky hand.

'Did you drink your tea?' she said, unblinking.

Slowly inching back, one foot at a time, fiddling with my phone in my hands, I said, 'I'm so sorry. I didn't mean to disrespect you. I was really hungover, sick from all the alcohol and lack of food. I'll drink the herbs now. I promise. I was going to suggest it, anyway.'

'I think we need to talk. Please take a seat,' she said, business-like, clasping her hands together.

I pulled up a chair and it scraped along the floor. The noise grated, breaking the stillness. I took my seat, placing my mobile on the table away from me so I wouldn't be tempted to fidget.

'I'm sorry I have to do this to you, but I think I have to be firmer from now on.' She sucked on her cigarette. 'Anna. I'm afraid I'm going to have to insist on no contact with the outside world. Not until we see positive results. That means no walks, no outside time whatsoever, and certainly no phone calls or messages.'

My hand reached for my mobile.

'I think it's best you hand me your phone.'

My finger tapped the phone for a few seconds, staring at Cassandra, trying to read her expression. She was deadly serious. Swallowing down the lump stuck in my throat, I stood up and gave it to her.

'I have to do what's best for you,' she said, her voice softening, her features mellowing.

'It's not working. The phone. It locked me out this morning,' I mumbled.

She placed it on the counter, next to the set of keys. 'I took the liberty and changed the code myself. I anticipated that you'd falter,' she smiled. 'I hope you don't mind, but I must insist on showing no signs of weakness when it comes to your husband. A positive decision was made last night, and we cannot possibly back track. Not now. Not ever.'

What if he messaged begging for forgiveness, pleading for me to come home? What if he wanted to prove to me that he could change, he *would* change? None of that was ever going to happen now, because I wasn't going to give him the chance.

It was actually OVER. I bit down hard on my lip to stop the tears from spilling out. I was not prepared for this.

'Do you not agree?'

I looked away.

'You wanted to be more assertive.'

'I know …'

'I'm helping you, Anna. Remember that. You must stick to the positive decisions you make and move forwards,' she said.

'Okay. I'll try,' I said. 'I'll try.'

'Don't look so deflated. Remember, he's been cheating on you.'

I picked at my annoying false nails.

'Let Matt go. Let him go,' she said, 'so you can move on and deal with the more pressing issues in your life.'

'But how will I cope on my own, without Matt?' My lips quivered.

'You're not alone, my dear. You have me. And after this programme is through, you'll be strong enough to take care of the situation yourself.' She turned away, placed the kettle onto the hob and stubbed her cigarette out in the cactus plant. 'You have my word.'

My tense shoulders relaxed. I breathed. She was right. I had two weeks to get better before I had to face the music. I'd be in a better head space to deal with it all then.

'Now for some tea,' she said, satisfied.

She dropped two bits of bark, which looked like cinnamon sticks, into a tall mug, added a teaspoon of something white from a small decorative jar which she retrieved from a cupboard above the sink, and opened a Ziploc bag with Chinese writing on it. Using a measuring cup, she fished one heaped cup of brown powder from the Ziploc bag into the mug, mixing it all in with boiling water. She stirred the concoction with a long silver spoon which had lost its shine. 'Here you go.' She placed the drink on the table in front of me.

The mixture had dissolved, apart from the woody bits, which were floating around. I sipped my tea while she smoked yet another cigarette and spoke enthusiastically about the next phase of the therapy programme. I drank and stayed quiet, listening to her talk.

After a while, her sentences started to sound weird and fragmented. It was hard to grasp what was being said. I finished my drink quickly, hoping it would make me feel better. Heat radiated from the back of my eyes. My brow was sweaty and my body clammy.

'I think I need to lie down on my bed for a while. I'm a little spaced.'

'Oh dear. Why don't you rest your head on the table, Anna? That might help.'

A profound drowsiness took a hold of me. Swishing sensations inside my head came and went, like waves lapping the shore. Cassandra peeled my head up off the table and helped me upright.

My eyes opened and closed. Opened and closed. I couldn't fight the sleep.

'You're in the perfect suggestible state of mind right now,' she said, closing the lids to my eyes with her long index finger. 'Perfect state for therapy. Just perfect. That's right, Anna. Let sleep consume you. Allow the trance state to take over. Go deeper and deeper within yourself.'

My head lolled, swaying to the motion of the sea.

'Anna. Take me back to your mother's flat, so we can continue with our good work.'

Chapter Forty-Three

'Are you there?' Cassandra asked.

'Yes. I'm inside the flat.' The skates were discarded on the landing and muddy skate tracks had dirtied the carpet. Prince played on the radio. Loud noises bellowed from downstairs. My heartbeat quickened. 'There are people downstairs, in Mary's bedroom.'

'Who are they, Anna?'

'I don't want to look.'

'What is it you refuse to see? Uncover the truth. Don't delay,' she said in her melodic lullaby voice. 'Do it today.'

I had to progress. Get better. I had to go downstairs, confront my demons and make Cassandra happy.

'Make me happy,' she said, reading my thoughts.

We were in sync. It was telepathy.

I walked down the stairs, in our upside down flat, towards Mary's bedroom, each footstep heavily weighted with a sense of doom. The closer I got to the bottom step, the more I wanted to turn around and run. Run as fast as I could. The closer I got, the louder the alarming noises became, until it was ringing in my ears and was all I could hear. It was deafening.

Crying. Yelling. Cheering.

Standing outside Mary's bedroom, trembling with fear, I pushed the door open. Standing in the doorway, I scrunched my eyes tightly shut and covered my ears with my hands. Desperate to stop the noise from entering my head and the images from imprinting on my brain.

However, every vibration had already been learnt off by heart. Every sordid disgusting detail had embedded itself inside of me. It had always been there. I'd always known the truth but was too scared to face it. I'd always known.

Peeling my trembling young hands away from my face, I flung my eyes wide open.

I had no choice. I had to see. *Make Cassandra happy.*

It took a while to digest the scene that was in front of me.

Mum was on the bed, naked. Beaten and bruised. Her right eye swollen. There were three men in the room with her. One sat on the dressing table stool, topless, another man cheered as he pulled his trousers up, buckling his belt, and the last man was on top of her, naked, savaging her. His clothes discarded on the floor.

The smell of violence and sex was overwhelming, filling my mouth and making me gag. Pungent and revolting.

The room was pulsing. Raging. Alive with a wild brutality.

Condensation ran from the window. My eyes wandered from the window to the wardrobe. I fixed my gaze at the ridiculous stacks of toilet paper she'd bought from the market piled up high on top of the wardrobe. Why did we need so many loo rolls?

The men didn't notice me standing there at first, but Mum did. She faced me, horror reflecting from her eyes. 'Help me,' she mouthed.

'I'm gonna fucking finish her off,' the man on top of her said.

'Dirty bitch. She loves it,' said the one standing over them both.

The topless man on the seat next to the dressing table, turned to look me square in the eye and whispered, 'You're next, beautiful.' He licked his lips in a vile, disgusting way.

Frozen to the spot, I stared vacantly for a moment as a trickle of pee escaped, wetting my knickers and blue striped shorts.

'Get help, Anna,' Mary screamed. 'GET HELP!'

The man standing nearest to me, spun around to face me.

Get help, Anna. I ran as fast as my legs could take me, out of the flat, down the concrete stairs of the tower block littered with trash, bypassing the smelly lift, straight to ground level. I didn't stop running until I reached the playground.

I sat on the swing, trembling with fear, waiting for my mum to call my name from the window, like she always did. It was fish finger Friday and she'd be calling me any minute.

Backwards and forwards I went, swinging like a pendulum, waiting for her to call. I stood on the swing and worked it with my legs until I was tired and had to sit back down. The other kids in the playground called me names: homeless, loser, creep, no shoes. But I just ignored them, waiting for Mary's call. Any minute she'd stick her head out of the window and shout, *dinner is ready, girl.*

I waited, and I swung, and I waited, and I waited, and I swung.

The kids got bored with the teasing and left. Everyone had left.

The estate became quiet under the gulf of the black sky.

That night, she never made it to the window.

Chapter Forty-Four

Opening my eyes, I burst into uncontrollable floods of tears. All those years I'd suppressed that memory. All those years I'd trapped that incident in the back of my mind. I should have helped Mary. I could have helped Mary. Why did I choose to do nothing? The burden pressed on my chest, crushing my ribcage, squeezing the air out of me. I found myself mentally falling, tumbling into a black hole, unable to get out. Swamped by the uncovered memory. Swamped by my guilt.

All I could see were the men's faces staring back at me. All I could hear was Mary's cries for help. All I could smell was the pungent act of violence thick in the air.

I wanted to bury the memory back down. Bury it. Bury it for good.

I was only a girl. I was only a girl. I didn't know any better.

With my head cradled in my hands, I sobbed like a baby, crying for the scared little girl I once was and crying for Mary. I cried for the lack of relationship I had with my mum, I cried for what could have been and what was. I cried for her pain and for her abuse, and I cried for mine. No child should have seen what I saw. No child should have been put in that impossible situation.

I continued to sob until there were no more tears left and I'd flatlined.

My heart ached and my face was numbed. My lungs emptied of air.

The room fell silent apart from a faint noise I recognised. I looked up, as though waking from a bad dream, taking in my surroundings. I was in the kitchen. The noise was coming from the rattly boiler. Cassandra was sitting next to me, looking concerned. Her big black eyes, dilated. A sea of black. Endless black.

'Anna?' She placed her hand on mine.

My skin prickled.

'Are you okay? Here, please take a tissue.'

She pushed her chair out. The noise was unbearable. Painful. Pins in my skull. She walked over to the counter and tore kitchen paper from the roll holder and handed it to me. I wiped my eyes, my face, and then crumpled the tissue in my hand, squeezing tightly.

'This is a positive step forward. We're finally unlocking the truth. The trigger,' she said, walking back to the counter and sparking up a cigarette. The room filled with dense smoke. 'This is only the beginning. There is so much more to do,' she said. 'So much more.'

My body ached. Burnt.

I dropped the tissue and held my hands out in front of my eyes. They were trembling. My ears were ringing. She continued to talk, but I only caught soundbites of what was being said.

'Your mother went through a terrible ordeal.'

It was impossible to concentrate.

'Do you feel you could have done more to help?' she asked.

'What?' I said, shaking.

'Anna?'

Dizziness came and went. The room refused to stop spinning. I rested my clammy head on the table. Some kind of fever or sickness was trickling its way into my system, through my veins.

'Is everything okay?'

'I was just a kid. I didn't know any better. I ...' I wanted to say more, to explain to her, but somehow, I couldn't form the words on my cracked lips.

'Do you think she blamed you?' she asked.

I attempted to lift my head up, but it was too heavy and collapsed back down. 'I was just a kid,' I slurred, disorientated.

'Anna? Can you hear me?'

She lifted my head up and touched my forehead. The cigarette made my eyes sting and water. 'Oh, my goodness. You're burning up.'

I looked up at her.

'Help me ...'

Her eyes were black, black, and I was drowning in them. Drowning.

'Let me help you to your room.'

She butted her cigarette out in the ashtray on the table and lifted me off the chair with ease. I put my arm around her shoulder for support. My legs were weak and about to give way. The room spun violently around me. She walked me along the oppressive corridor, carrying all my weight, and helped me up the stairs, one step at a time, to my bedroom.

Chapter Forty-Five

We were in the playground, the one next to Cassandra's house, and I was pushing Joshy on the swing. He was ebbing back and forth, gaining momentum. Way up high and way down low he swung. He let out a belly laugh as his little bottom lifted off the blue plastic seat when he reached dizzying heights. 'Look at me now,' he giggled.

His laughter was contagious and made me laugh too and suddenly I felt lighter, free. The burden lessened. Happier than I'd felt in months. 'You want to go higher?'

'Yes.'

'Higher?' I laughed, as I pushed.

A familiar voice boomed from behind me. 'Anna. Get yourself over here, girl. Your dinner's ready!'

All the hairs on the back of my neck stood on end. I stopped pushing the swing and turned my body, too afraid to look. 'Mary?'

There was no one there.

I turned to face Joshy. The swing swayed solo. He'd vanished. My eyes darted around the playground. The slide, empty. The climbing frame, empty. The roundabout, empty. There were no children anywhere and Joshy was nowhere in sight. I was alone in the playground.

Cassandra entered through the yellow gates, leaving muddy footprints on the path. She was barefoot, wearing a turquoise kaftan.

'I've lost Joshy. Have you seen him?' I wailed. 'Have you seen him?' I grabbed her by the scruff and shook her. 'HAVE YOU SEEN HIM?'

Her face remained neutral. Controlled.

Had someone snatched him? Had Mary taken him? Matt? Rosita?

'Anna. Stop your fussing, girl,' Cassandra said.

I woke, gasping for breath. I'd perspired so much, a pool of sweat rested on my chest. My nightie was drenched, and the sheets were clammy, sticky. I kicked them off and pulled myself up to sitting, resting my head against the soft headboard. My body ached, my breasts were swollen and sensitive to touch, and tears had gathered in my eyes.

'Good morning, sleepy head.'

I jumped at the sound of her voice.

Cassandra was sitting at the end of the bed, looking poised and pristine. Swallowing down my tears, I smiled at her. A cup and saucer rested on her lap. Judging by the smell, it was the Chinese herbs. My tummy turned.

'Are you okay?' There was a tender quality to her voice.

'I had a nightmare.'

'I could tell. You were restless. You've been running a fever.'

'Fever?'

'Yes. I fear your sickness may be psychosomatic.'

'I don't understand,' I said.

'Your body is in shock, caused by the trauma you've unlocked.'

'How long have I been asleep for?'

'Anna, my dear. You've been sleeping solidly for 24 hours.'

'Oh my God. How sick was I?'

'Very. It's quite extraordinary to see how rapidly your sickness has come on.'

283

'Will I start to see progress now that we know what happened to me?' I asked, trying to steady my voice.

'Unfortunately, it's too early to tell. How do you feel about your discovery?'

'I don't know what to make of it all.'

She placed the cup on the side table and shuffled closer. 'You're still in shock.'

'But ... shouldn't I be feeling ... something? Be lighter, somehow? You said I'd feel differently once I'd discovered the truth, less burdened. The trigger. Wasn't that the trigger?'

Cassandra picked at an imaginary thread on her trouser leg.

'Do you think I should be doing more as your therapist?' she whispered, locking eyes with me and holding me there.

'No. No.' I reached my arm out to her and then retracted back. 'No. I'm sorry. It's not what I meant.'

She looked away. I'd upset her. Me and my stupid mouth.

'Now we've discovered the truth, we need to work out why you buried this trauma, choosing to self-harm as your coping mechanism.' She paused. 'Of course, if you're dissatisfied with the progress and think you should be cured by now ...'

'No ...' I butted in.

'Maybe you'd like to be referred on to someone else. Perhaps you have qualms about the programme I specifically tailored for your needs?'

'No. Please. Don't do that,' I said. 'I need this programme. I want to do this. You've made me feel so welcome, you really have, and you've helped me so much. I need you now, more than ever. Especially since I've uncovered what happened. I'm sorry, I'm not thinking straight.'

'I believed we'd made a real connection the other night,' she looked at me, hurt.

'We did. We have. I couldn't be more grateful for what you've done for me, taking me into your home and helping me out like this. All that you're continuing to do for me.'

'I need to know you have faith in me and trust me. You must trust the programme, because if you don't, then all this work we're doing will be for nothing. Hypnosis can *only* be beneficial when the participant has faith and believes.'

'I know. I know. Of course, I trust you, and I trust the programme. I'm sorry.' God, I hated the word, sorry. 'Look, it's me. Not you. I'm sick.'

'It's best you rest up. Regain your strength,' she said, leaning in and touching my forehead. 'You're still hot. I'll fetch a wet flannel from the bathroom.'

She rushed to the bathroom and came back with a damp cloth, dabbing my forehead. She lifted my sleeves to cool my arms down. The cold gave me goosebumps. She placed the flannel on the bedside table.

Here she was, nursing me back to health, taking the time to sift through all the issues from my crappy childhood, and I was asking her why I wasn't getting better fast enough, like some ungrateful spoilt child, like somehow, it was all her fault!

I shuffled my weight around. 'I'm sure I'll feel better if I take a shower and clear my head. Can you help me up? I'm feeling weak.'

'Rest. Drink your tea and let it work its magic. Surrender yourself to the situation. You'll be up and about before you know it. Trust me. I know what I'm doing.' She pushed me back down. 'You need time to rest and heal. Rest and heal, Anna.'

I could shower later.

Chapter Forty-Six

My sickness carried on longer than I'd expected, and with it came a sort of delirium. Long days and nights stretched and expanded around me, and I was lost somewhere inside. I didn't recall ever having been that sick before, not since I'd had a high fever when I was twelve with whooping cough.

I stripped off my nightgown and stared at my reflection in the small mirror above the sink in the en suite. My hair was plastered to my head, my eyes were sunken despite all the sleeping, and my skin was ghostly pale. My mouth was furry and tasted like the gutter. I hadn't brushed my teeth in days and my false nails had come off somehow.

I tried to remember the dreams I'd had during my illness, but it was impossible to pinpoint specifics. They all merged into one continuous nightmare, Mary morphing into Cassandra morphing into Matt. Joshy missing. The playground. The flat.

I brushed my teeth and tongue vigorously, and took a long shower, washing away the remnants of the illness and brain fog. Changing into a fresh pair of jeans and t-shirt, I went downstairs to find Cassandra.

The radio was playing jazz in the kitchen. Cassandra sat by the pine table, smoking a cigarette and drinking coffee. The newspaper was sprawled open. Scrambled eggs and avocado with toast were plated up on the table, alongside a steaming cup of Chinese tea.

It was Sunday.

I was starving and couldn't recall the last time I'd eaten. Using a fork and my fingers to scoop, I gobbled up all the food. She was still holding back on the knives. Harming hadn't even occurred to me, so I guess her therapy was working on a deeper level that I didn't understand.

Even though over the past few days I had felt as though I'd fallen into a void and was never coming out, I took solace in the fact that she'd mentioned the first week of the programme was really tough. It was now week two, and I knew I'd start to feel better. Things would improve, especially since I'd uncovered my buried trauma – the trigger.

'It's good to see your appetite return.'

'Thank you, this is exactly what I need,' I said, finishing my plate of food.

'Drink your tea. It'll help.'

'What's in this? It tastes like mud,' I half-smiled, cautious not to offend.

'It's supposed to taste bitter. Like I said, it may cause some drowsiness, but that's to be expected.'

That was an understatement, I'd never wanted to sleep so much in my entire life.

She stubbed out her cigarette, stood up, brushed herself down and walked towards the counter, producing a hairbrush from a drawer. She returned, standing behind me.

'Do you mind?'

Her breath danced on the back of my neck, making my skin tingle. 'No,' I whispered.

She started to brush my wet hair away from my face. The tender strokes made my body rush. She smelt of lavender perfume and herbal cigarettes.

'I thought this might help,' she said, brush stroking my hair. 'Perhaps, if I adopt the role of your mother, you'll be able to open up more.'

'Okay.' I breathed out, melting into the chair.

'Close your eyes, relax. Imagine I'm Mary standing behind you, brushing your hair before school. Can you do that for me?' The brush lightly touched my scalp.

Nostalgic tears welled up in my eyes as I was taken back to the kitchen in Mum's flat. The radio played in the background, the traffic noise from Rossmore Road filtered through the flimsy window and Pebbles munched noisily from the cat bowl. I eased my head back into Cassandra's tummy, allowing the experience to engulf me. I could feel her heart beating, a rhythmic hypnotic drum. One two. One two. One two.

'If this makes you uncomfortable in any way, you must say.'

'No. It's nice,' I said, keeping my eyes shut. 'Comforting.'

'Anna. Use this opportunity to speak to Mary, tell her what you're thinking, how you're feeling. What would you say to your mother right now?'

'I ...'

'It's okay, Anna. Speak to me.'

'I miss you.'

'What else do you want to say?' she said, tenderly.

My head lulled. The brush strokes were sending me into a state of light hypnosis. I thought back to that awful day and the ordeal she'd endured. The pain, the horror.

'Is it all my fault?' I asked. My voice quivering.

Mary didn't respond.

'Should I have got help?' I could taste a thick coating of mud in the back of my throat. My face was wet with tears. 'Is that why you don't love me?'

The boiler burst into life and started rattling. She stopped brushing. Mary disappeared. I sensed Cassandra stepping away from me. The throb of her heartbeat faded, her breath no longer tickling my neck. Her perfume and cigarette scent evaporated into the air.

'You're riddled with guilt,' she said.

I opened my eyes and turned to face Cassandra. She was standing by the counter.

'You believe you failed your mother.' She placed the brush on the kitchen worktop. 'This is the root cause to all your problems.'

I hid my hands under the table and squeezed tightly.

'You need to learn to forgive yourself,' she said, walking towards me and pulling up a chair.

'Maybe I could speak to her? For real. What do you think?'

Cassandra sat upright.

I was ready to speak to Mary. I uncurled my fists and cleared my throat. 'It doesn't have to be a long phone call. I just want to tell her I've been thinking about her, that I miss her. Try and make amends before she dies. I think I'm ready. It might be the only chance I get.'

Cassandra stared at me with a blank expression on her face.

'Or maybe I could send a text message?'

'Oh Anna, Anna,' she said, shaking her head. 'Haven't you learnt anything?'

'Just one message. To let her know I'm thinking of her and am ready to talk when she is. That's all I'd have to say. And you can take my phone off me, straight after. I think it could help with my recovery, you know, with the guilt and stuff.' I scraped my hands along my jeans.

'It wouldn't be beneficial for you to make contact. Even a message could set you back.'

I stared at her, pleading with my eyes, praying she'd let me.

'It's not a good idea.'

'But why?'

She sighed loudly, like the way I'd sigh at Joshy for bombarding me with questions. How I missed the way he'd ramble on and on about the Gruffalo.

'Hypothetically speaking, let's imagine you messaged her to say you were thinking about her. What would happen next, hmm?'

'I suppose it would be an olive branch. Maybe it would make me feel better?' My chin trembled.

'Or it could make you feel worse.'

'How?'

'Annabelle. It's not a little role-playing exercise which you and I can control. It's real life. It's unpredictable. Your mother is unpredictable. She may respond negatively.'

'You don't know that for sure.'

'You're expecting a certain response from her. Yes? You're probably seeking validation from her. Reassurance. For her to tell you that she loves you, that she's always loved you. That it's all going to be okay. But let me ask you this. What's going to happen if she responds aggressively towards you? Responds with anger and bitterness? What if she's been harbouring bad feelings towards you for what you did to her when you were younger? Or she could be angry towards you because you haven't made contact with her since she fell ill. What if she wants an explanation from you and wants answers for herself? What if she feels abandoned by you, her only daughter? Feels crushed that you haven't returned any of her calls. What then?' she said. 'Let me ask you this, what happens if she doesn't respond at all?'

Every word she said was a hard blow to the stomach. I stared at the scene outside the window, chewing on my thumbnail.

'I don't believe you're ready for contact. You're not strong enough. Not yet. I cannot run the risk of your state of mind worsening.'

'Okay,' I said, swallowing back down the grief I felt. 'I understand. You're right.'

Chapter Forty-Seven

Cassandra placed her Montblanc pen on the coffee table and tore a sheet of paper out of the leather notebook, handing it over to me. 'I thought it would be beneficial to share my thoughts.'

I pulled myself up to sitting, taking the notes from her hand. We were in the art studio and I was still in my nightie, deeply disorientated after another heavy hypnosis session. I'd no idea how long I'd been under for, but judging by my stiff body and neck, it had been a while.

'It's a breakdown of what's happening to you,' she said, matter-of-factly. 'You can judge for yourself the progress you're making.'

Cassandra sat in her usual spot opposite, looking as sharp as her suit, her olive skin radiant, her eyebrows immaculately arched, her lips painted red, matching her fingernails. She leant over the coffee table, took her Gauloises packet and shook a cigarette out. 'Go ahead. Read it,' she said in a satisfactory sort of way, sparking up and leaning back into the chair, crossing one leg over the other. She was wearing her Louboutins. She hadn't worn them in a while. She blew a singular smoke ring into the room.

My body fizzed with anticipation as I looked down at the piece of paper in my hand. She was granting me access to her notes.

Finally, I was able to find out what she really thought of me and my situation.

Finally, she was unveiling her secrets.

The page was filled with diagrams, doodles and spidery, child-like handwriting. Framing the page, like a border, were sketches of smudged eyes and artistic doodles of swirls and patterns. Sentences were circled inside bubbles with arrows pointing to other sentences inside more bubbles, and at the centre was my name, Anna, circled again and again. It reminded me of the mind mapping exercises we used to do in English class, when we had to plan an essay. A spidergram, my teacher called it. This time, I was the subject matter.

Clinical Notes

Anna.

Self-harming stems from deep rooted feelings of shame. Guilt is the trigger.

Could Anna have done more to help her mother?

Anna has learnt to deal with mental pain by burying it and swapping it for physical pain which offers her release.

Self-mutilation, pleasurable – brain secretes endorphins into the nervous system.

Anna resistant to full recovery.

Subconsciously wants to continue learnt negative behaviour.

Destructive habits WILL continue.

Unaware of real danger to her own life and that of others, such as her son.

Must protect Anna from herself until full recovery.

Anna is currently too unwell to live a stable and independent life.

Rid of guilt. Rid of negative habits. Rid of ALL negative relationships.

Must increase daily sessions. Must push Anna to work longer, harder, deeper.

The room was stagnant, stuffy, like a sauna. My skin prickled and sweat dripped down my spine. The notes were held tightly in my grip. The glistening eyes on the ceiling stared, waiting for a reaction. Cassandra stared, waiting for a reaction.

The world shifted as I forced myself to stand. My toes curled as everything around me started to spin furiously. I resisted the urge to lie flat on the floor and feel the earth beneath my body. I had a deep longing to be outside amongst the trees, smelling the woodland, feeling the crunch from the twigs beneath the soles of my feet. I searched my mind for a smidgen of hope, something I could grasp onto.

For some reason *The Gruffalo* came to mind. The words of the book had been engraved in my head, having read it so often to Joshy. But for some reason, however hard I tried to conjure up the words, I couldn't remember them. *I couldn't remember them*!

My heart fluttered wildly, my body began to shake and there was a high-pitched ringing inside my ears.

Maybe I hadn't forgotten the words at all. Maybe, just maybe, I'd never known the words to the book in the first place. Maybe it was all an illusion and I'd never read to Joshy at night. Maybe it wasn't me, but Rosita. She knew the words. Not me.

Rosita knew the words!

'Don't despair. It's all fixable,' she said, blowing smoke into the airless stale room.

'Is it?' I said, my body swaying gently backwards and forwards.

'Everything is reversible.' She re-crossed her legs. 'Anna. Don't worry.'

'I can't remember.'

'Excuse me?'

'I can't remember the words. The words to *The Gruffalo*.'

'Anna? Would you like to lie back down on the chaise?'

'No. No. I'm fine,' I sniffed, ironing down the creases to the paper and flattening it out. 'I'm sorry. I shouldn't have …' My hands trembled.

'That's quite alright.' Cassandra stubbed out her cigarette. She'd left a red imprint of her lipstick on the filter. 'Why don't you take the rest of the day off? Take the notes to your room. Today's session has now terminated.'

'Okay,' I said, quivering.

'But first, let me make you tea.' Cassandra stood up, brushed her skirt down and started for the door. A strong tobacco and lavender scent lingered after her. 'Are you coming?' she asked, looking back at me, smiling.

Chapter Forty-Eight

Menstrual pains woke me up. It'd been ages since I'd suffered cramps that bad. My breasts were swollen and hurt like crazy. I switched the frilly bedside lamp on, and it cast shadows across the room. Stumbling out of bed, I tiptoed down the stairs as quietly as I possibly could in search of painkillers.

Light and smoke escaped from under the gap of the door to her mother's studio. I stood in the hallway, holding my breath, suppressing the urge to cough out loud. She didn't like me wandering the house alone. I inched away.

'I know you're there,' she said from beyond the door, her voice clipped.

Padding toward the studio, I opened the door, peering inside. She sat at her mother's desk with her back to the door, her head slumped. Dozens of candles lit up the room, making the ornamental eyes that hung from the ceiling glisten in the ambient glow. Cassandra was examining a photograph in her hand. More photos were scattered on the desk. A cigarette burnt in the ashtray.

'What do you want?' She swivelled her chair around to face me. Her eyes sparkled like black marbles. Her mascara had smudged, and her hair was unkept, messy.

'Have you … have you been crying?' I stuttered.

Long shadows danced around the floor and on her face.

'Would you care if I had?'

What was left of my fingernails bit into the palms of my hands. 'Of course, I care.'

'You pretend to care, but I know you don't, not deep down,' she said, placing the photo she'd been looking at face down on the desk next to what looked like my mobile.

'I've grown to care about you,' I whispered, taking a step closer into the room.

'Huh!' she spat, crossing one leg over the other and rocking her foot up and down. 'Anna, I'd like to share a secret with you.'

'Okay,' I said, feeling unsure.

'We're connected, you and I, like mother and child. I feel things you feel, hear things you hear, see things you see. I know you inside out, better than you know yourself. You can't hide anything from me,' she paused for a moment. 'So, don't *ever* lie to me.'

'You're freaking me out.'

'Why is that?'

Next to the ashtray was a bottle of wine and an empty glass.

'I know there's something playing on your mind,' she said, sucking on her cigarette.

'Well, there is … it's just … I thought I'd be a lot better by now, not worse.'

'I see.'

'I'm starting to worry about my recovery and I'm wondering why it's taking longer than expected. And, well … I'm starting to miss home …'

'You want to go back to him?' she hissed, smoke escaping her mouth, her foot bouncing around frantically, her eyes wild.

'I miss Joshy.' My voice trembled. 'And I miss …' I stopped myself from saying, *my life*, *my freedom*. I missed being able to walk out the front door. All the things I took for granted. I missed Joshy so much it physically hurt. I missed Mary, I desperately wanted to speak to her before she passed, and, of course, there was Matt. I still didn't know how I really felt about the text I'd sent him. Was it really over between us?

'You *do* want to go back home, to him, back to being downtrodden and controlled, where the only escape route is self-harm.'

'It's not what I meant,' I said, my voice barely audible.

'Hmmm,' said Cassandra.

'I want to be stronger, more independent. Really, I do,' I said, inching into the room one unsteady foot at a time. 'I know my progress is slow. Slower than we'd hoped. If you just tell me where I'm going wrong maybe I can fix things and it'll speed things up for me.'

'You must let go, Anna. Submit to me.'

'But I have. I'm doing everything you asked me to.'

'I'm sensing resistance.'

'I've been trying my best. I don't know what more I can do.'

'Anna. I'm afraid it's much worse than you think.'

I stared wide-eyed, mouth agape.

'We have a predicament on our hands.'

'What do you mean?' I took another step into the room.

'Your two weeks is up. The programme has officially ended.'

I flinched. My legs were about to buckle.

Two weeks. It had been the marker we were working towards. Two weeks. I was supposed to be better by now, not worse. Two weeks. The therapy was throwing up problems quicker than it was solving them. Two weeks. The thought of going home so messed up horrified me.

What would Matt think if he saw me in such a state?

She scrunched her cigarette into the ashtray. 'With your permission, I'd like to extend the programme a while longer.'

'What about Joshy?'

'Are you well enough to take care of him on your own?'

My heart ached. I rubbed my neck with my trembling hand.

'We must work harder. Starting from tomorrow. A fresh start. Let's make the next week count.'

'Okay,' I said, blinking away my desperate tears. It was a total fucking disaster. 'One more week.'

I stepped closer, craving warmth and comfort, wanting reassurance, needing hope.

'Please don't come any further,' she said flatly, gathering the pictures up into a pile.

'I'll just get paracetamol for my period pains and then head back to bed.' I turned around, heading towards the door with tears streaming down my face.

'Wait,' she said.

Hopeful, I quickly spun around to face her, wiping my wet face.

'You don't know where they're kept,' she said, standing up and brushing her messy hair down with her hands. She walked around the room, snuffing the candles with her fingers, until the room turned pitch black. 'Let's get those painkillers, shall we?'

I followed her into the kitchen. She fetched the paracetamol from the cupboard where the components of the herbal tea were kept and handed me two pills.

Chapter Forty-Nine

She was in the kitchen reading the Sunday newspaper. Jazz played on the radio and fresh coffee wafted from the pot. For the first time since I'd arrived, I'd experienced full blown insomnia and I was really groggy from lack of sleep. I'd spent the night stressed out of my head. An avalanche of thoughts crashed my mind, keeping me awake.

There was something I had to tell her. It wasn't going to be easy.

'You're still in your nightgown,' she said, looking up from the paper, a cigarette in one hand, a coffee cup in the other.

'I didn't ...' The smoke in the room made me feel sick. 'I just ...'

'Never mind that. Hope you're hungry,' she said. 'Come and sit down.'

I took my seat. In front of me was a plate of avocado and eggs, a knife and fork. My stomach filled with acid. 'Thank you for giving me a knife,' I said.

'That's quite alright. It's another positive step forward.'

I smiled. 'Look, about last night, when I walked in on you. Were you okay? It looked like you'd been crying.' I stared at the plate of food.

She leant her elbow on the table, her cigarette dangled in her hand, inches from my face. My eyes, which were already gritty from the lack of sleep and excessive crying, stung bad and began to water.

'I'm sorry, I shouldn't be prying,' I said, pulling my head back.

She dragged on her cigarette and blew the smoke in my direction. 'That's quite alright. You're coming from a good place. I know you're concerned for my well-being. Let me assure you there's nothing to worry about.'

My body tensed. I placed the utensils down on my plate and took a deep breath in. 'Cassandra, I have to tell you something.'

'Oh?' She sat back, removed her hand from the table and folded the newspaper.

'Well. I'm not sure. Not sure at all,' I said. 'I could be wrong, but I don't think I am. It's just that …' I fiddled with my necklace.

'Well?' she asked, looking at the clock. 'Come on. Don't be shy.'

There was no way out of it. She had to know. 'I have a sneaky suspicion I may be pregnant,' I blurted, before I could chicken out.

'Pregnant?' she said, curtly.

'I know,' I hung my head.

She stood up, walked over to the sink and ran her cigarette under the tap, keeping her back turned. 'I see,' she said, her voice clipped.

'I don't know what to say.'

'Are you certain?'

'Pretty sure. I haven't had a period for six, or maybe seven, weeks – and even then, when I did come on, it was light, lasting only a couple of days. I have the same symptoms as before. My breasts are swollen and I'm getting strange cramps. It was the same sort of pain when I fell pregnant with Joshy. I thought it was period pains back then too, but it wasn't, it was the uterus stretching out. Expanding, apparently, something like that anyway. Someone told me once, I can't remember who.' I stared at my unappealing food. 'I'm also feeling nauseated.'

She spun round to face me. Her features pinched.

'Have you finished?' She walked towards me and snatched the

plate without waiting for a reply, returning to the sink and dumping the whole lot in, including the food. It made a loud crashing sound, making me jump. I wondered whether she'd smashed the crockery.

'I'm sorry. I don't know how this happened,' I said, my head thumping from the hectic music coming from the radio and my jumbled thoughts.

'Would you like me to explain how one gets pregnant?' Her back was still turned.

I burst into tears.

'This should not jeopardise our work,' she said, after a beat.

I looked up, sucking in my tears.

She swirled around, took another cigarette and sparked up. 'We'll get you a pregnancy test to make absolutely certain. In the meantime, we shall put this little hiccup of yours to the backs of our minds and continue as we are. We will have to work much harder. Stronger. Deeper. More vigorously. Are you in agreement?'

'Shouldn't I visit the doctor? I think I need a check-up.'

'You want to end the programme, now? Now we're so close? Now that you've agreed to extend it for another week? It seems you need this programme more than ever.'

'But I'm not feeling great at the moment. I haven't been for a while, so maybe a doctor would help. There's something wrong. I know there is. Maybe it's the tea. It could be having an effect on me. I'm so tired all the time and I get confused. I forget things. It can't just be the trauma doing that to my brain. What if I'm allergic to the tea? Can that happen? What if it's harming the baby?'

Her face changed. Her lips pursed. Her brow creased. A small vein I'd never noticed before appeared on her neck.

There was something about her reaction that wasn't quite right, but I decided not to press her.

The excuses I made for her behaviour always flattened the doubt niggling away in the back of my mind. She was under pressure to get me better, more so than ever. She was worried for me, and my situation. I had complicated things. Being pregnant changed everything. She knew that, and so did I.

'Annabelle. You are, at the best of times, an unstable mother, and now that you're pregnant with your second child, I feel it's imperative you complete the therapy programme. The doctor can wait. The therapy programme can't.'

How would I cope with Joshy and a newborn alone? Was I even equipped to become a mum again after messing up with Joshy? She said that Joshy could be in danger if I didn't recover. That meant the unborn baby was in danger, too.

'We'll see the programme through. Are we in agreement?' Her voice was lighter.

I swallowed down my mounting panic. 'Yes.'

'Great,' she said, upbeat. Her features mellowed. She picked up the knife from the sink. 'Today is the day that will mark the breakthrough in therapy. You will turn a corner today. I'm convinced of it. Are you ready for your breakthrough?' she said, with an injection of optimism in her voice. 'Are you excited about the potential that lies ahead?'

I nodded, suppressing the desperate cries from within. I would make it work. I had to.

'Let's go.' She walked off, with the knife in her hand.

With one hand protectively clutching my belly, I followed her into her mother's studio.

Chapter Fifty

The photos from the night before, and my mobile, had been cleared away. She placed the knife on the cluttered coffee table alongside her leather notebook. 'Are you comfortable?' she asked, pulling up a chair opposite me.

'Yes.' My jaw clenched.

'We shall begin,' she said, changing the tone of her voice. 'I'd like to talk about the work we've undertaken so far. As I've previously explained, new pathways called synapses have been created in your brain, through constant repetitive suggestions. Your brain has learnt to latch onto these suggestions and has worked hard, unbeknownst to you, to form new habits.' She folded her hands on her lap. 'And at this point, I believe we need to test the brain. Make sure we're on the right path. Do you understand, Anna?'

I nodded, even though I wasn't quite sure. I felt jittery with nerves and anticipation.

'You truly are the best client I've ever had,' she said, smiling broadly. 'Now, close your eyes and sleep.'

Closing my eyes, my brain activity started to quieten, my nerves settled, and I drifted into a sleep-like state.

'Today, you will prove you can respond to anything I say.'

I tuned everything else out and listened to the hypnotic tone of her voice.

'Regress back to when you were fourteen years old, back to the first time you cut yourself. Go back to the day when you and your friends were huddled together in the arts supply cupboard. Think about it, remember it as if it were right now. *Feel it. Live it. Breathe it.* Sit with these feelings. Recreate the scene in your mind, as though it were in real time, as though it were happening today.'

I was transported back to school. Me and my mates were huddled together inside the arts supply cupboard. Someone said something funny, I couldn't recall what, but whatever it was, it made us all burst into laughter, cutting the spiky tension.

'Go on Anna. Do it, do it, do it!' Siobhan had said.

A mixture of apprehension and exhilaration buzzed through me.

'Deeper,' she said. 'Dig deep within yourself.'

I sank into her words. Her sentences were stretched, elongated. I didn't know where her voice ended, and my thoughts began. We had developed a strange telepathy over the months, and I swear she could read my mind. We were connected.

'It's been so long.' Did I say that out loud?

'Access your memory bank. Re-live the sensations one more time. The calm clarity it gives you.'

The knife she'd taken from the kitchen was cold in my hand. I pressed the sharp blade onto my bare leg, but not hard enough to break the skin. Tingles raced up and down my spine. Adrenaline surged through my body. I ached for the rush.

One more time wouldn't hurt.

'You're stronger now. You're in control. Prove it to me. To yourself.'

This was a test. She was testing my will. My chest tightened. Would I pass?

'Now, cut.'

My hand was shaking. I bit the inside of my lip so I wouldn't cry.

'You can do anything if you put your mind to it.'

Confused, I hiked my school skirt up and pressed the cold blade onto my leg. It was beyond my control. I was possessed. My old way of life had come back, I had travelled full circle. It was how it all began. The only way I could truly escape.

'That's right Anna. Deeper. Deeper.'

I sank deeper into myself. I couldn't control the urge.

'Is this enough?' I heard myself say.

'Do you think it's enough?'

'I want more. I want …'

'Unleash your deepest darkest desires, Anna. Feel free and safe to explore who you are, in this controlled environment. How deep do you want to go?'

The pressure built inside my brain. I wanted to explode. Release. I needed release.

'How do you feel?'

'Like I'm home,' I said.

Chapter Fifty-One

Joshy! He was gone.

I woke with a gasp, like I'd been held under water. I was lying in bed and the room was dark. I thought about him at home in his Gruffalo onesie and wondered whether he'd stopped loving me.

Cassandra, a dark shadow, approached, placing something heavy on the bed, beside my legs. She walked over to the window and opened the shutters but kept the window shut. The bright sun filtered through. With all the effort I could muster, I pulled myself up to sitting and leant my head against the headboard. Squinting, I adjusted my eyes to the light and rubbed the back of my sweaty neck.

I longed for fresh air, clean oxygen, and was desperate to go outside.

As she neared, the sun glistened on her olive skin, making it sparkle like diamonds. She looked radiant and healthy. Glowing.

It had been a few days since I'd told her I thought I was pregnant, and I'd been working extra hard on the hypnosis, submitting myself to her, like she'd asked, but still – *still* – there was no improvement in me. Was I doing it deliberately, on some level I didn't quite understand? Did a small part of me want to stay in the little bubble we'd created inside the house? The cocoon of endless sleep, hypnosis and dreams. Was I too afraid to face the world alone? To parent alone?

'I've brought you some food. You can eat in bed. We'll make a start on hypnosis afterwards,' she said. 'Did you take the pregnancy test?'

I nodded, looking towards the side table with tears welling up in my eyes. She took the test and stared for a while at the two red vertical lines.

'It's positive,' I said.

Without saying a word, she placed the test on the '70s-style retro tray which was on the bed. On the tray was her leather notepad, a mug of herbal tea, a plate of eggs and avocado, a fork *and* a knife.

'What day is it?' I asked.

'Why do you ask?' She placed the tray on my lap and retrieved her pad.

'Somehow, it feels like a Sunday. I know it can't be because Sunday was two days ago, or was it three? I've lost count,' I forced a smile, staring at the pregnancy test.

'It's Friday.'

My eyes threatened to fill up. I turned to face the window. More days lost.

'Maybe I'd make improvements if I went outside to clear my head? It's so hot in here all the time. My muscles are weak. I need some exercise, some movement in my body.' I slowly turned to Cassandra.

The warmth to her features had disappeared, replaced by a cold icy harshness. Her lips pursed. That weird vein appeared on her neck. A chill ran down my spine, despite the stifling heat.

She picked on a thread from one of the beads of her kaftan. The white bead came off in her hand. She placed it on the tray, and it rolled into a corner. 'Think back to your little excursion when you first arrived. It was a huge setback for you. Can we risk this happening again?' Her voice was razor sharp, slicing the minuscule confidence I had left.

'What about the garden?' The tray wobbled as I adjusted my legs, making the cutlery clink together.

She placed her hand on my jittery legs. 'Not today.'

I pushed the eggs around on my plate. My appetite had vanished, but I knew I had to eat for the baby's sake. 'I should contact Matt and let him know what's happening. He'll be worried. It's been almost three weeks now …'

'I contacted him on your behalf.'

My mouth opened. Her facial expression remained neutral, giving nothing away.

'I pretended the message was from you.'

'Can I read?' I mumbled.

'You know I can't allow you access.'

She pulled out her cigarettes from the deep pocket of her kaftan, tapping the Gauloises packet on the tray until a loose one came out. She lit up.

Breathing in the smoke and stale air into my lungs, I shakily asked, 'What did you say?'

'Don't you trust me?'

'I'd like to know.'

She looked at me blankly.

'In fact, there's a lot of things I'd like to know, like, did he ever respond to the message I sent him telling him it was over? Was he upset, glad? Does he want to make amends? And what's actually happening at home, is Joshy okay? Is he missing me? And what about Mary? Have there been any more updates on her illness from Uncle Jack? And why are you locking the windows all the time? It's so damn hot inside the house and stuffy, I can hardly breathe. What's so bad with having fresh air, anyway?' I said, gasping, my hand clinging onto the collar of my nightie, pulling it away from my neck.

Without saying a word, she stubbed the cigarette out on the plate of food and removed the tray, placing it on the floor. She folded her hands neatly on her lap. Her jaw hardened.

'Cassandra, I'm sorry. I don't know what came over me.' I looked at the tray on the floor, my eyes welling up.

She reached over to touch my forehead. I inched all the way back and pressed my head against the headboard.

'I'm wondering if you're getting sick, again,' she said in a flat tone.

'Yes. I know I'm sick. I think I need a doctor. A real doctor.'

'Anna. There's no need to panic,' she said. 'I believe you're suffering from post-traumatic stress disorder. A condition from mental, emotional and physical strain. It can occur as a result of a psychological shock. We don't need a GP to confirm what we already know.'

There was always a possibility that she was right. But what if she was wrong?

'Let's continue with the therapy and see if we can get you over this hurdle,' she said.

'What if I worsen?'

'We'll cross that bridge when we come to it.'

'Give me your word you'll let me go if there's no improvement, so I can get checked out.'

'Anna, of course,' she said, her voice softening, her features mellowing, empathy reflecting from her eyes. 'If there are no improvements, you have my word, I'll let you go.'

'When?'

'One more week and you'll be right as rain,' she said. 'You have my word. Trust me.'

'Okay. One more week,' I said, determined to keep track of time.

'Great. Now, let's not delay our therapy a moment longer. I would like to unlock further secrets from your past. With your permission,

I'd like to explore the second time you cut yourself. What propelled you to do it again. We need a deeper understanding as to why you decided to continue self-harming.'

I nodded and squeezed my eyes tightly shut.

One more week.

Chapter Fifty-Two

The days that followed on from the first time I'd cut myself were bliss. Mary let me have time off school and for the first time I could remember, we spent two whole days together on our own. We woke up late, stayed in our pyjamas all day eating beans on toast, watching trashy daytime TV. She chain-smoked, telling me her awful collection of rude jokes and I confessed to her that I had a crush on Shadi. It was as if we were the only two people on the planet that existed. The front door was kept locked, and her friends kept away. She told them she wanted to spend some quality time with her girl.

Her girl. It made me feel all warm and fuzzy inside.

But come 3.00 pm on Friday, things changed and the whole pamper process began. She took a long soak in the bath, poured herself a large vodka and orange cordial into a tumbler glass and sat, in her black tacky underwear, at her dressing table, putting heavy make-up on and fixing her hair. She plucked at her eyebrows so hard, it was like pulling weeds out of an overgrown garden. She dry-shaved her legs, covering herself with cheap moisturiser and talc afterwards.

By 6.00 pm, I was told to make myself scarce. 'What's a girl your age wanting to hang out with her ma for, anyway? Come on, girl.

Go and have some fun. Do what normal kids your age do. Go. Leave me in peace. Go.'

Johnny from Chequers House turned up with a bottle of Blue Nun and some weed. He wore a fake Rolex on his tattooed wrist, a Hawaiian shirt which was partially opened and sported a greasy Elvis haircut. His bottom front tooth was missing. He'd always given me the creeps. They left me alone in the kitchen and went downstairs to her bedroom, where they continued to giggle away like a couple of lovesick teenagers.

Why did she have to make a mockery of me? Didn't she care for *my* feelings?

Grabbing the first sharp object I could lay my hands on, a blunt kitchen knife, I screamed at the top of my lungs, filling up the void in my pathetic fourteen-year-old life. I howled so loud, Pebbles scarpered out of the kitchen and dashed down the stairs to hide. There was no way out. I took the knife to my forearm, dug it deep into my flesh and sliced diagonally. Blood wasted no time in pouring out, dripping onto the lino floor. Tears stung the backs of my eyes and snot ran from my nose. Loud footsteps thumped up the stairs. A commotion erupted. Mary and Johnny were back in the kitchen. Mary in her frilly underwear, Johnny holding the bottle of wine. Someone rapped hard on the kitchen window from outside: 'Is everything alright in there?'

'Anna. What have you done?' Mary shrieked.

'Ahhh. Mary, I think you have your hands full.' Johnny buttoned up his shirt and walked out of the kitchen with his half bottle of wine in his hand.

Helen from next door peered through the kitchen window. 'Is everything okay?'

Mary shouted back, 'Go home, Helen, love.'

Mary followed Johnny out of the flat. I could hear her apologising to him in the hallway, convincing him to stay, saying it would only take a minute. I was attention seeking, that was all. It was because I was bored and needed something to do.

Standing motionless, I held onto my bloodied arm, feeling angry as hell.

'Welcome back, Anna. Take a good stretch,' Cassandra said, pulling me out of the trance.

My pillow was wet with tears as I lay there on the bed, staring up at the pendant lantern and decorative ceiling rose. The back of my throat was rough like sandpaper, as though I'd been screaming for real.

Chapter Fifty-Three

A few days later, Cassandra helped me out of bed, leading me to the main bathroom of the house on the first floor. I hadn't left my bedroom in about a week. My legs wobbled as we stood side by side, facing the full-length mirror. She stared at her own reflection, striking a pose, like models do, with one hand on her hip. She'd applied red lipstick and looked sharp in her trouser suit and heels. I was beside her, child-like, unable to stand properly.

'My name is Cassandra and I'm a bad-ass bitch. Now, you say it,' she said, staring at me through the mirror, my forearm in her grip.

The words sounded strange coming out of her mouth. 'I can't. I just …'

'Yes, you can.' She lifted my arm in the air, like I'd won first prize in some competition. 'You're a strong independent woman, and you're a bad-ass bitch.'

I cringed.

'Now say it. Come on. Don't be shy, Anna. Be open.'

'I can't …' I squeezed my eyes tightly shut.

'You're a beautiful woman. Embrace it. Look at yourself. Say the words.'

Tears welled up in my eyes, clogging my sight. Droplets fell to the floor. She let go of my arm and I hugged myself, covering up as much surface area as possible.

I was standing in the bathroom in my underwear.

She'd wanted me stripped down naked, explaining I had to be laid bare in order for that particular exercise to work. The point was to stand in front of the mirror and tell myself I was beautiful. I had to learn to love myself in order to let go of the past baggage. I begged her to keep my underwear on. 'It'll have to do,' she'd said, not impressed with my prudishness.

My eyes fixed on the stranger's face reflecting back. I had dark rings under my eyes. I looked gaunt, much older than before, a ghost-like version of my former self. Refusing to let my eyes travel down over my body; I didn't want to see the rest of me.

I didn't want to see!

A spiky needle-like pain jabbed my insides. The blood from my head drained to my feet, and I felt dizzy. My head spinning and whizzing. Crashing down onto the cold floor, the cramps had intensified, like contractions, coming and going in waves. My body was shaking, maybe from the cold or the pain, perhaps from the shock of the situation I found myself in.

'Don't deflect, Anna.' She attempted to pull me up with her strong arms, but I resisted, pushing my weight down into the ground. 'Get up. Come on. Up.' She let go and placed her hands on her hips again. 'I've explained already, you need to go through this process. You want to get better, don't you?'

I looked up at her, hoping she'd let me off. I needed a pass. The pain struck more fiercely, corkscrewing its way deeper into me. I gripped my tummy tight and collapsed into a foetal position. The folds of my flesh squished between my fingers.

'Anna, where have you disappeared?' Her voice sounded distant.

'Huh?'

'Stay with me. Concentrate.' She tapped my head with her long finger.

'I'm trying …'

'Do you trust me?'

'What?'

'It's a simple enough question.'

'Yes.'

'Then prove it to me.' She crouched down to my level. 'You're distracted. Come on, concentrate. Get up. This is attention seeking behaviour. Come on. Up.'

Each time she spoke, it thrummed violently in my head. Uncurling myself off the floor, I stood up and stiffened my spine, keeping my focus at eye level.

'My name is Anna …' I froze. *Come on, bloody do it.* 'My name is Annabelle and I'm a bad-ass bitch.' I'd done it. There, I'd done it.

'It's Anna. Say Anna. Annabelle is no longer with us. She's dead.'

'What?'

'One more time,' she said. 'Come on. Say it. My name is Anna and I'm a bad-ass bitch.'

I opened my eyes, bit down hard on my lip until I tasted metallic blood, and like a programmed robot, said the words she wanted to hear.

'Good. Now, how do you feel? I bet you feel great.'

'Yes.' My hands were now stiffly by my sides. I breathed in, deep and slow, and allowed my eyes to scan my body. It was the first time I'd seen myself in a full-length mirror since arriving at Cassandra's.

I stared, frozen to the spot.

I was a freak of nature.

Skin and bone. My ribs visible, my collarbone protruding, my tummy weirdly bloated. But that wasn't all. My skin. Oh my God, my skin. I didn't want to look, but I couldn't tear my eyes away, compelled to see what I'd become.

My flesh had been marked. Deep cuts scored my arms and legs. Long jagged angry lines. My body was covered in wounds. I'd been sliced to shreds.

The room became stagnant. Toxic. I couldn't breathe.

What was going on?

A loud knocking rapped at the front door. A beat of silence followed. She hadn't had any visitors since I'd moved in. Both of us remained statue-still.

'It's best you stay here. It's probably the neighbour. I'll be right back.' She scurried towards the bathroom door. 'Don't make a sound.' Her eyes wide.

She looked rattled as she took the key from inside of the door and locked it from the outside. I was trapped.

Putting a towelling robe on to cover myself up, I paced the bathroom, questions firing at me. How had I not registered this before? Why had I not paid attention to my bloodied sheets recently?

A commotion erupted downstairs. Some kind of altercation. It was hard to hear. I placed my ear against the cold tiled wall. It was a man and he sounded agitated. Cassandra seemed more restrained.

The man's voice was deep and muffled. Straining to listen, I managed to catch snippets of sentences.

This is not going according to plan, he said.

My stomach started cramping. I began to sweat. I pushed through the pain, keeping my ear glued to the wall.

I have it under control. Trust me, said Cassandra, her voice steady.

This needs to end. Today, he snapped.

Give it a little more time, was her response.

I can't be here right now. I've got to go, Sandy, the man said.

The front door slammed. A car engine fired up outside. Silence. We were alone in the house once more.

A bolt of lightning charged through my body, startling me awake from the deep hypnotic sleep I was in, sparking one crystalised thought in my mind.

I wasn't healing. I was dying.

I slammed my fists hard against the door. 'Help me,' I cried. 'Somebody HELP ME. I'm locked upstairs in the bathroom. Please help me. HELP ME,' I wailed. 'I think I'm in danger. HELP.'

The door unlocked. Everything turned black.

Chapter Fifty-Four

The shutters were partially opened, letting sunshine into the room. I was in bed. The last thing I remembered was being in the bathroom shouting for help, and then, boom. Nothing. Blackout. My left eyelid was sensitive to the touch and felt swollen and puffy. I couldn't see out of it properly. It reminded me of my fall out with the Clancy twins in the playground on the estate. They were teasing me about Mary, calling her names. They'd wound me up so much, I picked up a large stone from the floor and hurled it towards Chantal as hard as I possibly could, catching her in the windpipe. I didn't mean to hurt her. I just wanted the teasing to stop. She doubled over, struggling to catch her breath and without any warning, her twin sister Clarice marched towards me and punched me in the eye.

Clambering out of bed, I stumbled my way towards the door. It was locked.

'Cassandra? What the hell is going on?' I rattled the door handle. 'Cassandra?' I cried.

I was met with silence.

My tummy spasmed as the nausea hit me. I crouched down, waiting for the pain and sick feeling to subside. The room spun, the pain continued, and the nausea travelled up to the back of my throat.

Crawling my way into the bathroom, I made it to the toilet just in time, opening the lid and spewing bile-like liquid into the bowl. I then crawled over to the sink and gripped the edges of the basin to help hoist myself up to standing. Splashing cold water on my face and into my mouth, I peered at my death-like reflection in the small mirror above the basin.

My eye *was* swollen and bruised. I had been struck.

I remembered when Mary spoke about destiny once, how our destiny was mapped out from the moment we were born. The stars aligned themselves in a certain way, determining our inevitable paths. Never believing her at the time, I'd thought she was talking her usual hippy rubbish, but as I glared at my broken face in the mirror, I couldn't help but wonder whether what she'd said was true. For as long as I could remember, I'd been chipping away at myself, piece by piece. Soon, there'd be nothing left of me. Was that my destiny?

I struggled to pinpoint the exact moment in time where it had all gone wrong with Cassandra. When did I start believing wholeheartedly that she was going to be the one to fix me? To protect me. To save me.

Not wanting to look at myself any longer, I punched the mirror as hard as I could, breaking the glass. I trusted Cassandra. I believed her. I loved her.

I took a hot shower and crawled back into the cesspit of a bed and waited for her to unlock the door, fighting the urge to sleep.

My eyes pinged open. Blood trickled down my arm. Cassandra sat on the edge of the bed. Her eyes dilated and wild. Pools of black penetrated through me, sending shivers up and down my spine. I felt like I was trapped in a bad dream. Lost inside. I looked down at my hand and realised I was holding a piece of glass from the broken bathroom mirror and my forearm had been sliced.

Silence pulsed in the room. We stared at one another.

The walls throbbed. Expanded and contracted. Expanded and contracted.

'Anna. Give it to me,' she said, cautiously reaching towards me.

Disorientated, I looked at the glass then back at her. Another piece of me gone.

'Anna. Do the right thing.' Her hand came closer. Closer still. 'Give me the glass, and I'll explain everything.' She leant over and took the piece of glass.

'Why aren't you stopping me?' I could hardly get the words out of my dehydrated lips.

'I've been trying, and it's a shame you're unable to acknowledge my efforts,' she said, wiping the blood from the glass onto her kaftan and placing the shard inside her pocket.

'You're allowing me to hurt myself while under the state of hypnosis.'

'Yes. Yes, I am,' she said, locking eyes with me. 'I'm testing you, but you're failing. Quite frankly, I think you're enjoying the attention.'

Although her voice was soothing and her features soft, her eyes glistening and still, there was something alarming about her quiet, calm demeanour – I could feel violence simmering beneath the surface.

My pulse raced as my mind went into overdrive. The bedroom door was open, but I couldn't trust myself to make a mad dash for it. I was too weak, in a bad way, and hadn't eaten in days.

'Cassandra. You need to let me go.' Red droplets of blood spilled from my arm onto the bed sheet, spreading like a blot of ink.

'Anna. My dear, Anna. You're so naïve,' she said, smiling. 'Do you think Matt will allow you to keep Joshua if he sees you like this? Do you think he's going to roll over and give you his son, and allow you to keep your baby once you've given birth? Look at the harm you've done to yourself. You're clearly unstable. Undoubtedly, a threat to his children.'

I pressed my fists into the sides of my head, remembering Matt's warning, telling me how he had to put Joshy's needs first, above all else. I swallowed down my mounting terror.

'Do you want to know what he said when he received the text telling him it was over?'

My heart stopped beating.

'He said, and I quote, *you'll never take Joshy away from me.*'

She picked up a mug from the floor and brought it to my lips. 'Now, have some tea. It'll settle your mind.'

I pursed my lips tightly together.

'Anna. It's for your own good.'

I shook my head, no.

She sighed heavily. 'Why are you defying me today?' She placed the cup on her lap.

'What have I been drinking?'

'It's your medicine. You need it to get better. Don't you want to get better and see your son?'

'It makes me ill,' I quivered.

'If you don't drink your medicine, you *will* get sick. Very sick. I guarantee you.'

'There's something in the tea. I know there is.'

'This is your paranoia speaking. Drink your medicine,' she said. 'Otherwise, I'll have to lock you inside the room until you come to your senses.'

'No.' I said, shaking. 'I have to protect the baby.'

She stood up, holding the herbal drink in her hand and edged towards the door. 'Have it your way. I'll be back later,' she spat.

The door closed. The lock turned.

'Wait. No!'

Chapter Fifty-Five

My skin was on fire, hot and sizzling. My tummy cramps had worsened, they felt different somehow, like there was something seriously wrong with the baby. The sheets were yellow in colouring, drenched from the filthy sweat that had seeped from my body.

A delirious withdrawal sickness had consumed me.

She'd been gone for hours. It felt like days, weeks, months even. Every second that passed was excruciating. Painful. I knew soon enough, if I didn't get the tea, my fix, I'd be in deep shit.

'Cassandra, come back. Come back. I need my tea. Cassandra!'

A deathly silence followed.

The air in the room tasted sickly sweet. Foul and unclean.

I curled myself up into a tight ball and wrapped the sticky sheets around me, trying to sleep it off, hoping to wake with more clarity, but I couldn't sleep, my bones were restless and my skin irritable. Every molecule in my body ached.

The sound of the squeaky key turning magnified inside my head, piercing my skull like an acute shooting pain. The door finally unlocked. I opened my eyes and watched her gliding into the room with a broad smile painted on her face, as though it were a dream. She'd changed into her business attire and I realised then how odd it was that I'd never seen any other clients. The diary I peeped through, void of hypnotherapy appointments.

I was such a fucking fool.

'Are you ready to drink the tea?' She perched on the edge of the bed with her back upright.

'No. Please. No more. I can't,' I said. 'I need a doctor. I'm not well. I need to see a doctor.' I reached out to her. 'The baby.'

'Anna, dearest. I'm your doctor now,' she smiled. 'Please, take your medicine so you can get better.'

I shook my head. 'I need a *real* doctor.'

'Drink. Your. Medicine.'

'Why are you doing this to me?'

She stood up with the tea in her hand. 'We can do this dance all day and night. It's up to you. Eventually you'll give in to your urges.' She turned her back to me and walked out the room, locking me inside.

'No! I'm sorry,' I yelled. 'Please? Come back. I'll drink it.'

Stupid, stupid, Anna!

The baby and I were going to die.

When my body couldn't hold out any longer, when the cravings and the shakes had gotten so bad, when my tummy convulsed and I vomited over the side of the bed, and my brain was about to explode, and I believed I was better off dead – the door unlocked.

She walked in, holding a cup of herbal medicine.

Helping me upright, she tipped the mug to my cracked lips, so there were no spillages, and this time, I didn't resist. It burnt on the way down, the liquid replenishing my dehydration. I could feel the poison, like a warm gooey syrup, trickling its way inside my body. I lay my head back down on the bed.

'Good girl, Anna.' She put the mug on the bedside.

'Why did you say Annabelle was dead?' I mumbled. My vision blurring.

She smiled. 'Annabelle. It's such a pretty name. Do you know where the name derives from?'

I stared into her eyes and could only see a black lagoon of emptiness.

'It's Gaelic. It means joy. Do you feel joy?'

Overcome with exhaustion, my eyes opened and closed. Opened and closed.

'That name is too exotic for a creature like yourself. You're more of an Anna,' she whispered, in a lullaby tone. 'Anna. Anna. Anna,' she sang.

She clasped my hand in hers.

'Do you know the meaning of Cassandra?' she asked. 'It means prophetess. Do you know what that even means, Anna? Did they teach you anything at school?' Her voice was soft, like a dull hum.

My eyes closed again.

'It means clairvoyant. Fortune teller. Would you like me to read your palm? See into your future?'

'I want to sleep.' My voice sounded like it was under water.

'Good girl. Sleep is good for you. It allows you to heal. And that's what we want, after all,' she said, holding my hand. 'Now, let's have a look.' She turned my hand over, so my palm was facing upwards. 'This line represents your head.'

She stroked the small crease, sending ripples throughout my entire body.

'This is your heartline. And right here, is your lifeline. Do you see?'

'Yes.'

'There's a break right in the middle of your lifeline. Do you see? Do you see now? It's inevitable, Anna.'

Her sharp fingernail scratched across the inside of my hand and stopped at my wrist.

Chapter Fifty-Six

My eyes pinged wide open. It was pitch black. I switched the frilly bedside lamp on. I was alone. Thank God. Tracing my memory back, I pieced the puzzle together. I'd drunk the tea and she'd read my palm. I kicked the covers off and scanned my body for cuts. I'd done it again. A new one had appeared on my right thigh. I glanced over to the bedside table. No tea, only a set of creepy notes.

Loss of control. Delusional episodes. Suicide risk. Imminent death.

My skin crawled. I ripped the piece of paper into shreds and flung my legs out to the side of the bed, flexing my toes, stretching my back. Rain pelted sideways against the window, making it rattle and water dripped from the leaky roof. It took all the will in the world to stand upright. The window shook as a draught blew across the room.

I sucked in the cold breeze, grabbing the little oxygen I could get. What I would do to be outside feeling the rain douse my skin, inhaling fresh air into my lungs.

The bedroom door banged against the framework, making a knocking sound. I stood in the middle of the room, vacantly staring, with my feet planted on the ground and my body swaying gently, every inch of me thrumming in pain. The door shook again as another gust of wind swept through the room. A crack of light appeared vertically between the door and framework. It was coming from the landing.

The door was unlocked.

Something shifted from deep within, something which Cassandra had overlooked. I may not have cared much about my own life, but I did care for the life of my unborn child and the child waiting for me at home. She had no idea what a mother's love could do. Within seconds I was standing on the landing, silently panting, looking from left to right. I had to act quickly before my pains worsened, my brain completely fogged over, and my withdrawal symptoms kicked in.

Holding my breath and my nerve, I tiptoed down the creaky stairs in the dark onto the first floor, cursing with every step. All the bedroom doors remained closed. I knew she was asleep because I could hear the faint sound of her breathing. Could I rush into her room and strike her? She was so freakishly strong, and I was so extremely weak. There'd be no prizes for guessing who'd come out on top. There had to be another way.

I continued my descent to ground level with no master plan, just a gut for survival. I knew it was futile, but I crept towards the front door just in case. It was Chubb-locked. I felt my way along the wall to the key box in the dark. It was empty. Next, I tried the door under the stairs which led to the basement clinic, but that was also locked. I was trapped inside. I thought about smashing the window in the front room and climbing out, but that was also risky, her bedroom was directly above, and she'd wake from the noise. Catch me in the act.

My phone! Even though I was locked out of it, I could still emergency call the police.

Stepping inside Cassandra's mum's art studio, I switched on the tall floor lamp next to the chaise. The ornamental eyes spun furiously from another draughty window. They watched me closely. My mobile wasn't anywhere. A stupid old-fashioned house phone with a rotary dial was on the cluttered desk. The line was dead. The desk drawer made a racket as I rattled it open in search of my mobile. My phone was in the top drawer, but was out of battery.

I wanted to belt out a scream of frustration.

Rooting inside the drawer for a charger, a clap of thunder startled me, lightning lit up the room. The eyes on the ceiling looked even more menacing as they twirled and glared. There it was, the charger! I knelt down on the floor to plug it into the socket on the wall, praying it would burst into life before Cassandra caught me red-handed.

If luck was on my side, I'd be able to call for help and get back upstairs into bed before she'd notice me gone. *Come on. Come on!*

I smelt the smoke before I heard any sound.

She was in the room.

Uncurling myself off the floor, I stood up, leaving the phone behind, praying it was obscured enough from her vision. Another thunderbolt rumbled in the sky.

'Anna?' She was standing in the doorway, wearing a deep red kaftan, keys dangling from one hand, a cigarette in the other. Her eyes were as black as the night.

'I can explain … I was looking for you and thought I'd check in here, but you weren't around and so I decided to …'

The desk drawer was open.

'So, you decided to invade my privacy,' she said, finishing my sentence. 'Did you find anything interesting?' She cocked her head to the side.

'Please don't be angry.' My eyes darted toward my phone which still hadn't switched on. She'd failed to notice.

'I'm not angry, Anna. Just discouraged by your actions.' She puffed out smoke, turned to the door and locked us both inside. The keys dangled from the keyhole.

Was the front door key attached to the set?

She inched closer towards me as I stood rooted to the spot. In my peripheral vision, I saw a flash of light appear. The iPhone had started charging. If she were to come any closer, I'd be done for. My brain scrambled for something to say, anything, I had to stop her approaching.

'I've been thinking about your mother's paintings and wanted to have a look,' I said, taking a few steps to my left away from the desk, towards the upright easel covered by a dust sheet. 'May I?' I asked, pulling the sheet off with my trembling hand, revealing the painting beneath.

She faced the painting. Her straight back relaxed and her shoulders slumped, her crow black eyes glossed over. The tension in her face and in the room mellowed somewhat.

Her mother was her weak spot.

'This is my favourite piece. It's me as a child,' she said, lost in her own thoughts. She stood admiring it as though in an art gallery.

I turned so we were standing side by side facing the painting.

My hand went to my mouth as I looked at the picture ahead, unable to comprehend what was in front of me. The painting. It didn't make sense. I swallowed hard. A grey barren landscape and blood red sky, moths formed the shape of a rain cloud and in the far distance, a small girl in red wellies was holding a limp teddy. The girl's eyes had been hollowed out. Black charcoal tears ran down her cheeks.

My legs almost buckled from the stress as I took a step back.

It was connected, somehow. The painting and the hypnosis sessions.

Standing very still, taking in shallow short breaths, I had the strongest sense of *déjà vu*. It wasn't the fact that I'd somehow managed

330

to conjure up the same imagery in my regression sessions, but there was something else familiar about the oil painting, something I couldn't quite put my finger on, like an itch I couldn't scratch, gnawing away at my flesh.

I knew that piece of art. I knew it well.

However much my brain scrambled to remember, it fired blanks.

'Do you like it?' she asked. Her features soft, glowing from the ambient light in the room.

'Yes,' I said.

'Mother loved to paint,' she said, 'sometimes I think she loved to paint more than she loved me.' Cassandra looked away.

I turned to face her. She was tearful. Tender. Human. Resembling her old self, the Cassandra I'd first met, the person I trusted, the person I loved.

We stood in silence staring at the painting.

It was going to be alright. She would see. I'd make her.

She'd let me call Matt, and he would come to collect me. We'd go to the doctors and have a scan, and the baby would be healthy. Joshy would be waiting for us at home and Rosita would make us one of her hearty meals and I'd gobble it all up and I'd even ask for seconds. Matt would put me to bed and tell me he loved me. Joshy would climb into bed with me and we'd snuggle, reading *The Gruffalo* together. It would be tough at first, but things would work themselves out. Matt would be remorseful about cheating, and he'd prove to me that he was sorry. Our lives would return to normal. I'd be able to cope on a day-to-day basis. Somehow, I'd manage, and we'd be happy. The baby would unite us as a family, and finally, I'd be home.

She turned her body to face me. 'Mummy issues, am I right?' She wiped her eyes and smiled warmly.

'Cassandra, I think I want to go home.'

331

Her smile dried up and her mood turned itself inside out.

In an instant, she'd become unrecognisable. Her face tensed, her eyes hardened, her lips pursed. That weird vein appeared on her neck, throbbing violently. Before I had a chance to back away, she grabbed my arm and stubbed her cigarette out onto my flesh, deep into layers of skin. I could smell the burn and hear the sizzle. I screamed as the pain catapulted through my body, hitting every nerve ending.

'You can't leave me,' she said. 'You can't go home. Not now,' she said.

Cassandra corkscrewed the cigarette in, butting it out into my forearm and then let go, allowing the stubbed-out cigarette to fall to the floor. I collapsed into a heap, cradling my injured arm, and cowered into a foetal position, shaking. She placed one foot onto my back and pressed down, applying pressure.

'Why do you want to leave me? What's the hurry?' she said, as she pushed her foot down.

My throat was constricted, making it hard to breathe. 'I ... I ...'

'Stop muttering under your breath, speak up,' she spat.

'I ...' I spluttered. My arm was on fire. My tummy screamed in pain. 'I need to go home ... I wouldn't be leaving you ... I'd just be returning home,' I cried.

She released some pressure. 'Why do you want to go back to him? Explain to me why you want to go back to a cheating husband?'

'I miss my son. I miss my family.'

'Haven't I taught you anything?'

'I think I'd like to fix things with Matt. Give it another go. For Joshy's sake. For the baby,' I quivered.

'You're so pathetically weak.'

'I'm not trying to be weak. I'm trying to be strong, assertive, like you taught me.'

'You'll go back to your old ways, within days. You'll fail. You're not equipped with the right tools to deal with your controlling cheating husband,' she scowled. 'YOU NEED ME TO HELP YOU.'

'I can try on my own. I'll tell him I won't stand for his shit anymore. Give him an ultimatum. One last chance to prove he's worthy of being with *me*. You've taught me well and I'm so grateful for everything you've done for me but it's time I go home. I can't stay here forever. Even you know this,' I cried. 'We can stay in contact and talk every day. I can come back for sessions. To the clinic, rather than at the house. Twice a week, three times, maybe? Whatever you think. Every day if you think I need it. Cassandra, please understand my time is up here. I need to be with my family.'

'Do you think you're able to make these decisions on your own, without my guidance?'

'Yes. I think so.'

'You believe that you're in the right state of mind?'

'Yes. Yes. Cassandra, please. You're scaring me.'

'Can you explain why you failed to mention your previous visits to Doctor Jacobs?' She removed her foot and crouched down next to me. 'Why didn't you tell me about the severity of your post-natal depression and the mania which followed?' she whispered.

'What do you mean? I told you about my awful visit to the doctor. My one and only visit,' I said. 'I told you!'

'What about the other times?'

'What other times?'

'Anna. The doctor treated you in the past, didn't he?'

'What? No!'

'Why are you lying to me?'

'I'm not. I swear I'm not lying to you.'

'We can't make the progress we need if you continue to lie to yourself. Don't you see this has been your problem all along; your grasp on reality, your inability to see the truth, your blackouts and suppressed memories. It's been impossible for us to make real progress when you refuse to recognise your own truth. You're consistently lying to yourself.'

'I don't understand what you're talking about. I haven't lied. I promise, I haven't lied about anything.'

My thoughts tumbled around me and my brain emptied out. But there was still something niggling away in the corner. Something I'd buried. I swiped it away.

She was wrong. She had to be!

'I know all about your previous appointments with Doctor Jacobs. You were his client for a long time. He treated you for post-natal depression and manic episodes six years ago, when your son was born.'

'No, that's simply not true. It can't be.'

'I'm sorry the truth is so hard for you to grasp, Anna.'

'You're messing with my head, confusing me deliberately. Twisting things around.'

'You've always had problems facing the truth.'

'No. No, you're lying. I know what's been happening to me. I know you're making me harm myself. I KNOW IT'S DOWN TO YOU. Suggesting things when I'm under hypnosis.'

'I've been trying to save you.'

'How? By encouraging me to self-harm and by burning my arm with a cigarette?' The words spilled out of my mouth, making them solid. Real. There was no doubt in my mind, I had to get away from her poison and brainwashing. Get away from her fucking warped lies.

I had to get away from HER.

'I'm sorry about your arm,' she said. 'You were acting out, again. Behaving erratically, I had to do something.'

'Stop with all the bullshit. Stop it.'

'Is the truth too unbearable to digest?'

'Stop it, I said. Stop it. Stop it.'

'Anna. Do you think our meeting was accidental?'

'What?' I sniffed.

'Nothing in life is accidental.'

'Why are you talking in riddles?'

She stood up, towering over me. 'How did you feel when my hypnotherapy leaflet landed through your letterbox? Did you think you were saved? Did you think your life would change forever?' she smirked.

'I don't understand what you're asking me.' I curled up in a small ball.

'Did you believe it was a miracle receiving my leaflet through the letterbox? Did it come at just the right moment in your life? Did you think it was some sort of divine intervention? Destiny?'

'Yes,' I whispered, wiping my eyes.

'You're so naive, Anna. You didn't find me. I found *you*.' She crouched down next to me.

'Please, let me go home,' I pleaded. Tears streamed down my face.

'Don't worry. You'll be freed in good time. Be patient.'

'Thank you,' I said.

Breathe in, breathe out.

She sat down on the floor in the middle of the room beside me and stretched her long legs out. Every single cut, graze and scab on my body was alive. The agitation biting, as though a thousand insects were crawling under my skin, feasting on me.

A familiar bleeping sound startled us both, followed by another bleeping noise, and then another. We both turned toward the direction of the sound. My phone! Someone was sending text messages. Cassandra's eyes darted from me and then back to the phone, which was by the far wall beyond the desk. The mobile bleeped and flashed. Before she could register what was happening, I scrambled beneath the desk towards it. She yanked at my legs, pulling me back and forced herself on top, mounting me and crushing me beneath her weight. She pulled my hair, holding me back.

Somehow, she'd managed to clamber over my head, squashing my face into the rug. She reached towards my phone, her fingertips almost touching it, managing to snatch it out of the socket. When she had it in her grip, she rolled off me.

Cassandra stood up and brushed her hair down with her hand. 'So, let's see. Who's messaging Anna?' She punched in the code. Her finger scrolled. 'Your uncle is texting about your mother.'

My heart pounded in my chest.

'Let's go to a more recent message, shall we. Hmmm. Matt,' she smiled at me. 'What has he got to say for himself?'

Her expression changed. Something about his message displeased her.

I managed to pull myself upright and leant my body against the far wall, shaking. 'Let me call Matt. He needs to come and get me. I need a doctor.'

'I'm afraid I can't let you do that.'

'You can't hold me prisoner. People will start to look for me. Matt will wonder what's happened.'

She placed the mobile on the desk and took a seat, swivelling her chair round so she was facing me. 'Who do you think urged me to take you in?' she asked.

'What do you mean?'

'You heard what I said.'

'I don't ...'

'Understand?' She mimicked me. 'There's so much for you to learn.'

'Please, Cassandra, I beg you. Give me my phone. I need to call Matt. NOW.'

As I attempted to stand, she booted me back down with her foot, making me lose my balance. My hands instinctively covered my stomach.

'Let me ask you again,' she leant forward. 'Who do you think is responsible for you being here?'

'What are you saying?'

'Who brought us together?'

'Please stop. I need to call Matt.'

'Think, stupid girl, think. Don't make me have to spell it out.'

'I don't understand.' My tummy was cramping. The baby.

'Boohoo, poor Anna, she doesn't understand,' she laughed and then suddenly stopped.

Silence followed.

'It's Matt. It's been Matt all along, Anna. He knows you're here.'

Chapter Fifty-Seven

'There's something delicious about keeping secrets, don't you agree?'
She kept tapping her long finger on the desk, her fingernail clicking
each time it made contact.

'I don't believe you.' I shook my head, positive I was trapped in
a nightmare.

'Anna. I'm so tired of keeping secrets. It's time you learnt the
truth.' She placed my phone back inside the top drawer and fished
out a cigarette and silver Zippo lighter, sparking up and blowing the
smoke into the airless room.

Matt knew I was here.

She crossed one leg over the other and dragged slowly. 'Matt and I
have been in contact,' she said, exhaling smoke. 'He was desperate and
asked for my help. He said he couldn't control you anymore. You were
getting out of hand and he needed my guidance. My expertise. He
suggested I post a leaflet through your letterbox as bait. You fell for it.
Let's just say, it wasn't hard to convince you to come for an appointment.'

'Are you telling me this was all a plan?'

'We can't leave anything to chance, can we, Anna?'

'But why would Matt want to do this to me? It doesn't make
sense. None of it makes sense.'

'Matt said he wanted *you* to make the decision to seek help. You just needed a little nudge,' she smiled. 'You needed saving and I appeared at the right time.'

'Wait a minute,' I said, my mind struggling to catch up. 'Was *he* at the front door the day you locked me in the bathroom?'

'How did you know?'

'The car engine,' I whispered.

'Yes, it was him.'

It was an ambush. My husband and my therapist, in on it together.

My mind raced back to that particular day and what I'd overheard. He'd called her Sandy. Sandy! It meant he knew her intimately. He'd said things weren't going according to plan. What plan? WHAT PLAN?

I slammed the back of my head against the wall as hard as I could.

'My husband made this all happen?' I asked, trembling.

'Yes,' she sighed, heavily. 'We came up with the programme together.' She sucked on the last bit of her cigarette, stubbing it out in the ashtray. 'He told me everything. All about your past. Even the things you hadn't disclosed.'

'What do you mean, things I hadn't disclosed? I told you everything. Everything.'

'We both know that's untrue,' she said, pausing. 'Matt explained to me how unwell you'd become after giving birth. How you rejected your own son. The housekeeper had to take over. You began to suffer manic depressive episodes and that's why you started treatment with Doctor Jacobs.'

'No. That's not true.'

'Matt was convinced it was happening all over again. He said you were displaying the same worrying signs. That's why he called me to intervene.'

'No. No. You're lying.'

'I am the shining light on the truth. On your truth, my darling, Anna.'

A series of images flashed up in my mind; Joshy in my arms wailing, rejecting my breast, rejecting me. Rosita sitting in the nursing chair cradling Joshy in her arms, rocking him back and forth to sleep, a bottle of formula in her hand. Dr Jacobs with his glasses on his head and small beady eyes staring at me, waiting for me to say something.

'Why didn't you disclose this in session? This was vital information,' she said.

'I … I don't know … I can't remember.'

'You've blanked out more than your childhood traumas, Anna. It's a cycle.'

It was true. It was all true.

Everything she'd said about me, when Joshy was born, was true.

I'd spent days on end in bed, wishing I was dead. Crying, endlessly crying. I couldn't face Matt, the world, and I couldn't face motherhood. I blamed myself for my failings. I was just like Mary, a hopeless mother. Matt took me to see Dr Jacobs. He prescribed some pills. Rosita moved in and took over. She'd always been there for Joshy. She'd always been the better mum.

That's when the self-harming flared up again – when Joshy was born – and I'd been harming intermittently ever since. Whenever I felt under pressure, my mind would shut down and I'd reach for the knife. It was my warped way of taking back control over my life. The only way I knew how. It became my coping mechanism and helped me put a lid on the deeper issues. As the weeks rolled into months and soon approached the first year of Joshy's life, I somehow pulled myself together. Baby steps were taken. I forced myself out of bed, forced myself to shower and to eat. I forced myself to take Joshy into my arms. I forced myself to walk outside into the world and I forced

340

myself to be intimate with Matt. Soon enough, life settled. I settled. The lid to my problems securely shut. Life ticked on.

'I've been attempting to help you, but it's been challenging to say the least.' She clasped her hands together. 'You're very uncooperative and I've had to resort to extreme measures in order to get you the help you need.'

'Does he know about my harming?' I stuttered.

'Yes, Anna. He's always known.'

I covered my mouth with my shaky hand.

'That's why he came to me. He believes you're a danger to Joshy.'

'Wake up,' I said to myself, pinching the burn on my arm. It made me wince in pain.

'I've been trying to save your life, don't you see?'

'How can you be saving my life when you've been encouraging me to hurt myself?'

'For the record, I haven't been encouraging you to harm. I took away all the knives, but you insisted that I trust you,' she said, flatly.

'Yeah, but …'

'You said I should trust you with a cutting implement. You said you would prove it to me in session, while under. Have you blanked this out of your memory too, like everything else?'

'No.' I put my hands to my ears. 'No.'

'This is the truth, Anna.'

'Wait until Matt hears about this. He won't be happy. He'll call the hypnotherapy society or whatever body you're associated with and have you struck off. Just you wait and see.'

She laughed at my empty threat. 'I'm telling you the truth. The truth you so desperately want to avoid.'

'Give me my phone. I want to call Matt myself.' I tried to pull myself up. 'Hand it over. NOW.'

'It was you who wanted to introduce the blade into the sessions. You persuaded me. How else would we know if you were better, you said? You wanted it, craved it. It's your addiction. You needed to cut yourself to feel normal again.'

'Liar!'

'Anna. You asked me to bring a knife into the session to demonstrate where it all began. You said it would help. I've been following your lead. Now I know it was foolish of me. I believed it would get you better, but it hasn't, it's only made you worse.'

'And you trusted what I said? In my state of mind? Are you crazy?'

The word crazy hung in the air between us. We stared at one another.

'I've always been on your side. I have your best interests at heart. Believe me, I do,' she finally said in her mellow soft tone.

'Side? Why are there sides all of a sudden?'

'I can't say any more than that. I'm sorry.'

'This is bullshit. Hand over the phone. I want to call my husband. I want to go home.' I reached my unsteady hand out. 'Cassandra. I mean it. Hand me my phone and let's put an end to this,' I said. 'You don't want me to lose my shit and start screaming, do you? Alarm the neighbour.'

Time was running out – the withdrawal.

'I'll give you what you want, Anna. However, there's something else you need to know before you make that call. Maybe if I could show you, you'll have a better understanding.' She put her hand inside the desk drawer and fished out a set of photographs. 'Take a look at these pictures. They'll clarify a few things.' She leaned over the side of her desk and passed them down to me.

They were the photos she'd been looking at, that night I found her crying.

Chapter Fifty-Eight

Placing the photos on the floor, I moved them around like pieces of a jigsaw puzzle, trying to slot them into place. Salty tears fell onto them. 'I don't understand,' I said, wiping the tears away so I could see the images clearer.

'You will. Take a closer look. It'll be okay. I'll be here for you. I want you to learn the truth.' She placed her foot on one of the pictures and pointed with her black nail-varnished big toe. 'Pick this one up.'

A man and woman both in their late twenties or early thirties were sharing a sun lounger on a white sandy beach with the turquoise sea behind them. They held up cocktails with umbrella sticks in their hands. They were somewhere glamorous, like the Bahamas or Mauritius, some-place I'd seen in one of my travel magazines and had always wanted to go. The couple looked happy and in love, like they were honeymooning.

I flipped the photo over. The stiff cursive writing on the back of the photo said, *Matt and Sandy 2009.* I recognised the handwriting. Turning the picture over again, I stared at the image of a younger version of my husband sitting next to a younger version of my hypno-therapist. Together, looking very much in love.

'Do you see now?' She pulled tissues from a box on the desk and crouched down beside me, offering them out.

My hands shook as I took the tissues, wiping my eyes. Each time I blinked new tears formed. I picked the rest of the batch up and studied them carefully, as if seeing for the very first time. Cassandra and Matt, together. She had long straight hair down to her waistline and was lean and model-like, exquisitely beautiful and exotic. Matt was baby-faced, with thick brown hair and dark sculpted brows. His cute little dimple showing in every shot, as he smiled. There were no lines on his forehead, his strong jawline was still prominent but the intense seriousness to his features and permanent frown was absent.

I recognised the setting to one of the photos, it was in my home, but not the home I knew. The glass coffee table was the same, but in place of the L-shaped grey sofa we currently had in the family room, was a large black leather monstrosity with matching black leather pillows, not our yellow scatter cushions, and instead of the slimline curved fifty-two-inch plasma screen on the wall, there was a bulky old-fashioned black box on a stand.

My hand clenched another photo, the edges curled. Cassandra was in Matt's home office, the one I'd been barred from, sitting on his desk, her head flinging back, laughing, looking very much like her mum. He must have taken the shot. On the wall behind her hung an oversized oil painting. The painting was still in the office now. A moody grey landscape, moths for a cloud, a blood red sky as a backdrop, and a girl in the distance with blacked out eyes, crying charcoal tears, holding a teddy.

The world raced away from me. I pushed my head back against the wall. Finally, I made the connection.

Why had I never joined the dots up? Was I so withdrawn and into my own self-misery I couldn't see the truth staring me straight in the face?

I'd always detested that piece of art, but Matt insisted on keeping it, saying it was a present from a *dear friend.* It was the same haunting painting that was in her mother's studio. The only difference being that the girl in Matt's painting was older.

Cassandra sat back down on her chair and lit up another Gauloise. The thick smoke in the room made me think back to the strange scent I sniffed on Matt once, late at night. It was an unfamiliar smell I couldn't quite place. Of course! It was the distinct smell of her exotic cigarettes. My brain raced to other events over the past few months. The text message he'd received, *do you think she knows?* His weekend break with Bill at The Grove; she'd gone AWOL, too. The receipt for dinner for two. All the late nights 'working'.

It hadn't been Rachel. It was Cassandra all along. She was the other woman.

'You must have been having a right laugh at my expense.' I pushed the pictures as far away from me as I could.

'I've grown very fond of you over the last few months. We are connected, you and I.'

'Save it, please. You've both been playing me for a fool.' I yanked the necklace she'd gifted me off my neck and threw it on the floor by her feet. 'I trusted you,' I whispered, shaking.

'Please listen to me carefully, as I'm about to tell you the truth,' she said, placing her cigarette in the ashtray and kneeling down next to me. 'He came to me for help and persuaded me to see you. It was his idea. He wanted to get inside your head. He used me. He's used us both. He manipulated me into posting one of my leaflets through your letterbox, to lure you to come and visit me. He knew you'd buckle. He wanted me to dig inside your head and find out what made you tick. Find your weaknesses and use them against you.'

I pulled away. 'Why would he do that? It doesn't make sense.'

'Because he wants to leave you.'

'What the fuck do you mean, leave me? What are you talking about?' She stood up and paced around the airless room.

'He came up with a plan. He wanted to destabilise you. Tamper with your head. But it's all got out of hand. All of it. I've grown very fond of you. I told him I wanted it to stop. Begged him to stop his games, but you know what Matt's like, he's got a persuasive charm.' She sat back down and swivelled around in her chair to face me.

'If he wanted to leave me, why didn't he just leave?'

'That's the thing, Anna,' she said. 'He wants *you* to be the one leaving.'

'But why all this? Why the games?'

'He wants to prove you're an unfit mother. He wants to take Joshua away from you. For good.'

A switch flicked inside my brain.

Sliding myself up the wall using my legs, I forced myself to stand. Without thinking, I charged towards Cassandra with my arms stretched out in front of me, flinging myself at her, while she sat on the swivel chair. The chair buckled from the force and she toppled backwards, hitting her head against the floor.

As she tried to turn her body around to crawl away from the chair, I threw my body on top of hers, trapping her beneath me.

I wanted to kill her. I wanted to kill my therapist!

Chapter Fifty-Nine

With my hands clasped around her throat, I squeezed as tight as I could. Panic washed over her face and horror reflected in her eyes. She opened her mouth and started silently gasping, digging her long fingernails into my hands in an attempt to loosen my grip. Her legs kicked beneath me, and her eyes started to bulge. She was in deep shit and she knew it.

No more games. No more lies. No more Cassandra.

'Why have you done this to me?' I screamed.

'Stop. Plea—'

'WHY?'

'Anna …'

'You've ruined my life,' I wailed. 'I was okay until I met you.' I squeezed. 'I was managing.'

'I can't …' She scratched at my face and tore at the skin. She kicked and flailed her arms. Her right leg shot up, catching me in the abdomen.

A stabbing pain pierced through my tummy. The baby! I instinctively let go of her and clutched my stomach. Suddenly, the tables had turned and she was on top of me, her legs either side of my torso and had my arms pinned down.

'You need to calm down,' she said, breathless. 'Calm down and I'll explain everything. You don't want to suffer a miscarriage, do you?'

I turned away from her and stared at the discarded necklace she'd given me, promising protection.

'Calmer now?'

'Why?'

'If you promise to stay calm. I'll explain everything to you. No more lies.' She loosened her grip on my arms. 'It's not only your well-being we need to think about now, is it? It's the baby, too.'

I nodded.

She uncurled herself off and sat beside me, leaning up against the wall.

I dragged myself up to sitting. 'How long have you two been together?'

'We've known each other for nearly fifteen years.' She rubbed her neck. It had a faint imprint of my hands.

'You've been having an affair all the time I've been married?'

She didn't answer.

'Do you love him?' I asked.

'Not anymore.'

'Does he love you?'

'I don't know if he's capable of loving anyone.' The colour had drained from her face. She looked beaten. 'He seduces you, draws you in until you're hooked. When he finds your weak spot, he uses it as a weapon against you. He has no moral compass and uses control to get what he wants,' she said. 'Ironically, he couldn't control you. You were different. Unpredictable. Believe it or not, you're stronger than you give yourself credit for.'

'But if you know all this, why are you with him?'

'He's *my* weakness. He promised we'd be together. He's been promising that for years. I've been an idiot to hold on for so long,' she said as tears gathered in her eyes. 'Matt said he needed you out of the picture and wanted it done in a specific way. He needed you sick. Very sick,' she said, shaking her head, as though in disbelief. 'The plan was to push you over the edge, little by little, until you buckled, so he could take Joshy away from you.'

My heart squeezed inside my chest. 'All this time you were making me ill.' I turned to look at her.

'Theoretically, yes.' Her voice cracked. She looked away from me. 'But the more time we spent in each other's company, the closer I've felt to you. There's a real connection between us. I know you feel it too.'

'How could you do this to me? How could he?' My voice trembled.

'There's more.'

I let out a desperate laugh.

'I'm sure you've guessed that you haven't been drinking just Chinese herbal tea.'

'What am I addicted to?'

'I'm afraid it's opiates.' she said. 'Matt has been giving me the pills to crush.'

'Oh my God.'

'You must believe me when I tell you, I've been attempting to stop it getting out of hand. I've been helping you in my own way, in a way he cannot detect. I've been training you to become more assertive. The therapy sessions we've embarked on have been genuine and you've made real progress.'

'Huh!'

'I wanted to help you get stronger, by giving you as many positive affirmations as I could, as an aid. Undetected by him. To help you make the right decisions in your life. Look at you now. You're standing up for yourself, aren't you? You're fighting back. This is good. This is positive.'

She rolled her head around, to loosen her neck. 'Remember, I encouraged you to send the text message telling him it was over. I was hoping he'd back off and let you go. I thought he'd back out of the plan all together. It should have made a difference. But Matt likes things done on his terms.'

Her features had mellowed. For the first time, she looked fragile, breakable.

'I'm sorry, Anna. I'm truly sorry for all the suffering I've caused you. It's all my fault and I completely understand if you never want to see me again. I've been weak. I'm weaker than you know,' she said, her voice breaking.

I recognised the look in her eyes, it was one of pain and despair.

'It's me who's the pushover,' I said.

'No. No. You mustn't say these terrible things. You've been amazingly strong.' She took hold of my hands. 'If you'll let me, I'll make it up to you. I'll put things right,' she said, looking deep into my eyes. 'I can't go through this charade any longer. It's over. All of it's over. I told him.'

Every word thrummed inside my skull and rang in my ears.

'I've realised, it's not me he loves and it's not you he loves. He only loves Joshy.' She let go of my hand, stood up and started to pace the room. 'I'm going to get you the help you need. I'll call the doctor in the morning and we'll get you weaned off the drugs. I'll call the police if I have to. Whatever you need me to do, I'll do it. I'll hand myself in, give them a statement. Tell them everything, from the very beginning. I don't care if I incriminate myself. This has to stop. I'll help you get as far away from him as possible.'

I could hear the words but couldn't string the sentences together.

'Look at what he's done to you. Look at what he's done to me. We can't allow him to get away with this any longer,' she said. 'If we unite, it'll make us stronger.'

Sweat dripped down the back of my neck. 'Cassandra. I don't feel so good …'

'Oh my God. The withdrawals.' She rushed over. 'I need to get your pills. Don't worry, I know what I'm doing. I'll give you a very mild dose to tide you over. Just enough to stop the pain. Trust me.'

'Please be quick.'

'Can I help you to the chaise? Maybe you could lie down and wait.'

'No! Don't move me. Please. hurry.'

'Okay, I'll be right back.' She scurried towards the door, unlocked it and darted out, leaving the door wide open. The keys dangling.

Every fibre in my body screamed. I twisted my body round onto all fours and crawled towards the chair by the desk. With each movement came a flash of new pain. Pulling myself up onto the swivel chair, I gripped the handles from the desk drawer to help hoist myself up to sitting. The drawer rattled open.

Inside next to my phone was a photo she'd held back. My hand reached inside and fished it out. I stared at it in disbelief, thinking the image would disappear somehow, like it was an optical illusion, but the image remained a constant.

The truth staring me in the face.

It was the photo that'd mysteriously gone missing from my purse months ago. She must have stolen it while I was under hypnosis.

The snap was taken on our last summer holiday together in the South of France. The three of us sat on the wall, holding ice creams, the sea behind us, the row of shops and restaurants in front. We'd just eaten dinner. I had Dover sole and Matt had rare steak, we ordered French fries for Joshy and he picked from both our plates. We walked along the promenade and stopped on the wall to enjoy the ice-creams. A passer-by offered to take our photo, using Matt's flashy Canon camera. Joshy was sandwiched in-between us, grinning wildly.

The picture only showed Matt and Joshy. She'd torn me out.

Chapter Sixty

Shaking from adrenaline, I placed the photo back inside the drawer. She returned, holding a glass of water and two tablets, leaving the door wide open. She glided towards me and handed the pills over, with a fixed smile on her face. Maintaining eye contact, I threw the pills into my mouth and secretly tucked them under my tongue. Taking the glass, I swallowed a little water, making sure that the tablets didn't travel down my throat. I then used my tongue to fish them around my mouth, placing them between the hollow of my cheek and gum.

'One's Xanax, the other's OxyContin.' She placed the glass on the desk 'Let me help you to the chaise. You can rest up until sunrise. We will deal with everything in the morning.'

Cassandra hauled me up and walked me over to the chaise. She returned to the desk and took something shiny out of the bottom drawer, placing it on the desk. With her back still turned, I spat the pills into my cupped hand and threw them under the sofa, before she had a chance to notice.

She dragged the office chair along the floor and positioned herself opposite, like she always did. 'Why don't we do some light hypnosis? One last time. It'll help settle your mind. Counting backwards. Deeper and deeper. Ten. Feeling heavier and heavier. Your body is tired. Your mind is willing to let go to the sound of my voice.'

My face was numbed. My body trembled. My mind had broken.

'Nine. Sinking deeper into yourself. Eight. Give yourself away, Anna. GIVE yourself to me. Seven. Deeper and deeper you descend. Six.'

I had to stay alert, but it was impossible to fight. The changing sound of her voice immediately sent me under. Greece was beckoning me.

I closed my eyes. One last time.

'Five. Four. Three. Deeper and deeper. Two. It'll all be over with soon, my dearest, Anna. Soon, the pain will disappear. One. You are now fully under my control.'

Silence.

Stay alert. Focused. Impossible. *Stay alert. Come on!* My mind swayed to-and-fro. *DON'T GO UNDER.* Drifting and drifting. Out to sea.

'Anna, allow your subconscious to do all the work for you. It knows what to do. Your subconscious mind has been preparing for this day ever since I met you.'

In the distance, somewhere out to sea, a distraction came hurtling towards me, pulling me back into the room. In the real world, outside of the trance state, my phone had pinged a message. My mind fought the trance, backwards and forwards it went, like a pendulum.

Stay awake. *Hypnotic sleep.* Stay awake. *Hypnotic sleep.*

The stillness returned and I began to drift out towards the anchored yachts.

'All your sessions have been leading up to this very moment in time. This will be our collaboration. Our masterpiece. One last time.'

Drifting. Another noise from the outside dragged me through the layers of my consciousness. *Drifting out to sea.* Ringing in my ears. *Towards the boats.* A ringtone. *Sleep. Sleep.* I recognised the sound.

354

Deeper and deeper. It was my ringtone. It was my phone. Someone was calling me. *Wake up, Annabelle! WAKE UP.*

She huffed loudly. I sensed her get up and walk away. She sat back down and continued to speak in her lullaby tone, whipping her clever words inside my head, but I'd already started to stir. The hypnotic spell was breaking.

Something heavy was placed on my lap. She guided my right hand, suggesting I pick the object up. A long cold blade with a jagged edge.

Home.

'Let it seduce you. Tease you,' she said in her rich velvety voice.

My home was with Joshy. The baby. Matt.

'You must do what needs to be done. This has always been your destiny. Releasing you from your long-term suffering. Only you can do it.'

More ringing, different this time. She got up. Sat back down. Huffed and puffed, mumbled something under her breath.

'Today, you will go all the way. It's inevitable,' she said.

She didn't need to ask because I knew what was expected of me. It's what I'd been programmed to do all along. She'd been compounding it in my head, over and over again, brainwashing me from the very first day she met me.

Cassandra turned my left hand round so the inside of my wrist was facing up. I could feel the drag of her long fingernail along the crease of my wrist. My body tingled.

I ached for the final rush. One last time.

Home.

'There's an area along your wrist which needs releasing.'

Her breathing was rapid. Edgy and hasty. No longer were we synchronised.

I imagined myself climbing up stairs to conscious awareness. I was almost there. I could see a crack of brilliant light up ahead. My heart pounded in my ears. I was almost at the top of the stairs to my conscious mind. The light dazzled. One more step and I'd be awake.

WAKE UP.

My eyes flung open. I blinked, clearing the fog from my vision.

'Anna, close your eyes. Concentrate.'

The knife held tightly in my grip for protection. Protection.

'Anna! Close your damn eyes.' Her eyes widened. 'Do it now.'

I became still.

Breathe in, breathe out. Breathe in, breathe out.

As I raised the knife in my hand, all the pent-up rage and anger and hurt and betrayal which had been stored up inside of me suddenly exploded out of the stillness, like splashes of brilliant colour. I lunged towards her with the blade in my hand, catching her jaw, slashing vertically. Slicing her face open from the jawline to the corner of her lip and up across her cheekbone. Blood gushed from her face, all over my hands and over me.

For a split second, it all went quiet. Her eyes stared blankly at me. More beats passed.

She opened her mouth and let out an ear-splitting laugh.

'You've done it now.' She clutched her face, throwing herself at me, laughing hysterically.

Ducking out of the way, I collapsed in a heap on the floor. She fell to her knees, grabbing at her hacked face, continuing to laugh.

'You've done it now,' she shrieked.

Blood poured onto the Persian rug.

It was coming from me. I turned my left hand over. She was right, I'd finally done it.

I'd sliced my wrist open. I let go of the knife.

Chapter Sixty-One

Blood spurted from my wounded wrist as I crawled towards the door of the studio.

'There's no escaping your imminent death,' she said from behind me.

Pushing my limitations to their outer edges, I continued to baby crawl. She stepped over me and stood in the doorway, blood pouring from her face, and took the keys which dangled in the door.

'You won't get far without the keys,' she laughed hysterically.

She stepped aside, allowing me to pass.

With all the will I could muster, I dragged myself into the corridor, gripping the sides of the runner with my hands, pulling myself towards the front door, leaving a bloody trail behind.

'Someone help,' I cried, my voice almost failing me.

A primitive scream howled out of me as I tried to gain the momentum I needed to continue. The bones inside my body felt brittle. Cassandra stamped on my back, rendering me helpless, my ribs crushing from the sheer force, the pain shooting from the centre of my back, spreading across my body. The foul stench of death hit the back of my throat.

'Where are they?' I screamed.

'What?'

'Recent. Photos. You. Matt. Where?' I said, staccato. 'Where?'

I growled, forcing the voice out of me. All the photos she'd shown me were old, before I'd even met Matt.

It didn't prove a thing.

'Are you delirious, Anna?' She stood over me with blood cascading down her face.

Knowing that I didn't have much fight left inside, I wriggled onto my back to look at her one last time, desperate to see something human in her black crow-like eyes, but what stared back at me was pure evil.

It was death.

The front door pounded. Someone was silhouetted outside and they were calling my name. My eyes opened and closed. I tried to scream but my voice was lost inside of me. She kicked me in the stomach and grabbed my hair, U-turning me around, so my head faced the direction of the studio, back to where I'd crawled from.

'You've always been in the way. Interfering. Why couldn't you behave yourself and do as you were told? I had it all planned out. Me and Matt were going to be a family,' she shrieked. 'You could never be a proper mother to that child. A proper wife to Matt. I was going to be the mother and wife they both deserved. But you ruined it all, by falling *pregnant*.'

She grabbed under my armpits, struggling to pull me back towards her mother's studio. I lay as heavy as I could, a dead weight, forcing myself into the ground. My bloodied hand grasping at the wall, at anything, trying to hold onto something so I could stop her.

Death was coming. It was coming.

Flashes appeared in my mind: reading *The Gruffalo* to Joshy in bed, Matt telling me he was going to fix things, Uncle Jack's market stall, the swing swaying solo, Mary's haunting eyes. I sat on Cassandra's front doorstep and tied up the laces to my roller skates. Using my front stoppers and holding onto the railing, I tiptoed down the external steps and onto the pavement, skating away from the house, as far from Abbey Gardens as I could, towards my home. Home. Where my family were waiting for me.

The front door to Cassandra's house was being pounded.

'It was going to be perfect. All I had to do was get you away from Matt and from Joshua. First, I needed to encourage you to walk away from your marriage, but you had such low self-esteem, the only way to do that was to build your confidence up first, using positive affirmations and suggestions during hypnosis. At the same time, I needed you to start questioning how you were parenting Joshy. It was a delicate situation. Giving you enough strength and courage to leave your cheating husband, as well as destabilising you, so you would believe you were a danger to your son,' she said, continuing to pull me towards the studio. 'You had to think you were as hopeless as your abusive mother!'

My eyes opened and closed, opened and closed.

'I had to find your weaknesses. It was easier than I thought. You had so many. My personal favourite being the self-harming. Your biggest weakness came wrapped in a pretty red bow. Your childhood trauma – the reason why you harmed. I couldn't believe my luck. You handed yourself to me on a silver platter,' she said, stopping to catch her breath, blood gushing from her wound. 'But you kept holding on, didn't you? Your love for your son. Your need to stay with your husband. Your desire for a secure family unit. A home. You were showing very little sign of actually wanting to leave. So, I encouraged you to come and live with me for a while, so I could work on you without any distractions. Get you away from Joshua, from Matt, from your home. Get you away from your mother.'

The front door was pounded again. My name. I could hear the faint sound of a man calling my name. Cassandra was too absorbed in her words, lost in her evil plot to destroy my life, to notice the commotion coming from outside.

'During your stay, all I had to do was send you back to the place of your horrors through regression, and repeat the ordeal over and over again, making you relive that terrible day as if it were happening afresh. Trapped in an endless cycle of terror. Compounding the trauma should have been enough to tip you over the edge,' she said. 'However, the day you told me you were pregnant, things changed. I had to work quickly. You left me no choice. You *had* to start self-harming again while under hypnosis,' she spat. 'I realised that *Matt* had to see what a danger you'd become to yourself and to your children.' She pulled at my hair, yanking me further into the studio. 'He had to know who you really were.'

'Help me,' I mouthed silently.

We were at the foot of the studio. She let go from under my arms and stepped back into the room. I forced my eyes to stay open, cocking my head to the side to see what she was doing. Everything was fuzzy, blurry, as though it wasn't real.

She stood in front of me, cut up and bloodied, deranged with hatred, holding the blade in her hand. 'Anna, dearest. You're going to die.'

It all happened so quickly. The front door burst open. 'Quick, in here. They're in here,' someone said.

My eyes shot back open. I was still alive.

Police officers stormed the house. 'Put the knife down!' The male officer with a deep voice shouted at Cassandra. He reached out towards her and took her down.

'Where are the paramedics?' someone bellowed.

'Annabelle. Annabelle. Can you hear me? Can you hear me, Annabelle?'

Oh my God. It was Matt and he was crying.

'Paramedics are on their way,' said a female officer.

'Annabelle, my darling, what has she done? What has she done? Somebody, please help her. She's dying.'

I turned to see a distressed Matt getting shoved out of the way by another officer.

'Annabelle, can you hear me? Nod, if you can hear me?' An officer with a kind face, kneeling beside me, asked. 'That's great. Stay with me, Annabelle. Help is on its way. Stay with me. Focus on my voice. Everything is going to be okay,' they said, taking my hand in theirs. 'Focus on my voice.'

'Please sir, we need to secure the scene. Please step outside. Someone get the husband out of here!'

'She was trying to kill me,' shrieked Cassandra from somewhere in the room. 'My own client, trying to kill me. She's crazy. Delusional. Look what she's done to my face. She's crazy. Take a look at my clinic notes. They're over there. You'll see. Check my clinic notes and see for yourself how unhinged she is. What a danger she's become to those around her. To herself!'

More police entered.

'Annabelle, baby. Wake up. Wake up,' Matt cried. 'She's dying. Somebody please help her,' he yelled. 'Darling. Darling. I had no idea what was going on. I'm so sorry. She said she was helping you,' Matt sobbed. 'SHE SAID SHE WAS HELPING!'

'Matt why are you saying this?' shrieked Cassandra.

'Sir. Come this way, come with me. We can talk outside. I'll need to take a full statement.'

'Annabelle? Wake up. Please wake up.' Matt's voice faded into the distance.

My eyes closed.

Chapter Sixty-Two

Today's the first day I'm walking Joshy to school on my own and I'm taking my time trudging up the steep hill. With his hand gripped in mine, I near the school gates, while the usual school-run chaos unfolds. Four by fours pulling up on the zigzags, kids crashing around in the playground and mums in huddles, like wolfpacks, in their gym gear, gossiping.

Then there's me, the freak who was brainwashed by her hypnotherapist.

Cassandra was sentenced to fifteen years and is now serving her time at Bronzefield high security prison, found guilty of false imprisonment, assault, consumption by fraudulent means causing mental impairment, and coercive control. The court case caused a media frenzy with national coverage and our faces were plastered all over the front pages. Tabloid headlines such as *Mum brainwashed at the hands of crazed hypnotherapist*, *Hypnotherapist uses mind control in the name of love* and *Hypnotherapy is a dangerous practice.* She was in her element, lapping up the attention, despite the permanent scar I inflicted on her face.

The clinical notes she'd kept on file were complete mumbo jumbo, according to the experts in court. Pages and pages of drivel that didn't make any sense. Ironically, it was her clinic notes that helped to convict her, displaying her unstable state of mind and her intentions towards me. In her head, she believed they were professional assessment notes, but in reality, her notebook was filled with doodles, drawings and incoherent scribblings.

The most unexpected thing to come out of the trial was the story behind her parents. Cassandra echoed her father. Her mother was mentally ill and her father, a clinical psychiatrist, kept his wife imprisoned in the house while he treated her, apparently drugging her for years. Her mother's only escape route was to paint. Cassandra was eighteen when she raised the alarm with the neighbour, the day her mum slit her wrists. She was put on the witness stand to testify against her father. He was arrested and charged, and later hanged himself in prison.

Cassandra boasted of her successful 'experimental hypnotherapy programme' with a sense of pride. The judge claimed she had delusions of grandeur, displayed signs of narcissistic personality disorder and was fully aware of her actions at the time, showing no signs of remorse for what she'd done to me.

The thing people don't understand is, I loved her, and I trusted her with my life. During my time in the house, I kept making up excuses for her behaviour. I was blinded and I didn't want to admit to the truth. Ha! She always said I had a problem recognising the truth. I guess she was spot on.

Cassandra had undertaken a diploma course in hypnotherapy seven years previously, when I met Matt, and hung her certificate on the wall in her dad's unused clinic. There were no other courses taken and no other qualifications to add. She was clearly skilled in the art of hypnosis (the drugs helped in the house, of course), but she'd no other clients, apart from me.

What a fool I was.

It'll take a while to get back to normal, but I'm determined to get there. The one positive thing she taught me was how to be assertive, which is exactly what I'm doing. I have the baby to think about now. She's due next month and is healthy, giving me bad heartburn and kicking around like crazy. I won't be surprised if she pops out early.

Matt is involved, but we are no longer together. We've decided to be adult about the whole thing and co-parent for the children's sake. He's still living at the house, sleeping in one of the spare rooms, and says he's finally found himself a suitable flat close by to move into. He's been looking for a while.

We've spoken at length over the months and he's told me everything. They were together for years. She could never have children and Matt desperately wanted to be a father. They split up when he met me. He said he knew I was the one the day we met. We quickly fell in love and I accidentally fell pregnant. Cassandra felt pushed out and watched Matt create a family of his own. She became obsessed with him and obsessed with me. She planted the hypnotherapy leaflet because she wanted to meet 'the other woman'. She still believes to this day that they're an item. She contacted Matt after my second visit and he naively agreed to the programme because he was desperate. He believed he was getting the help I needed, especially since he failed with Dr Jacobs. He had no idea of the abuse going on inside the house. He swears on Joshy's life that he slept with Cassandra only once, the weekend at The Grove hotel – his moment of weakness.

Sometimes, late at night when Joshy's sound asleep and Matt's taken himself to bed in the spare bedroom, the house falls silent and Cassandra appears from the shadows. She stands in front of me, back poised, looking sharp in her suit and Louboutin patent heels. Blood cascades from her open wound and her black haunted eyes pierce right through me. Her melodic voice, with its lullaby tones, whispers in my ear, *Matt wanted you out of the way.*

But come the morning when the shadows disappear and I look at my beautiful Joshy and rub my belly, counting my blessings that have kept me alive, I realise that her words were used as a weapon to derail me, and I swipe the doubt from my mind. I know Matt may be many things – a control freak, old fashioned and a cheat to name a few – but I know deep down he's not malicious or cruel, and he'd never want to cause me harm. He loves his family more than anything. After all, it was him who raised the alarm, calling the authorities, ultimately saving my life. Even the police dismissed him as a suspect pretty much straight away.

Cassandra simply spun her web and trapped him, too.

I've been told part of the healing process is learning to understand and forgive someone's actions. I'm learning to forgive Matt for his involvement and infidelity, learning to forgive Mary for my terrible upbringing, and I'm learning to forgive myself, too. However, I don't think I'll ever bring myself to forgive Cassandra. She was callous and evil and used my vulnerabilities against me. She almost destroyed my life. Almost.

Online, people have called me *gullible, stupid, weak,* saying things like, *didn't she know what she was doing? Why didn't she just walk out the door? She must have enjoyed it. She was a masochist.* The comments get to me sometimes, but real therapy has taught me how to dull the white noise and concentrate on what matters – Joshy and my baby.

I try not to think about Mary too much. It's too painful. She passed away a few months ago and I only got to see her one more time. She hardly recognised me, so it wasn't the reconciliation I was hoping for. But with death comes new life and new beginnings, and today is another brand-new day.

Joshy grips onto my hand a little tighter as we enter the school gates. The cold February air bites and I wish I had a thicker coat on. I breathe in the crisp air, filling my lungs, and walk towards the pack of mums. Rachel is talking loudly, as per usual, speaking about her boyfriend, Frederick, whisking her away to Paris for the weekend. As I approach, she stops talking, spins on her heel and stares. The mums look towards me. No one says anything. Joshy sees Leo, let's go of my hand and runs off. Saskia smiles, places her hand on my shoulder, steps back, making room for me in their huddle. I relax a little.

It'll take a while, but I'm sure soon enough the gossip will subside, and somehow, my scars will heal.

After saying goodbye to Joshy, I waddle back down the hill towards my house and lock the door behind me, double bolting and Chubb locking for extra security. I rest the back of my head against the door. I did it! I took him to school.

Something posts through the letterbox. My heart leaps into my mouth and my legs turn to jelly. I take a moment, breathing deeply, and look down past my tummy towards my feet and the doormat.

It's a letter – not a leaflet.

A sense of relief passes over me as I crouch down to pick it up, my rotund belly is in the way. It's addressed to Matt. Since he parted ways with Bill and moved offices, he's been receiving a lot of work-related mail at home. I leave the letter on the console for him to collect, but something pops out at me. A stamp.

HM Prison Bronzefield.

Cassandra!

My chest tightens as I gasp for air.

With my trembling hands, I tear the letter open. On the page, I see Cassandra's spidery child-like handwriting and I think I'm about to throw up. Swallowing down the nausea, I begin to read.

My dearest Matthew,

I know you said I shouldn't contact you, and that you'd be in touch when things have calmed down, but I cannot possibly wait any longer. I miss you, my darling. You're all I think about, day and night, and you're the only thing keeping me from going insane in this godforsaken place. When will you come and visit? When will you write? Why have you abandoned me in such a way?

I did everything you asked of me and more, and I almost succeeded. We almost won.

Why did you pull out of our plan, right at the end? Is it because she's carrying your child?

What's going to happen when she starts having doubts, late at night? What will she do when she finally finds out the truth?

Will she reach for the knife? Who will she harm this time? Matthew, please don't allow history to repeat itself.

You and I were always meant to be together. It was always only ever meant to be us.

With a heavy heart, yours forever, Sandy xxx

My heart clenches. The letter slips from my hand and helicopters to the floor by my feet. My stomach twinges, as the baby moves inside. I slowly inch backwards, stepping away from her contamination, her toxicity, my eyes are fogged with tears, as doubt clouds my mind.

I remember back to the house, the day Matt visited, the day she humiliated me in my underwear and locked me inside the bathroom.

That day, I'd overheard him say, *things aren't going according to plan.* When I queried him about it a few months later, he'd said that he was referring to the hypnotherapy programme he genuinely believed he'd signed up for and was worried for my well-being.

As my mind grapples, trying to make sense of her letter, I can almost feel her breath dancing on my face, teasing my cheek. *What will she do when she finally finds out the truth?*

Reason and logic and common sense tell me that Matt wouldn't lie. The police found nothing to link Matt to the abuse going on inside the house. Nothing. At the time, she confessed to everything and he was quickly dismissed as a suspect.

It's her – she's always been delusional.

As I stand rigid in the corridor, with tight fists by my sides, and stare down at the letter on the floor, I realise that Cassandra *still* holds all the power. She has the power to delve inside my mind and manipulate my thoughts – even from prison.

The letter's a plant. It has to be.

She wants to get at me one final time, meddle with my head, triggering me in hope I do some irreversible damage. All she needs to do is plant a little seed of doubt and watch from afar as that seed takes shape and form, as I feed it daily with my paranoia, until it swells and grows, turning into an uncontrollable monster. With a knife in my hand, God only knows what damage I'd do this time.

It's just a game to her. It's always been a game.

But this isn't a game. This is my life!

I storm past the stairs, ignoring the baby kicking inside my stomach, along the corridor and head towards Matt's office. I haven't had the courage to step inside since I returned home from the hospital.

I fling the door open and look straight ahead of me.

Terror catches in my throat and suddenly, I can't breathe. The room shrinks, the walls cave in, the ceiling tumbles down, and I'm being crushed, crushed, crushed, trampled from all angles, and my brain is smashing into pieces.

I fall to my knees.

There it is in front of me, staring me in the face – the crying girl with the blacked-out eyes.

Why hasn't he taken the painting down?

Scanning the room, I take in my surroundings. Nothing is boxed up. Everything is still in its place. He has no intention of moving out! I think back to the day when the hypnotherapy leaflet was taken out of the trash can and placed back in the snug.

Maybe it *was* his plan all along?

Standing up, I start pulling everything off the bookshelves, mindlessly searching, looking for anything incriminating. I flick through the boring economics and business books and wrench paperwork out from the boxed files and folders. I search inside his storage cupboards, scattering all the contents to the floor, delving into the waste-paper bin.

Nothing! There's nothing!

My head is spinning, and I want to scream.

Next, I scramble to his desk and force his drawers open, pulling everything out, flinging the contents across the room. Letterhead paper, Sellotape, two hole-punchers, pens, envelopes, blank paper, scissors and a Father's Day card Joshy made him last year, and at the bottom of the drawer, under all his crap, is a letter opener.

There's nothing compromising. Nothing which links him to Cassandra.

Sitting in a heap on the floor, the room ransacked, I'm so angry now.

How could I let her get to me, again?

This is what she wants.

I stare at the wall. One thing remains intact – the picture of the girl with blacked-out eyes.

My vision clouds, and before I know it, I've taken the letter opener and I'm hacking away at the painting, tearing at the face of the girl, Cassandra as a child, ripping it to shreds, screaming at the top of my lungs, like some crazed lunatic. I can no longer hold it all in. I want Cassandra completely out of my life. I want her gone for good. I hack and hack and hack until the image of her as a child has disappeared.

Ripping what's left of the picture off the wall, I hurl it across the room. It crashes against the door and the wooden frame breaks and snaps.

Two pill bottles hang off some Sellotape attached to the back of the frame.

Time stands still, as I inch closer and closer towards the bottles on the floor, dropping the letter opener in my hand. Peeling the bottles off the tape, I gather them up and read the labels.

Xanax and OxyContin.

The drugs used in the house.

Matt.

Ice travels down my spine and spreads throughout my body. It trickles into my veins, freezing my blood and my beating heart. It freezes every single molecule and atom. It freezes my entire existence. I stare at the bottles in my cupped hands.

Matt.

The words of her letter ring in my ears; *I did everything you asked of me. We almost won. Why have you abandoned me in such a way? History is repeating itself. Did you pull out of the plan because she's carrying your child?*

Did you pull out of the plan because she's carrying your child?

The ice begins to thaw. It cracks and breaks, melting bit by bit.

My heart begins to beat, and I can feel blood beginning to pump through my veins. The baby kicks.

Suddenly, a small fire is burning inside of me.

Matt.

The ground beneath my feet shifts. The world spins on its axis. Everything that I thought was the truth was in fact, a lie.

But somewhere in the back of my mind, something dark is niggling away. A flash of memory. A spark of something old. I'm ripping Matt's office apart, piece by piece, and he's standing in the doorway, looking alarmed. Joshy is sitting by my side on the floor, crying. I'm manic again, not listening to reason, searching for goodness knows what, accusing Matt of trying to poison me. He's telling me to calm down, asking if we need to see Dr Jacobs. I take the letter opener which is inside the desk drawer. Matt inches into the room. I grab Joshy in my arms, warning Matt off. He begs me to calm down. He only wants to take Joshy. Make sure he's safe.

I push the memory back down.

It's Matt. The father of my children. *He's* the monster. *He's* been behind Cassandra all along. It's the only thing that makes sense.

Matt is to blame.

He used her skillset in an evil plot to destroy my life and make me go mad, perhaps going as far as brainwashing me into killing myself, guaranteeing Joshy remains with him. As Cassandra stated in the letter, they almost succeeded. They almost won. Almost. He must have got cold feet because of the unexpected pregnancy and instead, painted himself the big hero, saving my life, and getting her sent down.

The fire inside me starts to burn, gathering momentum, brighter and brighter, the flames flicker and dance. It grows quickly, until it's raging inside my very core, and I find myself laughing out loud in disbelief, laughing so hard it hurts. I think about Cassandra in prison, alone, forever waiting for Matt, desperately hoping for that relationship to flourish into something more. He never had any intention of being with her. He played us both!

Matt only loves two things in life, his children – his flesh and blood – and himself.

With the flames fully ignited and adrenaline pumping inside of me, giving me the courage that I've lacked for so many years, I know there is only one thing left to do.

Taking in a long slow deep breath to compose myself, I fish my mobile out of my back pocket and dial 999.

Today is the day I change my life, forever.

Acknowledgements

I'm eternally grateful to my amazing agent Madeleine Milburn for choosing me as her first ever mentee and signing me. Thank you so much for having faith in me as a writer and believing in my story. You really have changed my life forever. Thank you!

To the rest of the incredible team at Madeleine Milburn who rallied round and helped with my edits and queries and wobbles, thanks so much for shaping the novel into what it is today. Liv Maidment, Rachel Yeoh and Georgia McVeigh, you guys are the dream team. And to everyone else involved in the Mentorship scheme, Giles, Hayley, Chloe and all – I have so much gratitude.

To James Faktor, Publishing Director at Lume Books, I am so thrilled to have worked alongside you on this novel. Thank you for loving this story. Lume is the perfect home for my debut (my baby).

When I started writing this book back in 2019, I had no idea how many people would play key roles in the completion of *The Call of Cassandra Rose*. Writing may be a solitary occupation, but completing a novel takes a small army!

Here are some of the other people I'd like to thank:

To the five brilliant MM mentees, who have now become close friends. Thank you for being there and sharing this surreal experience with me. I couldn't have done it without you. Ronali Collings (it feels like I've known you all my life), sweet Sophie Jo, my amazing US buddies, Avione and Nigar, and of course, Francesca (I've finally met someone who swears as much as I do). I can't wait to see all your novels out in the world.

To my fellow Debut2022 authors – you guys are so talented, I'm in awe. Eve Ainsworth and the online writing community out there. A special thanks to Anna Wharton, Zoe Rosi and Susannah Wise – you guys have kept me sane.

To everyone at Faber Academy, your course was truly the best six months of my life. To Shelley Weiner, my tutor at Faber who championed me right from the start and who taught me how to write from within. And to the wonderful class of 2019, who I still meet up with. Jenny, Geraldine, Alexandra, Naomi, Tara, Barbs, Helen, Kathryn, Michelle and all. LOVE you guys so much!

There's nothing like having fellow writers as friends.

I'm so grateful for my beta readers who helped me navigate my way through early drafts of the story. Sarah Lawton, may we forever be discussing 'how to get away with murder', Angela Sweeney my partner at Faber, Lola May Coker, and my best buddy Joanna Constantindes. Other early readers included Nikki Roberts and Maria Marzocchi. A thousand thanks, guys. Hope you enjoy the final version!

I'd like to raise a glass to some other important people in my life. My besties, Maria Charalambous and Claire Bibaud, who've had to listen to me go on and on and on about my book every single day (I'll be calling you both tomorrow!). My mum Stella, the kindest, most generous person I know. My dad Sergio, thank you for the laughs over the years and that one outrageous joke that comes out every Xmas. And to my brother Christopher, a bright spark, who's always filled with creative ideas. The 'Cousins Group' – the other members of my family, Theo, Hatty, Andy and Miri – oh man, you guys are nuts! Thank you for making me laugh hard and for all the fun nights out we've had. Love you all.

To my pets (sorry – I had to), thanks for keeping me company during the day when I'm tapping furiously at the keys or swearing at the computer or scrolling Twitter.

I'd like to thank my two beautiful children, Luciano and Arabella, to whom this book is dedicated. Guys, you can do anything you want to in life if you put your minds to it – just as long as you work your butts off, listen to advice and have faith in your abilities. Love you both with all my heart (please put some socks on!).

To my husband Byron, my biggest cheerleader, my partner in crime, my rock (n' roll), the person who's believed in me more than I've ever believed in myself! I love you, babe!

And finally, a note to self – to the working-class girl with olive skin, frizzy hair and roller skates glued to her feet, the girl who came from an immigrant family, who grew up on Lisson Green council estate in London. Remember, be proud of where you've come from, who you've become and what you've achieved. *You have done good.*

CPSIA information can be obtained
at www.ICGtesting.com
Printed in the USA
BVHW091049021122
650938BV00005B/107